# The
# Wake
# Up

# Also by Catherine Ryan Hyde

# The
# Wake
# Up

## Catherine Ryan Hyde

*A Novel*

LAKE UNION
PUBLISHING

Text copyright © 2017 by Catherine Ryan Hyde

Published by Lake Union Publishing, Seattle

www.apub.com

Amazon, the Amazon logo, and Lake Union Publishing are trademarks of Amazon.com, Inc., or its affiliates.

ISBN-13: 9781542047951
ISBN-10: 1542047951

Cover design by Shasti O'Leary Soudant

Printed in the United States of America

# The
# Wake
# Up

# PART ONE

## AIDEN DELACORTE AT AGE FORTY

### PRESENT DAY

# Chapter One

## Clouds and Shadows

The phone jangled Aiden out of sleep. His heart raced, and he knocked over a plastic drinking glass and the alarm clock while reaching to grab the receiver.

His panic didn't last. The voice on the other end of the line soothed him on contact. It felt like a drink of cold water, its relief spreading down through his gut on a hot and dusty day.

It was only one word. But it repaired everything.

"Hey."

It was feminine and smooth, that word. It felt like everything in the world Aiden had found to love. Or maybe that's genuinely what it was. He could feel his heart expand, or at least the sensation of it filling. Swelling. It ached. It was painful in a very real way, but Aiden wouldn't have traded it for anything.

"Oh," he mumbled, still mostly asleep. "Gwen. Hey."

"I'm sorry. I know it's late. I know I woke you up. I knew I would, but . . ."

Aiden sat up on the edge of the bed. He was wearing only boxer shorts, and the air in the room felt blissfully cool against his bare chest and back.

"But what? Are you okay?"

In the silence that followed, he watched shadows cast by the branches of scrub oak trees sway on his bedroom wall. He looked through his window to see the dark shapes of his sleeping brood mares in the nearest pasture.

"I guess so," she said. "I guess I just needed some reassurance."

"About what?"

"Tomorrow."

"What about it?"

"You're not worried about it?"

"No. Not at all. Why would I be? I'm looking forward to it."

"Just . . . you know." There was a lot that could be read into her voice. Aiden knew that. He listened as hard as he could to every word she didn't say. "You meeting the kids and all."

"You're worried they won't like me?"

"More that you won't like them. It's hard. You know. When you have kids and you meet somebody new."

"I'm going to love them. I like kids. I told you."

"I know," she said. But she didn't sound as though that settled much. "I should have had you meet them sooner. I was a little surprised you didn't press the issue."

For a moment nobody said anything more.

"What can I say to reassure you?" he asked.

"Nothing, I guess. Tomorrow just has to get here. I'm sorry I woke you up for no real reason."

"No, it's okay."

"Go back to sleep."

"I will."

He didn't, though. He thought he would but he didn't. Something about her tone. About the subtext of her words. She was worried. Not just mildly insecure. Genuinely worried.

Maybe she was worried about nothing. But Aiden couldn't shake the thought that maybe she knew something he didn't.

———

He purposely did his food shopping before 10:00 a.m., to be sure he would get a grocery checker who was not Gwen. Not because he didn't want to see her—he did. But he would, soon enough. Meanwhile he did not want to see her in that context. He did not care to put her in the position of having to serve him.

Marge was his checker that morning—a jolly middle-aged woman with glowing cheeks and quick and frequent smiles. Her eyes came up to his face and lingered a couple of beats longer than normal.

"Aiden Delacorte, I swear," she began, "I have never seen a smile that big on your face as long as I've known you. And how long have I known you? Forever?"

It surprised him. He hadn't realized he was smiling.

"Pretty close, Marge. More than thirty years, anyway."

"And all this fancy food. Shrimp. Cocktail sauce. Parmesan cheese. Fancy fresh pasta. If I didn't know better, I'd think you had a date."

"I might have a date," he said, a little embarrassed.

He didn't say with whom, because she knew. It was a small town. Marge was Gwen's coworker. It went without saying. As he spoke the words, he became aware of his own smile. Hyperaware of it, in fact.

"I didn't know you could cook," she said.

"Don't know for a fact that I can, but I'm going to give it a go."

"Now I just know the frozen macaroni and cheese can't be part of this fancy date. That must be for you, then. Right? To tide you over till dinner?"

"No, that's for her kids. Just as sort of a fallback. You know. In case they don't like what I'm making."

A moment transpired. It was silent, but there was more to it than that. Something rolled in. It reminded Aiden of a cloud suddenly moving across the sun. Bringing coolness and making everything a little darker.

"You've met Gwen's kids," Marge said. "Right?"

Meanwhile her hands continued to run groceries across the scanner. A bottle of wine that Aiden would not drink, but that Gwen might want with her dinner. Soda and milk for the kids. A frozen pie for dessert.

"No. Tonight will be the first time I meet them. Why?"

"No reason. No reason."

She totaled up his groceries and he squinted at the price and pulled his wallet out of his back pocket. Counted out three twenties. Still, something sat on the moment. Weighed on the heads of both the people involved in this conversation. Aiden had no idea what it was, and felt ambivalent about poking it to find out.

"You know Gwen's kids?" he asked her when it all got too heavy.

"Yeah. She's brought them in the shop a few times."

"They nice kids?"

"Elizabeth is a doll. Just about the sweetest girl you'll ever meet. And very mature for thirteen. You find yourself talking to her just like she's an adult. Milo, now . . ."

She allowed the sentence to drift off. Meanwhile she placed Aiden's change in his palm. Three singles and a few coins. She folded his hand around the money and held his fist in both of her hands. He met her eyes, though it felt potentially dangerous to do so.

"You'll work it out," she said. "If you really care for each other, you'll work it out."

Aiden felt his limbs grow firm and immobile, as though they'd been made of fresh plaster of Paris and were now beginning to set up. The bag boy had finished placing his groceries in two sturdy paper sacks and had pushed them in Aiden's direction, but Aiden made no move to pick them up.

"Want help out with these?" the boy asked.

Probably not because Aiden didn't look every bit the strong and healthy rancher. Aiden was obviously fit and quite capable of dealing with the physical world. Probably the boy asked because Aiden did not move or speak. Maybe the boy correctly sensed that Aiden was lost in a moment of his life.

"No, I've got it," he said.

As he lifted the bags, he braved another glance at Marge. She shot him a smile that was clearly intended to be bracing. But it looked as though she was scared for him. Which made Aiden's gut feel the tiniest bit wobbly, though only for a second.

He left the store without glancing back.

———

Aiden arrived back at his ranch to find an unfamiliar truck at the end of the driveway. Parked in front of the locked gate, with its engine off but the radio blaring country-western, windows fully rolled down in the midmorning heat.

Aiden pulled up beside it and powered down the passenger window of his beefy one-ton pickup.

The man behind the wheel was a good ten years older than Aiden, and unfamiliar. So clearly not someone who lived around here, or Aiden would have known him. The man lifted up his battered cowboy hat and scratched his mostly bald scalp.

"Can I help you?" Aiden called over.

"Thought maybe I could take a look at that quarter horse you got up for sale. Saw your ad in the paper."

Aiden sighed.

"Which horse?"

"Sorrel gelding? Three-year-old?"

Aiden didn't want to show anyone a horse. Not today. That would involve pulling his head around to business. His head balked at the prospect. All he wanted to do was clean the house for his guests and get started on the food preparation. He wanted to stay in that dreamy land of having a date with Gwen. The rest of life could wait outside the gate forever as far as he was concerned.

"Most people call on the phone and set up an appointment."

"I called. Didn't get an answer. Had some business down the road a few miles. Had to drive here from Fresno, so I thought I'd take a chance on catching you."

Aiden sighed again.

"Okay," he said. "I got a few minutes, I suppose."

———

He haltered the three-year-old sorrel gelding and led him out into the dappled sunlight in front of the barn.

"Solid for his age," the man said. Aiden hadn't bothered to ask his name.

"Yeah, he's going to be big. Stocky big. Not too tall to work cattle. Probably no taller than he is now, which I'd say is fifteen-two. I never put a measuring stick to him or anything. I've probably got my nerve calling him a roping prospect, because he's not even under saddle yet. But both the stallion and the brood mare were born to rope. Champions, both."

The man looked the horse up and down. Ran a hand down the animal's side. Picked up a rear hoof and looked at the bottom of it. Aiden wasn't sure what he was trying to see.

"Yeah, I heard good things about these horses. Same ones your daddy used to breed, right? Harris Delacorte?"

"It's his same line, yeah. You from around here?"

"Fresno."

"Right. You said that. Sorry. Glad word's traveled that far."

The man dropped the hoof and straightened his back. Stiffly, as though it hurt from too much ranch work and holding too many hooves. He stared at Aiden and said nothing. Aiden felt the need to fill the silent air.

"Until pretty recently I'd always start the three-year-olds myself. Much too long a story to explain why I don't anymore."

*And not a story I'd consider telling to a stranger. Or would enjoy telling to anyone.*

"Start 'em?"

"Under saddle," Aiden said. "Yeah."

"You mean break 'em." With an argumentative emphasis on the word "break."

A pause as the unspoken parts of the disagreement settled in.

"I don't like that word myself. I don't look at it that way. I mean, the horse should still be in one piece after you're successfully sitting in that saddle on his back. If not, I'd say you're doing something wrong."

Aiden felt the man bristle. Felt a return of that same shadow of dark cloud that had been dogging his day.

"Can't say as I agree with you there. Horse has a spirit that tells him to go his own way. Please himself and not you. You don't break that, you're just heading for a world of hurt."

A moment of silence, during which an energy crackled in the air between them. Even the gelding caught it. Aiden saw the animal's head come up, and his eye open wider—saw the dark brown iris partially ringed with white.

"Not a point worth arguing," Aiden said. "Because the horse is not for sale. None of my horses are for sale."

"But you put him up for sale with an ad in the paper."

"Oops."

The man just waited. Maybe to see if Aiden would say more. Maybe deciding whether to blow his top or not.

"I hate it when that happens," Aiden continued. "When your horse is not for sale and you accidentally tell the classified ads people at the paper that he is."

"Right," the man said, his eyebrows pressing down over his darkening eyes. "I get the message. I know when I'm not wanted."

"That's a good quality in a person," Aiden replied.

The man stamped back to his truck, the soles of his boots kicking up miniature dust storms in the arid dirt.

Aiden tried to pull his attention back to his day. Tried to force the feeling of elation back into place. Of course it didn't work.

There was a pall over everything now. A lingering sense of some small pending doom. And it wasn't about the sorrel gelding, Aiden realized as he walked him back into the barn. There was far more at stake than an argument with a buyer. The man gunning his engine and tearing away was the least of Aiden's worries.

He wished he had a better bead on the greater worries, but they eluded him. Just shadows. Ghosts. Unknowable and indistinct. And yet so very . . . *there*.

# Chapter Two

## Falling and Breaking

When Aiden swung his front door wide, all he could see for a minute was her. Though it was not a full minute in actual fact—it was two or three seconds that felt stretchy and overextended, as though they had caused time to falter.

He knew he should look down at the two children who stood one on either side of her. But all he could see was Gwen.

Her hair, naturally jet black, was swept up into a soft do, her eyes so dark as to be nearly black as well. And deep, as if he could swim right through them to what mattered most inside her. She wore a deep-red dress that managed somehow to be modest and show off her full curves at the same time.

"Hey," he said, and felt his face flush with embarrassment. Because her children were watching him look at her as though she were the only thing in the world that mattered to him.

Had he ever felt this way about a woman before? Nothing came to mind. Everything before a couple of months ago felt like a muddled blank when he tried to reach for it.

"Hey yourself," she said. "This is Elizabeth . . ."

Aiden lowered his eyes to the girl.

She was a slim, shy-looking teen who bore no resemblance to her mother. Same with the boy, he could now see in his peripheral vision. They were redheads. Muted red hair and light, freckled complexions. Which could only mean one thing, and it was a thing that made Aiden's stomach roil: the kids took after that horrible, abusive man Gwen had just divorced. By the look of it, they were more part of him than of her. He had pictured them as miniatures of Gwen. It was a disappointment, because he'd thought they would feel familiar to him, and they did not.

"Elizabeth," he said, and held his hand out for her to shake.

She accepted the offer. Her grip was tentative and light. It made her smile hesitantly to shake his hand. Still, it was a lovely smile. Toothy, braces and all, and real. The kind that makes you smile back whether smiles come easily to you or not.

"And this is Milo," Gwen continued.

Aiden reached his hand out to Milo, who was younger and smaller than his sister. The boy stood with his head purposely angled away, as if he thought he could pretend not to see Aiden's offer. Gwen bumped his shoulder with her arm, but it only caused the boy to back up a step. As if retreat were the only move he knew.

He was strangely thin, Aiden now saw. Sickly thin. He had bags under his eyes, deep circles. As if he hadn't slept for a week. Or as if he were allergic to something. Or maybe everything. The whole world.

"Okay," Aiden said, though everyone present seemed to know it was not okay. "You folks should all come in."

Meanwhile, as he spoke, he found himself seized with a strange thought. Well, not even a thought so much. He did not think it through in his brain, nor did he go there on purpose. It was more of an image, flooding in uninvited, of his adoptive father the first time Aiden had met him. He'd been standing in the doorway with his hair slicked back and flowers in his arms. Obviously deeply taken with Aiden's mother, and more than aware that her two children stood as walls that would need to be scaled if he was to be with her. All the fear of that knowledge etched into his face.

It was a memory from a time he'd been sure he could not remember. And yet there it was.

*Ironic,* Aiden's brain said to him. *Thirty-four years later you know exactly how he felt. Poor guy.*

———

"I can make Milo some macaroni and cheese," Aiden said. As he spoke, he rose out of his chair on his way to leaving the table.

"No, really, Aiden," Gwen said. "Don't." She put her hand on his arm, and he sank back down. Aiden looked up to see both children staring at the spot where Gwen's hand intersected with his white shirtsleeve. "He won't eat that, either. It's not about what you made. It's good. And Milo likes chicken and pasta. Usually. He just doesn't eat when he's nervous."

"I'm not nervous," Milo said, still staring at his plate.

It was the first the boy had spoken. Aiden was literally hearing Milo's voice for the first time. It hadn't changed yet—well, of course it hadn't; he was only ten—but somehow Aiden had been unprepared for the high flimsiness of it. It made the boy sound more innocent than he looked.

He did not look innocent. Not at all. He looked shifty and suspicious. Unbalanced by his fear of everything around him.

"I'll rephrase," Gwen said. "When Milo is in an unfamiliar situation, he doesn't eat."

"Or any other situation," Elizabeth added. "He just never eats." Then she glanced up and around, was caught by her mother's eyes, and decisively clammed up.

"I hate to sit here and eat while he starves," Aiden said.

But he placed his cloth napkin back in his lap, because he had no idea of a better way to proceed through the moment.

"It's his choice," Gwen said. "You served him a lovely meal. He'll either eat it or he won't. I won't have you jump up and make him something else, because he's just as likely to turn his nose up at that, too."

They ate in silence for a few minutes. Well, three of them ate.

"I thought maybe after dinner," Aiden said, "we could all go for a ride. I have some really nice, quiet horses. You kids like horses?"

"Yes," Elizabeth said.

"No," Milo said.

Their words erupted simultaneously and more or less canceled each other out.

"Well, Elizabeth and Gwen can go for a ride, and Milo and I can stay here and get to know each other better," Aiden said, refusing to let the dread of that statement come through in his tone. "We have lots of time before it gets dark tonight. Second-longest day of the year. Did you know that?"

He looked to Elizabeth as he asked the question. It just seemed safer.

"I did, actually," she said, sounding eager. "Summer solstice is tomorrow. So, do you have cows here, too? Or just horses?"

"Elizabeth," Gwen said, and shot her daughter another look, as though the girl had said something wrong.

"What?"

"Aiden might think that's too personal."

"How can cows be personal?"

"No, they're not," Aiden said, setting his fork down. "It's not too personal a question at all. So don't feel bad for bringing it up. It's just that your mother happens to know that I'm . . . in between on some things. And she probably thought I wouldn't want to talk about it. But it's okay. I still have a couple hundred head of cattle. And this used to be a working cattle ranch. Just three months ago it was. But then I went through some . . . Oh, I don't know. A change of heart, I guess. And now I'm not sure if that's what I want to do anymore. I also breed quarter horses. So I might just do that instead. You know. Only that."

He looked up to see the girl staring into his eyes with an unguarded intensity. It made him realize that he was not nearly as ready for this meeting as he had thought. But ready or not, here it was. And Aiden was going to see it through.

"So what will you do with all the cows you already have?" she asked.

"I . . . haven't quite decided that yet."

"That's enough of giving poor Aiden the third degree," Gwen said.

"No, it's okay, Gwen. Really it is. The idea was for the four of us to get to know each other. Right? So questions have to be okay."

But he breathed a quiet sigh of relief when no more questions seemed forthcoming.

———

Aiden picked up Milo's plate. The food on it literally had not been touched. The boy hadn't even pushed it around with his fork. In fact . . . had he even picked up his fork? Not that Aiden could remember.

He carried the plate out onto his front porch and whistled for Buddy.

"Hey, Buddy. Here, boy."

Gwen came out onto the porch and hooked her arm through his.

"How can you have a dog and I don't even know it?"

"I guess because he's only been hanging around two or three days. The cats told him to come around for a handout, I swear. All these cats who hang out here and beg off me for meals. I think they all belong to the same club. They tell each other who's the biggest sap within walking distance. I'm kidding, of course. Well. I'm half-kidding. They've got my number, no matter how they manage to do it."

Buddy wagged his way up onto the porch, and Aiden set the plate on the boards. Buddy wolfed down the chicken almost without stopping to chew. Then he began lapping at the pasta.

"Poor baby," Gwen said, pressing more tightly to Aiden's side. "He's so thin and raggedy. And he hardly has any hair."

"Yeah. I think he's been on the road awhile. But you're not on the road anymore, are you, Buddy? You found your sap now."

"What kind of dog d'you think he is?"

"Now that's hard to say. I'm tempted to say every kind. But I actually think he's got some border collie or maybe some Aussie shepherd. I'll know more when his hair grows back some. I gave him a flea bath. Hopefully that'll help. Hopefully it's not the mange, but we'll see. Where are the kids?"

"Milo had to use the bathroom. And Elizabeth volunteered to wait and make sure he got back out here with no trouble."

Aiden almost asked what kind of trouble she was anticipating. But the words wouldn't pass through him.

"He's not a bad boy," she said, when it was clear Aiden was not about to speak. "He's difficult. These days. But he's not bad. I know him. I know he's not. He was the sweetest little guy until . . . It's not in his nature. His dad was really awful to him. And it's just left him . . ."

But before she could finish the sentence, the kids joined them out on the porch. And their chance to talk evaporated. Just like that.

Just when they were getting to the part Aiden really needed to know.

———

Looking back, Aiden would find it hard to pinpoint the moment when Milo slipped out of sight.

It could have been while Aiden was assuaging the last of the nervousness of two novice riders about to mount. He knew he'd seen Milo out of the corner of his eye a moment earlier as he'd fitted Elizabeth with a helmet she could wear to ride. He'd given her a helmet because he felt responsible for her. Because it had been his idea to put her on a horse. He'd noted the presence of Milo because of the pressure it made him feel.

He had claimed that he and the boy would get to know each other better. Which Aiden—and probably everybody else—knew to be a euphemism for "We will suffer quietly until you're done riding."

"They're good horses," Aiden told them over and over.

But was Milo right there listening with him? Looking back, it was hard to say.

He remembered that Gwen and Elizabeth were riding in circles in the big roping pen in the front yard—the one in which Aiden's life had so recently fallen apart. Because they were afraid to ride out on the trail without him, without something or someone to help them feel more in control of their own safety. He remembered their laughter as they nudged the horses into a trot.

Gwen was riding Pharaoh, a big bay with a black muzzle and black legs from the knees down. A real gentle giant of a horse. He had put Elizabeth on Penny, the little gray mare. At fourteen hands she was technically a pony. No matter what her size she would never harm a soul. She would protect her rider, up to and including slowing down and stopping if her rider seemed off-balance or physically insecure.

"Can we canter?" Elizabeth called to him as they trotted by, both bouncing comically in the saddle. Both holding on to the horn as if it were the only thing keeping them from landing in the dirt. "Or lope? Or whatever western riders call it?"

"You can," Aiden called back. "Use a little inside rein. Then nudge 'em with the outside foot. And kiss 'em. They'll go right into it."

Both riders reined their horses to a stop and stared at him.

And no, looking back, Milo was not there. Aiden had lost track of him. Everybody had lost track of him.

His new love and her teenage girl rode their horses to where he stood at the pipe fence.

"My daughter and I think our ears need a good cleaning," Gwen said. "Because we're both pretty sure you said we have to kiss the horses if we want them to canter."

Aiden laughed. It was a genuine thing that rose up out of his belly and surprised him. He hadn't laughed from that place in as long as he could remember. Or maybe he never had.

"It's an expression," he said. "Which I forgot you would not be familiar with. Kiss 'em means you make this little noise at the horse."

He pursed his lips and made a little kissing sound that just about anyone, even if only from having seen western movies, would identify as encouraging a horse to move faster.

"Got it," Elizabeth said.

Then they were loping around the big pen, and Aiden was happy. Genuinely happy. He watched the way they held the saddle horn with both hands—meaning they weren't steering at all—and the way his good horses correctly assumed they were to follow the pipe rail around in a circle, and complied.

He glanced at the sun, which had sunk nearly down over the tops of the trees on the forested western edge of his land. He noted the way the scrub oak leaves had built up on the orangey California tile roof of his one-story stucco ranch house. And even though it meant he would have to clean them off to keep the rain gutters unclogged, it still made him happy. Because this was his home.

And it was a big thing, to be happy. A huge thing. It was something Aiden had sought after all his life, but it had always stayed a few steps ahead. And every time he had reached out to grab it, it had disappeared around a corner, leaving Aiden to start over.

And now here it was.

He felt so good that he thought he could bring himself to try having a conversation with Milo. Who, quite honestly, he had forgotten all about.

Aiden turned 360 degrees, looking for Milo.

The boy was nowhere to be seen.

Aiden caught Gwen's eye and held up one finger to let her know he'd be gone a moment. She reined Pharaoh down to a walk and cupped her hands around her mouth, yelling out, "Where's Milo?"

And that good horse did not even spook.

"That's what I'm about to go figure out," Aiden called back.

—

Aiden found Milo out behind the house, where Aiden had built his new rabbit hutch. The rabbits were surrounded by a tall fence of sturdy four-by-fours and closely hatched welded wire. Because wild animals love to get in and slaughter your rabbits. So you have to build a fence that might stand a chance at stopping them.

But now, Aiden realized, they had all come face to face with a wild animal no one had anticipated.

Before he even truly understood the scene before him, Aiden felt it. Felt the rabbits' panic. It surged through his own gut and he experienced it just as surely as the animals did.

Because that's what his life was these days. That was Aiden's curse.

Milo had scaled the seven-foot fence and sat straddling the top rail, securely up above the rabbits, waiting. Holding something in his right hand. The rabbits crouched inside their shelter, despite the fact that there were still several heads of lettuce outside in their feed pan in the corner. They should have been out gorging themselves. But there was a predator in their midst. So they huddled inside.

As Aiden crossed the ground from the house to the fence, a bold rabbit stuck its head out into the unguarded air.

Milo's right hand drew back, and he lobbed something at that innocent head. It missed the rabbit—who jolted backward inside the shelter—and tumbled harmlessly into a corner of the hutch. A rock about the size of a golf ball.

"Hey!" Aiden shouted, and broke into a run.

He expected Milo to clamber down from the fence, but no such thing happened. Instead the boy reached into his jeans pocket and produced another rock.

Aiden reached the fence and wrapped his fingers through the wire. He had to. It was how he kept his hands off the predator. Which he felt constrained to do, despite the fact that his absolute synchronicity with the rabbits' fear put Aiden squarely on their side.

"Milo," Aiden said, trying to calm his voice. He looked up and saw mostly the boy's blue-jeaned butt. "Get down from there. Now. I won't have this."

Milo did not get down.

Instead the boy cocked his arm back for another throw.

Aiden reached up as high as he could, which involved a jump. A lifting of his feet off the ground. He grabbed the offending arm and pulled it back again. Stopped its forward trajectory.

But then the trouble came.

Aiden was still holding the boy's arm as his jump was inevitably overcome by gravity. And when Aiden came down—when his feet touched earth again—he pulled down on the small arm without meaning to.

The boy tumbled off the fence.

Aiden watched him fall as if in slow motion. He watched the rock come free from Milo's hand.

Aiden still had hold of Milo's arm. And somehow—misguidedly, in retrospect—he thought his grip on the arm was a good thing. He thought it meant he still had a chance to break the boy's fall. So he pulled up on the arm as if to save him. Spare him the bulk of the impact.

It was a singularly wrong move.

Aiden knew he'd made a big mistake as soon as Milo thumped into the dirt. Because the impact happened anyway. But it happened with the boy's arm twisted up into an unnatural position.

Aiden let go.

He stood a moment, too shocked to know how to proceed. Just looking down at the boy. Hoping in spite of all evidence that Milo would jump up, dust off, give him the finger, and saunter away.

"Milo," Aiden said quietly. "You okay?"

For a moment, nothing.

Then Milo split the air with a cry. Something that might spring from a wounded animal. A wild, unrestrained shriek of pain.

# Chapter Three

## Owning and Answering

Aiden sat beside Gwen in the hospital waiting room, and she held his hand. Which, as best he could figure, was the only thing good to be said about his world in that moment.

Elizabeth had fallen asleep in her hard plastic chair on the other side of the long, narrow room—head back, mouth yawning open. Long hair falling across her face. She looked like an angel. A sleeping angel with braces on her teeth.

"I never meant for this to happen," Aiden said again. It might have been the tenth time he'd said it. It might have been the twentieth.

"You don't have to keep saying that, Aiden. I know. I know you."

"Thank you," he said, and gave her hand a squeeze.

It felt good to hear her say she didn't blame him. It had felt good every one of the ten or twenty times she had said it. But she was standing a few steps away from him now, figuratively speaking, in some indefinable place inside herself. And, worse yet, she had closed the door to that place, leaving him alone on the outside. Exactly where he had been his whole life, minus a couple of wonderful months.

"I'll take care of the bill," he said. "Don't worry. I don't know what you have for insurance, but I won't let any of it fall on you."

"But how? You're not exactly—"

"I don't know, but I will. I'll figure it out."

It flitted through his mind that just an hour or so earlier he had been happy. But it felt unreal, impossible. So he let it go again. He sat staring at his hand entwined with hers, and at the finely patterned hospital linoleum beyond.

"The evening wasn't a total loss," Gwen said.

"How do you figure?"

"Elizabeth just adores you."

Aiden burst out laughing. It was a bitter laugh. It did not come from that place inside that feels genuine happiness. Or genuine anything.

"I'm sorry," he said. "I shouldn't laugh. Nothing is funny right now."

"It's okay, I know you're not laughing at him getting hurt. What? What seemed funny?"

"I was just thinking of that joke. That old one-line joke. 'But other than that, Mrs. Lincoln, how did you enjoy the play?'"

Aiden saw a movement above him and glanced up.

Standing over him was Jed Donovan, in uniform. Jed was a sheriff's deputy in this county. Had been for twenty years or more.

"Aiden," Jed said as their eyes connected.

"Jed," Aiden said in return. "Please tell me you just saw me sitting here and came by to say hello."

"Wish I could, Aiden. But we both know it's not gonna be like that. I need to ask you some questions."

———

Jed stood outside his patrol car in the parking lot, puffing on a comically fat cigar. Aiden sat on the edge of the back seat of the vehicle, with the back door standing wide open.

It was full-on dark by then, but their meeting was illuminated by light poles in the hospital parking area. Even the second-longest day of the year had to end sometime. Aiden wasn't sorry to see this one go.

"So what you're saying, then, Aiden," Jed mumbled around the butt of his cigar, "is that you pulled the kid down off a high fence to protect a rabbit."

"No," Aiden said. "No, no, no." It was one "no" for every time he had told the story and Jed had recited it back to him slanted and wrong. "I just took hold of his arm to stop him getting off another throw. The rest was pure accident. I swear."

"Why didn't you just tell him to get down off the fence?"

"I did. He paid me no mind."

"I see."

Jed opened the driver's side door of his patrol car and reached his upper body across the front seat. He emerged with a clipboard.

For a few moments the deputy made notes in silence.

"Okay," Jed said, as if talking to his clipboard. "Okay."

Then he looked down at Aiden. Their eyes met. But with the deputy's face backlit by the parking lot lights it was hard to know what was there in his eyes. Aiden wondered if Jed could see his own eyes clearly and, if so, what he thought he saw there.

"You know why I have to ask these questions," Jed said. "Right?"

"Yes and no."

"It's a legal requirement in a case like this. Kid shows up at a hospital with a broken arm. If he's been riding a horse or a bicycle, maybe we let that go by. Stuff happens with kids, after all. But when we hear it happened in the course of a dispute with his mom's new boyfriend, well . . . that just puts us in a different territory. That sets off what you might call alarm bells."

"I understand that," Aiden said. "The part I don't understand is . . . well, it's me, Jed. It's *me*. I've lived in these parts thirty-four years. Since

I was six years old. You know me. When have you ever known me to cause any trouble?"

Aiden looked up into the deputy's mostly shadowed face and thought he might have seen Jed's eyes narrow. Or it might have been an illusion. A trick of the light.

"Yeah, I do know you, Aiden. And I hate like hell to say it, but that's part of our issue here. Everybody in these parts knows you, and we all know you've changed of late. This real sudden change nobody can understand or follow. That's another red flag, my friend. A sudden change in personality, or . . . I don't know. Beliefs? Habits? I don't even know what to call it. If I understood it, we might be done with this little talk by now."

"But it's just the opposite," Aiden said, paddling hard within himself. As if swimming against a strong current. As if only just realizing what he was up against. How deeply he was sinking into this mess. "I changed into a person *less* likely to do violence to anyone or anything. Not *more*."

"Yeah, I catch your drift, but it doesn't set my mind to rest. All of a sudden you're changeable. Maybe it goes back and forth, how do I know? All I know is . . . I just have no idea what I should expect from you anymore."

They sat silent for a time. Well, Aiden sat. Jed stood silent.

Aiden looked up to see that the moon had risen, huge and filmy over the top of the rise to the east. Just a couple of days off full.

"What do I have to do to prove this was an accident?" he asked after a time.

"Don't know as you can. But at the same time nobody else can prove it wasn't. There was nobody there to witness it except you and the boy. The rabbits aren't talking."

Aiden wasn't sure if that had been intended as a joke. He did not laugh.

"What's Milo saying happened?"

"He's not saying anything at all. He's a recalcitrant little bastard. Don't think I don't know his story, too. Barely over three months in town and already the department's been called to the school twice to sort out some disaster of that kid's making."

"What kind of disaster?"

"That I would not be at liberty to say. But you got your work cut out for you with that one. I'll just say that much and leave it. I don't envy you having that little miscreant suddenly dropped into your life. Hope you really love his mom a lot, because something's got to pay you back for what he'll put you through. But enough about that, because it's only my opinion anyway."

Jed's hand came up to his cigar. He pulled it from his lips for a moment, spat a shred of tobacco off the end of his tongue, then shoved it back into the corner of his mouth again, clamping down on it with his molars.

"Now as far as tonight," he continued, "we more or less take you at your word. For now. You say it was an accident and nobody else says otherwise. But it's a suspicious accident. I'm not gonna lie about that. But there's not much evidence to charge you with anything. But if something like this were to happen again . . ."

"It won't," Aiden said quickly.

"You don't know that. I might know this boy better than you do, though I don't claim to know him well. Disasters follow him around. People get mad in his presence. Nothing good comes of it."

"We'll be fine," Aiden said. Then, after an awkward silence, he added, "Are we done here?"

"Not quite. I'm going to make you a suggestion. I'm going to advise you to get some help with your anger."

"I don't have trouble with anger. Never did."

"Fine. Call it what you want. But even you admit that all of a sudden there was this big change in you recently. You don't even care to know why?"

"Are you talking about . . . ?" But then Aiden couldn't bring himself to pin it down in words.

"Psychiatric help. Yeah. I can't insist. I'm not a judge. What I can do is tell you that if we find ourselves in this bind again, it'll go well with me to know you been making an effort to get your own self figured out. Get what I'm saying?"

"Yeah," Aiden said, and pulled to his feet. "Yeah, I got it."

———

They drove back to Aiden's ranch in silence, Aiden occasionally glancing over at the side of Gwen's face. Especially as they passed under street-lights on the two-lane backcountry highway.

Both kids were sleeping on the small back seat of Aiden's extra-cab pickup, Milo with a ridiculously bulky cast on his right arm. Aiden had carried the sleeping Elizabeth out to the truck over his shoulder. Milo had climbed in of his own accord, but the painkillers had knocked him out as soon as the hum of the driving settled in.

"Are we okay?" Aiden finally asked Gwen.

It made her jump. They had both been so solidified into that silence.

"Of course," she said.

But it wasn't entirely true—he could hear that it wasn't. She probably wanted it to be true. But she was still on the other side of that invisible door. Maybe she couldn't even help it, but those were the facts. Aiden needed only to be present to know it.

"I know things happen with Milo," she said. "Not usually things with animals. He never hurt an animal before. But it's always something. Just different things with different people. I don't know how to say it any better than that. Perfectly nice people get into bad situations with him. People who would never have trouble with anybody else they meet. It's like he brings out the worst in people. Just in the last few years. I really think he can get past it, because it wasn't always like this."

"That sounds like . . ."

"What?"

"Like you're saying you think it wasn't an accident."

"No, I didn't mean it like that. At all. I just mean . . . oh, hell, Aiden. I don't even know what I mean."

And because it had been such a miserable evening—because he had run out of emotional energy and had nothing left to give to the moment—Aiden didn't try to press the conversation to a more satisfactory ending.

—

She called him not ten minutes after leaving his ranch. She must have just walked in her own door.

"You weren't in bed yet, were you?" she asked without bothering to say hello.

"No."

It wasn't entirely true. He was in bed. But not anywhere approaching sleep, so he decided that was close enough.

"I figure I've woken you up out of a sound sleep enough for one lifetime."

"Only once," he said.

"That's enough."

A long silence fell. It felt more awkward than an in-person silence, because there were no visuals to help him judge the tone of her. Her mood.

"It's not what you're thinking," she said.

"What's not what I'm thinking?"

"I know I've been kind of quiet tonight. And kind of . . . I know you think I'm mad at you, or that I blame you. But it's not that."

She fell silent again, and Aiden only waited. To see what it was, if not that. He did not feel he had a right to ask her. He was not sure what rights he had, if any—not only with her, but in the world in general. So he waited.

"It's that I'm scared now. That you're going to drop me."

"Why would I drop you?"

"You know why. Because of Milo. The more you know about him . . . He has a way of getting under people's skin. He always seems to know the one thing that'll bother a person most. The one thing they can't take. Like with you it was the thing with animals. He sensed that right away. And I just don't know that we've got enough water under our bridge, you and me, that you're going to want to walk through all that to be with me. I just worry it's something that gets worse from here."

Aiden breathed for a moment before answering, weighing and measuring the uncharted iceberg floating just under the surface of this discussion. Reimagining his terrible night as a mere jumping-off place for a situation that had only begun to fester.

"We'll work it out," he said, hoping he sounded fairly sure.

"That's nice to hear you say." And a more satisfied, and satisfying, silence followed. "I also called because . . . well, I forgot to ask. There was so much going on right when you got back from talking to that sheriff. You didn't get in any legal trouble, did you?"

"No. Nothing that . . . I mean, if it all stays peaceful from here, no harm done on that account."

"I'll let you get to sleep, then."

And with that she left Aiden alone. Left him to face the fact that sleep likely could not be gotten to. Not anytime soon.

—

It was after eleven when Aiden sat straight up in bed, remembering the rabbits. He felt bad because he had not thought to check on them sooner. On the other hand, it was a good sign that he had forgotten them, and he knew it. If they were afraid, or in pain, he would not have been able to turn his attention elsewhere.

He would have known.

Still, he found his big battery-powered lantern in the pantry and walked out back in nothing but boxer shorts, a robe, and his cowboy boots. He let himself into their enclosure and sat cross-legged on the hard ground, waiting. It was better to let them come to him. Especially after their tough evening.

In time two or three of their white or light-brown heads appeared, reaching out from the open doorway of the hutch. With little hops of their back legs, they made their way over to him. A few of them did. Some came closer than others. It was always that way. Not everyone responds to fear with the same behaviors.

He held the lantern close to them, one by one, and checked them for blood, and ran his hands along their heads and sides if they let him. He could find no sign that any of them had been hit. He turned off the lantern and stretched out in the cold dirt, feeling like Gulliver as they climbed onto his chest and nestled in the spaces between his arms and his sides.

"Sorry, guys," he said.

He wanted to say more. That it was all over now. That nothing like it would happen again. But he wasn't sure if that would prove to be the truth.

———

Several hours later he woke on the hard soil, slightly cold and a little stiff from his awkward position.

All the rabbits had gone back inside their hutch for warmth. Except one. One lone brown rabbit was sleeping with his head tucked into Aiden's armpit. And Aiden didn't want to disturb him. He felt as though he'd been given an honor, a compliment, that he was not ready to give back.

So he put his head down again and let sleep take him for a few hours more.

# Chapter Four

## Tearing Open Everything

Aiden looked up suddenly to see her standing in the open doorway between her office and the waiting room—a woman who must have been the psychiatrist. She stood surveying the waiting room where Aiden sat fidgeting.

"I'm Hannah," the doctor said. "You must be Aiden."

She was somewhere between sixty and seventy, he guessed, with gray hair piled neatly on her head, and a face that seemed to have one crease or crow's-foot for every figurative mountain she had climbed or lesson she had learned the hard way. Then Aiden wondered where that thought had come from. She wore a skirt and blouse in a deep, rich color of red that made Aiden's gut relax.

It reminded him of Gwen's red dress, he realized a moment later. The one she had worn to his house that night. That horrible night. The relaxation dissipated.

"I don't call you Dr. Rutledge?"

"You can if you like. Whatever makes you most comfortable. But Hannah is fine with me."

Aiden stood and walked into her office. Just for a moment he almost turned around and walked out again. But he had driven nearly an hour to get here. And he would probably owe her for the session anyway. It seemed like a waste.

He sat in a deep, comfortable leather wing chair. It was huge, and well padded, and he sank into its cushions. It made him feel like a child.

For several moments he didn't speak. Just nursed an uneasy feeling that she was assessing him in some wordless way. He stared out the window at the freeway and the industrial-looking buildings of this section of urban Bakersfield.

The doctor had a clock that ticked. It made it hard for Aiden to think.

"I hate cities," he said. "After all these years out in the sticks, I can't stand looking at all that concrete and steel."

"I feel exactly the same."

"Why live here, then?"

"I don't. I just have my office here. I live in Tehachapi and commute."

"Lot of driving."

"It is. But it's worth it to me. Correct me if I'm wrong, but I get the impression that you're a man who never imagined himself seeing a psychiatrist."

"You got that right."

"I know you'll tell me what drove you to come here. But before you do, I'm curious about one thing. Why did you choose to see a woman psychiatrist?"

"Oh," he said. "That."

He stared out the window for another moment. Tried to see the buildings differently, now that he knew she didn't like them, either. Tried to see *her* differently. It felt strange to think they had anything in common. Even something small like that.

"Only if you care to say," she added.

"I just thought . . . based on what I need to say here . . . I thought a woman would be more likely to understand." He knew as he said it that he was referring more to what he called "the wake up" and less to Milo. "No, wait. I'll be even more honest than that. I thought a man would laugh at me. Maybe not right out loud, but I would know. And that would be bad enough."

Then he pulled his attention back to the subject at hand. Or at least what he wanted to be the subject. He had come here to talk about Milo. Not himself. Aiden was not the problem. Milo was the problem.

———

"So you were ordered to come here by a judge?" Hannah asked, after Aiden had told her the story of his disastrous first meeting with Milo.

"No. Not ordered. And no judge. It was just something that was . . . highly recommended. I think it was kind of hinted at . . . you know . . . that things would go easier on me if anything like this ever happened again. I think the world sees me now as having anger issues. Which I don't. Well. My little corner of the world, anyway. Which I guess isn't much world. But it's what I've got."

"Did you come here only to get the law off your case?"

"No. Not entirely. I'm feeling more than a little bit lost these days. I could use some help sorting all this stuff out."

"Good," Hannah said. "Good. I'm glad to hear you say that. I think we can go with that. I think that's enough to work with for now."

———

"It was Gwen who pointed out that somehow this kid had found my Achilles' heel," Aiden said a few minutes later in the session. "He'd just met me, but he knew the one thing I couldn't take. And he was all too happy to use it against me."

"I understand," Hannah said. "And I hope you understand what I'm about to say next. For the purposes of this therapy, Milo is not as important as you think he is. He's important to you; I get that. You have to learn to get along with him if you want your new relationship to move forward. And we can certainly deal with that. But people come into our lives and point things out to us for a reason. Right now I'm more interested in why this issue with animals is such an Achilles' heel for you. Not that anyone wouldn't want to protect their animals. Don't get me wrong. But I'm sensing there's something more here."

"Oh yeah," Aiden said. "There's more. There's definitely more." He sighed. Paused as long as he felt he reasonably could. "I guess I need to tell you about the wake up."

"The wake up? That's an interesting expression."

"Yeah, well. That's what I call it. When I have to talk about it. If I had my way I wouldn't call it anything at all. Because I wouldn't even bring it up. Or better yet, it wouldn't have happened in the first place."

"But you're going to tell me about it now. Right?"

"Yeah," Aiden said with another sigh. "I guess I am."

He sat in silence for a moment, listening to the clock ticking, and nursing an uneasy feeling. Why was he opening this can of worms?

He'd come here, he now realized, for an easy answer. What he would get would be far messier, less exact, and more complicated than he could possibly have imagined. He could feel that now.

He would have to tear open everything.

# PART TWO

## AIDEN DELACORTE AT AGE FORTY

### THREE MONTHS EARLIER

# Chapter Five

## The Wake Up

There *was* something different about that day. There was. Even before it became painfully obvious. Even before it left Aiden no choice but to fully live it through.

He felt the something in question as he bent down to catch the cinch and pull it up around his horse's barrel. He felt it again as he leaned forward to clip the breast collar to the bottom of the cinch. Almost as though the blood rushing to Aiden's brain gave it power.

It was just a nagging thing, back then. A sense that something stood close behind his shoulder, crowding him. An unsettling feeling that he was holding something at bay. Maybe he always was. Maybe he always had been. But somehow, in that moment, its presence felt less inchoate, more dense and problematic.

He straightened up to see Derek sitting his bay gelding nearby, staring at Aiden as though amused by what he saw.

"What the hell're you doing, Aiden?"

"I'm going hunting," Aiden said. "You never saw a man go hunting before?"

"I'm not sure I ever saw a man spend ten hours riding cattle and otherwise nailing his ass into a hard saddle, then turn around and choose to do something just for the hell of it that requires more riding. No. I do believe this might be a first."

"I've just been wanting to go. That's all."

"Some people take their trucks hunting," Derek added.

*Not to this spot they don't,* Aiden thought. But he didn't want to share his special spot with Derek or anybody else. The last thing any hunter wanted was for that kind of information to get out.

He said nothing.

"You ain't got but an hour or two till sundown."

"That's a good time to go," Aiden said, asking his horse to take the bit.

"Trucks have lights. In case you didn't know. Horses not so much. You could get stuck out in those woods for the night if you don't play your cards right."

"Like that would be the most terrible thing in the world," Aiden said.

He pictured himself lying on his back on two saddle blankets in the warm spring night, staring up at a riot of stars.

"Whatever, man," Derek said, neck-reining his bay gelding back toward the house. "You always were a little crazy."

———

Aiden rode through the woods, allowing the slant of light through the dense trees to settle his spirits. He rode his stallion, Dusty, a solidly built gray quarter horse that he used for breeding great cow horses. He ponied his sorrel gelding Leo along behind, harnessed instead of saddled and pulling a drag sled. What the Native Americans would call a travois. But the Indians made them from the trunks of narrow saplings. This one had been made with two-by-twos from the hardware store.

Aiden could hear the distinctive thumps it made as the gelding dragged it over rocks.

For a flicker of a moment he thought he felt it again—some kind of rattling uneasiness. Something that wanted to turn him back. That was why he had to go, and he knew it. He had pushed himself into this trip for precisely that reason: to answer that nagging subconscious request with a strong and solid no.

———

Aiden walked upstream until he was several hundred yards from the spot where he'd tied his horses.

There was a special clearing, a break in the woods. If you looked closely, you could see the faint trail left by the deer on their way to and from the stream. They came down in the evening to drink.

*Everybody and everything has to drink.*

Aiden set down his deer rifle and dipped his cupped hands into the cold, flowing water. He was thirsty. He hadn't so much as popped a can of soda during that long, hot day of riding. He hadn't bothered to feel his thirst then. He felt it now.

He sat a few minutes, enjoying the way the wind blew the leaves over his head, shifting the dappled light that fell into his eyes. He could hear that wind, and the water tumbling over stones, but nothing more.

A movement caught his eye, and his hand instinctively found the weapon again.

He looked up to see a doe leading her young fawn down to the water. Very young, that fawn. Probably no more than a month old. Aiden had no intention of shooting a fawn that young, nor did he plan to leave one on its own to be slaughtered in the forest. There was hunting, and then there was just plain cruel. It was a line he was not about to cross.

His hand loosened on the stock of the rifle.

Not a second later he saw it. The buck. The one who changed everything. Broad chest. Flash of white on its muzzle and belly. Eight points on its rack of horns.

Aiden raised the rifle and sighted, centering the buck's heart in his crosshairs.

He pulled the trigger.

Pain exploded in Aiden's chest, nearly a foot from the spot where the rifle butt kicked against his shoulder. It ripped through, erasing everything in the world that was not that pain. Searing, with pressure. It knocked him backward. Threw him over.

He blacked out so quickly that, as far as Aiden's conscious mind was concerned, he never hit the ground.

———

Aiden opened his eyes.

Very little time had elapsed. He knew so from the angle of the sun. At first he remembered nothing. And there was nothing to help him remember.

There was no pain.

He sat up, and gradually the memory returned to him. His hand came up to his chest. He looked down, expecting it to come away bloody.

There was no blood.

Aiden pulled his shirt away from his skin and looked underneath. No bruising. He felt everywhere. Nothing hurt. He breathed deeply, searching for any shortness of breath that might indicate a heart attack. His breathing was fine. His heart seemed to beat normally.

It was as if nothing had happened.

Well, not even *as if*. Nothing had happened.

So what the hell had happened?

"What the hell," Aiden said out loud. It was not a question. It was a criticism of the moment. A complaint about the unpredictability, the sheer senselessness, of the world at times. Though, frankly, at no other time had it ever made as little sense as this.

He stumbled to his feet.

He looked in the direction of the buck. The buck was down. A perfect shot. One bullet hole, squarely in his chest. Aiden had taken him with one exacting shot through the heart. No pain. Or, if there had been pain, it must have been brief.

*So why was I the one who felt it?* a voice asked in Aiden's brain. A voice that felt vaguely apart from him. Like a second Aiden, hovering over the first with its unwanted presence.

Aiden pushed the thought away again.

—

Aiden led Leo to the spot where the buck lay beside the water. As he did so, he listened to the occasional thump of the drag sled and comforted himself with the feeling that all had returned to normal.

The congratulatory moment did not last long.

When they reached the buck, or close enough to the animal to see and smell it, the gelding paused in his tracks. Just one beat, but a sudden fearful jolt tore through Aiden's gut like another phantom gunshot. On any previous day he likely would not have noticed the pause at all. On that day, fear struck Aiden's body. A variety of terrified dread.

He looked over at Leo and saw just the slightest widening of the horse's eye.

The gelding was afraid.

The gelding smelled blood.

The gelding understood death.

The gelding was afraid of death. Even the death of an animal unrelated to himself. Even the death of a non-equine.

And Aiden felt himself overwhelmed with that same fear. That's when he knew it was not over. Not even close.

—

He arrived back at the ranch to find that Derek had not yet gone home. His other ranch hand, Trey, had driven away. Derek was sitting in his battered flatbed pickup truck, lighting a cigarette and letting the engine warm up.

The sun was recently down, the dusk thick, warm. Dry.

Aiden rode up near Derek's open driver's window, still ponying the gelding, the sled, the buck.

"Damn," Derek said. "Lookit what you got. Sure didn't take you long, neither. You weren't gone but an hour."

"Wasn't I?"

"That's a nice-lookin' beast you bagged."

"You want it?"

For several moments Derek just smoked and smiled. He seemed not to know much about the nature of the joke, yet appeared convinced it must be a joke of one sort or another.

Then he must have gotten tired of waiting for the punch line, because he frowned.

"What, seriously?"

"Yeah. Seriously. You want it?"

Derek narrowed his eyes with suspicion. "What's wrong with it?"

"Nothing's wrong with it."

"Wait. Don't tell me. Let me guess. You blew right through the guts and now you think the meat is tainted."

"No. Not at all. Right into the heart."

"Well, what's wrong with it, then?"

"I told you. Nothing."

Aiden swung down from his stallion's saddle. Derek held his cigarette between his lips and opened his truck door, stepping into the dirt.

They stood over the body of the buck where it lay lashed to the drag sled, head lolling.

"Why don't you want it, then?"

"I can't say exactly. I just don't."

"You didn't field-dress it."

"No. I didn't."

"Why didn't you field-dress it? Not like you not to."

"I just didn't want to, that's all."

"And why d'you want to give it away now?"

"I told you. I just don't want it."

Derek pushed his hat back on his head, revealing half of his sweat-slicked hair. "Why shoot it in the first place if you don't want it?"

"I guess I thought I wanted it then," Aiden said.

"Livie's gonna kill you if she finds out you shot it but she won't be eating any of it."

"I expect."

They stood in silence for a time. Long enough that Aiden felt he could watch the twilight darken. But that might only have been his imagination.

"I think you've gone and lost what little bit was left of your mind," Derek said at last. "But if you're crazy enough to give away this much meat, I'm smart enough to take it. Come on. Help me get it on my truck."

———

Aiden stood in line at the local market, three people in front of him but no one behind. That was what happened when you got a slow start into town after the working day.

In his cart was a frozen lasagna, a bottle of wine that was for Livie and not for himself, and a bag of navel oranges.

He looked up at the ceiling fans as he waited. He did not think about anything. There was nothing safe to think about.

The checker was a woman he had not seen before. In these parts, new people did not happen along every day. Oh, maybe standing beside their cars at a filling station, they did. But not so much working at the local businesses.

She had long dark hair, pinned up on her head. Eyes so dark they were almost black. She was not the image of fashion model slimness like Livie. Neither was she particularly big. Just full. Round where women have curves.

Then Aiden questioned what he was doing looking at her curves, and the line shifted forward by one shopper.

Her name tag said "Gwen."

When he finally got up to Gwen to have his scant groceries scanned, she lifted her eyes to his and smiled. That in itself was nothing much. Warner's Market probably encouraged such behavior. But the smile itself was a deeper moment. Not intimate, but as though she actually saw him. That startled Aiden, and made him take a figurative step backward to protect his delicate insides.

Insides that he had thought to be quite sturdy until just a little earlier that day.

"Dinner?" she asked, nodding at his lasagna. Probably just to have something to say.

"Looks that way." He opened his wallet and pulled out two twenties. Then, to fill an awkward vacuum of words, he added, "You're new here."

"I am."

"Just got to town?"

"About a week ago, but this is only my third day on the job."

Meanwhile, as they tried to conduct this simple conversation, there was the issue of the dog breaking through to Aiden's conscious mind.

Someone had tied a dog to a newspaper vending box out in front of the market, and the doors were open to take in the evening cool. This was not a supermarket with automatic doors. Aiden would have had to drive more than forty miles into Bakersfield to find one of those, and what would have been the point of doing so? This local market was just a little storefront business letting out onto the pedestrian sidewalk, on which a shopper had tied his or her dog. It was an animal Aiden had not seen around these parts before.

The dog was whining.

Aiden had been aware of his own discomfort, but only in that moment did the cause of the stress become conscious. It escalated the sensation, to know. It felt like someone had tightened a vise clamp on his large intestines.

"Welcome, anyway," Aiden said, realizing he had left his end of the conversation alone too long.

"You okay?" Gwen asked, lifting her eyes to him again in that manner that made him feel bare.

"Yeah," he mumbled. It did not sound convincing. He looked around to see if another shopper was waiting in line behind him wishing he would hurry things along. There was no one there. "Just . . . ," he began. Then he stalled briefly. "That dog was just bothering me."

"Aw," she said, as if to dismiss his statement, "he's just lonely. Not even being that loud."

"No, I didn't mean it like that. I didn't mean the dog shouldn't be whining. Or that he was bothering me with his . . . I just meant . . . oh, hell, what *did* I mean? He just sounds so uncomfortable. I was feeling for his situation. It was making me uncomfortable, too."

"Well, aren't you sweet?" Gwen said, her voice rising into a distinctly feminine range that made Aiden's heart hurt.

Aiden sensed movement and looked around to see Trey, his other ranch hand, step into line behind him with a six-pack.

Meanwhile Gwen was still speaking in that voice.

"You just know he'll feel all better when his person gets back to him."

"*He* doesn't know that, though," Aiden said. He didn't want to say it with Trey listening, but he did anyway. "He thinks it might be forever this time."

He looked up to see Gwen staring into his eyes. Curiously. Only then did he realize he had overstepped his own borders.

"What makes you say that?"

"Oh, you know. Just how dogs are."

It wasn't the truth. But it was the level of truth you share with a new grocery checker at the market. Like when they ask how you are and you say you're fine. No matter how you are. And that's all they really wanted from you anyway.

"That's true," she said, and handed him the change and his receipt.

Before he stepped away from the checkout counter, Aiden looked around at his ranch hand.

"Trey," he said. A simple greeting.

Trey raised his eyebrows but nothing more.

Aiden stepped out onto the street and stood at the curb under a post light, holding his rapidly defrosting lasagna and staring down at the dog. A yellow lab, maybe, only not a full one. Sixty pounds easily. The dog stared up at Aiden and wagged cautiously. Aiden didn't want to touch the dog, because he didn't know for a fact that it wouldn't bite. Neither did he want to leave it alone to its fear.

A moment later Trey appeared near his left arm and began to untie the dog's leash.

"This your dog, Trey?"

"It is. Yeah."

"How come I never saw him before?"

"Just got 'im."

"What happened to your other dog?"

"Useless cur," Trey said, like spitting out something bad tasting. "Doesn't even bark at noises. Licks burglars, I swear. Gave 'im to my stepmom. Hey. Aiden. You do remember you have a girlfriend. Right?"

Aiden felt his back stiffen. "How could I not remember that?"

"Good question. How could you not? Watching you talk to that pretty new checker, seemed like it might've slipped your mind. Her name is Olivia, by the way, your girlfriend. Just to refresh your memory. If you ever decide you don't want her, I'll be happy to take 'er off your hands."

"*Take her off my hands?* She's not a sack of cornmeal, Trey."

"I know it. Just sayin'."

Then Trey took the end of his leash and his new dog and his six-pack and disappeared into the dark of the evening.

———

Livie arrived at eight, walked straight into Aiden's kitchen, and opened the oven door, peering inside.

She was wearing those skinny jeans and a top that showed off her midsection. Her dark-blonde hair was disorganized and casual in a premeditated way, one it might have taken her a good part of the afternoon to achieve.

"Frozen lasagna?" she asked. It was clear by her tone what she thought of frozen lasagna, and it was not good.

"What's wrong with that?" he asked, leaning in the kitchen doorway.

"Trey said you went hunting at the end of the day."

"When did you talk to Trey?"

"He calls now and again."

"Does he now? You think that's appropriate?"

"Do I think what's appropriate?"

She closed the oven door at long last. It settled something in Aiden's stomach. He hadn't liked all that heat getting out. But Livie tended not to take well to any sort of correction.

"Him calling you," Aiden said.

"He's harmless enough. My point is, I kind of had my mouth all set for that venison sausage you make."

"You have any idea how long it takes to process out the meat like that?"

"Would have been nice to at least see that process . . . in . . . you know. Process. So you came home empty-handed?"

"Yeah," Aiden said. "I did."

For a moment he was looking at something else. Through the kitchen window at a movement in the pasture that proved only to be two of the brood mares scuffling over a hay feeder. Then her silence drew his attention back. He looked into her face to see it steaming with fury. It made something inside him shut down. Hang out the "Closed" sign and switch off all the lights.

"I can't believe you, Aiden."

"What can't you believe?" he asked, because it would have been dangerous to say nothing.

"I can't believe you just looked right into my face and lied to me."

*Actually,* Aiden thought, *I was looking out the window at the time.* As he thought it, he did so again.

"I didn't lie," he said, wondering, as he said it, if he could somehow twist it into being true.

"So you didn't bag an eight-point buck out there today? Because I heard you did. I heard you gave it away. And that you brought it back not even dressed out, and nobody can figure why, because usually you're so damned predictable about things like that. All about your routines. And did you ever think before you gave it away that *I* might have wanted venison?"

Aiden wanted to ask how. *How* had she heard all that? But it would have been a pointless question. One person had known. Derek. In a small town full of cell phones and small-town interests, the travel of information never took long.

"I didn't lie," Aiden said again. "I didn't say I didn't bag anything. You asked if I got home empty-handed. This is my home. This house. And by the time I got back to the house, I had nothing."

A silence, during which he did not dare look into her face.

"That is absolutely pathetic," she said.

*Yes,* he thought. *That was pathetic.*

"I might just spend tonight on my own," she added.

"Take this bottle of wine," Aiden said. "You know I won't drink it."

In the crackling silence that followed, he realized he had said the wrong thing. He should have said, "No, Livie. Don't go." But the idea of spending the evening alone—not affronted, not on thin ice, unguarded—felt positively compelling to Aiden. Something he would have actively sought had he realized he was within his rights to want it.

She shook her head and stomped to the door, ignoring the bottle of wine that he held in her direction. At the door she stopped and leveled him with another look. He forced himself to meet her eyes. Her left one was slightly askew, looking too much toward her own nose. Normally Aiden found it adorable. In that moment it only looked like a flaw.

"What else do you lie to me about?"

"I don't lie to you."

"That's what I used to think, but now I don't know. Trey said you seem a little sweet on that new checker at Warner's."

"That's ridiculous."

"Is it? Why?"

"Because all she did was ring up my groceries and we talked a few sentences about a whining dog. Trey is sweet on *you*, in case you haven't noticed, and if there's anything he can say to drive a wedge between us, then that's what he'll say. I didn't lie about the buck. Just didn't go into every detail. It wasn't something I wanted to talk about much. Not right then, anyway."

He watched her for a time. Watched her shoulders soften. For a moment he thought she might stay, which felt disappointing. He needed to be alone. Needed it sorely. More than he could entirely fathom. Certainly more than he could have communicated.

"Tell me the truth *now*, then," Livie said. "Why'd you bring that damn thing home without even dressing it out? Why'd you give it away to Derek when you know fresh venison's my favorite?"

Aiden sighed. He backed up a few steps to the couch and sank down into a seat. Sighed again. Pressed his face into his hands briefly.

"I just didn't want to cut into it. Him. Into his . . . body. It was his *body*. I can't explain it any better than that. I didn't want his blood all over me. I didn't want to see his guts. Can you understand that?"

"Sure," she said. "Sure, Aiden. I can understand that fine. Just not from you. How many deer you dressed out in your time? A hundred?"

"Maybe."

"So what changed all of a sudden today?"

"I wish I knew."

He looked at the rug for a long moment. Not up at Livie. Not in any way.

A minute later he heard the door thump closed. When he looked up, she was gone. A load of stress drained out of his belly.

He sighed and closed his eyes as he felt it go.

—

Aiden ate the frozen lasagna. All of it. Even though it was clearly intended to serve two.

It was still a little bit frozen in the middle.

He ate it anyway.

# Chapter Six

## The Roundup

It was the following week, eight in the morning on roundup day, and summer had decided to arrive early—when the calendar said barely spring. It was already over eighty degrees. Not a cloud in the sky. The bake of the sun was a bear, even at its distinct morning slant.

Aiden's property was dotted with three-quarter-ton and one-ton pickup trucks hitched to stock trailers, left to sit with their trailers' rear gates yawning open. The neighboring ranchers came on roundup day, and they brought their horses. They brought their families. They helped rope and tag and castrate. Then Aiden would feed them a good barbecue and all the beer they could drink, and when *their* roundup time came, he would return the favor.

It's just the way things were done. Had always been done.

Aiden sat his paint gelding, Mather, in the roping pen, swinging his rope, surrounded by a shifting sea of cattle. Lowing, bellowing cattle. About a hundred head. The sound of their comments was ceaseless. They could and would express themselves all damn day.

He used his legs to guide the horse, who was in a distinctly skittish mood. It was unlike the paint to be skittish. It was unlike any of his horses to be anything but quietly resigned to his or her work.

Aiden let the rope fly and caught a calf around his back legs. He pulled the rope tight and it took the animal off his feet. The calf landed with an audible thump and a puff of dry dirt. Aiden winced. For a moment he just sat his horse and held the rope taut. In that moment he did not do what was needed of him next.

His job, along with both his ranch hands and one older next-door neighbor named Roger, was to drag the calves by their back legs to the men who would tie their legs up in front, tag their ears, castrate the males.

Even the act of dragging the calf across the pen felt unthinkable.

The calf thrashed and kicked and tried to regain his feet, and Aiden felt the animal's fear like a knife wound. A brand-new wound to add to all the others. The paint danced beneath him, wanting to know why Aiden was afraid. Trying to understand whether Aiden knew something he did not.

*You'll get through this,* Aiden said to himself for the hundredth time that morning. *Swallow it down and do what you need to do.*

He pressed his heels to the paint's sides.

The gelding surged forward too suddenly, dragging the calf violently through the dirt for several feet. The calf bellowed out in panic, and Aiden caught it like a cold, only more immediate. Aiden's horse spun and stood facing the calf, which was not a tenable position. A grown steer ran between Aiden and his calf, catching his horns on the rope, pulling it sideways, pressing the rope against a front leg of the gelding, who surged forward again into a full-on spook—and stumbled badly.

Aiden's gut jolted with panic. Partly because he thought the horse would go down. Partly because Mather felt a jolt of panic thinking he would go down.

The gelding caught himself, regained his balance—then exploded into bucking.

Aiden grabbed the saddle horn, squeezed with his legs, and sat the first three spirited bucks. The fourth sent him flying. He landed in the dirt, wrenching his shoulder and smacking his head hard enough to see stars.

He drew up onto his knees and reached for his hat, vaguely hearing hoots of laughter in his ears. They sounded far away. He watched the gelding tear around the big pipe corral, dragging the bellowing calf behind, cattle dashing out of their way like water parting. Now and then one tripped on the rope or stepped on the calf as he was dragged by.

"What the hell was that, Aiden?" Derek's voice made its way across the pen to him. "I watched you ride four, five years now and never saw no gelding set you on your ass in the dirt like that."

Aiden felt his face redden. He pulled to his feet, though it hurt to do so. Though he could have used more time to stitch himself together. He likely had a concussion from the feel of it. But it was humiliating to come off your horse in front of just about everybody you knew—roundup, of all days—and nothing was more important than to prove you were tough enough to shake it off. Whether that was the truth of the situation or not.

"I don't know," Aiden called back, smacking his hat against his jeaned thigh to dust it off. "I don't know what he's got up his butt today."

"Not like Mather to be that way," Derek said.

"No. It's not."

Aiden jumped in front of the horse on the next pass and extended his arms on both sides. The beast skidded to a stop. Aiden took hold of the reins just behind the bit.

"Stop it," he said, leaning close to the horse's ear and speaking low. "Work with me here."

He moved down the gelding's left side to mount. But no sooner did he put his foot in the stirrup than the horse crow-hopped away again, leaving Aiden yanking on the reins with one hand and struggling to half run along, half get his foot back. He pulled free of the stirrup just in time—just as he was about to be taken off his feet. The gelding yanked the reins out of his hand and ran off, still dragging the calf in the dirt behind.

Aiden leaned on his knees and breathed for a moment. Then he looked up. No one was laughing. Everyone had stopped doing what they'd been doing. No one's hands moved. The women had stopped buttering garlic bread and marinating tri tip. The men had reined their own mounts to a halt or knelt frozen in the dirt, hovering over downed calves.

Just about everybody who lived in these parts was staring at Aiden. As though they couldn't possibly understand the difficulty. As though they felt sorry for him. They seemed to know they should look away again but just couldn't bring themselves to stop staring.

Even their horses stood still and watched, far too mature and professional to let the panic of one misguided cow pony throw them off their game.

Aiden grabbed the reins of his gelding, who had stopped by the pipe fence and was standing with his head down, blowing through wide nostrils, neck foamed with sweat. He undid the rope at the saddle and let the calf loose. With slack in the rope, the animal kicked free and stumbled to his feet, plainly traumatized.

"I'm gonna put Mather away and get Turbo instead," Aiden said loudly. Not to anyone in particular.

——

"Okay, so this isn't going well," Aiden told Turbo as he saddled the big bay. "Not even as well as I thought it would, and I didn't have what you might call high expectations. So cut me a little slack today, huh, buddy? Pay me back for all that hay I fed you all these years."

Aiden looked up to see the bay's eye open wide, showing a hint of white all the way around.

"Crap," Aiden said out loud.

Nothing is much worse on a horse than a scared rider, and Aiden knew it well. Had known it since he was a child. Only, normally it did not apply to him. Aiden did not ride his horses scared. Or at least, he never had before. A horse is a herd animal, and Aiden's horses looked to him to be their leader. If they sensed fear in him, it stood to reason they would assume there was something to fear.

Aiden put his foot in the stirrup and swung up from the ground. The horse jerked forward before Aiden could even swing a leg over, nearly leaving him in the dirt. He yanked the reins back too suddenly, and Turbo planted his front hooves and stopped, throwing Aiden down over his neck.

Aiden sighed. Straightened. Swung into the saddle.

"Damn it all to hell," he said out loud, more or less to the horse. "This's gonna be one long damn day."

——

The second time he fell off his horse and hit the dirt—twice shattering a seven-year record of staying on, including while breaking these good horses—Aiden simply handed the reins off to his neighbor Roger's teen-age granddaughter. Then he did what he had inwardly vowed he would not do: he joined the team working the calves on the ground.

The team that had to inflict the big hurt.

He felt the sickening panic roil in his gut as Derek dragged a calf to where he and Trey waited. Somehow Derek had the calf by the front legs, which was an unusual way to rope one. As soon as Derek reined his horse to a halt the calf struggled to his feet. Aiden body-slammed the animal and wrestled him onto his side again. He wrapped and tied the back legs together with one lightning-fast motion of his rope. Then he pulled back just slightly, sat halfway up—and made a colossal mistake.

That is, if it was accidental at all. Later he would look back on the moment and wonder.

The most important element to his current task was to keep the rope taut at all times. Keep the hind legs not only tied together but drawn back. Immobile.

Aiden allowed the rope to slack.

The calf thrashed his hind legs violently—tied together into one lethal club—and kicked out, striking Aiden hard in the side. Breaking more than one of his ribs. No one had to tell Aiden his ribs had just been broken. No X-ray required. Aiden felt at least two of them give.

He landed on his tailbone in the dirt and just sat. Just froze there, immobile, experiencing the pain. Allowing it. Because there was nothing else to be done about it. No point trying to do battle with something that's already won.

Everything stopped around him. All activity ceased, at least from the sound of things. Even the cattle seemed to settle, now that the ropes and the horses held still. Aiden figured everybody was staring at him again, but he might have been wrong. He never did look around.

It's unlikely that he was wrong.

"You okay, buddy?"

Aiden looked up into the hot sun to see Derek peering down at him from the back of his horse.

"Not so much, no."

"He break some ribs with that kick?"

"I believe he did."

"Okay, then," Derek said, swinging down from his mount. "You win the award for worst single day ever. While we get your trophy ready maybe Livie can drive you over to that county hospital and see what they can do for your situation."

"Livie won't even be here till she gets off work," Aiden said, surprised at how much it hurt to talk.

"Okay, then," Derek said again. "I'll just have to take a break and do the deed my own self."

He reached a hooked elbow down, and Aiden took hold of it with his left arm—the less broken-up side. As he pulled to his feet he felt jolted by the pain, which made him so nauseous he thought he might vomit. When the feeling passed, something else replaced it. Something entirely different.

Relief.

Aiden had just gotten out of roundup day the only way possible. You either worked roundup or they carried you out on a stretcher. Now Aiden was out. Guilt free. Explanation free.

Gone.

At least, Aiden himself was free. He could still feel the fear and pain of the young steers long after Derek drove him off the ranch.

———

Aiden looked out the truck window, breathed as shallowly as possible, and watched the land roll by. It all looked pretty much the same. Board or wire fences. Rolling golden hills. Scrub oaks. Patches of thick evergreen forest.

"Those hills were green about a minute ago," Aiden said to Derek. Probably just to have something to say.

"Yeah, and that's how long they stay green, too. About a minute."

"This drought's gonna be the death of us."

A silence. Derek pulled a cigarette out of the pack with his teeth and fired it up with the dashboard lighter.

"What the hell happened out there today, buddy?" he asked Aiden after a time.

"Anybody can have a bad day. Horses and humans both."

"Kind of a coincidence, though. Don't you think? You and two of your horses? All having a bad day at the same time? Those horses are solid as the hills. All the years I been working with those two I never once seen 'em so much as spook big. If my daddy was here he'd say if two of your horses are having a bad day on the same day, *you're* having a bad day."

"Glad he's not here then," Aiden said, speaking quietly so as not to jostle his injuries with too much breath.

"You can talk to me, you know, Aiden."

"No, I can't."

He hadn't planned to say it. But all he could think about was the pain, and in the midst of that distraction other issues slipped through the gate.

"Why would you say a thing like that?"

"Last week when I brought that buck home. You said to me, you said something like 'Livie's gonna kill you if she finds out you shot it and she doesn't get to eat it.' *If. If* she finds out, you said. Not two hours later she comes by my house and sets a trap for me to walk into, and she already knows everything. Everything. How many points that buck had. How I didn't dress it out."

It was a lot of words for Aiden. A lot of truth. More than he sometimes said in a day. If he could help it.

"I didn't tell Livie."

"You didn't have to. You told Trey and he's like a telegraph wire right into her ear, and you know it. He loves any excuse to talk to her, the less flattering to me, the better."

Derek smoked in silence for maybe a mile. Maybe two.

"I'm sorry you feel that way," he said at last. "I figured we were friends."

Aiden opened his mouth to answer, but he was in too much pain. And it was too much trouble.

It was just all too much.

—

At least four hours had passed by the time Aiden made it back home to the ranch. Maybe closer to five. They had stopped at a pharmacy near the hospital and filled the prescription he'd been given. He'd popped two of those pills in the truck on the ride home. To say he was feeling their effects would be understating the case.

He climbed gingerly down from Derek's truck. Walked in what he hoped was a more or less straight line to the pipe corral, relieved to see that all the work had been done and the crowd had moved on to the barbecue portion of the proceedings. He had skipped breakfast due to nerves, and his hunger added to that lightheaded feeling. And it might have been exaggerating the effects of the drug.

Of course, he was grateful the roundup was over for much larger reasons than just barbecue.

Something caught his eye, though, and he stood at the pipe fence a minute, trying to make sense of what he saw.

That calf was still down. The one that had kicked him. At least, Aiden thought it was the same calf. He was hog-tied, all four of his legs lashed together in one desperate bundle. He lay on his side in the sun, in the hottest part of the afternoon. His tongue lolled out, touching the dry dirt. If not for his heaving sides, Aiden might have assumed the animal was dead. The rest of the herd had been released from the pen. They had moved on up the hill to nurse their fresh wounds and ease away their terror, leaving this one calf unable to follow.

Aiden could clearly see that the calf had not yet been gelded.

Trey walked up behind him and clapped him on the shoulder. Aiden winced silently.

"We saved him for you," Trey said.

"What?"

"We saved him. We figured after he broke your ribs you'd want to take his manhood personally. Or . . . his bull-hood, I guess I should say. So we left him for you to do."

"You left him lying tied up in the sun for almost *five hours*? With the other cattle stepping on him and nothing to drink?"

Aiden heard his own voice coming up to a shout. But he couldn't seem to stop it. He was outside himself now, watching from afar. His emotion was a rubber band wound up until it snapped. The ends would fly. Nothing would come back together. Not now. Not anymore.

Aiden looked up to see everyone staring at him. A little bit of déjà vu in that. But now they were all at rest, sitting in lawn chairs and on blankets, guzzling beer and watching the tri tips cook. And all eyes had turned to Aiden.

Derek appeared from nowhere, hooking an arm around his shoulder and leading him toward the house.

"All righty, then," Derek said. "Somebody's a little hopped up on pain meds and needs a good old-fashioned lie down. He doesn't know what he's saying, folks."

"I know exactly what I'm saying," Aiden shouted, ducking out from under the arm. "What the hell is *with* you people? Not one person here spoke up and said this is wrong?"

The silence rang out. Sharp and clear. Growing. Taking on a life of its own.

"He broke your ribs," Trey said in time. He sounded hurt. Like a little boy whose gift was received with less gratitude than he felt it deserved.

"We tied him up so we could cut him, Trey. With no anesthetic. If I came at you to do the same, would you kick me if you could? And then how about if I'm extra violent with you because you tried to get out of it? He's a freaking calf! He doesn't know any better! Besides . . . he's right!"

Aiden pulled the buck knife out of its sheath on his belt and marched back to the pipe corral. There was pain on each step, but it felt almost as though someone else were having it. He ducked between the pipes. With his ribs compressed with a wrap, it wasn't easy.

The calf had been panicked for so long that he had exhausted himself. The animal could feel nothing anymore, because he had not an ounce of energy left to burn. Or at least that seemed to be his situation as Aiden approached him. But as Aiden leaned over him, reaching out with the knife, the calf bucked up from the dirt, committing to a spasm of motion in what he thought was one last attempt to save his own life.

Aiden slid the blade of the knife under the rope and sliced through it. All four wraps of it. The calf lurched to his feet, leapt forward, fell again, then stumbled up and ran away as best he could.

"There," Aiden said, turning back to the crowd, most of whom sat with their mouths open. "That one gets to grow up to be a nice big bull. Who the hell cares? Who the hell cares about any of this? Why do we even do this? There must be a better way to make a living than torturing cattle all day."

He threw the knife down in the dirt, point first, and walked into his house.

It was several degrees cooler inside, and he cranked up the air conditioning and drank his fill of water from the faucet.

He could hear the hooves of visiting horses clatter up onto the floors of their stock trailers. He could hear pickup truck engines start up and run.

Several minutes later, when he felt he had calmed himself enough, he stepped outside again. To apologize to any remaining neighbors. Maybe clarify what he had meant to say.

The tri tips lay burned to crispy black charcoal on the barbecue.

Everyone, even his ranch hands, had gone.

—

Aiden ate garlic bread for his combination lunch and dinner, popped two more pills, and put himself to bed at three in the afternoon with the air conditioner roaring. Still fully dressed and filthy.

He slept until morning. Livie never showed.

# Chapter Seven

## The Falling Down

Aiden woke suddenly to a burst of light through his eyelids and a violent ache in his skull.

"Rise and shine, sleeping beauty," a familiar male voice said. "You got fences to mend."

He opened his eyes to see Derek standing by his bedroom window, pulling back the drapes.

Aiden tried to swing up into a sitting position on the edge of the bed. It didn't pan out at all. He had forgotten about the ribs. He let out a pained grunt and lay back down again.

"I don't think I'm in much of a fence-mending condition."

"I wasn't referring to actual fences. Oh, that too, coincidentally, but it's just one little section on the north property line and Trey and I can get to that today. I meant mending fences with your neighbors."

"What's wrong with me and my neighbors?"

"Uh-oh. It's like that, is it? Okay, I'm gonna go on in the kitchen and fix you a great big pot of my famous coffee. Only you don't wanna know what it's famous for. Couple cups of that and we'll check back again and see what you recall."

———

"Two words," Derek said, settling on the other side of Aiden's kitchen table. "Damage control."

"Okay. What's that look like in your head?"

Aiden sipped the blazingly strong coffee. Unfortunately he remembered now. Everything.

"Let's say I drive you around to the ranches in question. And you have yourself a little sit-down talk with the people involved. What're you gonna say? Just gimme a light preview so I can see where we stand."

"Hmm," Aiden said. He sipped at the coffee again. His head hurt fiercely. More than his ribs. He wanted to ask Derek to find his painkillers, but he couldn't seem to peel his attention away from the disaster at hand. "I guess I'd say I didn't ever intend to demean their livelihood."

"That's a damn good start."

"I know most of what we do to these calves is just what needs doing. They all can't grow up to be bulls. Whole breed lines would be ruined. I mostly was upset about that one calf lying tied up all that time. And the idea I'd want to take some kind of revenge on him—that seemed like cruel and unusual punishment to me. The rest of what we do is mostly . . . although . . . you know, really, when you think about it, cutting them without any kind of painkiller . . . isn't that almost the dictionary definition of cruel?"

They both knew it was legal to castrate without painkillers in calves up to two months. They also both knew Aiden wasn't talking about legalities.

"We're moving in an undesirable direction here," Derek said.

Aiden set his head gently in his hands. "I think I have a concussion."

"Okay, that's good. That'll help explain a lot."

"No, I mean I think I have a concussion, Derek. I'm not rehearsing anymore. I'm telling you, right now."

"You didn't get kicked in the head, though."

"No, but I landed on it twice."

"Oh, that's right—you did, didn't you? My brain was so focused on the grand finale of the disaster that was our roundup yesterday, I almost forgot all the ways it sucked early on."

"Go and see where my painkiller pills got off to, will you?"

Derek sighed. Pulled to his feet. "Why do I have a feeling this's gonna be another crap day?"

Aiden looked up and met Derek's eyes. But his mind was not on the question at hand. He had moved on.

"You got any idea why Livie never showed up here yesterday?"

"Well, Aiden. It's like this. I would allow for the possibility it might've made it back to her ears that this was not the happening spot to be."

"She could have come to support me. I would've done as much for her."

"If you want a supportive-type girlfriend you're gonna have to let go of Livie and pick again. You know that as well as I do, buddy."

"Yeah," Aiden said. "I guess that's a decent point."

———

Aiden stood at the fence behind the barn and watched his cow horses lope up the golden-brown hill. He had opened the stall doors in the barn. Not even haltered them. Not even led them with a rope. Just opened the doors and trusted them to move in the direction of grass, through the wide-open gate and into the horse pasture. And they had not let him down.

Dusty was another story. Aiden didn't like the idea of turning a stud out with all those geldings, right on the other side of the fence from the brood mares. So Dusty would stay in. Aiden would have to think of a bigger place to house him, or a way to get him worked.

He heard the four-wheeler, heard its engine. It was coming closer, but he didn't bother to look around. Just stared at his horses. Watched them go. Felt it like a loss in his belly. They were still his, and yet not the way they had been just a few days ago.

An order of business had been broken. A way of living. Gone.

Derek drove the four-wheeler up beside him and cut the engine.

"Nice to see you up and around," he said to Aiden.

Aiden said nothing in reply.

"Why'd you turn 'em out?"

"So they can get some exercise."

"You don't figure they'll get their exercise the old-fashioned way?"

"No. I don't figure they will."

"How long you think it'll be before you ride again?"

"Remains to be seen."

"What'd the doctor say?"

"It's not about what the doctor said and you know it."

A long silence. Derek stepped down from the four-wheeler and they stood at the fence together, staring at nothing. The horses had disappeared over the rise.

"You ever gonna tell me what's going on?" Derek asked after a time. Then, when Aiden didn't answer, he said, "Oh, that's right. I forgot. We're not friends like that anymore. Or maybe we never were. I just don't know."

More silence. Aiden had not bothered to put his hat on, and the sun burned where it baked his scalp. A reminder that his hair had gone a little thin of late.

"Let me ask you a question, then, Aiden. I still got a job with you?"

"For the moment, yeah. Of course you do."

"And after the moment?"

"I don't know, Derek. I really don't know what happens from here."

—

Aiden waited until nearly 1:00 p.m. before driving into town. Partly because he wanted the bulk of the painkillers to wear off before he got behind the wheel. Mostly because Livie took her lunch break at 1:00.

He parked perpendicular on the street outside the salon. Eased out of the truck and onto the curb at about one-tenth the rate of speed he might've shown on any previous day.

When he swung the salon door open with his left hand, all eyes came up to him—both the women cutting and styling hair and the women having their hair cut and styled. They all looked at Aiden. They all stopped talking. Aiden stood holding the door open into all that toxic silence and wondered if this was his world from here on out. Everybody staring at him in utter, wordless disbelief.

Livie stood in the far corner of the shop fussing over a pot of coffee. But Aiden sensed she had seen him. She was moving with that fierce determination that suggested she had some outrage to grasp and control.

Aiden moved through the sea of silence and caught up with her in the back.

"What're you doing here, Aiden?"

"Nice to see you, too."

"I heard you were banged up pretty good. Didn't expect to see you out and around."

"And you couldn't even come by to see if I was okay?"

Her eyes came up to him then. Burned through his outer layers and scorched him all along his gut. It was unlike her, tough as she could be. Something had cut her more deeply than usual. There must have been a wound to her pride.

"I don't have time for this," she said. "I'm working."

"Looks to me like that coffee is all made. I think it can do the rest on its own."

Livie did not cut or style hair. She greeted customers, made appointments. Coffee. Made the hair on the floor go away. Ordered supplies.

"I don't need you to be snide with me, Aiden. I got things to do."

"You take your lunch yet? I thought we'd go over to Dennison's. Eat. Talk."

"I can't get away. Nobody to cover me. Besides, I brought my lunch in a bag."

"I could go to the take-out place and get us something. We could eat it here."

"I just told you I brought my lunch in a bag!"

Her voice had come up, and he could feel everybody listening. Maybe everybody had been listening all along. Aiden hadn't heard a single voice that was not his or Livie's. Not since stepping through the door.

"Maybe we could just talk outside. One minute. We'll stand on the sidewalk out front. If a customer comes in, you'll see it."

Livie sighed a loud and dramatic sigh.

Yeah. It was worse than usual this time. He just didn't know why yet.

"Fine," she said. But she spat the word as though it wasn't fine at all. As though it didn't even rise to the level of acceptability.

She poured coffee into a Styrofoam cup and Aiden followed her to the door. The people they passed, the hairdressers and their customers, pretended to look away. But Aiden believed their gazes still followed him. Just more peripherally.

She banged through the door and they stood on the sidewalk together in the waves of rising heat, not looking at each other. She sipped at the coffee that Aiden had hoped was for him.

"I could use a cup of coffee," he said gently.

"Fine. Take this one." She thrust it in his direction.

"Never mind," he said, pushing it back. "We okay?" He knew they were not.

"You tell me, Aiden."

"I don't know how to answer. I don't really know what's going on with you."

"*You?* Don't know what's going on with *me?* I think the question here is what's going on with *you*. Every single person I've bumped into today has asked me, 'What's wrong with Aiden?' 'What's going on?' 'What's got into him?' Then three people I didn't bump into called on the phone to ask. You got any idea how humiliating it is to have to tell them I don't know? To have to more or less admit that you haven't bothered to share that information with me?"

He watched a one-ton truck go by and slow. Behind the wheel was Charley Ross, who had worked the roundup the day before. Aiden met his eyes briefly, and Charley shook his head and gunned it, driving on.

"You're right," Aiden said quietly. "I should tell you what's what."

A silence as she waited. She sipped the coffee again and took to tapping her foot, which made it difficult to think.

"It's hard, though," he said. "Because I don't really understand it very well myself."

"Try," she said.

"Okay." He stared down at the hot sidewalk as he spoke. "Something changed in me just recently. And now it's like . . . like when I'm near an animal . . . dog, horse, steer, buck, whatever . . . when they feel something unusual—really big or really sudden—if they're scared, or in pain, I feel it too. I don't want it. I don't want this to be happening to me, but it just is. I can't help it. I can't make it stop."

He looked up from the concrete and into her face. She looked mad. He hadn't expected that. He'd expected his honesty to make things better. To bring out her gentler side. She did have one. He'd seen it. Just not for a while.

"And what am *I* feeling?" she asked, still tapping that infernal foot.

"You look mad."

"But you don't know."

"Not really. You look and sound mad. But I don't really know why."

"So what you're telling me, Aiden Delacorte, is that your heart breaks for every dog or calf you see, but you have no more idea what's going on with me than you ever did. Which is a pretty sorry amount to know."

*Oh,* he thought. *That's why she's mad.*

He could almost see her point about that. But there was not much he could do. It's not like he pulled the strings on what he did and did not know.

Meanwhile he was not answering.

"You got nothing to say about that, I see."

"I told you, Livie. I don't want the damn thing. I've just got it. I don't know why it doesn't work on people, too. I don't know anything about it. I just can't make it go away."

Livie shook her head. "I need a break," she said.

"From what?"

"Us, Aiden. A break from us."

Then she threw the rest of the coffee into the street just outside the curb and marched back inside the shop.

Aiden did not follow.

—

Aiden stood in the market, staring into the freezer case. He had no idea how long he'd been staring. Several minutes at least. He had no idea what he was looking for, which likely explained why he wasn't finding it. The pain had ratcheted up three or four levels of volume, but he didn't want to take more pills until he was safely home.

"Need help finding something?"

Aiden turned his head to the voice. Gwen was standing by his right shoulder, staring into the case with him.

"Oh. Gwen. Hey."

"I never did catch *your* name."

"Aiden Delacorte."

"Oh, *you're Aiden*," she said.

He didn't have to ask what she meant by that. The subtext was obvious. It spoke for itself.

He didn't answer.

"Can I help you find something?"

"I doubt it. Since I have no idea what I want."

"Hmm. Yeah. That *would* make it harder."

"Thing is, I had my mouth all set for Dennison's. They have this really good baked brie with slivered almonds. And French bread they make fresh. And their fish-and-chips is something else."

Aiden liked their ribs, too. But he didn't add them to his out-loud list. Because he knew he would not have ordered them. Something about chewing on the bones of a steer. It was not the way this day was destined to go.

"Fish? Around here? It is fresh, even?"

"Oh yeah. We get good fish in these parts. The coast is less than a three-hour drive from here."

"You should go," she said, sounding very sure.

"To the coast?"

"No, silly." She bumped his right shoulder with her own. It hurt, but he didn't let on. "Dennison's."

"Oh. Right. See, I'm not good at that. It's not a takeout place. It's a real sit-down restaurant. I was never one of those people who could walk into a restaurant alone and sit at a table all by myself. It's too awkward. I never know where to look. I always feel like everyone's staring at me."

*Yeah,* Aiden thought. *That would be the worst. Everyone staring at me.*

"I bet they'd make you something to take out," Gwen said. "I think any restaurant will. Takeout place or not."

He looked over at her. Right into her face for the first time. A little something stirred inside him as he met her eyes. Something that felt nervous, yet not unpleasant at all.

"You're right," he said. "They would. I just have to go ask."

They held each other's gaze for a split second longer. Then Aiden looked away. They moved off together toward the door. As they stepped out of the air conditioning and into the outdoor heat, Aiden looked over at her again.

"You're leaving?" he asked.

"Yeah, I just got off my shift."

"I thought you worked evenings."

"No. Not usually. Usually I work days. That one evening when you saw me here, I took over a shift for Maura. She had a cold. It was my only day off, but I needed the money. That's how it is when you have two kids and you're on your own. You always need the money. But then subtract the money for the babysitter and I didn't net much."

"You eaten?"

"No," she said, tentatively, the end of the word coming up like a question. She seemed to sense where he was going with his questions.

"Come with me to Dennison's then."

"Oh. Well . . . yeah. I guess I could. It would be nice to actually get to know somebody. For a change. And the kids don't get off school until three. Thanks. I'll take you up on that."

It would get back to Livie by the end of the day. If not by the end of the lunch.

He did it anyway.

———

They sat across the table from each other, a table with a nice white tablecloth and a fresh-flower centerpiece and leather-covered menus. The way people ate when they had the time to treat themselves well.

If Aiden hadn't been dealing with a concussion and two broken ribs, unmedicated, it might have been a lovely moment.

"Oh," he said, picking up the printed card with the specials on it. "Salmon fish-and-chips today. I know what I want."

"I'm thinking bacon avocado cheeseburger. I know. Don't say it. If I ate like that every day, I'd be as big as a house. But I'm thinking of this as more of a special occasion."

"I wasn't going to say anything of the sort." Then, before he could say more on the subject, he looked up to see his neighbor Roger walk in with his wife, Nadine. In the middle of a weekday, no less. "Crap," he breathed out loud.

"What?"

Aiden held the menu up in front of his face. "Somebody I just had a little falling-out with."

For a few seconds, she said nothing. Then, "Won't you have to put that menu down when the food comes?"

Aiden laughed a bitter bark of a laugh and dropped the menu onto the table.

"Sorry," Gwen said.

"Don't be. Do *not* be sorry for pointing out when I'm being an idiot."

"So . . . maybe I shouldn't ask, Aiden. I don't know. And you don't have to answer, of course. But a lot of people were talking about you in the market today."

"Yeah. They hate me."

"I don't think they hate you. I think they're worried about you."

"No, I mostly think they hate me."

A long silence fell, during which the waitress came to take their order. Aiden thought she stared at him a few beats too long, but it might have been paranoia building up.

Then again, it might not have been.

—

"Okay," he said to Gwen when the waitress left them alone again. "You deserve an explanation."

"You don't owe me anything."

"Common courtesy."

There was a plant by his right shoulder, a big fiddle-leaf fig, and he felt like it was crowding him. It also needed water, which was a disturbing thing to be able to feel. The condition of its leaves had not visually tipped him off, and Aiden had no special bond with plants. At least, he never had before. Plus there was music playing, just a hair too loud. It made it hard to organize his thoughts.

"Truth is, I made a big public statement over the weekend. I guess I pissed some people off and hurt some feelings. I basically said cattle ranching is cruel. Or . . . I guess it doesn't have to be, but . . . seems mostly it is."

"Yeah," Gwen said. "That could make some waves. Around here. So what do *you* do for a living?"

"I'm a cattle rancher."

That just sat on the table for a moment. On the clean, starched white cloth. Aiden tracked Roger and Nadine from the corner of his eye. It did not appear they had seen him.

"How long you been in the business?"

"Twenty-two years."

"Oh, come on. You're not even old enough."

"My dad died when I was fourteen. Not my birth dad, but I thought of him as my dad. He was my stepdad from the time I was six, and then he adopted me. When he died, he left me this ranch I live on. And operate. But it went into a trust. I got it on the day I turned eighteen. Uh-oh. Roger just spotted me."

Aiden pulled halfway up from his chair as Roger stormed the twenty or so steps across the dining room. At first Aiden's hands balled up into fists, but then he decided that if Roger wanted to batter him, he would not fight back. He would take whatever his community thought was his due. His debt to pay.

Roger did not assault him. He stopped two or three steps away and unclenched his own fists. The two men stared into each other's eyes for the count of three.

Nadine came and pulled her husband away.

"Stop it, Roger," she said. "We'll go someplace else for lunch."

Aiden remembered then why his neighbors might be out having a fancier-than-average lunch on a Monday. It was Nadine's birthday. She was sixty-four today.

Roger turned away and stomped out the door.

Nadine stayed.

She put a hand on Aiden's shoulder before speaking. "Honey, how are you? We're all worried about you."

"I don't think Roger's worried about me," Aiden said. His voice was a tiny bit shaky from the leftover adrenaline of what could have been a fistfight, but he didn't think it was audible.

"Roger's a hothead and we both know it. How long have we known you, Aiden? Since you were six years old. And you have *not* been yourself lately. And I'm worried."

Aiden glanced at Gwen, who returned something of an "I told you so" look.

"It's just been a hard week, Nadine. You better go talk to Roger. He'll be pissed if you're more worried about me than him."

"There. See?" Nadine reached out and touched his cheek. "You always were a thoughtful boy."

But Aiden knew she was giving him undeserved credit.

"Happy birthday," he said.

She smiled sadly and then rejoined her husband on the street.

Aiden looked up at Gwen again.

"Sorry about all that."

"It's okay. I think. I mean, I don't know what it is, but . . ."

"How good are you at keeping a secret?" Aiden asked.

—

When Aiden had told her everything he was willing to tell about his week, they ate in silence for a time. Two or three minutes at least.

Aiden figured this would be the last he would see of her. After what he'd admitted. Then again, what did it matter? He had a girlfriend anyway. Even if they were on a break. It's not like this was going anywhere special.

"It's not a bad thing, you know," she said. Startling him.

For a moment he only stared.

"It's a terrible thing."

"Well, I'm sure it feels bad. But to have that kind of empathy with what a helpless animal is feeling? That's good. I wish my own son could be more like that. The world would be better. You know? We couldn't do as much harm if people could feel what they were doing."

Aiden swallowed his mouthful of salmon and stared at her for another beat or two. He could tell that his mouth was slightly open. He didn't speak.

"Why are you looking at me like that?"

"Oh. Sorry. I guess because . . . what you're saying never even occurred to me. I never once saw it as anything but a curse. It's been a curse, really. I feel like my whole life is coming down all around me. Stuff it took decades to build."

"I'm sorry," she said.

One of her hands, her right one, slid across the table and landed lightly on Aiden's arm. His skin tingled where her skin touched it. They both stared at the hand for a second or two, shocked the way static electricity shocks. At least, Aiden felt it that way. Then she quickly pulled back again.

"I think I should have said this before," Aiden said quietly, and his tone made her face flush red. Or something did. "And I'm sorry if I waited too long. But . . . I have a girlfriend."

"Oh," she said. As though trying to sound casual, and not hurt. She sounded hurt.

*Oh crap,* Aiden thought. *Now I've gone and messed things up again.*

"At least, I *think* I have a girlfriend. She just told me she wants a break from me. But I don't think that means I'm free to get too close to somebody else."

"It doesn't."

"I'm sorry if I should've said that right up front."

"Don't be silly. It's just a friendly lunch."

"Right," Aiden said.

But it wasn't. Or, at least, it was beginning not to feel that way.

"Won't she be mad when she finds out you took me out to eat?"

"Oh yeah. Very."

"Why even do it, then?"

"That's actually a really good question. So I'm not going to answer off the top of my head. I'm going to think on that for a minute."

They ate in silence for a time. Aiden had mostly lost his appetite, and he could not keep his mind off the pain and getting home to the medication that would ease it. But he just kept shoveling in the food out of habit.

The music made it hard to think. It was as though Aiden could no longer ask his brain to do more than one thing at a time.

"I needed to talk to somebody," he said. It wasn't the result of any apparent thought process. It just came out. "I tried to talk to her, but she wasn't having any of it. She does this thing where she controls people with her anger. She wants life a certain way. If you don't do everything just right, she'll punish you with her anger."

"Punish?"

"Not like that. Not physically. She'll just make your life so damned uncomfortable by being mad at you. And . . . I hate the turmoil. Always have. Can't stand any kind of fighting. So I tend to give in and do what she wants. But when she said she wanted a break today . . . it was like I had nothing left to lose anymore. Like maybe I could just be me. It felt good. It was this amazing experience to do what I wanted. What was best for *me*. And if she gets mad, then she does. I hope you don't feel like that's using you. I didn't mean for it to be that way."

"No. Not at all. I'm glad I could be somebody for you to talk to."

"Me, too. Because I'm fresh out of that."

"I think you have people all around you who want you to talk to them."

"Maybe," he said. "Maybe they wish I could. But I can't. It's just not something they could ever understand."

———

As he walked her to her car, she said it.

"You could see somebody, you know."

Aiden didn't know what she meant by it. Not at first. He thought she was saying he was free to date, which they had both agreed he was not.

"See somebody?"

"Like a professional."

"A professional what?"

"For a year or two before I left Sacramento I was seeing a . . . counselor. You know. You don't have to be crazy—that's a common mistake. You can just be somebody who's under stress or can't quite figure out your life right in that moment. It helped me. It helped me see I had to leave my marriage."

They stood in the street together for a moment, near the driver's door of her car. It was an older Toyota. Green. Aiden was thinking you didn't see a lot of green cars anymore. Everybody went for black or white or silver these days. He purposely ignored the cars and trucks that passed them by, because he assumed their drivers were mad at him. Or worse yet, wanted him to confide in them regarding his recent troubles.

"I'm sorry," she said, probably because he wasn't answering. "Maybe I shouldn't have suggested it."

"No, it's okay. It's another one of those things I never would have thought of in a million years. But it's not a bad idea."

"Okay, good. I was afraid I offended you. Well. Thanks for lunch."

"Thanks for having it with me."

"And don't worry. I don't even know anybody yet. Around here. Except you. And even if I did . . . I mean, when I do . . . I'm not one to tell tales."

"Thanks."

Aiden had no idea what to say, or how to end their meeting. He couldn't just turn and walk away. He wanted to say something like "Okay, 'bye" and make a break for it. But his mouth wasn't working right.

He stepped in and gave her a quick, awkward hug. She hugged back, just for a second, and it was all he could do not to cry out in pain. But he kept it to himself.

"See you," she said.

"Yeah."

As he turned back to his pickup truck, he saw her. Livie, who absolutely should have been at work—who wouldn't take off to have lunch with him because there was no one to cover her job—was sitting in her car at the end of the block. Watching him.

———

When he got home, Aiden took two of the painkillers and turned off his phone, then napped briefly on the couch.

When he woke up, he turned on the phone again. There was a message from Livie. As he'd known there would be.

He played it. Wincing. Trying to listen and not listen at the same time.

"We're through, Aiden. Through. I'll box up anything that's yours in my house and give it to Trey and you do the same. But don't try to call me or talk to me. It's over."

*Right,* Aiden thought, clicking to delete the message. *I knew that. Everything else I thought I wanted is over, so why not?*

# Chapter Eight

## The Parting

A couple of days later Aiden woke in the morning and decided he couldn't tolerate his neighbors' rabbit situation a moment longer.

At first it had bothered him only as he was driving by his neighbors' property. Especially if one of them was being culled for slaughter. Or had been recently. Or was about to be. But the moments of panic had gotten more protracted, and closer together. And now Aiden could feel it even when he was home in bed.

He rose, dressed quickly, combed his hair, and drove his truck to the ranch closest to his own. About half a mile down the road.

Aiden honked at the gate, because it was padlocked.

His neighbor Benny came out of the barn and waved to him. A little suspicious but not downright hostile. Benny walked closer.

"Wait a minute," he called to Aiden. "I'll go inside and get the key."

"Don't bother," Aiden called back. "I'll come see you on my feet."

He shut down the truck's engine and stepped out, ducking gingerly through the boards of his neighbors' fence.

"What can I do for you, Aiden?"

"I came to talk to you about your rabbits."

Benny tipped his cowboy hat back on his head. As if his brain needed fresh air to comprehend a conversation. "What about 'em?"

Aiden took a deep breath and noted that all was still. The rabbits seemed to rest in a state of relaxation. Relatively speaking.

"How many have you got?"

"Twenty-some, but I couldn't tell you exactly. Depends on who gave birth and if all the kits survived."

"You eat them yourself or sell them for food?"

"They're just for me and Estelle."

"Would you consider selling me the whole lot of them?"

"Um." Benny paused. Scratched his head in front of his battered hat. "I suppose. If the price was right."

"Well, you tell me then, Benny. You make me a special price. For what it would cost to sell me every rabbit you got and not buy any more."

"I don't follow."

"It's pretty simple, really. You sell me all your rabbits and go out of the business of raising them. If you get a taste for rabbit, you can buy one somebody else raised and slaughtered. You just tell me what it's worth to you to make that happen."

———

As he pulled off the road and onto his ranch's long dirt driveway, he saw Derek and Trey waiting for him. Standing with their arms crossed. Aiden could practically smell a confrontation waiting to happen. Smell it like coffee brewing.

He parked his truck in front of the barn and turned off the engine, stepping down into the dirt.

"What?" he said simply.

"This true what we're hearing?" Derek asked. He seemed to have appointed himself ringleader. Of a very small ring.

"Now how the hell do I know what you're hearing?"

But he knew.

"Something about how the cattle's feelings are more important than ours all of a sudden?"

"Who told you that?"

"Who do you think?"

Aiden's mind swirled with anger. And disappointment. He had thought he could trust Gwen. But why had he been so sure? His head and ribs hurt. He wanted to go inside and hit the medication bottle, but this mess required sorting out.

"She swore she didn't tell tales," he said bitterly.

"Of course she tells tales, Aiden. Come on. You've known her four years. When have you known her to miss out on a good piece of gossip?"

Aiden's insides cleared. Just like that. Like silty water when the sludge settles out, but faster. Suddenly you can see the bottom. See everything.

Meanwhile Trey had said nothing. He only stood silent, two steps behind Derek. Like the coward he had always been.

"Livie told you," Aiden said.

"Of course Livie told us. Who else did you think? Look, to some extent your business is your business, Aiden, but you're not the only one whose livelihood depends on this little operation. Trey and I got bills, too. So we got one question for you. We're supposed to take forty head to the feedlot tomorrow. That's how you make payroll, in case you forgot. We taking 'em there or not? I hate to tell you, but if we do, they'll fatten 'em up and send 'em on to the hamburger factory. You have to be man enough to face that fact, I guess."

"Don't press your luck with me, Derek," Aiden said, his voice steady.

"Right. Whatever. Sorry, I guess. Do we take 'em?"

"*You* can," Aiden said. "I'm still on painkillers and not much fit to help."

It would be a terrible morning, even if Aiden stayed inside the house. A nightmarish morning. But Derek was right. It needed to be done.

And meanwhile everybody was so upset with everybody that nobody even bothered to ask Aiden why there were ten metal cages full of rabbits clearly visible in the bed of his pickup truck.

———

Aiden woke suddenly to the sound of frightened lowing, and a feeling in his body and gut as if in danger of being crushed from both sides.

The sun was not even fully up.

He wrapped a pillow around his ears and tried to make it all go away.

It did not go.

It did not rely on his sense of hearing. It was something else entirely. And even a few seconds of the feeling was more than Aiden could stand.

He pulled himself stiffly out of bed and ran to the front door, still wearing only boxer shorts and the compression wrap around his ribs. Out into the cool, mostly dark morning. Feeling terrified. Battered. Unable to hold still in his panic. Feeling as though he had no space to breathe.

As though his life were almost over.

Derek and Trey had the stock trailer filled with ten or so steers, and they had just put the truck in gear and begun to drive.

"Stop!" he shouted after them.

The truck and trailer braked with a puff of dirt, and Aiden felt the jolt of bodies trying to balance. Felt the fear of being trampled if he went down.

Aiden caught up with the truck and flipped the lever that allowed the trailer gate to unlatch. He swung the door wide, more concerned about the terror in his mind than the pain in his ribs. He stood as far back as possible to keep his bare feet safe from trampling hooves.

The cattle came surging out.

They ran to the gate, hoping to rejoin the herd in their familiar pasture. The gate was closed. But they settled there. They settled on the inside of themselves, waiting to be let back in. So Aiden settled, too.

He looked up to see Derek standing in the dirt in the dim light, not three paces away.

"Open the gate and let them back in," Aiden said.

"Hell I will. You want 'em back in, *you* put 'em back in."

Aiden walked to the pipe fence. He didn't want to push through the cattle to the gate, because his feet were still bare. So he cut a wide path around them, climbed over the fence, and opened the gate from the inside.

The steers loped up the hill to rejoin their herd.

As he latched and chained the gate, he saw both Derek and Trey moving in his direction. He tried to feel nothing about the fight headed his way. How had he used to do that? Why couldn't he anymore?

"So, you want to tell us how you plan to make payroll?"

Derek had spoken. Trey was still hanging back.

"I can cover you guys for a month at least."

"In other words, this's our notice."

Aiden stood a moment, gulping air. Realizing how nearly naked he was. Asking his brain to grasp the moment. Still waking up, really.

"I suppose it is. I'm sorry, guys."

"So it's true. You care about them now more than you care about us."

"You're grown men. You'll find work."

Derek moved in. Close enough to engage Aiden's eyes in the dim barely dawn light. Close enough that Aiden assumed a fist might be about to swing in his direction.

He cut his eyes away to telegraph that he did not want to fight.

"I remember your daddy, Aiden. I knew Harris. Don't forget that. This was his legacy. If he could see you right now, he'd be ashamed."

For a moment—just for the flash of a fraction of a second—it was almost Aiden's fist that swung. Almost. He told himself, silently, *Don't you dare.*

"Get the hell off my property," Aiden said, sounding reasonably composed. Far more composed than he felt. "Don't come back."

"So now you're revoking notice."

"You revoked it for yourself, when you said what you just said to me."

They stood, almost nose to nose, for another tense second.

Then Derek peeled away.

"I take it back," he called out to Trey. "I said don't tell him. I was wrong. Tell him."

Aiden almost said, "Tell me what?" He wisely refrained. There was no need to push. Whatever this news turned out to be, it was speeding toward him like a freight train. You don't tell the train that's bearing down on you to hurry up.

"I asked your ex-girlfriend out on a date," Trey called, his voice full of puffed-up arrogance. "And she's so mad at you, she actually said yes."

It hit Aiden's gut the way the two men had clearly expected it to hit. It roiled and twisted in his stomach like a nauseous cramp. It was over with her, so it shouldn't have mattered. But it did. He had lost a battle, and now the winner was gloating. It couldn't not hurt.

He refused to let them see.

"Well, I'm glad she at least has some good reason for it. It sure as hell wasn't going to be for your good looks or your sparkling personality."

For a moment or two, Trey behaved like a windup toy. He came toward Aiden, he jerked away. He balled his fists, he let them drop.

"Forget it, Trey," Derek said. "Let's just go."

And they did.

They left Aiden alone, barefoot and nearly naked, in the near dark, on what had used to be a small but thriving cattle ranch.

What it was now, Aiden couldn't say.

# PART THREE

AIDEN DELACORTE AT AGE FORTY

PRESENT DAY

# *Chapter Nine*

## *The Remembering*

By the time he had given Hannah what he thought was a brief just-the-facts outline of the recent turmoil that was his life, he looked at the ticking clock and saw that forty minutes of his session had flown away.

"These are fifty-minute hours," he said. "Right?"

"That's right."

"So my time is almost up. Just telling you about why I think I need some help here."

"True. But that background is something you only need to share once."

"What do you think it's all about?"

"Which? The troubles with the boy?"

"Well . . . that needs dealing with, all right. But actually I meant the part about the wake up. I mean . . . for starters."

It was veering in a new direction for him, but that could not be helped. Granted, he had not wanted to talk about it. But now that he had, he needed to know what she thought.

"I wouldn't want to make a determination based on that little bit of input."

"What if you had to guess, though? I mean, do you think I had some kind of . . . that thing with the buck. I haven't told anybody else that. They'd think I was crazy. Do you think I'm crazy? Or . . . do you think I had some kind of . . . otherworldly experience?"

The doctor sat back in her chair. Stopped taking notes. She did not answer for a time. Aiden wanted to ask her to hurry, but he didn't wish to be rude. But they only had nine minutes.

"How do you stand the ticking of that clock?" he asked instead.

"I like it. It makes time seem very orderly to me. You know how time can play tricks? For me, hearing a tick for every second keeps things regular and manageable. But I can put it out in the waiting room if it bothers you."

"No. Don't do that. It's your clock. I didn't come here to rearrange your furniture."

"I'm going to tell you where my thinking lies right now, Aiden, but it's important you not see this as a diagnosis. At this point it's more of an educated guess. I think you're likely an empath. An extraordinarily sensitive person."

"I never was before."

"Not even when you were a child?"

"I don't remember anything from back then."

"Sometimes an empath can be quite purposely shut off to what they might otherwise feel. For some it's possible to compartmentalize. Stand away from those emotions. Then the person can be viewed as numb. Almost dead to the world. Because knowing what others are feeling can be absolutely overwhelming. You have no memories at all of your childhood?"

"Not before I was seven. We lived with my birth father until I was four. And then my mom took me and my sister and left, but I don't remember any of that. I just remember being told about it. My mom met a new guy. The man I think of as my father. I was six when we went to live with him. He was a cattle rancher. We lived on the same property I've got now."

"Can he help you with remembering your childhood?"

"He died when I was fourteen."

"Oh. I'm sorry. Is your mother still alive?"

"She is. But she can't help me. She has dementia. Some days she can't remember what she had for breakfast. It's hard. She lives back east, in Buffalo where she grew up, with her brother. My uncle Edgar. I go see her once a year at Christmas."

"What about your sister?"

"I don't talk to her. I'd have to think on whether it would be worth it to me to talk to her now."

They sat in silence for a few moments. Aiden wasn't sure how long it would take to convince her that he didn't want to say more. The silence didn't seem to bother Hannah. It bothered him.

"Tell me the oldest memory you have," she said at last. "When you were seven. Why does that stand out when so much else is gone?"

"Oh. Okay. Well. I think it's possible that before this I didn't get on all that well with my stepdad. Adopted dad. Stepdad at the time. I'm not even sure why I say that, because I don't remember how we got on at first. But I remember accepting him that night, so I guess that's why I figure I didn't before. He had these quarter horses. Really nice horses. I still have them. Well, not those exact horses. This was thirty-three years ago. But I still breed his same line. It was the middle of the night and he came and dragged me out of bed. I didn't want to go. I was sleepy and it was cold out. But he insisted. He said he wanted me to see how life started.

"He takes me out into the barn, just the two of us, and this brood mare of his, she's foaling. He has me watch this amazing little thing being born. Watch him pull this colt right out of his momma. And then, just as this skinny, wet little thing is stumbling to his feet, my stepdad says, 'What're you gonna name your colt?'"

"He gave the colt to you?"

"He did."

"I can see how that would stay with you. Seven is awfully young for horse ownership, though."

"He was right there with me on it, though. He taught me everything as we went along. How to get him used to being handled, how to teach him to lift his hooves for picking. How to halterbreak him and train him to tie. And then of course we had to break him. As we used to call it. You know. To ride. Not one person ever rode that horse but me. Not even for a minute. After that, I looked up to my dad. Idolized him. I followed him everywhere. I did everything he did. He went hunting, I begged to come along. He rode the roundup, I wanted to ride. I wanted to be just like him."

"Was he a fairly unemotional man?"

"I . . . I don't know. Just normal, I guess. I never really thought about it. Why?"

"Never mind. We'll come back to that. You broke a horse to ride when you were seven?"

"No, I was ten by then. You start them when they're three. Give or take. Different schools of thought on it."

"I see."

"Everything after that night I remember so clearly. I mean, not every minute of every day, of course. But I remember so much from that day on. Before that it's like trying to reach around a brick wall. It's funny, but . . . looking back on it now, it feels almost like my life started that night. Like that's the night I was born."

A brief silence filled only by the ticking of the clock.

"Which makes this a terrible moment to have to tell you our time is up," she said. "I'm sorry."

"That's okay," he said. But it wasn't. "I just ran my mouth a lot today, I guess. Which I usually don't. Well, lately more than usual. Used to, I could go a month without saying as many words as I said to you today."

"Things are changing very fast for you."

"Yes, ma'am."

He rose from his deep, soft chair. Walked with her to her office door. Just a dozen or so steps. But in those few seconds, Aiden experienced a full-on hailstorm of emotion. He didn't want to go. He might have found a refuge here. He needed someone to know for him. To understand what he did not. He did not want to leave the safe cocoon of her office and reenter his own world.

"I'm wondering if you'd be willing to commit to two sessions a week," she said.

"Yeah. Sure. If you think that's the way to go."

"Just out of curiosity, what did you name your colt?"

"I called him Magic."

"Because of the feeling you got watching him being born?"

"I don't suppose I would have put it like that at the time, but yeah."

"Nice," she said. "Well done."

"I had him right up until a handful of months ago. And you know, now that I think about it, I've had a much tougher time of things since he died. But I guess that's a subject for next session."

"Yes," she said. "I think it is."

—

Aiden walked out into the bright, hot sun, shocked to see that the world had waited for him, unchanged.

He felt utterly unequipped to go home. Forcing himself back into a world that had put him in some role of authority felt akin to turning a puppy loose on a busy highway.

He drove home anyway.

Because, really, what else was he going to do?

—

He had let himself back inside his own gate when he saw her. He had parked his truck and stepped out into the midday heat. He'd reached down to give Buddy's head a pat. Watched the whole dog wag as he did so. Then, when Aiden straightened up, he saw a slim figure standing outside his fence. A girl, down a few dozen yards from the gate. It was hard to tell from this distance—and through the waves of rising heat—but it looked like Gwen's daughter, Elizabeth.

He squinted into the sun, shielded his eyes with one hand, and tried to look more closely. Or, at least, more effectively.

She raised one hand to him and waved shyly. Well, she didn't wave the hand, exactly. Just held it up like a stop sign.

Aiden walked toward the gate and so did she.

"Elizabeth," he said.

"Hi," she said, purposely avoiding his eyes. Either that, or the dry dirt beneath her untied sneakers was an endless source of fascination for her.

He opened the gate again and let her through.

"What are you doing here?" he asked.

"I could leave if you don't have time."

"No, it's fine. I just meant . . . where's your mom?"

"At work."

"How did you get here?"

"Walked."

"Walked? It's almost five miles."

"I like to walk. I walk all day sometimes."

"In this heat, though? You need to come in and have something to drink."

———

"Who's looking after Milo?" he asked as he poured a can of soda over ice.

"My mom hired a babysitter. But she told the lady I can go for a hike if I want to."

"Oh," Aiden said.

Then he clammed up, fresh out of words to speak. He handed her the cold drink. He knew she must have something to say to him. Some reason for seeking him out. But he had no more idea how to approach that situation than he had a plan for flying up into the trees like a bird.

They stood in awkward silence for a time. Aiden wanted a cold soda, too, but he had forgotten to stop at the store on the way home, and he had given the girl his last one.

Then they sat on the couch in his living room, Aiden respectfully backed up into the far corner to give the girl her space. She wore cutoff jean shorts, and her legs were skinny, red from the sun, and about a yard long from the look of it. She would be a tall girl.

"Remember when my mom said Milo doesn't hurt animals?" Her voice startled him. He had been deeply dug into the silence. "Or anyway, she said he never did before."

"I remember that. But I'm a little confused about the fact that you remember it. We thought you were asleep."

"Part of the time I was. But I woke up on the way home."

"Oh," Aiden said. "Okay. Well. What about it?"

"It's not really true. She thinks it is, but it's not. Our dad gave Milo a BB gun. And my mom took it away. Because . . . well, you know. Milo and a gun. Holy cow. Bad mix. So she threw it out. But my dad got it out of the trash. And he showed Milo a good place to hide it. So when my mom used to leave to go to her therapy appointments, Milo would get it out. And he used to stand out in the backyard. Really still. And then he'd shoot at birds. Then he'd hide the BB gun again before she got home. She doesn't know. She never found out."

*Now we're getting down to it,* Aiden thought. He'd known she must have walked all the way out here for a reason. It set up a tingle in his belly, the gravity of it. He wondered how deep they were about to dig down today. What percentage of the underwater mass of the iceberg would be revealed. And why everything seemed like so much more of a problem once you dredged it up above the waterline.

"And you never told her?"

"No," she said, and swung her face away. It made a swoop of long hair fall over one eye. "I feel kinda bad about that. Like the birds were my fault. But it's weird to tell on somebody. It's hard. And my dad would've made me pay, believe me. It would have been telling on my dad, too, not just Milo. That's something you just don't do. You'd have to know him to understand."

"So what did he do with the birds? Milo, I mean. He couldn't have just left them in the yard or she would have figured out that something was going on."

"He's a bad shot. Really bad. That helps. But we had a lot of birds. So sooner or later he was bound to hit a couple."

"Did he sneak them into the trash or something?"

For a long, strange moment, silence. No answer. He wondered what could be so bad about the answer, to delay its arrival for so long.

"It was weird, what he did." Aiden braced himself for the worst. Tried to guard against it without picturing it. "He buried them."

"That's not so weird."

"But not just . . . I don't mean he just put them under the dirt. I mean he had these . . . funerals. He'd put them in a little box, like a crayon box or a model car box. He'd wrap them up first in one of our father's good silk handkerchiefs. He just kept stealing them out of Dad's dresser drawer, and I guess Dad must have thought he lost them or something. Then he'd bury them—Milo, I mean—and say these words over them. I never got close enough to hear what he said. And he had this little bamboo flute, and he'd play a tune . . ."

He waited, but the girl seemed to have run out of steam.

"Okay, that's fairly weird," Aiden said.

But then he didn't know how to go on. He wanted to know if that was the whole reason she had come all this way. And how it felt to live with a person like Milo as a brother. He wanted to know if she had come to warn Aiden because she worried about him, or if she'd come to unburden herself to Aiden because she worried about herself. And a few other things that were harder to pin down.

"We're going to have to move," Elizabeth said, before he could make his way through those thoughts.

"Already? You've only been in that place a few months. Is the owner selling it?"

"No, it's getting repossessed. The bank is taking it."

"Oooh," Aiden said, drawing the word out long. "That's low."

"Well. They're a bank."

"That's not what I meant. I meant the owner should have told you that before he rented to you. You have to be behind in your payments for quite a few months before the bank starts foreclosure proceedings. Makes me think that's something that should have been disclosed. How long before you have to find a new place?"

"Three days."

"*Three days?*"

"Yeah. Sheriff came by last night and told us we have three days to get out. Served us some kind of notice. He was sorry about it and all. Because he knows it's not us who got behind with the bank. But there's nothing he can do. And now my mom is all worried because she thinks we won't be able to find anything to rent around here. Because . . . you know. It's such a small town. Not much for rent." She levered herself suddenly to her feet. Swung onto those long, skinny legs like a foal standing up for the first time. "So, I just wanted to tell you all that," she said on her way to the door. "Because I like you. But don't tell my mom I told you, okay?"

"Wait," Aiden said, and stood to follow her.

"What?"

"At least let me give you a ride back into town."

———

"What do you think of your new school?" Aiden asked her on the drive.

Then he kicked himself a dozen times over. Because it was such a stupid thing to ask. Such a typical question for a grown-up to pose to a kid. Just the kind they despise because they've heard it so many times before.

"I hate it," she said with a wry little smile.

"Oh. That's too bad."

"But I hated my other school, too. Before we moved. So it's not a step down or anything. I just hate school."

"I used to hate school," Aiden said.

And then, just like that, he pulled up in front of their rental house. The short drive was over. Aiden felt relieved. He liked Elizabeth. He just had no idea how to talk to her.

She didn't jump out of his truck. Not right away. She just sat there and stared at him, as if taking some kind of measure of him. At first he avoided her eyes out of embarrassment. Then he quickly glanced over to see how he was measuring up.

Fairly well, from the look of things.

"Grown-ups never say things like that," Elizabeth said.

"What? That they hated school?"

"Right. That. They always say it was the best time of their lives."

"Hmm," Aiden said. And sighed out some tension. It wouldn't pay to be on his guard around this girl. She'd be with him a lot as time wore on. At least, she would if things went well with Gwen as he hoped. "Some of them, it might be the truth. Maybe school was something they could handle. They were popular and smart, so they had school on a string. And school was the only life they knew, so they thought they had life on a string. And then later they found out life is a lot harder than that, and now they spend their lives wishing they could go back. Others I think hated school at the time, but they have terrible memories. But a lot of people lie to kids. Tell them what they figure kids should hear instead of what's true."

"That's what *I* think!" She sounded happy now, and excited. As if she had dug down to the underside of him and found just what she was looking for. "Especially that last part. About the lying."

A silence fell.

It was time for her to jump out, and they both knew it. He didn't want to give her a hug, because it was too physical and personal. And a handshake seemed formal and staid after all they had just shared. So he formed his right hand into a fist and reached it across the seat, and she smiled and bumped his fist with her own.

"So don't tell my mom I came to talk to you, okay?"

"If you don't want me to, I won't."

She smiled again and jumped out, slamming the truck door behind her.

Aiden watched her go. As he did, it formed in his head, wordlessly, that she was a gift being given to him. Something rich and good coming into his life to make up for Milo and the rest of this mess. To give him back a little of the peace that was being stripped down and hauled away.

—

"Well, well," Marge said. "If it isn't your knight in shining armor."

Aiden was standing in the market when she said it, looking at Gwen's back. Waiting for her to turn around and see him. And yet it didn't occur to him that Marge might be talking about him.

"Gwen," Marge added. "I mean you."

Gwen turned around. Her hands stopped moving—froze in space with a bag of barbecue potato chips in one and a pint of vanilla ice cream in the other. And just for that moment, she caught his eye and did not scan anything. But the belt kept rolling, and the groceries began to bunch up at the register.

Her face lit up when she saw him there.

He wanted to be happy about that. Or just happy in general. But all he could think was how she was about to be out on the street with her kids. And maybe about to move to someplace too far away. Someplace he couldn't see her the way he could now. At least, if his plan to prevent such a catastrophe failed.

"What're you doing here?" she asked, but not in a bad way.

"I thought you were about to get off work."

"I am."

"Okay, good. I wanted to show you something."

"Ooh," Marge said. "Sounds mysterious."

"Ten minutes," Gwen said.

Then she went back to scanning groceries.

———

"But I have my car here," she said as he walked her out to his truck.

He had one hand on the small of her back, gently. Barely touching. Maybe because he wanted to touch her but couldn't think of a right and proper context in which to do so.

"I'll drive you back to your car."

"What's it all about, Aiden? Really."

"Just trust me for a minute, okay?"

He opened the passenger door of the truck for her, and she climbed in.

Aiden hopped in and fired up the engine, and they drove in silence for a time. He turned the air conditioning up full blast to make it more livable inside the truck's cab. He turned down the radio because the combination of the fan on high and country-western music made it hard to think.

She reached her hand across the seat and he took it and held it.

"Sorry I haven't been keeping in touch so well the last couple of days," she said.

"It's all right."

"I'm not having second thoughts about us. I hope you know that."

"I do."

But it wasn't true. He had worried some about it.

"I just sort of felt like . . . I thought maybe *you* were having second thoughts. And I wanted to give you some time and some space to have them."

"I don't need time or space. I know what I want and it's just what I've wanted all along."

She gave his hand a comfortable little squeeze.

A mile or two passed in silence.

"So, I had my first session with that psychiatrist today," he said.

"Oh. Right! How did it go?"

"Okay, I guess. I'm not really sure about . . . well, I guess I don't even know how to say it. I told her a bunch of stuff about my life, and maybe now I'm wondering how that's supposed to change anything. But I like her."

"I felt that way, too. At first. With my counselor. It takes a while. But you'll start to feel the difference it makes. Honest you will."

"I'm glad you told me you had a good experience with counseling, or I swear I never would have tried it. Sheriff or no sheriff. The whole idea was just so foreign to me."

He pulled up in front of his own gate. Jumped out and opened it.

As he climbed back into the truck, he braved a quick glance at her face. She looked curious. A little nervous. But not as though she were about to ask questions.

He swung left at the house and took the graded dirt road that wound around the roping pen and up the hill.

"What's back here?" she asked.

"You'll see in about a second."

Sure enough, before he could even finish the sentence they had crested the hill, and the caretaker's cabin came into view.

It was smaller than the house. Much smaller. But it had the same orangey tile roof and stucco sides. The same rustic wooden door and window frames. The same shutters. Like a miniature of his ranch house.

He pulled up in front of it and set the hand brake. Turned off the engine.

They sat in silence for a second. Maybe two.

"What's this?" she asked. As if it could be poisonous.

"It's a little house I used to offer to a ranch hand. Usually the main one. The guy who was most useful to me. That way if I needed to go out of town for any reason, there was always somebody here to look after the stock. But my last hand, Derek, he had his own house in town that he liked. So he never moved in. So nobody's lived here for five years at least. It'd take some fixing up."

He opened the door of his truck and stepped down into the dirt.

A moment later she stood at his side. She tried to look into his eyes, but he kept them averted.

"Somebody told you," she said. "Who told you?"

"Well. Small town. You know. Somebody rents out their place just as the bank's about to foreclose—that's gonna get around. You know how it is."

"I suppose," she said. "Yeah."

"It's small." He walked to the door, and she followed. He wiped the dirt off the soles of his boots on the dusty mat, but it might have made them worse, not better. "Only one bedroom. So I don't know how you fit three people in only one bedroom. But the thing about it is, it's available now. So if you've got a place to live now, but it's small, and you have to figure out how to do better, well . . . seems to me that's less of a problem. I mean, you've got a roof over your head at the end of the day. A door that locks."

As he spoke, he sorted through the keys in his hand. When he found the right one, he reached out to place it in the lock. Her hand touched his arm—touched bare skin where his sleeve was rolled back—and he froze.

"You know," she said. Then she didn't go on for a few seconds. "If you hear I'm having a problem, you don't have to step in and fix it for me."

Aiden felt his face redden. Still, he froze there, one hand reaching the key out toward the lock on the cabin door.

"I know that," he said. "I know you're absolutely capable of solving your own problems. I know you can always make a home for yourself and those kids. But it likely won't be around here, and we both know it. Not much for rent around here. So if anything, I'm being selfish. I just don't want you to move away, okay?"

Her hand left his arm and dropped to her side. In time he glanced up at her face. She seemed to teeter just on the edge of tears.

"The place we're just leaving is only one bedroom," she said.

"Is it? I didn't know that."

"Elizabeth and I have been sharing the bedroom and Milo sleeps on the couch."

"So this won't be a step down."

"Not at all," she said, and then breathed deeply a few times before saying more. "Let's take a look, then."

He turned the key in the lock and let the door swing wide.

It was dusty inside. He could have written his name with one finger on just about any piece of furniture. Rustic wood chairs and coffee table and a big battered leather sofa mostly covered with a Native American blanket. Kitchen table in more of a nook of a kitchen than its own room.

"It'll need a good cleaning," he said.

"I'm not worried about that."

"What are you worried about, then?"

Gwen sighed. Then she began to wander around the place, looking at the dusty furniture close up. It didn't take long.

"We're pretty new for this. You and me, I mean."

"For living together, yeah. I agree. It would be too soon. But you can't even see this place from the main house. And it's not like I'd be popping in all the time, acting like your life is mine because it's on my property. I'd let you have your privacy. And if it doesn't work out, well then . . . whatever. It doesn't work out. It's still a place for you three to be in the meantime. It still gives you more time to figure out where you can live long term."

She didn't answer for a strange length of time. Just stood in the swirling dust motes, in a beam of light from the open front door. She was looking up slightly, toward the ceiling. As if waiting for something to be delivered from on high.

Aiden didn't know what to say, or even if he should disturb her.

"And how much would it cost us to live here?" she asked in a small voice.

"Oh, come on, Gwen. It's just sitting here and you know it."

That look came across her face again. As if she might be about to cry. It made him look away, though he couldn't quite figure why.

A second later she rushed him. Appeared right in his line of vision and just kept coming, and he threw his arms wide to receive her, and she wrapped herself around him. He breathed deeply and held her in return.

Everything that had been weighing on him fell away, and he was okay. The kind of okay he'd been trying for all his life.

"You know this means Milo would be living here on your ranch," she said into his ear.

"I know that."

"With all your animals."

His muscles tightened, and he wondered if she could feel it. Strangely, he hadn't thought things through that far.

"Not that he usually hurts animals," she added quickly. "But I just had to say it. Make sure you know what you're getting yourself into. But that thing with the rabbits, well . . . like I said. Nothing like that ever happened before."

Still holding her, Aiden felt all that recently gained okayness drain away again. Abandon him.

An image filled his head. Milo standing over the freshly dug grave of a bird he had personally murdered. Playing a tune on some kind of child's wind instrument.

"We'll figure it out," he breathed near her ear. "It'll be okay. Everything's going to be okay."

# Chapter Ten

## The Tightening

Aiden could hear the sound of the television program Milo was watching. It was raucous and disturbing. Aiden was standing in his own kitchen, trying not to be troubled by the noise, and working up the nerve to go in there and start some kind of conversation with the boy.

Maybe having them here at his house—instead of at their new cabin with a babysitter—had been a bad idea. And yet it was Aiden who had insisted.

He pulled a deep breath and straightened his back. Somehow Milo was his new family now. He couldn't avoid these interactions indefinitely.

He marched into the TV room, a converted spare bedroom.

Milo raised his eyes to Aiden's eyes and then quickly looked away again. He was sitting slumped on the sofa, his back curled, his head tilted forward at what must have been an uncomfortable angle, his chin nearly touching his collarbone. He was wearing shorts, and his legs looked so impossibly thin that Aiden felt a pang of empathy for the boy. Those legs didn't look much wider than the bones that ran through them. The cast on his arm was so huge it seemed to swallow him up. Overshadow him.

"Where's Elizabeth?" Aiden asked, shouting to be heard over the too-loud television blare.

Milo muttered something, but it was much too quiet to hear.

Aiden moved closer and sat down on the far end of the couch from Milo. The boy moved farther away, though there wasn't much farther to be had. Still, he scooted his butt over until he was pressed into the very corner of the couch, as far from Aiden as possible.

Aiden slid his hand over and grabbed the remote control. He punched the volume down by four or five notches.

"There," he said. "Now I stand a chance of hearing . . . well, anything but what's on TV. Where did you say she was?"

"Out in the barn talking to the horses," Milo mumbled. Even at close range, and even with the TV at normal volume, the boy's words came out so wispy and small that Aiden could only just catch them. They barely took their rightful place in the air.

"The horses aren't in the barn. Except two or three. They're almost all in those two pastures between the house and your cabin."

Milo only shrugged. It was a stiff, overdone gesture that pulled his shoulders up too high around his ears and held them there too long. Meanwhile the boy's eyes never left the screen.

"What are we watching?" Aiden asked, trying to sound breezy. Light and normal. Not unduly stressed by the conversation.

It didn't go well.

Milo shot him a brief glance. He held it just long enough that Aiden could see the derision in the boy's eyes. As if the idea that "we" could do anything together was absurd. Offensive, even.

"*I* am watching cartoons," Milo said after a time, a strangely mature formality in his words and an ominous emphasis on the word "I." He could not have stated it any more clearly. Whatever he was doing, Aiden's participation—his mere presence—was not invited.

"Listen," Aiden began, "I just want to say again that I'm sorry for—"

He never got to finish the sentence. Milo leapt upright, landed on his feet, and began moving. Away.

Aiden followed him to the front door, but the boy was surprisingly fast.

Milo threw the door wide. He strode out into the warm and sunny morning without bothering to close the door behind him. Aiden followed, calling his name and gaining ground.

"Milo! Milo, wait!"

Milo did not wait.

"I don't want you going back to your cabin. I mean it. I promised your mom I'd watch you, and we're going to do that at the big house. So come back in. Now."

Milo kept walking.

It struck Aiden that it would be a terrible mistake to let him go. The boy was testing him. If Aiden stated very clearly how he needed something to be—as he just had—and then allowed Milo to do the opposite, it would set a terrible precedent for their relationship. He could be sunk before they ever really started.

He decided it was time to act parental. However that was supposed to work.

"Milo," he said again, and surged forward. He grabbed a handful of the back of the boy's shirt.

Milo hit the end of that tether, strained for a moment, then came to the desired halt.

"Look, I get it," Aiden said. "I was trying to talk to you and you don't want me to. Fine. I won't do it anymore. But you have to come back into the house."

Milo broke into a sudden flurry of forward activity. Except none of it resulted in his moving forward. But he thrashed against the restraint of his shirt in Aiden's fist. Unsuccessfully.

Then Milo did something Aiden had not seen coming. Something that could only be described as a meltdown.

He screamed. Shrieked, really. He dissolved into a heap at Aiden's feet, thrashing his legs and his unbroken left arm. Pushing out a noise that pierced Aiden's eardrums and psyche like a nearby siren. Keening.

Aiden stood hunched above him, wincing, still holding a handful of the boy's shirt, utterly unclear on how to proceed.

After a terrible moment Elizabeth appeared at Aiden's side. Aiden had never been so happy to see anyone. At least, not that he could recall.

"What happened to him?" Aiden asked her, shouting to be heard over the siren wail of Milo's panicky tantrum.

She leaned close to his ear to answer. To give him half a chance to hear her.

"Anytime somebody makes him feel . . . like, when they take hold of him . . . so he can't get away . . . and they have power over him like that, he freaks out."

"Oh. I'm sorry. I didn't know."

Aiden released his handful of the boy's shirt.

Silence fell. It felt shocking. As if the very air were vibrating, stunned to have all that sound subtracted so quickly.

"I just need him to go back in the house," Aiden said. "My house. I agreed to watch him at my house, and I need him to stay there."

"Okay," Elizabeth said. "No worries."

She knelt down beside her brother and spoke a few words into his ear. Aiden couldn't hear them and didn't try.

Next thing he knew she was helping Milo to his feet, one arm around the boy as if to shelter him from the world. From everything. The two walked together back toward Aiden's house. Aiden stood rigid in the sun and breathed, and tried to shake the feeling of being deeply rattled. But you don't simply shake off a thing like that. It's too bad you can't, but you can't. It's in your bones, it's in your cells. It needs time to move through you.

A moment later he looked up to see Elizabeth walking back in his direction. Alone.

"Hey," he said, relieved that it was only her.

"Hey," she said back.

"Is he okay?"

"Yeah. He'll be all right. He's back in front of his cartoons."

"Think we can trust him to stay there?"

"He hasn't moved off the couch all day. He kind of hasn't moved off the couch since his arm got broken, except just now when you tried to talk to him. So I figure, yeah. He'll probably stay put."

"Did you find the horses? Milo said you were going out to see the horses."

"I didn't find too many of them. There are three in the barn. I like that big gray."

"Oh yeah. That's Smokey. He's my stallion. He's the daddy of all these horses I breed here. And quite a few others around the county."

They turned and walked toward the barn together, as if following some invisible prearranged agreement. As if they could move in a sort of living choreography without any discussion before the fact.

"And then there was a young-looking one in there," she said, words spilling out of her in a fairly typical teenage rhythm. "And one that looks really fat. No offense."

Aiden laughed. "None taken," he said. "That's one of my brood mares, Misty. She's with foal."

"Pregnant?"

"Yeah. Pregnant."

They stepped into the barn together. Then they both stopped. It was more of that natural choreography that came so easily to them. It was cool in the shade of the barn aisle, and moist feeling. The air had a tropical feel and an earthy smell.

"You probably should have let my mom get the babysitter," she said.

"I don't know," Aiden said. "Seemed like a shame for her to spend all that money. I mean . . . I'm right here. And I want to get to know you two anyway." He paused, realizing he had just told a small untruth.

He wanted to get to know Elizabeth. He needed to get to know Milo, but he dreaded it. "Why? Did I just mess him up really bad?"

"No, I didn't mean that. He'll be okay. He'd be just as likely to have that much trouble with the babysitter. I just meant . . . for you. You might be sorry you offered."

Smokey nickered softly in his stall, impatient because he could hear Aiden's voice. Aiden instinctively moved down the aisle to where the stallion stood with his head extended over the stall door. He stroked the animal's long face.

"I'm not sorry I offered," he said.

It wasn't true. Not really. But he wanted it to be true so badly. Maybe he could make it true. Grow into it somehow.

The girl came closer to Smokey and reached a tentative hand out, and Smokey extended his soft nose to meet it.

"What happened to him?" Aiden asked. Then he wished he could snatch the words back again.

"Well. Our dad. You know . . . abused him."

Aiden wanted to ask, "Abused him how?" And also he did not want to ask it. Above all he knew it was not his business to ask such a thing. And that if he ever felt it was, he should ask Gwen. Not her daughter.

"Yeah. Got it. Never mind. None of my business anyway. You want to ride?"

*"Smokey?"* she asked, her eyes wide with fear.

"No. No, I didn't mean Smokey. He might be a little above your pay grade, if you know what I mean. I was thinking that little pony mare you rode the first time you were here."

"Yes! I want to. I'd love to. Where is she?"

"Out in pasture. But she'll come when I call. Just do me a favor. I'll go get her and tack her up. But run inside for a minute and make sure Milo is right where we left him. Okay?"

—

By the time Elizabeth came back, Aiden had the little gray mare, Penny, tied to the hitching post in front of the barn. The pony stood with her head down—as far down as the lead rope would allow—eyes partly closed.

The girl gave Aiden a thumbs-up, and he felt something in his gut relax.

"He's just watching TV," she said.

"Good. Come on in the barn. I'll show you how to tack up your own horse, so you can ride whenever you want."

They walked into the barn together, and Aiden opened the tack room door. They stepped into a sea of western saddles on racks, bridles—some plain and serviceable, some show-fancy—hackamores, breast collars, cinches. Lassos and other, more everyday ropes.

"Is he sick?" Aiden asked. It surprised him. He'd had no idea that he was about to mention Milo, or even that he still had the boy on his mind. "Physically, I mean. He's just so skinny. I know he doesn't eat much, but . . . does anybody know why not?"

"My mom had him to the doctor about a hundred times." She was looking up and around at all the tack as though he'd led her into a room full of gold and jewels and told her to take what she wanted. "But they don't really know. They said he had something called 'failure to thrive.' Or at least one doctor did, anyway. But nobody knows exactly what that is. I mean . . . the doctors must know *something* about it. But they just use those words to cover up the fact that they don't know *why* he isn't. Thriving. That's what I think, anyway. But they can't find anything real. Or, you know . . . in his actual body. So we figure it's more about what upsets him. Not about being really sick."

"Maybe I shouldn't have asked. I didn't mean to pry."

"No, it's okay. I didn't mind. *He* would've minded. If he was here. He hates it when people talk about him like that. But he's in the house, so what's the difference?"

Aiden nodded, suddenly needing to know for a fact that Milo was indeed in the house. He took down the mare's saddle and hung a bridle over its horn.

"Here," he said. "Carry this out to where I have her tied. I'll be right back."

He waited a moment after handing it to her, to make sure she was up to its weight. But she hoisted it above waist level and lugged it out into the sun.

He walked quickly to the house. Threw the front door wide. The raucous sound of the TV greeted him again. It had been turned back up to max. Slowly—and quietly for reasons that made no real sense—Aiden crept to the doorway of the TV room. With a jolt to his belly, he felt himself suddenly sure that the room would be empty. That Milo would be outside somewhere. Missing.

He could already feel the sense of déjà vu. That nagging feeling that when he finally tracked the boy down he would be sorely sorry he had taken his eyes off Milo. Even for a few minutes.

Just like last time.

He stuck his head through the door.

Milo was collapsed on the couch, much as before, his eyes glued to the screen. He looked up at Aiden for just a brief second. Maybe even a fraction of one. Then he looked away.

———

Once he got Elizabeth up into the saddle, Aiden no longer felt comfortable leaving her alone to go check on Milo. Although one time he had her ride beside him right up to the front door, then stuck his head inside and listened for the TV. He could see one sneakered foot through the doorway into the TV room.

"We're good," he told her.

They began to do their best to let the girl ride.

What he really wanted was to mount a horse of his own—Smokey, oddly enough for a stallion, was the one who had grown to tolerate his fear reactions—and ride with her. They could have gone all through the woods, up the hills and down again. They could have waded through streams. It would have been something like the old days, when Aiden's new stepfather had gone riding with him.

In other words, if only there were no such thing as Milo. Or, more charitably, if only Milo had wanted to ride as well. Aiden consciously corrected his brain onto a more magnanimous course of thinking.

"Ride her down to that creek," Aiden said. "You can gallop if you want. But when you get down there, give her a free rein and let her take a drink if she needs one."

"What creek?" Elizabeth asked, squinting into the sun and shading her eyes with one hand. Her helmet was comically floppy. She had to hoist it up off her right eyebrow now and then.

"Well, you can't see the creek from here. But you can see that line of trees."

"Oh. Right."

"And I can see you from here. So I'll know you're okay."

"I can gallop?"

"Sure. Just be aware of your pony. It's okay if she gets a little sweaty. We'll cool her off and give her a nice sponge-down after. But watch her nostrils. And listen. If she's blowing, that's too much. If you can feel her sides heaving, walk her. Right away. That would mean you're overdoing it. If you tune in to her, you'll know. You're on her back. You have no idea how much she knows about you when you're on her back. The slightest shift of your weight. If you're afraid. Try to be almost that sensitive to her."

He looked up to see Elizabeth staring at him, a curious look on her face.

"She knows when I'm afraid?"

"Absolutely she does."

"How does she know what I'm feeling?"

"There are little tells. There'll be more tension in your thighs. You'll grip her sides more tightly without realizing it. Your hands'll harden on the reins. But . . . I don't know. There might be more to it than that. I think they literally sense us in some ways I can't explain. Any time an animal is domesticated . . . well, their whole life is about getting along with people. But we can't talk to each other. So they learn us in other ways. It's like if a person loses their sight. Their other senses become stronger. I think we develop whatever senses we need to get by in the world."

"Hmm," Elizabeth said.

She was not riding away. She did not seem inclined to ride away.

"'Hmm,' what?"

"I wonder why it doesn't work both ways. We can't talk to them. Why don't *we* grow extra senses to know what *they're* feeling?"

Aiden sat with the question for a moment. Not really thinking of an answer. Just letting it rattle around inside him. He could tell her that it wasn't unheard of. That it occasionally worked both ways.

And he would, most likely. But not today.

"Because we're on top," he said. "Unfair but true. They have to please us. Not so much the other way around."

"I want to please this pony," she said.

"Good."

"Maybe she doesn't want to gallop down to the creek."

"Ask her."

"How?"

"Put your heels to her sides and ask her to do it. If you're paying attention, you'll know if she's enjoying herself or not."

Without taking time to reply, Elizabeth lifted the reins and galloped off. He watched them grow smaller in the shimmering sun. She stopped the pony at the creek, and seemed to wait. But the gray did not drop her neck and drink. Aiden hadn't assumed that she would. He just wanted to train the girl well. Right from the start.

They rode back to him again at a bouncy trot.

"She likes to run," Elizabeth announced proudly.

"Not surprised," Aiden said. "It's in her nature."

———

It might have been the third trip to the creek and back when Aiden began to get the uneasy feeling, or it might have been the fourth. It was hard to remember, even in the moment. And there was no outward tell of trouble. No clear sign that anything was wrong.

It was more a rising sense of panic in Aiden's gut.

It was a familiar panic. It wasn't his. That was also familiar—to feel something that clearly did not belong to him. That came to him across the space between himself and other living things.

Elizabeth was out of shouting range, but he waved his arms wildly to get her attention. He wanted her to ride back to him, and fast, so he could go check on Milo.

She didn't see him.

The discomfort spiked in his belly. And in his chest. He felt breathless.

He thought of leaving her alone. Running inside to see if the boy was still in front of the TV. But maybe it was nothing. Maybe it was a couple of his mares squaring off over some issue of a hay feeder or dominance in a group pasture.

What if Elizabeth fell while he was gone? Got in some kind of trouble? And then what if it turned out that there was no real reason to leave her alone in the first place? How would he explain himself? To Gwen, to his own conscience? To the deputy sheriff, if there was another hospital visit involved?

Aiden broke into a sprint in the hot sun. The moments, his strides, stretched out. Time began playing that trick Hannah had warned him about. He wished he had her ticking clock with him now, to keep the seconds right-size. Scrub oak trees flashed by in his peripheral vision, their leaves streaked by motion and lack of focus.

His chest began to heave—the warning sign he had told Elizabeth to watch for in her horse. He ignored it.

"Elizabeth!" he shouted when he thought he might be in range. When it made sense to do so.

Her pony spooked and skittered sideways three steps, but the girl stayed on.

"What? What's wrong?"

"Jump down. Walk your pony back. I have to go check on Milo."

He froze for a second or two. Maybe three. He had to watch her feet touch the ground. He had to know she was safe. He was responsible for her.

Then again, he was responsible for Milo. And he had left the boy alone.

There was an agonizing pause as the girl considered dismounting. She seemed to approach it like a puzzle. Take a minute to make a plan. Though it was likely more of a second. Still, it felt hours long to Aiden.

Then she swung a leg off the little mare's back, and her foot touched the earth.

Aiden ran for the house.

About halfway there, he heard it. A yelp of pain. A sharp cry that split the air, that cleaved something in Aiden's midsection.

It was not a human cry.

Aiden followed the sound. He found Milo in the front yard.

With Buddy.

The boy had found a rope lasso, which he had looped around the poor trusting dog's neck. That in itself might not have been so bad. It might almost have been a decent collar-and-leash substitute if Aiden had used it. But it was prone to tighten if pulled. It needed to be handled with care. Milo was handling it with rage. Yanking the dog back and forth, so much so that poor Buddy had to splay his legs and swing his body to keep from flying off in one direction or the other and choking from the pressure. The dog could not seem to override the tendency to pull back to get away, which tightened the rope further.

As Aiden ran, before he could reach out to them, before he could stop it, Milo looked over his shoulder. Looked right into Aiden's face.

Then he gave the rope another sharp tug.

The dog yelped in pain, and Aiden felt that pain from the base of his throat all the way down to his groin and down the insides of his thighs. As though someone were splitting him with a sharp knife.

Then he was upon the boy, but he didn't apply his own brakes. He just crashed right into Milo, and the boy went down. It wasn't until Milo was sent flying through the air that Aiden remembered the broken arm, and the chance of reinjuring it. But through some unearned moment of luck, the boy landed on his left side.

The rope tumbled out of Milo's hand.

Aiden grabbed the end of the lasso and hurried to Buddy, who wagged his tail. It was firmly tucked between the dog's hind legs, mostly hidden under his rounded, bony back. But still he wagged it. Aiden loosened the rope and pulled it free, and the dog lowered his head and gasped air.

Aiden examined Buddy's neck carefully.

He had a couple of rope burns, one that was just deep enough to weep a clear fluid and a little blood. If the dog had come here with more of a hair coat, it might have protected him. As it stood, Buddy was scraped up. Okay on balance, but slightly injured.

Aiden straightened and turned back to Milo, utterly blind in his rage. The boy was still sprawled in the dirt. He looked up at Aiden. Aiden looked down at him. The boy was smart enough to be afraid.

Aiden leaned down and lassoed Milo around the neck with the rope.

He would go back a hundred times and explain that he wanted only to show the boy how it felt to be so afraid. So abused. That he only wanted Milo to feel the fear that Buddy had felt.

And it was true that he had no intention to injure Milo. But the truth in that moment was that Aiden had lost control. He was outside his body and out of his mind.

Anything could have happened.

Milo stumbled to his feet, eyes wide.

"You think that's fun?" Aiden shouted, leaning close, his fist tight on the rope. The boy's eyes blinked and squinted at the ferocity of the words. "You like hurting things? You think it's a hobby to hurt my dog? How would you feel? How does it feel to you? To have someone hold this kind of power over you? And abuse it?"

And just for a split second, Aiden almost snugged up the rope.

But he didn't. Thank God he didn't.

A few things happened, nearly at once.

He looked into Milo's eyes and saw far more fear than he had ever intended to inspire. He saw that he had swayed far over the line between lesson teacher and aggressor. And just in that moment Milo began to cry pitifully.

Then Aiden saw movement at the corner of his eye and looked up to see Elizabeth standing at the corner of the house, watching him. Holding the reins of her pony, who was also watching.

Aiden dropped the rope.

Milo scrambled to get it off his neck, desperate and flailing, as if the rope were a boa constrictor or a thousand spiders. As it landed in the dirt with a whump and a puff of dust, the boy ran sobbing into the house.

Aiden stood. Stood almost as though unable to do anything else besides stand. Stood as if rooted to the dry ground as surely as the scrub oaks. He looked up into Elizabeth's eyes.

"I wasn't going to hurt him," he said. "I didn't want to hurt him."

The second sentence was absolutely true. The first may have involved some wishful thinking. He certainly had never wanted to. But there was some luck involved in the fact that he hadn't.

"Is the dog okay?" she asked. Shyly.

For one horrible moment, Aiden assumed she was gone from him. That she would never trust him again. That he now had two potential stepchildren who neither liked nor trusted him. Two wedges where there should have been family forming. Where there could have been love.

"He has some rope burns on his neck," Aiden said. He looked down to see Buddy crouched at his side. The dog was leaning against Aiden's leg, and Aiden hadn't felt him. Not physically. He still felt the dog's pain and fear, but that was everywhere. Aiden had not been aware of the actual leaning pressure of the dog's presence. He reached a hand down and placed it on Buddy's head. Reassuringly, he hoped. "Not too bad. I mean, he'll be okay. But maybe he'll only be okay because I got there when I did. I just wanted him to know how that feels. Milo, I mean. I didn't want to hurt him. I just wanted him to see what it feels like to be that afraid."

"He knows," Elizabeth said.

And it was true. Aiden had seen it in the boy's eyes. But how could someone do that, if they knew? He wanted to ask, but he had no right relying on Elizabeth to explain the world to him. And besides, his adrenaline had drained away and his words failed him.

"I'm sorry," he said, forcing himself to speak.

Yes, he would have to go inside and say it to Milo. But first he said it to Milo's sister.

"You don't have to be sorry," she said. "I know how he makes people feel. And you didn't pull it tight or anything. It's not like you hurt him."

"But I was right there. I was right on the edge of it. I could have done it."

"But you didn't," Elizabeth said.

—

When Aiden walked into the house, Milo was back on the couch in the TV room. Hunched over himself. Hugging his own knees and crying.

Aiden stood over the boy, who withdrew further into himself.

*This little missing person,* someone said in his head.

It was something he remembered. Someone had said it, sometime. But he couldn't remember when or who. But it was a thing. A real thing, that he knew. Like a belonging he had misplaced years ago and hadn't thought about since, but recognized immediately when he saw it again.

He heard a noise behind him, and turned to see that Elizabeth had followed him into the room. He looked into her face and she smiled sadly and looked away.

"Lock us in here," he said. "Please."

She looked up at him again but said nothing.

Meanwhile Milo cried harder, and with more force. "No!" the boy shrieked. "Don't leave me with him, Lizzie!"

"I won't hurt him. I promise. I just need to know he's going to stay in this room with me."

"But if you're right here with him . . ." She trailed off.

"But if he gets up and walks out, what am I supposed to do? I can't physically stop him without setting him off."

"Oh. Right."

Meanwhile Milo cried into his own knees and said nothing.

"How do I lock you in?" she asked, peering at the outside of the door. "There's no lock."

"Get one of the chairs from the kitchen table and wedge it under the knob. Can you untack the pony and put her away by yourself?"

"I think so. Where do I put her?"

"You can put her in an empty stall in the barn for now. And give Buddy some reassurance. Please. I'll take care of that rope burn as soon as I get out. Come knock every once in a while, okay? In case one of us needs to go to the bathroom or something. Otherwise we'll stay right here until your mother gets back."

Elizabeth nodded mutely. Then she stepped out and closed the door. A minute later Aiden heard the scrape of the chair being wedged under the knob.

"No!" Milo screamed, startling Aiden and hurting his ears. "No, don't leave me with him, Lizzie!"

"I won't hurt him," Aiden called to her through the door.

"He will! I know he will! He's going to kill me!"

"I'm not going to kill him," Aiden said as calmly as possible. "I'm not even going to touch him. I just need to know where he is." A long silence. Then Aiden said, looking right at Milo but loud enough for Elizabeth to hear, "If I was going to hurt him, it would have been out there. I've had time to cool off now."

"I know you won't," Elizabeth said through the door. Barely audible.

Milo's only answer was to scoot off the couch and run behind an upholstered chair, where he crouched on the floor, back up against a corner, skinny legs and sneakered feet sticking out.

Time stretched out from that moment into something so slow as to be nearly impossible to bear.

The idea, as far as Aiden could tell, had been to spend this time talking to the boy. Even though he knew the chances of talking *with* him were close to none. But Aiden could still say what he wanted Milo to know. He just had to give up on the idea that he would know how his words were being received.

But Aiden felt so entirely overwhelmed by the otherness, the "missingness," of the boy in his care, that it played out as several painfully long hours of neither of them speaking any words to the other at all.

It wasn't until they had sat there together—in a very loose sense of the word—for the better part of an hour that Aiden realized his hands were shaking. Had been shaking for some while. He figured they would stop within a reasonable space of time.

He was wrong.

—

Aiden could not have guessed how much time had passed before he heard the chair scrape away from the knob again. The door opened, and Gwen leaned her head into the room.

She looked at Milo's feet sticking out from behind the chair, then at Aiden, then back to Milo again.

Aiden had not properly spent the afternoon considering what he would say to Gwen. How he would explain their horrible day.

As it turned out, not much explanation was required. The look that passed between them said all Aiden had planned to communicate, along with quite a few things he would have preferred to keep to himself.

# Chapter Eleven

## The Unearthing

"But you didn't," Hannah said, pulling Aiden's gaze away from the downtown Bakersfield skyline. "You stopped yourself in time. I think you get credit for that. Don't you?"

"That's pretty much what Elizabeth said, too."

"Smart girl."

"She's amazing," Aiden said. He could feel the wonder that filled his voice when he spoke about her, along with the lifting of the dark cloud left by Milo. "She's such a great kid. She makes me feel . . ." But then he realized he had no ending to that sentence. If the thought had concluding words, he didn't know them. Yet.

"What? She makes you feel what?"

"Like . . ."—and then there it was. Just like that—"a father. Like I could be a father. It's really nice."

"So you're saying she makes it easy to love her."

"Yes, exactly."

"And Milo makes it hard to love him. But he still needs you to."

"I don't think Milo even *wants* me to love him."

"He wants *somebody* to."

"His mother loves him."

"Good. Then there's hope. Elizabeth was right. You don't have to pay for what you didn't do. What did Gwen say about the whole incident?"

"The same. That I didn't hurt him and that's what matters."

"Did you know your hands are shaking?"

"Oh," Aiden said. "Yeah."

He pressed his palms together and wedged them between his thighs. That didn't stop them from shaking. But at least it put them out of sight.

"How long has that been going on?"

"Since that incident I was just telling you about."

"This whole time?"

"I'm afraid so."

"Okay. Sorry. I didn't mean to get us off track. We were talking about Elizabeth."

"Oh, right. She said something else interesting. I said I wanted Milo to know how it felt. What he did to that poor dog. You know. The fear. She said, 'He knows.'"

"Again . . . smart girl."

Aiden thought once more of Elizabeth's quick forgiveness of him. Standing at the corner of the house, holding the reins of her pony, saying the same sort of things Hannah said for a living. The cloud returned.

"I don't see why I should get credit for the fact that I didn't, though. Tighten the rope, I mean. I don't think it's fair to let me off the hook. I *could* have done it."

He spoke with his gaze trained out the window. He hadn't met her eyes once since coming through the door.

"Okay. Here's why. Because I don't want to live in a world where we have to punish ourselves for things that we could have done but didn't. And I'm guessing you don't either, if you really stopped to think about it."

"I just . . . ," Aiden began. Then he ran out of steam. Out of words. Out of ideas from which to form words. He braved a quick glance into her eyes. Then he looked away again. The words volunteered their services. "I don't want to be someone who's capable of violence."

"But you are," Hannah said. "You are capable of violence."

Aiden felt a flare of anger that surprised him. Ambushed him, in fact. He could have said many things—he even knew what some of them were—but he refused to speak until the wave of rage had passed. He felt his face flush red. He stared out the window again until the heat of the emotion drained away and left him feeling more tired and defeated than anything else.

"I don't know where you get off saying that to me," Aiden said in a strangely quiet and calm voice. "You barely know me. How do you know?"

"Because you're a human being and you're alive. Everybody is capable of violence. Just most people never commit it. Look. I know what's troubling you. I really do. It's a turning-point moment in people's lives, when you look yourself in the face like that and realize that who you are, and who you become, and what you do seem to rely on a combination of factors that are partly out of your control. It's not whether a person could ever commit a violent act that's a reasonable question, but more how far you would have to push that person to bring it out. Be glad you passed the test this time. But I get it. It scared you. Plus it opened up some other unfortunate cans of worms."

Aiden chewed that over for a moment or two. Then he hit a wall in his head. He realized he had no idea what other cans of worms it opened. He didn't know what she meant.

"Like what, for example?"

"Well. Now that you know you could be pushed over the edge, in which case you would have been a decent person doing a terrible thing, you need to consider whether you can see Milo in the light of that same humanity."

"No. I can't. And I won't. Because he didn't stop himself."

"Right, no. He didn't. But he's not you. He may have been through some things you haven't. So you have to ask yourself if you're absolutely sure you could go through the experiences he's been through in his short life and not act out with violence. I'm not saying it's an impossible thing to do, or that everyone would react the same way. Some people can absorb a lot of abuse without outer-directing their anger. They turn it in on themselves, usually, instead. So here's another thought to blow your poor mind, and I'm sure you won't feel ready for it, but here goes. Milo's abusive father probably suffered a great deal in his life and reacted to it by outer-directing his rage. If we'd somehow seen him as a young boy being abused, we'd feel terribly sorry for him. We'd properly see that younger version of him as an innocent victim. But now he's all grown up and acting out the shape he's been twisted into being, and we have nothing for him but our hatred."

Aiden tried to take a step in the direction of that thought, but he had to stop and back away from it again. In fact, it was hard not to resent Hannah for asking him to try to approach such a thing.

"How do you know the kid's not just mean?" But even as he asked, Aiden remembered what Gwen had told him. What a sweet boy Milo had been before the trouble with his dad. How all this acting out had been more recent.

"I've never met anybody who was mean for no reason," Hannah said. "I've met some people who were mean for reasons I may never know. But I never met anyone who I think was born that way. I've never met a mean baby. Have you?"

"I've completely lost track of how this relates to my situation," he said.

It was only partly true. It was mostly a way of deflecting the more troublesome aspects of the conversation and sending things off in a better direction. Or an easier direction, in any case.

"Okay. We'll pull back a bit. If you can't see Milo with his full humanity now, that's okay. I'd rather you be honest about it. It's something you can sit with. Think over. Maybe you'll make your peace with it over time and maybe not. But a caution: Until you get it that's he's only what his experience has shaped him to be, you're seeing him as subhuman. As 'other' somehow. And the danger in the meantime is that he'll see that. He'll know how you view him. When you see a child as 'less than,' it's not long before self-fulfilling prophecy comes into play."

"Right," Aiden said. "Got it."

And, unfortunately, he did.

They listened to the ticking of the clock in silence for a few moments.

"Tell me what you think of this," Aiden said. "Elizabeth told me something strange about him. She said he used to shoot birds with his BB gun. And then he would give the birds these little funerals. Wrap them in silk handkerchiefs and put them in boxes in the ground and play a tune over them on a flute. What do you make of a thing like that?"

He watched her scribble notes on her pad for a few seconds. Then she set her pen down and sighed.

"Without seeing him and talking to him, it's hard to know. Could be he has a morbid fascination with death and dying. Could be he feels guilty afterward and wants to do something to make it up to his victims. Also, the two are not mutually exclusive. Could be both. If you want to know what's going on with him, I suggest you bring him in here."

*"Bring him in here?"*

Aiden only stared at her for a few seconds. He could feel that he was blinking too much. Too fast.

"Has he had any counseling, ever?"

"I . . . you know, I don't know. I never felt right asking. I wasn't sure it was any of my business. I don't know how I'm supposed to get him in here if he doesn't want to go. And I'm pretty sure he doesn't want to go."

Hannah sighed again.

"Theoretically, it's not that hard to compel a child to come to a place like this. The problem is that when you get him here, we can't compel him to open up to us. But it still might be better than nothing. He'll hear what we say, even if he never opens his mouth. I might gather a little information just by watching his reactions. He might sit here for a year and do nothing but resist, and then we might get a crack in his shell. I've seen it happen."

They sat in silence for a moment. Aiden wanted to glance at the clock, but he couldn't bring himself to do it. What if their session was nearly over? Then he would have to get up and walk out of this room and go back to handling his life for himself. He would have to be the grown-up who knew what to do.

In his head, he tried the mantle of humanity on Milo like a costume on a mannequin. It fell away again. As if it had never belonged there and refused to stay. As if humanity and Milo were two opposing magnetic poles.

"I just don't know how to get through to that boy," he said.

Then he froze, stopped talking, and just listened. Listened to those words echo around the room. Bounce around in his head. They had not felt like his own words. He had heard them somewhere. He was repeating something he had heard. He wasn't sure how he knew. But he knew.

"Hmm," he said. "That's interesting."

Hannah didn't ask him what was interesting. She waited. She trusted him to say.

"That's the second time that's happened to me in just a handful of days. The first time it was a thought. An internal thought. This time it came out of my mouth. But both times, it was something familiar. Something I'd heard somewhere. But I don't know where."

"What was the first one?"

"'This little missing person.' I think my mother said that. But I might be wrong."

"And this second one? 'I just don't know how to get through to that boy.' Do you know who said that?"

"My stepfather."

"About you?"

"Must have been. I was the only boy around. So he must have been exasperated with me. But I have no idea why. What could I have done that was so terrible?"

"I don't know. But it opens up another interesting can of worms. Your stepfather was exasperated with you. Made the same statement about being unable to deal with you that you just made about Milo. Hard not to see a parallel there."

"I wasn't nearly as bad as Milo," Aiden said.

But then he had to wonder how he could know. How he could feel as sure as he definitely felt. If he didn't remember.

"I'm guessing that's true," Hannah said. "Most kids aren't. But I don't think it's about *the degree*. I think you can understand the frustration with a stepchild without negating the insight on the grounds that the severity of the problem is not equal. I hope you know what I mean by that."

He did. But his brain had already moved off in a different direction.

"I had another thing happen not too long ago. I just thought of it again. When Gwen came to the door with her kids, I had this image of my stepfather the first time I met him. But that was when I was six. I never remember back that far. I mean, all my life up until just recently I couldn't. So does this mean I'm starting to remember things? Things from that time before I thought I could remember?"

"Looks that way," Hannah said.

"But I never could before."

"You could never feel your empathy before, either. Everything changes. You should be getting that, right about now."

# PART FOUR

## AIDEN DELACORTE AS A CHILD

## MORE THAN THIRTY YEARS EARLIER

# Chapter Twelve

## *Aiden at Age Four*

He woke in a darkened room, sitting up in bed. His heart was calm, in spite of the dream. It did not hammer as it often did in his waking life. And yet it had been horrid, the dream. All-encompassing and dreadful.

He padded barefoot down the hall to his parents' room.

It was tricky, crawling into bed with his parents. He could talk to his mother. Tell her he'd had a bad dream. If his dad stayed asleep, it would be as easy as that. If not, if his dad woke up, he would have to help his mom get around the man and his opinions, working in ways he didn't fully understand with his thinking mind. It was a little like moving through a darkened room. It was something you did one step at a time, working purely by feel.

The door creaked when he opened it.

Both his parents raised their heads and blinked at him in the mostly dark.

He froze a moment, teetering in the doorway.

Then his father put his head back down and closed his eyes. Maybe he was too sleepy to deal with what was happening. Aiden hoped so.

He crossed the cold wooden floorboards to his mother's side of the big bed.

Her eyes were closed. As if she'd gone back to sleep. But her arms reached out and gathered him closer. He stood, his bare feet cold and tingly, feeling the front of himself pressed up against the side of the mattress, and allowed her to wrap him in warmth.

"You have a bad dream, honey?"

Aiden only nodded. He wasn't sure where his voice had gone, or how to go about finding it.

"What did you dream?"

Aiden shrugged.

There had been a dream. He was not making that up. But it was not something he could pin down in words. Even if he had known where his words were hiding.

The dream was always the same. In the dream, there was him. And there was the Earth. The planet. But either Aiden was much bigger or the planet was much smaller, because he could see and feel the curve of its sphere under his feet, like the globe on his dresser, but bigger. And that was not all he could feel. The Earth seemed to groan with the weight of its own emotion. It was angry. It was afraid. It was in pain. Physical pain, but other, more nebulous types of pain as well. And Aiden could not separate himself. He had wanted to jump off. In the dream, he had tried to jump. To fly free. But his feet had been forever rooted to the desperate soil.

Now how exactly was a four-year-old supposed to describe a thing like that with his words?

"Tell me about it," his mother said quietly. "Anything you remember."

"Sad," Aiden said. He forced his voice out of hiding with the assurance that it would not need to do much difficult work.

"Doesn't sound like a nightmare, honey. Nightmares are scary."

"Yeah. Also that."

She sighed. Then she pulled back the covers and allowed him in. He crawled in on the outside, away from his father, and made himself as small as humanly possible. She rolled away, and he moved close. He could feel the warmth of the small of her back. He could draw from it. Use that warmth. It sustained him through the moment. He knew then that he could be okay. That okay was at least possible.

"Such a sensitive boy," she mumbled.

She shouldn't have. She should have let the moment lie still.

"*Too* sensitive," his father said, his voice strong. Definitely awake.

"Leave him alone, Eddie."

"There's nothing wrong with wanting him to be a man."

"He's four years old. There's everything wrong with it."

"I'd like to see us headed for that at least."

"Go back to sleep."

Silence. Stillness. Aiden lay curled and frozen, waiting to see if the moment would hold.

Sometime after that he must have fallen asleep again. But it was something that happened outside his awareness. It was rare—a blessing—for something to happen that Aiden could not feel.

—

He woke slowly, aware of pain across his ribs. He was being carried, a strong arm wrapped underneath his midsection. His arms and legs dangled free, almost dragging onto the hardwood of the hall floor. He tried to lift his head, but it was too difficult. Gravity and sleepiness fought him too effectively.

Then he was let go, dumped unceremoniously. He winced, expecting to hit hard wood. But he landed with a light bounce on his own bed.

"This is where you sleep," his father said simply.

Then he walked out, closing Aiden's bedroom door with a thump.

Aiden lay awake, shivering, for several minutes. It was not cold. They were not that kind of shivers. He willed himself to stay awake, but in time sleep caught him and dragged him under.

The Earth was still there. Waiting for him. Sobbing. Raging. Gasping. And still he could not get away. He could not jump off.

———

The following day Aiden sat in the backyard grass, under the rosebushes that lined the fence on all four sides, and watched his sister, Valerie, play.

She was a bigger kid than Aiden. Nearly six. She attended kindergarten in the morning, which commanded a great deal of Aiden's grudging respect. But now she had arrived home for the afternoon. He wondered, though not in specific words, how it would feel to live a life so heavy with responsibility.

Her hair was done up in two braids, but it had gone messy. She had been changed out of her good school dress and into khaki shorts and a pink tank top. She stood in the driveway, under the giant maple tree, picking up whirlybirds—the little seed pods that spun down like helicopters when thrown into the air—and releasing them to the warm wind with evident joy. Evident to him, anyway. He could feel her joy. Yet sometimes Aiden would say a thing like that out loud—how obvious it was what someone was feeling—only to be met with a look of confusion. Now and then she stopped gathering long enough to do a strange dance, stomping the concrete of the driveway in front of their garage.

Aiden eased closer to see what she was stomping, his stomach suddenly a panicky knot of stress. If she was stepping on bugs, it would be too much. It would be more than Aiden's heart could bear.

Valerie paid him no attention as he crept closer, crawling on his belly to see the concrete near her feet at closer range. When he saw what was happening, he stopped. Froze, in more ways than one. His gut turned to ice water at the sight of the disaster.

It was even worse than Aiden had feared. It was *ants*.

Aiden had an ant farm in his bedroom, and he watched the industrious little heroes for hours a day. Every time his father, who had been laid off from his job and was feeling extra touchy, sent Aiden to his room for being "weird," Aiden watched his ants. They were real, like us. They had jobs. They had a world.

Now their world was in a state of catastrophic disarray, like the scene of an epic battle in a war. Their dead lay everywhere. Live ants mobilized around each tiny corpse, lifting it by one end and attempting to drag it away. But there were so many. Too many. And Valerie was still stomping.

Just for a split second, Aiden felt overwhelmed with the sick dread of the scene. Then he bolted to his feet and pushed Valerie. Rammed her with his shoulder, hard, and pushed her into the rose-bush-lined fence. She shrieked as the thorns scratched her bare arms and legs and snagged her clothing. Then she bounced forward off the chain link and fell onto her face in the driveway. When she sat up, her nose was bleeding. Bright-red blood ran down her upper lip. Shockingly red. A drop landed on the front of her pink top. She held her hands out, as if to show them to Aiden. But more likely she was assessing the damage herself. The heels of both hands had been scraped raw. For a beat or two of time they looked white. Strangely white. Then blood rose in individual drops.

Valerie burst into tears.

"You little creep! I'm telling!" She struggled to her feet and ran for the house. "Mo-o-o-om! Daddy!"

Aiden watched her go, thinking only about the ants she was running over on her way.

There was punishment in his future, but he couldn't focus on it. Not yet. He would make his way inside and face it. Get it over with. But first he had to figure out how to cross the concrete without slaughtering any more ants.

He reached his face down and blew lightly on the pavement. The ants lifted away and flew. That could not be pleasant for them, certainly. But which was worse? To be blown several feet away by a strong and sudden wind? Or to be crushed into oblivion, never to see the light of another day? He was doing the best he could for them.

He set one sneakered foot down in the clear space he had created. Then he reached his face down and blew again. Stepped again.

The world went dark. Or darker, anyway. A shadow fell across him, like a sudden cloud blocking out the sun. Aiden looked up to see his father standing in his path. Standing on ants.

"Look out for—" he began.

He was never able to finish.

The back of his father's hand caught him across the face and sent him flying. He landed on his back on the driveway, smacking his head hard. On the whirlybirds. And yes, of course, on more ants. There was nothing he could do.

"Leave your sister alone," his father said, his voice booming. An instrument to erase all doubt.

Then he seemed to go. Aiden thought he could hear him go.

He reached a hand to his face. He felt a tickle of something underneath his nose. He touched there. It was wet. He drew his hand back again and saw blood. And an ant. An ant was walking on that hand, desperately seeking refuge from all the carnage.

He brought the hand closer to his face again.

"I'm sorry," he whispered to the ant. "I'm really sorry."

—

Aiden spent the rest of the day in his room playing with his horses. They were not real horses, of course. Just some kind of molded plastic. But imagination could do a lot. Great things.

He couldn't bear to look at his ant farm.

He had washed the blood off his face with moistened toilet paper and held the bridge of his nose until the bleeding stopped. Because he knew that's what his mother would do. His nose had bled before and she had cleaned it just like that.

He had his horses all laid out on the rug, one palomino mare at the front of the herd, the others arranged facing her. An audience. As if she had something important to say.

The door to his room opened and his mother came in.

His eyes came up to hers, and Aiden saw shock there. She was shocked to see his face. Aiden hadn't seen his own face recently. Not since he'd wiped off the blood. But it must have looked bad. Maybe it was swollen. Maybe it was bruised. It felt a little swollen. But the color of a bruise is nothing you can feel.

It was interesting. It tickled at his mind and perplexed him—how some things only could be seen with your eyes. They had no sensation. Most things had a sensation. Too much of one.

"What?" he asked her.

She sat on the end of his bed. Gingerly, it seemed. As though she might hurt the bed, or herself, by doing so.

"Come sit with me," she said.

Aiden did as he had been told.

She looped an arm over his shoulders. It felt like coming home. Like being saved. Like the end of all strife.

If only it had been the end of all strife. If only it hadn't been the beginning.

"This is not like you," she said. "What happened?"

"With Bally?"

He called his sister "Bally" because he could not wrap his mouth around her full name.

"Yes."

"She was stepping on ants."

"It's hard to avoid them sometimes."

"Oh no," Aiden said. Sure and authoritative. "She was stepping on ants on purpose."

"I see. Well. I know you like them. But don't you like your sister, too?"

"Not really," Aiden said, "no."

"Aiden! How can you say that?"

"'Cause it's true."

"Just because she stepped on some ants? You always used to like her."

"No," Aiden said, shaking his head with solemn gravity. "I never really did."

"That's distressing news."

"I don't know what that means."

"It means I don't like to hear that."

"Oh," Aiden said. Feeling bad now. "I'm sorry."

"Still. No matter how you feel about her. It's not right to hurt her. I know you feel bad for the ants. But don't you feel bad for her, too? She got hurt. You pushed her down in the driveway. She was bleeding."

"I didn't really push her down. I pushed her back into the fence. The fence pushed her down."

"That's not an excuse, Aiden, and I think you know it. I still want to know why you felt sorrier for those ants than you did for your own sister."

"I don't know," Aiden said. "But I didn't mean for her to get hurt. I just wanted to make it stop."

His mother sighed. Her arm disappeared from around his shoulders, which felt tragic.

"It was wrong, what you did. Do you understand that, Aiden?"

"Yes, ma'am." But he wasn't entirely sure he did understand. Not in this case. Not with countless lives to be saved.

"And it was almost as wrong of her to hit you back, but I understand it more. I think you brought it on yourself."

"Bally didn't hit me."

"Then what happened to your nose? You look like somebody hit you in the face."

"Daddy," he said simply.

He dared to look up at her face. It was whiter than he was used to seeing it. Still pretty, but white. And getting whiter as he watched.

"Excuse me," she said. "I have to go have a talk with your father."

———

It was only a few minutes later when everything fell to ruin. Aiden's whole life. Everything he had known.

He had rearranged his horses so they were all running in one direction, following the palomino mare. As if running to safety. Which seemed prescient, looking back.

Aiden heard a little cry, like a gasp of pain or fear. Or maybe it didn't start out little. Maybe it had gotten smaller as it made its way up the stairs and reached him. It was followed by a thump and a crashing sound like breaking glass. He ran out of his bedroom to the top of the stairs, where he froze.

He got there just in time to see the last of his father's back walking out the door. He waited, unsure of how to proceed and too frightened to move, until he heard his father's car start up, and the sound of its engine disappearing from the driveway. Then he crept down the stairs.

His mother lay sprawled against the wall under a living room window. She had pulled the curtain down around herself with the fall. A vase had been broken, and somehow she had fallen with one hand, her left, braced on its shards. Blood ran into the fibers of the carpet. Aiden felt his body waver, sway as though his bones had turned to rubber. The world went white at its edges, like being forced into a dream when you weren't even sleeping.

She looked up at his face. Her left eye, or rather the area around the outside of it, was swelling. And something had happened to cause that eye to bleed inside. Aiden could see the red stain spreading in the part that should be only white.

In that moment, suddenly, Aiden felt . . . nothing. Well, not nothing. But not enough. Not a normal amount. He loved his mother more than he loved anyone or anything. But as he reached for his feelings about what was happening, they ran farther away. Following the palomino mare to safety, maybe.

"What should I do?" he asked her. His voice sounded strangely calm.

"Call my friend Donna."

"How do you call on a phone?" he asked.

He had not yet mastered the art of a simple phone call, and if she had been thinking more clearly, she would have known that. He was struggling with learning to tell time. He could count to ten forward and backward, and that was huge, like scaling Mount Everest. It was a source of pride.

He was only four.

"Just bring me the phone," she said. "And go get me a clean rag or a towel or something. Please. Good boy."

The phone needed to plug into the wall, but it had a longish cord. And then the receiver was on a cord as well, but one that spiraled. It was twisted, and wouldn't stretch far enough. He had to unsnarl it. As he did so, he registered a distant feeling that he should hurry, and that the pressure of that time crunch should be causing fear. But he felt solid inside, as if stuffed with something from head to toe that did not react.

It was such a relief.

She got tired of waiting, maybe. Because she slid a few feet across the floor toward the phone, carefully brushing away the porcelain shards.

He handed her the receiver and ran to the linen closet for a towel. As he did, he heard her on the phone, talking to Donna. She called his father a bad name. She told Donna she needed her help. Right away.

The towels were too high for him to reach, so he brought her two washcloths.

She kissed his forehead when he delivered them, and she was crying.

———

"Where's Valerie?" Donna asked, her voice crisp.

She was pacing around the house, looking for his mother's purse. She reminded Aiden of the policemen on TV, looking through a house that might still contain a bad guy. She was a big woman, years older than his mom, with carefully styled, bleached-blonde hair and solid bones. She looked as though she could take care of herself, and not just because of her size, either. Some of that formidable presence lived on the inside.

"She's staying overnight at her friend Martha's," his mother said. She had a nonstick pad for wounds, and a roll of gauze, and some of that white tape you can use on skin. She was trying to stop the bleeding and cover the cuts on her palm. But the blood was already soaking through.

"Okay. Fine. We'll get her in the morning. Look. May." That was his mother's name. May. "The most important thing we can do right now is get out of here. I'll come back later for your things. I'll bring the police with me if I have to. I'll do whatever I need to do to keep you and the kids safe. But you have to make me a promise. You swore this was the first time he ever hit you. Is that really the truth?"

A tingle filled Aiden's gut. Well, not even filled it. It stayed fairly small. But it was there, lighting up the middle of all that otherwise-inert stuffing. He hadn't realized. He had somehow managed to believe it had all been a terrible accident.

"I swear it on a stack of Bibles, Donna. This never happened before. If it had, I wouldn't be here."

"Okay, good. That's what I want you to promise me. I'll help you. I'll do anything. But you have to promise me this is the *last* time, too. That you won't give him the chance to hurt you again."

"I promise," his mother said.

Aiden wasn't entirely sure he knew what it all meant. What it added up to. But he felt next to nothing. The inside of his head felt like the dead air of a television station when broadcasting ends for the night.

Empty static. White noise. A fancy form of nothing.

—

They rode in Donna's car, Aiden in the back seat. He stared out the window, his mind miles away. But where it was, he didn't know. There were no thoughts. Or at least none he could pin down.

Donna and his mom were talking. And they were close enough that Aiden heard everything. But he hadn't focused—or put any weight—on their words. Until his name came up.

Donna asked, "What brought it on all of a sudden? I mean, if he's never done this before?"

"He hit Aiden in the face earlier today. I wasn't there. There'd been some kind of scuffle between the kids, but I don't really know what happened. But I had to confront him about it. I had to tell him you don't do that to him. I mean, a swat on the butt, maybe. If it's really called for. But in the *face*! You saw his face. His nose is all bruised and swollen. It bled. I found the bloody toilet paper in the bathroom trash. He wiped it up all on his own. It was heartbreaking."

A return of that tingle in the center of Aiden's blankness. But it didn't grow, or stay. Shocked as he was by the suggestion that he had done something to break his mother's heart, he couldn't imagine or understand it. So the moment slid away.

And still his mother was talking.

"He worries about Aiden because he thinks he's too sensitive. My God, he's *four*. Just let him grow up, you know? Which is not to say I don't worry sometimes, too. I worry *for him*. Because it's a hard way to be. But then Eddie socks him in the face for being too rough with his sister. So make up your mind, right? You either want him to be a macho boy or you don't." A weighted pause. "I think it's the being laid off from work. He's proud about that sort of thing. Being the breadwinner and all. He's been on a short fuse."

"Uh-oh," Donna interjected. "That's the kind of thing women say right before they go back and give the guy another chance: 'He was just under extra pressure.'"

"I'm not doing that, Donna. I'm not stupid. He'll be under pressure again in his life. And now I've seen the full range of how he can be."

"Good," Donna said. "Good for you for using your head."

They drove in silence for a time. They weren't going to Donna's house. Aiden knew because he had been to Donna's house. Many times.

"I must admit I'm surprised," Donna said, startling the very air in the car, which had grown accustomed to the silence. "You were awfully quick to see. Didn't even need time to think about it."

"Nobody hits me twice," his mother said. Her voice was tinged with a strange conviction. A strength, maybe even a hardness, he had not heard in her before. "But, really," she added, more softly now, "it's not sudden at all. Things haven't been right with our marriage for years. Maybe more so than I've let on—I'm not sure. But every morning I wake up knowing it. And I have a choice. I can force a change that day, or I can get through the day and pass it off till tomorrow. Just keep kicking it down the road like an old can."

"I understand," Donna said.

Aiden didn't. He was too young. But in another way, he did. Not in the words, but in the way they were spoken. In the silences. In the air of that car. They were going away. And Aiden's father had somehow slipped into the past.

Donna's car pulled into a parking lot, and Aiden saw a sign on a building, but he was not a good enough reader to know what it said.

"Where are we?" he asked, somehow adjusted to his new world. Accepting of the fact that everything from here on out would be different. Unfamiliar.

"We're at the hospital," Donna said. "Your mom needs some stitches in that hand. And then you'll come to my house for the night. Okay?"

"Okay," Aiden said. "That's fine."

And it was. Or, at least, if it wasn't, Aiden had no way of knowing it wasn't. It was no longer something he could feel.

—

It wasn't until after the hand was stitched and they were on their way to Donna's that Aiden noticed he was hardly breathing. He had to take in some oxygen, of course, to keep himself alive. But it wasn't much.

# *Chapter Thirteen*

## *Aiden at Age Six*

His mother's face was strangely close to his own, and he could see her eyes and the shadow that had fallen across them as she worked. She was nervous. But Aiden had no idea what about.

She was on her knees in front of him, tying a Windsor knot in a blue necktie around Aiden's neck. Working with a strange precision. As if she would soon be harshly judged on the results. She snugged up the tie, and Aiden instinctively put a hand to his throat and used one finger to loosen the knot again.

"Ow," he said.

But it wasn't really an "ow" situation. It didn't hurt. It was just uncomfortable. And a little scary. It made him feel as though the tiny bits of air he was accustomed to inhaling might be further limited. He'd been barely breathing anyway these last couple of years.

She made a tsk sound with her tongue and gently snugged it again.

"Why do I have to wear a tie?" he asked, sounding a little whiny to his own ears. Almost like Valerie, and that was something worth avoiding.

"Because it's important."

"Why is it important?"

"It's a nice restaurant. Nicer than we've ever been to before."

"Does the restaurant check and make sure your tie is nice and tight?"

"No," she said lightly, looking at him as though he were being quite silly. "Of course not."

"Then why is it important?"

She had just begun to peel away from him. She had made it partway to her feet, and her body was turned half around, as if ready to tackle some other untidy kid-related disaster. But she stopped. Sank to her knees again. Looked deeply into his eyes. Or tried to, anyway. Aiden turned his own face away. The last thing he wanted was a two-way connection with anybody's eyes. The more he cared for the person, the less he wanted them seeing inside.

"Listen," she said. "It's not about the restaurant. It's about this man. Harris. He's my new . . . friend. He's the reason I've been leaving you with Grandma in the evenings and going out. I want you and Valerie to make a good impression. Oh, wait. That's not the best way to say it, is it now? That just ups the pressure on you. I just want you to give him a chance. Okay?"

But Aiden sensed that the first of her statements was more accurate. More honest. Because a necktie might make a good impression. But it could not be helpful when attempting to give someone a chance.

He tried to loosen the tie, just ever so slightly, without her noticing.

She noticed.

"Please," she said, snugging and straightening it again, but more gently. Leaving it tidy but a bit less severe. "I like this man. Please just go along with this, and we'll have a nice dinner. I just want him to like you and Valerie, and I want you to like him. It's important to me. He's a good man. The kind that doesn't come along every day. Do you understand?"

Aiden nodded.

He did not understand, of course. He was six. He did understand that his mother was uneasy, and that it was in his hands to please or disappoint her. He also understood that, even in the course of this brief conversation about neckties, he had skimmed dangerously near the disaster of letting her down in some indefinable way.

"I'll be good," he said.

She kissed him on the forehead and rose to her feet, hurrying away.

He wondered why he couldn't just wear the clip-on necktie he wore when they attended Grandma's church on Sundays, and at Grandpa's funeral. It was hard to imagine that a dinner with this stranger could be more important than burying your own grandfather.

He didn't ask. Because he had skated close enough to that line of hurting her. He could not bring himself to risk crossing it now.

—

"Is he coming here to pick you up?" Grandma asked.

She was a big, soft woman, given to wearing loose housedresses—half-covered with cardigan sweaters—for comfort. She had been slimmer and better dressed before Grandpa died last year, but some thread within her had been working its way loose since then.

"Of course he's picking us up," Aiden's mother said. She sounded insulted.

"Glad to hear it. That's a sign of good breeding, you know."

"Right. As if you didn't inject that under my skin like a tattoo while I was growing up. Look. Mom. You can't fault this guy on manners. Nobody can outdo him in that department."

"Then why didn't you bring him around sooner?"

"I'm bringing him around now, Mother. Can we get off this?"

They had been living here with Grandma for two years now. Here in California, where it never snowed. In a hot valley in the central part of the state, with no big cities. His mother had taken a secretarial job, hoping they could soon afford a place of their own. But everything was expensive, and besides, Grandpa had died. Grandma needed extra help.

"I'm still your mother, you know," Grandma said, apparently not ready to get off it.

"Like you'd ever let me forget."

"I just want you to think about the children."

"I *am* thinking about them, Mom. They need a father again. Especially Aiden. Poor Aiden. Living in a house with three women. And now, since Dad passed away . . . He needs somebody to teach him how to be a man."

"I guess I can't argue with you there," Grandma said. It seemed to trouble her, to be unable to find disagreement.

"Look. Mom. He's a little older than me, Harris, and I don't want any gibes about that. All right? Not in his presence, anyway. Wait till—"

Just then a knock on the door stopped everything. His grandma's sharply honed comments. His mother's nearly perpetual motion. Even Aiden's heart, though only for one beat. Whatever—whoever—waited on the other side of that door was life-changingly important. Even six-year-old Aiden could recognize that clearly enough.

His mother smoothed the front of her dress, which had been plenty smooth enough to begin with, and threw the door wide.

The man in the doorway beamed a wide, shy smile. He held flowers. Nothing formal like roses. A sunny, springlike mixture of blooms. His trousers had been pressed into neat creases in the front. He wore a sport jacket, and a blue necktie not unlike Aiden's. His gray hair was recently cut, from the look of it. Neat and short, carefully combed back along his head, and thinning at the temples. His eyes were a light but brilliant color of blue, shiny and twinkling, like the stars at night. Aiden wondered how you got a pair of eyes to do a thing like twinkling. At the outside corner of each eye, Aiden saw a network of lines radiating out along the man's skin.

"A *little* older?" Aiden heard his grandma mutter under her breath. He did not think it was projected loudly enough to reach the site of the open door.

Aiden looked over at Valerie, who sat on the couch in ankle socks and a yellow dress, looking bored. She rolled her eyes at Aiden.

"Aiden," his mother said, startling him. "Come and meet my friend."

Aiden walked to the door. Carefully, in case anything might be dangerous. He stood at the man's feet and looked up into his face. He was not a tall man, but he seemed solidly built. Then again, everyone is tall when you're six.

The man held his hand out for Aiden to shake.

"Aiden, this is Harris Delacorte. Harris, my son, Aiden."

Aiden took the hand and shook it. It was calloused and strong. It held his own small hand firmly, as if to make the point that this was a man who could be trusted to commit to a thing like a handshake. But it did not hurt.

"Well, you seem like a fine young man," Harris Delacorte said, his blue eyes doing that nighttime star thing again.

"I'm not a young man," Aiden said, because it sounded like a strange description of him. He was a kid. A boy.

"Of course you're a young man," his mother said, hurrying close. Aiden caught a quiet warning in her tone, and a desperation. "That's what you call a boy in a more formal sense. But the more important thing, Aiden, is that Harris just paid you a compliment. He said you seem fine."

"Yes, sir," Aiden said. Because he figured he did seem that way. Then he caught his mother's eye and added, "Thank you, sir."

He pulled a deep breath, one he feared everyone could hear, and vowed to do better. To be a better boy tonight, on better behavior. For the sake of his mom.

—

The restaurant was indeed fancy. Too much so, Aiden thought. His mother had been giving Valerie and him lessons—on and off for the better part of a week. How to place your napkin across your lap. Which fork was for your salad, which for your dessert. Aiden stared at the mass of silver and glassware and remembered none of it. His brain had receded somehow. Gone on vacation elsewhere.

He stared at his menu but didn't know what to order. None of the words he saw listed looked like food. He was only just learning to read, but he was surprisingly good at it. If he had seen "hot dogs" or "macaroni," he would have recognized them. There was nothing here to recognize.

"They have trout here, Aiden," his mother said. "You like trout."

"I do?"

"Yes, don't you remember? That time we all went camping? And you went fishing in the lake at dawn with your dad, and then we had grilled trout for breakfast? You said it was the best thing you'd ever eaten."

"Oh. I don't remember."

It was true in one respect and untrue in another. He did not remember eating trout and liking it. But he remembered going fishing with his dad. Suddenly, just when she said it. He remembered how he'd caught only one and insisted on putting it back into the water. How his father had caught several, and Aiden had silently apologized to each and every one of the poor, doomed fish.

It all seemed strange and long ago now, and he couldn't remember what there had been to get so upset about. Nor did he try.

He set down his menu, figuring he would order trout. You can't do much better than the best thing ever. And the fate of the fish no longer troubled him, he decided. That had been a different time, back when he was silly and little.

"Harris owns a cattle ranch," his mother said, seeming to need to fill the air with words.

"I do," Harris said. His voice was deep, like a man who wields power, yet at the same time kind. But maybe the kindness was plastered on when talking to kids. Especially the kids of the pretty new woman you had been seeing. Aiden vaguely, wordlessly wondered over its sincerity. "And it has a forest of evergreen and scrub oak on one end of the land, eighty acres of it, with a year-round stream running through. We have cutthroat trout and steelhead. If you ever wanted to go fishing."

"Where is it?" Aiden asked, not knowing what else to ask about a cattle ranch.

"Only about twenty miles from here. You like horses?"

"Aiden loves horses," his mother said, barely allowing him the chance to speak.

"Well," Aiden said. He felt hesitant to correct her, but some things needed saying. "I like my model horses. I never knew a real horse. I met one *once*. Just over a fence is all. Never really rode one or anything."

"You come to my place, you could ride horseback all day long if you wanted. On the weekends, anyway," he added, seeming to remember about school.

Aiden wasn't sure how to respond to that. It sounded scary and almost painfully fun in equal measure.

He looked up and around. Let the sounds into his head—the chattering of the other diners, the clink of forks and glasses. He glanced over at Valerie, who was still staring at her menu, and caught her gaze. She rolled her eyes again.

"He might be a bit young for that," Aiden's mother said. "He's only six."

"I have horses I'd trust with a six-year-old," Harris Delacorte said. "I have one horse, I could put a toddler on her back and she'd go slow and take pains to be extra careful with him. I'd bet my life on it."

Aiden turned his attention back to the man.

A sentence he had heard earlier that evening streamed back into his head again. As if Aiden were hearing it for the first time.

*He needs somebody to teach him how to be a man.*

That was an interesting thought. If not through this sudden new Harris Delacorte, a near stranger, how would Aiden know what it was to be a man? His mother couldn't teach him what she didn't know. Grandma and Bally would be no help to him at all.

He looked into the grown man's face, his gaze steadily returned. Just for a moment, Aiden thought he felt something open inside himself. Like a door that had been closed, locked, bolted, and barricaded with a chair. Guarded that way for a long time. Too long. He looked into those twinkling blue eyes and felt as though that might be about to change now.

And then it happened.

Aiden reached for his glass of water. But he should have been looking. He should have taken his eyes off the man's twinkly blue ones and watched his own hand wrap around the glass. Instead, he knocked it with the ends of his fingers and tipped it over, spilling water everywhere. On the cloth napkins. On the leather-covered menus. On his mother's tiny, fancy, beaded clutch purse.

His mother leapt to her feet and began wiping up the mess.

Aiden's door closed again. Silently, inside himself, he locked it. And set the bolt in place. And wedged a chair against it.

Harris Delacorte would not want him now. He would not teach him how to be a man, because Aiden was clearly unteachable. Harris Delacorte did things the careful, right way. Aiden had seen that in his eyes. Harris Delacorte was not clumsy, or prone to foolish mistakes.

Aiden felt his face redden with shame.

He said nothing for the rest of the meal. Not even when spoken to directly. When asked a question, he only nodded, or shook his head, or shrugged. He did not look into those blue man eyes again, because they would surely act as too much of a mirror. He did not want to see the reflection of the fool he had made of himself. He did not want to think about the chance he had squandered.

Men like Harris Delacorte didn't come along every day. Hadn't his mother said that, or something like it?

And in one careless move, it can all be undone.

—

After dinner they went to see a movie. It was rated G and supposed to be for the whole family, but it was boring. Aiden fell asleep halfway through.

Harris Delacorte toted him to the car, Aiden drooped over his shoulder in a fireman's carry. Aiden woke up on the walk back to the parking lot. But he didn't let on. He just hung there, limply. Partly because he was still very sleepy. Partly because he wanted the terrible night to be over.

He kept his eyes closed as the stocky man snugged him into his seat belt, next to his sister, in the back seat of his big American car. A Chrysler, Aiden thought he remembered.

They drove through darkened streets. Aiden flickered his eyes open in between streetlights. He saw that his mother had moved over closer to Harris Delacorte on the bench seat of the Chrysler. She was in the middle of the seat, right next to the driver, who had his arm around her shoulders.

"I worry about Aiden," he heard her say.

"How so?"

It hurt to hear them speaking about him. As if he were laid out on a table for no other purpose but their inspection. To invite their judgment. There were no words in his head to accompany this observation. But the muted buzz of feeling was undeniable. And denying what was there to be felt had become something of a specialty of Aiden's.

"He's just so shut down. If you had known him before we left his father . . . he seems like a different boy. He used to be so sensitive. He cared about everything. Maybe too much, I used to think. For his own sake, I mean. Now I don't even know where he is. It's like he drew all the curtains and I can't see in. I know he must be in there somewhere, but I feel like I haven't even seen him for two years."

A silence. As though her words required chewing before digestion.

"He'll come around, I expect," Harris Delacorte said simply.

"It's been two years, Harris. A third of his life. Sometimes I feel like this is the way he'll always be now. This little missing person."

Aiden focused on the buzz in his belly. It tried to grow, but he shut it down again instead. It really wasn't hard once you got the hang of it. Just breathe even less, if such a thing is possible, and let everything slip behind the wall. Where it can't find you, so it can't hurt you.

"It's been a tough time for him is all, May. Bring him out to the ranch. We'll do some fishing and horseback riding. Someone just needs to take an interest in him. He'll come out of his shell."

She didn't answer. Didn't offer any odds as to how right or wrong she thought Harris Delacorte might prove to be. She only laid her head down on the man's solid shoulder.

Aiden knew he would not come out of his shell. Because he could not be himself in the presence of Harris Delacorte. Because he had humiliated himself in front of the man. And that was a strike Aiden knew would be held against him, whether the man admitted so or not. Harris Delacorte did not knock over glasses or spill water over all those nice things. Harris Delacorte didn't make stupid mistakes. Harris Delacorte would never truly accept him because Aiden was not worth the acceptance. He did not deserve such consideration.

And, because he knew he never would be truly accepted, Aiden decided the relationship was not worth seeking. That the older man would not earn Aiden's trust.

In his six-year-old brain, though, it existed as a simpler thing: Aiden didn't like Harris Delacorte.

He would go along with dinners and movies and rides on horses because it was not in him to hurt his mother's feelings, or let down her hopes. But he would stay inside himself where it was safe. In the cautious blank space Aiden had constructed for himself. Where he belonged.

—

His sister came into his room at about seven o'clock the following morning. Which was weird all in itself, because she never sought him out. In fact, rarely did she deign to notice him at all.

He was still in bed, due to the lateness of the previous night. He didn't want her to see him in his pajamas because they had cartoon characters on them, and he thought she would make fun of him for that. So he just sat halfway up, the blanket pulled up to his throat, and stared daggers at her.

She chose not to notice.

"So what do you think of this new guy?" she asked him, fingering the model horses on his dresser as a way of keeping her eyes well away from his.

"What are you doing in my room, Bally?"

"I'm asking you a question."

"But you never come in my room."

"Well, today I did. I don't like him."

"Why don't you?"

"Well . . . he's not our father. Is he?"

"No," Aiden said. "He's not."

But he couldn't help wondering if not being their father was an unexpected point in the man's favor.

The sun had mostly risen outside Aiden's bedroom window, and it glinted off the glass of the hummingbird feeder that hung there. Shone into Aiden's eyes. He squinted as best he could, and tried to ignore it, but it made him feel vulnerable. Everything did.

"Would you please get out of my room, Bally?"

"So you like him?"

"No," Aiden said. "I don't."

"Well, we better think of something to do, and fast. Because they're probably going to get married. And then we'll be told that he's our dad and we have to call him that, and listen to him when he tells us what to do."

"They won't get married. That's stupid."

"No, *you're* stupid, Aiden. It's true. I heard her talking to Grandma about it."

So there it was. Another whole segment of his life, spinning away. Another father who found him defective and unworthy of love, slipped into place. And there was nothing he could do about it. There was never anything he could do about it. Except put it away.

Valerie was standing in front of him now with her knees pressed against the bed, staring at his face at close range.

"You don't even care," she said. "Do you?"

"Not really."

"You don't care about anything."

"No."

"You've been so weird. Ever since we left Dad. I can't even figure you out anymore. It's like you're not even my brother."

"You didn't like me the old way anyway."

"Well, I don't like you the new way, either," she said, and flounced out.

It was the most attention he'd received from his sister in as long as he could remember. That seemed sad. Or at least it would have, if sadness had been something Aiden could feel.

# Chapter Fourteen

## Aiden at Age Six and a Half

Aiden was just preparing to mount that good quarter horse mare, Bonnie. Might have been the twentieth time he'd ridden her, or it might have been the twenty-fifth. It was summer, with no school, and Aiden and his sister were being pushed onto Harris Delacorte's cattle ranch more and more often. Close to every day now, while their mother worked.

Aiden didn't mind it, because he liked to ride Bonnie. He would have preferred to go out alone, but it seemed he wasn't allowed. Nobody had said straight out that he wasn't allowed. But Alfie, the seventeen-year-old son of a ranch hand, always seemed to want to go riding at the exact same moment.

Once, Aiden had bravely suggested to Harris Delacorte that he might go out alone, but was told not to hurt Alfie's feelings.

Aiden swung into the saddle using two wooden crates as a mounting block. He looked back at Alfie and saw Harris Delacorte taking the reins of Wiley, the horse Alfie always rode. Taking them away as if he planned to ride the horse instead.

"I thought I'd go out with Aiden today," he heard the older man say.

Aiden felt his face flush, hot and red. He figured he was in some kind of trouble he knew nothing about.

He pressed his heels into Bonnie's sides. The heels of the now-scuffed cowboy boots Harris Delacorte had given him for a present. The mare surged forward. Aiden pressed again, urging the mare into a trot. Thinking he could leave this new father-person behind. But a moment later he heard the loping hoofbeats closing the distance between them.

"Slow down, Turbo," the older man said.

Aiden sighed and reined Bonnie back into a walk.

"Why?" he asked as Harris Delacorte rode up beside him.

"Why what?"

"Why you and not Alfie?"

"I thought we could have a talk."

Aiden's body set about tingling. His face and his gut exploded with it. He didn't want to talk about whatever the older man had in mind. So he filled the air with safer words.

"But you said Alfie loves to go out riding and that he likes having somebody to go with, and you said it would hurt his feelings if we don't let him come along."

They rode in silence for a few seconds. Aiden wondered if he should say more. Keep up more of a steady word wall against whatever was headed his way. But his mind felt blank. Strangely blank, like a freshly painted white wall.

"You're six years old, Aiden."

"Six and a half."

"Right. Six and a half."

"Almost seven."

"Fine, whatever you say. My point is, your mom doesn't want you riding alone."

So there it was. Aiden had known it. In some deep part of himself, he had. It still hurt to have it forced to the surface.

They rode in silence, headed up the hill toward the evergreen and scrub oak forest that formed the west half of Harris Delacorte's ranch. Aiden wanted to turn back to the house, but he knew it wouldn't help. The man would only follow.

"So . . . ," Harris Delacorte began. Hesitantly. With enough trepidation that Aiden caught the fear. Nothing seemed to frighten or trouble this man. So if Harris Delacorte was afraid of it, it must be a hell of a thing. "I guess you know that your mom and I have been seeing each other for a while now."

If Aiden hadn't been on a horse, he might have pressed both hands to his ears. But he didn't want to drop the reins. So he tried to shut off his ears from the inside. The same way he shut off everything else.

"And we care a lot about each other. I love your mother. And I think I'm safe in believing she loves me in return."

"Why are you telling me this?" Aiden's irritation burst up and out like a volcanic eruption. "I don't want to hear this."

"But you need to hear it, actually."

Harris Delacorte reined his horse to a halt, then turned the gelding with near-invisible leg pressure to face Aiden. Aiden's horse had stopped, even though he hadn't asked her to. Bonnie seemed to obey her real owner more faithfully than she did the kid in the saddle.

"I'm trying to tell you something important, Aiden."

"Well, I don't want to know it."

"You need to know it anyway. Because it's going to happen, and you'll know it then. I would think you'd rather have some fair idea of what's coming."

Aiden squeezed his eyes shut and said nothing. He tried to disappear. It only worked about halfway.

"Last night I asked your mom to marry me."

Silence.

"She said yes."

More silence.

"But I'm telling you, Aiden, there's nothing in the world more important to me than making that woman happy. And it's not lost on me that you're not my biggest fan. You're not the first boy who ever felt that way about a new dad. I think that's how just about any boy would feel. But May—your mother—is only going to be happy if she thinks you're happy. If we're getting along, you and me. So I'm hoping you'll give us your blessing."

For what might have been almost a minute, the world consisted of nothing but the hard feel of the saddle under his bones and the hollow sound of wind blowing across his ears.

Then Aiden surprised himself by speaking.

"I don't know what that is."

"Which part of the thing?"

"The blessing."

Actually, Aiden had heard the word many times in church, but he could not imagine it meant the same in this context. If it did, how could it be within Aiden's power to give it? He wasn't God, nor a pastor.

"It means . . . how do I say it? It means you tell us you're good with it. Like giving your permission. Not that we actually need permission from anybody, but you're so important that we'd feel better having it all the same."

Aiden took a few seconds to try to make sense of the moment. But that's the problem with shutting everything down. You can more or less understand a thing in your head, but you don't have your feelings about it to guide you. So it all ends up looking blank and muddy, like something you could stare at all day without it ever coming clear.

"I want to go back now," he said.

"But we only just started our ride."

"I don't want to ride anymore."

In the silence that followed, Aiden stole a glance at the older man's face. He looked crestfallen. Like a soldier in a war movie after a losing battle—a defeat that Aiden could read in the older man's eyes.

Aiden did something in that moment that did not seem to spring from a thought. He watched himself do it with surprise, as if viewing the behavior of a stranger. He drummed his heels into Bonnie's sides and flicked her flank hard with the ends of the reins. The mare took off at a gallop. They headed for the woods.

He glanced over his shoulder to see Harris Delacorte closing in fast. Aiden leaned over the saddle horn, over the mare's neck, flicking her again and again with the rein ends, elbows flapping. He waited for hoofbeats to overtake him from behind but they never did.

In time he glanced again over his shoulder.

Harris Delacorte had dismounted, and was leading his horse back toward the barn.

*So he doesn't really care about me being out here alone,* Aiden thought.

He galloped on.

———

It might have been a half hour of trotting later when he finally found his way to a road. But what road, and leading to where? He reined the mare to a halt, feeling her sides heaving, and looked up and down the dirt byway. He saw a mailbox at the end of a graded driveway, at the break in a white board fence. In the other direction, nothing at all.

Aiden urged the horse into a trot in the direction of the mailbox. It wasn't Harris Delacorte's mailbox, but it was somebody's. It was the first sign of life Aiden had seen since galloping away. And he was well and truly lost. He had known it for some time.

He rode Bonnie up to the mailbox, but saw no signs of life. No house could be seen from his vantage point on the road. Not even when he stood up in the stirrups. The gate was closed.

Did he dare open it?

"Your horse looks hot."

The voice made him jump. So much so that he almost lost his balance in the saddle. He turned to see a man trimming one of the many trees that lined the property inside the fence. He was a younger man than Harris Delacorte, but not young by Aiden's standards. He had a long face, like a horse, and smiling eyes.

"Yes, sir," Aiden said, though he had no idea how a horse shows heat, and how you can see it just by looking.

"You want to water that horse?"

"Yes, sir," Aiden replied. Because he had made a connection with someone who might help him get found again, and he didn't want to break it.

"What about you? Glass of lemonade?"

"That would be nice, sir. Thank you."

Aiden swung down off his horse and dropped into the dirt. He took the reins over her head the way he'd watched the ranch hands do it, and she lowered her head to allow it. He led her to the gate. As he did, he noticed her neck was foamed with sweat where the reins had brushed it. And her chest was wet with it. That must be how horses show heat. Her nostrils were flared wide. Aiden could hear the exaggerated sound of her breath blowing through them, flaring them even further.

The man opened the gate for him.

Aiden led the mare, who followed a step behind him, onto the man's property.

"Where do I put the horse?"

"Nowhere till you cool her down proper."

"How do I do that?"

"You have to hot-walk her."

"I don't know what that is."

"You just walk her around till she cools down and stops blowing. You don't give a horse a drink of water when she's this hot. You have to cool her down first. Especially if she's an old girl like Bonnie."

"Oh," Aiden said. "I didn't know that. How do you know her name? And how old she is?"

"I know all Harris's horses. I've ridden many a roundup next to Bonnie. She's a good mare and she deserves proper care. You just walk her around in a big circle. Right here in front of the barn. I'll go inside and ask Nadine to make up a glass of lemonade. But first you get the horse cool and watered. That's the most important rule of horsemanship. First you make sure your horse is okay. Then you take care of your own needs."

"Why does the horse come first?"

"Because the horse has no choice in the matter. The horse is trained to do what you ask, up to and including running too fast and for too long. So we have a responsibility not to take advantage."

"Yes, sir," Aiden said.

Aiden had not realized, until that moment, that there was any such thing as too much running for a horse. They were horses. Aiden had thought they could do anything, all day long.

The man disappeared inside the house, and Aiden walked around in a circle, as he had been instructed, Bonnie following faithfully behind like an old dog.

When Aiden got tired, and the sun got too hot, and he thought he couldn't go another step, he stopped just long enough to draw a few extra breaths. Bonnie caught up with him, and dropped her head down over his shoulder, as if inviting his affection. Aiden wrapped his arms around the huge, bony head and held it. He almost kissed her, but decided that was not a boy thing to do.

Then he walked again, even though it was hard. But he learned something in that moment, something he would never forget: the difference between a horse and a person. A good old horse won't hold your mistakes against you. The horse will let you have another chance.

—

The man's wife gave him cookies. They were from the store, but still tasty. And she put the sugar bowl next to his lemonade glass, which he appreciated. Because he wanted it much sweeter than she had made it.

"You must be May's boy," she said.

The man had mentioned his wife's name, but Aiden could no longer remember it. And he wouldn't have called her by it anyway. That would have been rude.

"You know my mom?"

"Not really. I've heard about her."

She placed one hand on his head and ruffled his hair, which Aiden thought was strange. He went stock-still and cold inside, and she quickly took the hand back. Aiden wasn't big on people who touched. Or stood too close.

She smiled in a crooked way and bustled out of the kitchen.

A few minutes later he heard a voice that made his heart skip one beat. A familiar voice.

"Thanks for calling me, Roger," it said.

"I knew that couldn't be right. Little slip of a thing out by himself like that? Why, he's not much bigger than a grasshopper."

"I don't know what I'm supposed to do with that boy."

The comment made Aiden's ears tingle and burn. Not that he hadn't known that Harris Delacorte didn't like him. Of course he'd known. But there's knowing and then there's knowing. And, as it turned out, one of the varieties hurt more than the other.

"He seems like a nice enough little guy, Harris. Stepkids are always hard at first. Give him some time."

Aiden found himself leaning in his seat. Sideways, toward the kitchen door. Hoping to hear more, and also hoping not to. If his new stepfather had a comment on Roger's advice, Aiden never heard it.

Seconds later Harris Delacorte was standing in the kitchen doorway. Suddenly, just like that. Aiden straightened up quickly and tried to pretend he had not been listening. Meanwhile he felt his insides solidify, like concrete setting up and curing.

Harris Delacorte sighed. Then he sat down across the table, picked up a cookie from the plate, and tried to catch Aiden's eye. Aiden made sure that didn't happen.

"You can't even look at me?" the older man asked after a time.

Aiden stared down at his plate and didn't answer.

"You know how old that mare is?"

"What's a mare?"

"A female horse."

"Oh."

"You know how old she is?"

Aiden said and did nothing. But he could feel the weight of the older man's stare, even though he wasn't looking. So he shook his head. Not much. As little as he could get away with and still have it be noticed.

"She's twenty-seven."

"That's not old. That man whose house this is said she was old."

"Because she is."

"Twenty-seven's not old."

"It is if you're a horse. Horses only live to be about thirty. Sometimes not even that."

"Oh," Aiden said. "Why?"

"Why what?"

"Why do they only live to be thirty?"

"I don't know. How can I know that? I'm not God. That's just how long they live. It's just the way things are. I'm trying to make a point here, boy. You could have killed her running her that hard. That's my point. Her heart might have given out. Plus I'd just told you how your mom thinks you're too young to go out riding alone. And she's right, by the way. Plus, when I tried to catch up to you, Wiley stuck his foot in a squirrel hole and now he's lame. Thank God we pulled up before he broke his leg. But he's favoring it, and I don't know how bad it is until the vet comes out, which won't be till tomorrow. And all that trouble because you couldn't just hold still and listen to what I had to say."

A long, stinging silence.

That would be it for this new life of theirs, and maybe that would be for the best. Harris Delacorte would abandon his mom because Aiden came along in the bargain, and that was no longer an acceptable price to pay. It would hurt her, and he was sorry for that. But in time maybe she would see that they had been okay on their own. That all they really needed was each other.

"Do you care?" The man's voice was booming and sharp, and it made Aiden jump.

"About what?" he asked. The two words sounded tentative. But inside he felt nothing, as far as he could tell.

"I thought you liked that horse you've been riding. Bonnie."

"I do."

"Do you care that you could have hurt her?"

"She's okay. I walked her until she wasn't sweaty. She's outside drinking water and resting."

"You got lucky. Do you care about Wiley? Who's lame now?"

Aiden never answered. Just stared down at his plate and wondered why people seemed to think that was an easy question. It wasn't. Why were people always asking him what he did or did not care about? Aiden had no idea what people expected of him when they asked it. How was he even supposed to know? His sister had done it, too, but in that case it had been less of a question and more of an accusation.

In time Harris Delacorte seemed to tire of waiting for answers that never came.

"Come on," he said. "We're going home."

But Aiden wasn't sure what he meant by it. Which home he had in mind. He guessed the man was referring to his cattle ranch, a place that did not feel like Aiden's home in any way.

He didn't ask.

He followed Harris Delacorte to the front door.

As he scuffed across the living room rug, barely lifting his feet, the husband and wife who had briefly hosted him stood watching. When he looked up at them they both smiled in a way that looked sad. Especially the woman.

"Thank you for the cookies and the lemonade," he said. "They were good. After I put in more sugar. In the lemonade, that is. The cookies had enough. And thanks for showing me about walking Bonnie around. I didn't know."

Both neighbors turned their eyes to Harris Delacorte. They said nothing, but their eyes seemed to plead with the man to give Aiden another chance. "See?" those looks said. "He's a nice enough little guy. He's trying, anyway."

They stepped out into the midday heat together, Aiden and his regrettable new dad.

Harris Delacorte's truck sat parked in the loop of dirt driveway, a two-horse trailer hitched to the back.

"Wait for me in the truck," he said simply.

Aiden silently did as he'd been told.

The windows were rolled down on both sides. All the way down. But still it was hot. The sun baked him through the windshield, but he sat. Because he didn't deserve better. He had not earned the right to complain.

He watched in the side-view mirror, through shimmering waves of heat, as Harris Delacorte loaded Bonnie into the trailer.

Then they drove home in silence. Crushing, stomach-churning silence.

—

The following morning, while his sister slept in, Aiden tried to come down the stairs for breakfast. It didn't quite work out.

That man was already here. Harris Delacorte. He was already in the kitchen with Aiden's mother. Which would not necessarily have been enough to stop Aiden from going in, especially since he was hungry. But their words stopped him. Their words were more than enough.

"I just don't know how to get through to that boy," Harris Delacorte said. "I can't figure out how to find any caring in him. I'm not saying there's no decent boy in there, May. Don't get me wrong. I take you at your word on that. But I can't seem to reach in there and get to him. He won't let me."

Aiden sat down hard on the stairs. The carpet runner that covered the middle of each step was scratchy against the backs of his bare legs— the part his shorts didn't cover.

"But you're the one who tried to assure me he'd come around," he heard his mother say.

"And I'm not saying now that he won't. I'm saying I can't test out the matter on my horses. I don't think I can let him ride my horses, May. They're not machines. They have feelings. They can get hurt. They did get hurt, or one of them did, at least. Not the mare he was riding, but Wiley. The one I tried to go after him on. The vet's been out already this morning, and he's got a pulled tendon. He'll be on hand-walking for months. Can't be ridden. I just can't trust that boy with my horses."

"Maybe he could ride but only with supervision."

"He was riding with supervision yesterday, May. He always is. He galloped away. There was nothing I could do to stop him."

While he waited for his mother to answer, Aiden wondered what on earth he was supposed to do at Harris Delacorte's ranch if he couldn't ride. Stare at the wall? Watch other people ride? And they'd be moving there soon. When his mother got married.

Then he thought about Wiley. Pictured the poor guy only able to be walked on a lead rope by hand. Aiden tried to feel something about it, but he couldn't. It just didn't feel real.

"But if you don't trust him," Aiden's mother said, "then how can he ever earn your trust? I mean . . . I understand how you feel, Harris. I'm not saying you're wrong. But if you keep sending him the message that he's not trustworthy, he'll believe it. And the more he believes it, the more it'll be true."

"I don't know, May. I don't know what the answer is. I only know it can't involve putting my horses in harm's way."

Aiden strained to hear what she would say. Leaned over until his head was pressed against the bannister. He heard his mother say there would be time to think about all this, and to work it out, because they'd be going to Buffalo to visit Uncle Edgar for a week of the summer break. Then their voices grew quieter and more muffled, as if they had moved closer together, or were whispering to avoid being overheard.

Aiden crept down the stairs and stole a glance into the kitchen. The man who wouldn't give him a chance was holding his mother in a tender embrace. Speaking words intended for—and delivered to—only her. Words that would never make it to Aiden's ears.

Shoulders slumped, Aiden moved back to the stairs and collapsed on the bottom step. Braced his elbows on his knees and set his chin in his hands.

A moment later he looked up to see Harris Delacorte walking out of the kitchen. Just as the older man passed the stairs—as it struck him that Aiden was there, was listening—their eyes met.

Aiden expected to see all manner of judgment against his own character. Expected to be looked down upon, in more than just the literal sense. He braced himself to feel like nothing in the older man's eyes. A speck of dust maybe.

Instead he saw something he had not in any way expected.

At the time he had no words for it. Later, looking back, he would realize he had seen Harris Delacorte's shame. His inability to cope with a stumbling block in his life. His grudging acknowledgment of his own shortcomings.

That was how their new relationship became a two-way street. That was the moment when both their failings lay on full display, and it was up to each of them to decide what they would do with the vulnerability of the other.

# Chapter Fifteen

## Aiden at Age Seven

"Wake up," someone said.

But Aiden couldn't seem to manage to do as the dreamlike voice suggested.

He felt a big, rough hand shaking his shoulder. But still the sleep, the dream—whatever it was—pulled him back under like quicksand.

Then he was sitting up, but not of his own accord. His stepfather was holding him in a sitting position. Aiden's eyes were open, but that didn't mean he was awake. But it did seem to be his stepfather in front of him. He saw that as his brain cleared.

"What?" Aiden said. "I'm asleep."

"You need to get up. You need to come with me."

"I want to go back to sleep."

"It's important. Do this for me. Please."

Aiden sat a moment, shaking sleep out of his brain. The more he came around, the more afraid he became. There was a gravity in the older man's tone, in his movements. And they had not been getting along for . . . well . . . ever. So Aiden had a bad feeling about what came next.

But he breathed hardly at all, and slipped the fear down behind the partition that kept him safe from everything.

"Put your jacket on," Harris Delacorte said.

It was winter—as much as it was ever winter here in California—between Christmas and New Year's Day. It never snowed, but it was cold enough at night.

Aiden threw back the covers, and found that it was nippy even in his room. He hopped a little on the cold wooden floorboards. He put on his warm slippers, or tried to.

But his stepdad said, "No. Real boots."

So he pulled on jeans right over his pajamas, and the sweater that made him feel most safe. And his cowboy boots and down jacket.

"Where are we going?" he asked at last, heart pounding.

"There's something I want you to see."

Aiden's brain filled with a sudden image of one of his grandmother's neighbors and her dog. She house-trained the dog—or tried to, anyway—by dragging it over to the spot of an accident and then thrashing it.

Aiden assumed he was about to be thrashed. For what exactly, he didn't know. He ran through the previous day in his mind, through any previous day he could reach out to grasp and remember. He could not recall doing anything bad.

But maybe it wasn't any one thing. Maybe it was the sum of Aiden. Maybe he was about to be punished for all he was, all he had been, since dropping into this man's life to spoil everything.

They stepped out into the front yard of Harris Delacorte's sprawling cattle ranch. The biting air stung Aiden's face and ears and hands. And because he was still so sleepy, he felt too vulnerable to bear that discomfort.

"I'm cold," he said, hearing more panic in his voice than he realized he was feeling. "I want to go back to bed."

"How can you be cold? You have that big down jacket on."

"Only on part of me."

"Come in the barn. It'll be better in the barn. I have a heater on."

Aiden followed a step or two behind.

He could see from their path that the barn was almost dark. Just a soft glow from within, maybe created by something like a flashlight or a lantern. He didn't turn around and look at the house behind him, but he could feel it back there. It felt like safe harbor.

Maybe Harris Delacorte was taking him into the barn so he could do something Aiden's mother would never see. Maybe he was about to get the beating of his life.

He stopped dead in his tracks in the cold night, hearing nothing but a light wind blowing by his ears and his own blood beating inside them.

Maybe his stepfather was going to kill him.

It would be so easy. His mother would never have to know. Harris Delacorte could simply say Aiden had disappeared from his bed that night. Run away, maybe. It was a mystery that would never be solved.

His stepfather's life would be so much better without him. All of the older man's problems would be solved. Because Aiden comprised all of the older man's problems, so far as he knew.

For one long, strange, silent moment there in the dark, Aiden didn't blame the man for what was about to occur.

Then the older man's hand took hold of the shoulder of his down jacket and pulled him along.

"We need to get a move on," Harris Delacorte said. "She might need my help."

Aiden had no idea who "she" was. But the sense of dread lifted slightly, replaced by curiosity. He allowed himself to be towed into the barn.

They stepped together into the largest stall, the one his stepdad called the foaling stall. A sorrel horse was down on its side, clearly distressed. Harris Delacorte moved a big battery-powered lantern closer, and closed them into the stall with the horse.

Aiden could see the animal lift its head and crane its neck around to bump at its own swelled side. As if trying to point to the cause of all that discomfort.

"What's wrong with him?" Aiden asked, his fear left behind in the dirt. He did not even recall that there had been fear, or that he had recently shed it.

"She's not a him. She's a her. A mare. And she's about to foal."

"I don't know what that means."

"She's going to have a baby."

"Right now?" Aiden asked, his eyes widening.

"Pretty darn soon, yes."

Harris Delacorte lifted the lantern and set it down near the animal's tail.

"Look at this," he said to Aiden.

Aiden leaned in close and was startled by what he saw.

Something was protruding from an area under the mare's tail. But it didn't look like a baby. It didn't look like a living thing of any sort. It looked like she was giving birth to a ghost. Whatever was being expelled from her seemed to be sealed into some kind of bag, a whitish covering that kept Aiden from identifying anything that might look like a baby horse. He had no idea what part of a foal he might be viewing. He wasn't even sure that his stepfather was correct to pronounce that it was a foal.

"This is how life begins," Harris Delacorte said. "I wanted you to see it."

Aiden said nothing in reply. He was too busy watching the mare. Watching her strain. She seemed to be trying to push. She was sweating in the cold night. Aiden knew now what it meant when a horse sweated. The little propane heater out in the barn aisle, blowing the tiniest bit of warmth under the stall door, could not have been the reason. It barely took the edge off the cold. The mare's sweat could only have been a result of exertion.

Just for a moment, Aiden felt her pain. It felt natural and familiar and scary and unfamiliar at the same time. It overwhelmed him, so he slowed his breathing almost to a stop and tried to put it away again. It only worked about halfway. Now and then the mare's discomfort peered out around the partition and startled him.

Aiden backed up into a corner of the stall.

"Don't you want to see close-up?" his stepfather asked.

Aiden shook his head in silence.

The mare committed herself to a huge burst of energy, and struggled. Aiden could see her sides heave. The bagged ghost grew longer. Aiden thought he could see two separate sections of whatever was inside the bag, but he couldn't identify what they were, either one of them.

"That's the head," his stepfather said.

"I don't see a head."

"You will."

For what could have been ten minutes, or could have been an hour, Aiden leaned into a corner of the stall, his back up against the cold boards. His stepfather stayed close to the mare, but did not interfere.

And then suddenly the older man changed his tack.

"Okay, girl," Harris Delacorte said. "I thought you could do this on your own, but I get the message."

Aiden leaned in, transfixed.

He watched his stepfather take a firm grasp of something solid inside the ghostly bag. The mare seemed to understand. Aiden could feel her gear herself up for one gigantic push.

With a deep groan that Aiden could feel all the way from his throat down to his groin, like a tingling pain, the mare pushed, and Harris Delacorte pulled.

Everything came out in a rush. Things Aiden had never seen before and never cared to see again. The solid, ghostly bundle. Blood, and other fluids he did not understand. Torn and stretched long threads of the whitish covering. It all flowed out, just like that.

The mare pulled to her feet and stepped away.

Harris Delacorte moved in at once and used both hands to tear at the white covering. Where he ripped it and pulled it away, Aiden saw something amazing. Something he would never forget. An equine head. Its eyes were open, its ears perfectly shaped. Aiden could even see its markings. Patchy blond and white markings.

It was alive. It was perfect. It was real. And a split second ago, it hadn't existed in the world, not in any way Aiden could grasp. And now here it was. This new living thing.

"It's a little paint," Harris Delacorte said.

As he spoke, he ran his thumbs down both sides of the baby's long face. Down to the nostrils and a little bit beyond. As if the foal had a stuffy nose and Harris Delacorte was helping to clear its passages.

Then his stepfather tore away more of the covering.

Aiden could see the baby's front legs. They were bizarrely long. Impossibly long. The hooves looked soft and barely formed. The baby had its front legs together and braced against the straw of the stall floor, knees up toward the sky, as if ready to attempt to stand.

Aiden moved closer and looked into the foal's eyes, and the foal looked back. And saw him. And was not afraid as far as Aiden could tell. They just looked at each other. And Aiden was shocked, because the foal was so fully formed and so aware. Nothing like the baby puppies he had once seen, limbs thrashing, eyes squeezed closed, searching to nurse at their mother by feel. This animal was open eyed and fully aware—and still looked for all the world as if it were about to struggle to its feet.

"It's a colt," he heard Harris Delacorte say.

"Well, of course it's a colt," Aiden said, still staring transfixed into the baby's intelligent eyes. "What else would it be?"

"No, that's not what I mean. Of course it's a *foal*. Any baby horse is a foal. But a colt is a boy. A filly is a girl."

"Oh," Aiden said, but to the colt and not to the man. "You're a boy."

The colt's mother came back. Came around with her head low, and bumped the baby with her muzzle, several times. All over.

Aiden reached out and touched the colt's neck. It was wet, and the strange fluid coated his hand, but he didn't care.

———

"You can go back in and go to bed if you want," his stepfather said. "I just wanted you to see that moment when life begins."

Aiden ignored the substance of the comment completely.

"He looks like he's trying to get up," Aiden said. Even though he was sure such a thing was impossible.

It was maybe an hour later. Time had become liquid and strange, a hard thing to judge.

"He *is* trying to get up."

"Doesn't he know he was just born?"

"That doesn't matter with horses. They stand up pretty much straightaway."

The colt lay with his front hooves dug into the straw, knees up at a sharp angle out in front of his face, and tried to lever itself up with those brand-new limbs. But he was still too far over on his hip in the back, hind legs sprawled out forever, and it seemed impossible that he could ever harness those spindly hind limbs and pull them underneath his body. Make them work for him.

*And who said he should even try?* Aiden thought, though perhaps not in words, or at least not in those exact ones. How about a minute to get used to being alive?

Still he stared into the big, dark pools of the animal's brand-new eyes. Now and again he was sure the foal looked back at him. Really saw him. Without fear. Without fear in either one of them.

The mare moved in a slow circle around her foal, forcing Aiden to scramble out of her way. She reached down and used her long, bony face to nudge the foal's back end, literally push in a series of little urgings until the foal was more centered over his own hips.

In one sudden, rickety, lurching movement, the foal was standing, comically long legs skewed out at ridiculous angles. Aiden gasped out loud. Then the foal nearly lost his balance and fell, but he caught himself, thanks in large part to the support of his mother's well-placed head. The baby took a clumsy step or two, as if on brand-new stilts, and bumped underneath his mother's belly with his wet nose.

"What are you going to name your colt?" Harris Delacorte asked.

The words startled Aiden. He had been deep in concentration and not expecting them. Then, when they came along, he didn't let them in or fully understand them.

"What colt?" he asked, as if in a dream.

"What do you mean, what colt? The one right in front of you."

"He's not my colt."

"What if he was, though?"

"But he's not."

"You're not getting what I'm saying, boy. I'm saying he's your colt now."

Aiden looked away from the animal for the first time since his knowing eye had emerged from that ghostly sack. He looked at his stepfather in the lantern light, but the man's face lay in shadow. Whatever lived there was beyond Aiden's ability to see.

"You're giving him to me?"

"I think I am, yes."

"That doesn't make any sense. You don't trust me with your horses."

"But this isn't one of my horses. This is *your* horse. I'm counting on that to make a difference. I'm banking on the fact that you'll love him and be proud of him because he's yours. It's different when they're yours. When you take care of your own horse, maybe you'll love him and understand him in a different way. That's my gamble, anyway. I've thought about it and thought about it, and I just now decided. I'm taking a chance on you, boy. That you'll take good care of this colt and not let me down. Or at least not let *him* down."

Aiden's mind and gut swam with a panicked uncertainty.

"But I don't know how to take care of a colt."

"That doesn't matter. I'll teach you. I'll show you everything you need to know. All you have to do is *care*. You need to have the heart for the job. I'll make sure you have everything else you need. Think you can step up to that?"

Truthfully, Aiden wasn't sure. He couldn't imagine what it would feel like to step up to a task with his heart. But that liquid-eyed, brand-new colt could be *his* now. And so he just would. He would not miss a chance like this. He would do it even if it was the hardest thing he had ever done. Even if it was impossible, he would defeat impossibility and manage somehow.

"Yes, sir," Aiden said. "I'll take real good care of him if you'll show me how."

"Good. Now come on back to bed."

"No, sir. Please. I'd like to stay here with my colt a little longer."

His stepfather clapped a hand onto Aiden's down-padded shoulder and then left him alone. And yet not alone. Because he had his magic new companion, and the baby's devoted mother.

He had more than he'd ever had before in his life.

It almost hurt to try to take it all in.

———

When Aiden woke in the morning, his mother and stepfather were standing over him. Standing hand in hand, staring down at him as he slept.

He was on his side on the straw bedding of the foaling stall, one arm thrown over his magic colt, who slept with his head thrown over Aiden's side. The weight of that head felt uncomfortable on his ribs, and the hard dirt of the barn floor felt cold and pinching against his hip, but he would have stayed in that position all day long and at least another night if such an opportunity presented itself.

"Come in for breakfast now, honey," his mother said.

"I can't yet. I have to feed my colt."

"Aren't you hungry?"

"Yeah, but he must be hungry, too. You have to take care of your horse first. And then yourself. I learned that. I know that part of taking care of a horse already."

"You don't have to feed him," his stepfather said. "He's nursing. His mother will feed him for now. Later, when he's ready to be weaned, I'll show you how to feed him. Your mother's right. The colt is fine. Come in for breakfast."

"Okay," Aiden said. "In a minute. I just want to say goodbye to my colt."

Though, truthfully, he could not imagine where he would find the courage to tear himself away.

They walked off and left him in the stall, where Aiden struggled to his feet. The colt took it as an invitation to struggle to his own hooves as well, and they stood side by side for a couple of minutes. Aiden wrapped his arms around the colt's now-dry neck, and the colt bumped at Aiden's side with his muzzle, and played at grabbing Aiden's jacket with his lips.

"I'll be back right after breakfast," Aiden said. "You go get breakfast from your mom. Then I'll be right back."

But still he could not step away. Not in that moment.

Without thinking it out in words or sentences, Aiden flashed back to the previous night—the bad part of it. That long, cold walk out to the barn, when he'd thought his stepfather might have been about to kill him.

He had thought his life was over. That he was about to die. But it was just the opposite. He could feel it. Instead, his life had begun.

Just as surely as his colt, Aiden had been born.

# Chapter Sixteen

## Aiden at Age Eight

Aiden was on his way out to the barn to feed his yearling when he saw them. Aiden's new father was warming up his pickup truck in the pre-dawn dark, his friend Teddy Flannigan in the passenger seat beside him.

Aiden moved closer.

They didn't see him, so he rapped on the window. Both men jumped, then laughed out loud at themselves. As if it were a source of amazement and humor that something could startle them.

Aiden's father rolled down the window. As he did, Aiden saw that the gun rack in the back of the cab, which normally sat empty, held two rifles.

"What're you doing up so early, boy?"

"Going to feed Magic."

"Why don't you stay in bed and wait another half hour or so and the ranch hands'll do it? They feed all the horses, you know."

"Yes, sir. I know they do. But Magic isn't their yearling. He's mine. So his feed should come from me. That's what I think, anyway."

"Suit yourself, son. Say good morning to Teddy Flannigan."

"Morning, Mr. Flannigan."

Teddy tipped his hat to Aiden. The man had a smile on his face that suggested everything Aiden did was funny to him. Getting up early. Feeding his own horse. Being eight. It was all a big joke to Teddy Flannigan.

"Where're you guys going?" Aiden asked, trying to keep the longing out of his voice. It didn't work.

For nearly a year, Aiden had been following his stepfather around like an old dog. Wanting in on everything. Any time Aiden caught the man doing something that left him on the outside, it brought a desperate physical pain down the middle of Aiden's chest. Like a sword swallower, but without whatever trick they used to make sure it didn't hurt. Assuming they had a trick.

Or maybe they just hurt, like Aiden.

"We're going hunting," his father said.

"I want to go hunting!"

It came out sharp and loud. And too high. Almost like a girl to his ears. Or maybe like an excited boy, but definitely not the man he was trying so hard to be.

In that moment, Aiden had never meant anything more. Even though he knew in some part of himself that it was a ridiculous thing for him to want to do.

But Harris Delacorte went hunting. So Aiden wanted to go hunting, too.

"*You?*" His stepfather exchanged a silent glance with the man in the passenger seat. "*You* want to go hunting?"

It burned Aiden's face and made his guts tingle, to be so shamed. Probably no shame had been intended. But still Aiden felt as though his claims to manhood were being negated, shredded before his eyes and ears.

"Yes, sir."

"I thought you didn't like to see anything get hurt. Your momma told me you were real sensitive about stuff like that."

"No, sir. I mean, that was before. You know. Back when I was dumb. I was just a little kid."

The men laughed at him. Not in a mean way, but as though Aiden had told a good joke. They both got it and he didn't.

"Oh, I see," his father said. "Before you were all grown up like you are now."

"Yes, sir. I can go hunting."

"No you can't." Then Harris Delacorte seemed to notice the pain this conversation was causing his stepson. Because he softened his tone and changed his conversational tack. "I mean, not this morning, you can't. Because you've never handled a firearm before. And you don't have a license. You need a license to hunt. But . . . tell you what. While we're gone today, you think extra hard on whether this is really something you want. And can manage. You know. On the emotional side of things. And if you're sure, I'll start teaching you to handle a gun safely. And how to shoot clean and true. And then we'll have to enroll you in a hunter safety class. You got to have that in this state to get your license. And then if you want to see it through all the way to the licensing phase of things, then yes. I'll take you."

It helped and it didn't help. To an eight-year-old, it was something like having been told, "Yes, I'll give you what you want. Sometime next century."

But the news must have softened Aiden's face some, because his father smiled at him in the dim light, and tousled Aiden's hair through the open truck window.

"Now go feed that nice-looking paint yearling of yours."

That formed a painful sword, too. It hurt both ways, both times—when he was left out, when he was loved. Both sliced down through his chest. But at least that was the only place, the only manner, in which he felt any pain.

As he walked away toward the barn, he heard his father and Teddy talking. The truck window was still down. Their voices carried.

"Thought that boy was all shut down where you couldn't get to 'im."

"Not now, Teddy. Not anymore. Not since I gave him that paint colt. Now he wants nothing more than to be just like me. Why, he'd climb right into my boots if I'd let him."

The men didn't really sound all that critical of the situation. But it made Aiden's face burn all the same. Until he paused slightly, and strained his hearing, and tuned in to catch Harris Delacorte's next words.

"It's kinda nice. Kinda warms your heart, you know?"

That was the moment, at least as far as Aiden was concerned, when his obsession with his new father morphed into a reciprocal bond.

—

"Hey, Magic," Aiden said when he stepped into the barn.

Magic answered him. Magic always answered him. It was the most wonderful greeting in the world, the best sound Aiden knew. A deep, satisfied nicker, throaty and rumbly.

Aiden pulled a flake of alfalfa hay off an opened bale and tipped it into his horse's feeder.

It was still dark, and there was no electricity in the barn. But Aiden's eyes had adjusted to the dimness, and he could see as much of his colt as he needed to see.

Magic was tall now, his withers coming up to about Aiden's nose. And he was beginning to fill out. He was getting a chest, and hindquarters. Not the ones he would have as an adult horse. But he wasn't a spindly foal who couldn't seem to control his own legs. Not anymore. He ran like a flash flood when turned out in pasture, and his blond-and-white painted coat was furry and long for winter. He wore a green rope halter at all times because he was just learning to lead and tie, and it could be hard to catch the colt to put it on.

Aiden let himself into the stall and draped his arms over the yearling's spine as he ate his hay. Leaned his weight on that warm back, lightly.

"So, I'm going hunting," he told his horse.

Magic swung his head around, jaw working with his chewing. He seemed to look at Aiden curiously, but that was probably reading too much into the situation. After all, it was dark. And Magic was a horse. Then he turned back to his hay.

"I know it doesn't sound quite right. But it'll be okay. My dad does it, and he gave me you. So if he does it, it must be a good thing to do. But don't worry. I would never hurt a horse. It's different with a deer. It's just all different."

Aiden was grateful that Magic didn't swing his neck around again. He would have hated to be called upon to explain why it was so very different.

———

When Aiden stepped back into the house after his first firearms lesson, his sister, Valerie, was standing in the front parlor. Shooting daggers at him with her eyes.

He ignored her and walked into his room.

In his head he could still hear and see everything. The crack of the rifle, leaving his ears ringing and mostly deaf for several seconds afterward. The ping of the soda can when Aiden finally hit it. The way it jumped slightly, popped up off the fence before falling. The little whoop his father made when he did it right.

He stood looking out the window at the cattle grazing in the north pasture, and ran the moments over and over in his head. He picked up his baseball glove, because it was something his father had given him. Took the ball out of it and smacked it back into the glove again and again, enjoying the hard impact of it. Imagined his father giving that little whoop because he had caught a high pop fly in a big, important game.

Something pinged against his head and he cried out loud from the pain of it.

"Ow!"

He turned to the open doorway of his room, rubbing a stinging spot behind his ear. Valerie was there, a bowl of walnuts—still in the shell—in her left hand.

"What the hell, Bally?"

"You cursed."

"And you hit me in the head with a walnut. That's worse."

"You deserved it."

"Why? What did I do?"

"I thought you were on my side. I asked you if you liked the guy, and you said you didn't."

"That was a long time ago. I changed my mind."

Valerie let another walnut fly. It caught him just above the left eyebrow.

"Ow! Stop doing that!"

"You always were a traitor. I never liked you."

Just for a moment, Aiden almost said he'd never liked her, either. It was true enough. He probably loved her, in some deep place in himself. Some inaccessible place. He had probably loved her since he was a baby, far too young to know she would only torment him and never love him—always make him feel bad about what he was, about who he could not help being. Or maybe you had no choice but to love your sister. Maybe it was impossible not to. But you could dislike her. Aiden knew that for a fact.

He didn't say it. He couldn't. It wouldn't come out of his mouth. It was just meaner than he could bring himself to be. So Aiden said nothing.

"I can't believe you think you want to go hunting. You used to cry if I stepped on bugs."

"Did not."

"You did, too, you idiot. I was there. Ask Mom. You used to cry like a baby if anything died. Even an ant or a fly."

Just as he opened his mouth to issue another denial, some tiny scrap of memory opened up to him. And he could no longer deny it.

"Well . . . that was before. I was stupid and young."

"And now you're older and even more stupid. You won't be able to shoot a duck or a deer. I can't believe you think you can. You'll cry all the way home."

She lobbed another walnut at his head, but he ducked it.

Then she was done tormenting him for the moment. He could tell because she turned and walked away. If she was there with him, there was torment. If she left, she was done and he could relax. For the time being.

Except this time she left him with a nagging doubt.

Could he shoot a duck or a deer? Or would he cry all the way home?

———

It was probably six weeks later, or it might have been seven or eight, when Aiden lay in the woods just before dawn with his father and Teddy Flannigan.

They had found a downed tree, and were stretched out on their bellies in front of it, only their heads and hands and rifles protruding over the top of its broad trunk.

Aiden had to stretch his upper body higher than the men did, to see over. There were bugs on the log. Ants and pill bugs, and maybe some other living things that Aiden would not have wanted walking on him. So he lifted his chin still higher, even though it was making his neck hurt.

It was cold. It was all Aiden could do to keep his teeth from chattering. He couldn't stop it, but he tried to chatter silently. His bare hands shook. But he knew in some deep part of himself that it could be ninety degrees out here and his hands would still be shaking.

"Cold, boy?" Teddy Flannigan whispered.

You always whispered when you were hunting. Because the deer have good ears.

"Yes, sir," Aiden breathed back. Barely moving his numb lips.

"I got just the thing for that."

The older man reached into his coat pocket and brought out a small, flat bottle. A fifth of whiskey.

"Teddy," Aiden's father whispered. "He's eight."

"One snort. Just a good swallow. It'll warm him up some."

Aiden took the bottle. Felt the warmth of it on his hand. It had been pressed closely to Teddy Flannigan's side, and it was warmer than everything around it.

In that moment, even before he sipped at it, Aiden already knew. He knew he had found the answer to something that had eluded him.

Maybe they called it spirits because it really did have a spirit to it. Like a living being. Because as Aiden unscrewed the cap and the smell came up to greet him, he seemed to get a message from it.

*I have what you need.*

He took a deep swallow.

It burned going down. But it didn't matter. It felt good to be burned. He did not cough. Just lay still, eyes stretched wide, and felt the heat of it radiate all the way down through his gut.

Both men were watching him. They seemed to be waiting for a reaction that never came.

"What?" Aiden asked, looking first to one and then the other.

"I'll be damned," his father said.

"Thought he'd cough that right up again," Teddy added. "Didn't you?"

Aiden tipped the bottle back and took another long swallow.

"Ho, ho, whoa, boy," his father said. A little too loudly, what with the deer and all. "Go easy on that."

"Natural born drinker," Teddy said. "Got to watch that."

"Don't give him any more, Teddy. Or it'll be us that gets shot. Either out here in the woods, by him, or later when I bring him home drunk to his mom."

But it didn't matter.

Aiden had swallowed the exact amount of whiskey he needed. And he would never forget the feeling. He knew he wouldn't. You didn't need too much. You needed just enough.

His hands stopped shaking. He could breathe more deeply. There was no sense of any emotion about anything trying to sneak through. Nothing poked out from behind the partition. Everything lay down inside him, perfect and smooth.

And twenty minutes later, when a long parade of deer came ambling through, their hooves crunching in the dry leaves, and Aiden was allowed to take the first shot, the shot he took was perfect.

He had been practicing for weeks, and he did it just the way he had practiced it. The deer went down. Just like that.

If it was in any way different from plinking cans off a fence, Aiden couldn't feel how. He couldn't feel much of anything. Which was perfect.

He did not cry all the way home.

———

When it came time to learn to dress out the deer, it was light and warm out. Teddy Flannigan had taken off his jacket and hung it on the limb of a standing dead tree. Aiden slipped the bottle out of the jacket pocket and took another long swallow.

Nobody noticed.

Nothing hurt.

# PART FIVE

AIDEN DELACORTE AT AGE FORTY

PRESENT DAY

# *Chapter Seventeen*

*Tesserae*

Aiden sat back on the couch and watched Hannah take notes. It was four sessions later, unless it was five and he was remembering wrong. One session seemed to blend into the next. Each had been used to fill in the newly remembered details of his childhood. Some details had seemed to be remembered almost the moment he'd spoken them. And surely there was still more he was forgetting. But four or five fifty-minute sessions added up to a lot of details. Especially for a man who had forgotten his own past for so many years.

"Hmm," Hannah said, and bit down on the end of her pen. She stared at her notes for a second or two. "I think we can agree that's awfully young to start drinking. I don't mean it as a judgment. And I'm certainly not suggesting you're the first."

"I didn't drink a lot, though," Aiden said.

He didn't say it defensively. He didn't say much of anything defensively anymore. Not to Hannah. They had shared too many sessions for that. He had told her too many things. Her office had become too safe a space for such worries.

"I guess my point was that any alcohol at all is a lot for an eight-year-old."

"Looking back, that sure feels true enough. At the time I guess it just felt . . . normal. Weirdly normal."

"I can't imagine you were able to get your hands on much at that age."

"Oh, you'd be surprised." He stared out the window and into other windows in other large, impersonal office buildings in downtown Bakersfield. Into the lives of other people. Was he the only one tearing his own life apart? Opening it for inspection and possible repair? "Because I didn't need that much, so it wasn't hard to hide whatever I was taking. I mean . . . two good swallows. When I was little, that is. Later, just two drinks. Two beers or two shots. That's all I really needed. I already had the talent of barely breathing. If you can call that a talent."

"I'm not sure if I would, but it's a common tool people use when they don't want to feel. Especially kids. Because kids don't have a lot of tools at their disposal. How much do you drink now?"

"I don't."

"Not at all?"

"No. Not at all."

He expected her to ask why. Instead they fell into a calm silence that directed Aiden's attention to the ticking of the clock. He hadn't been aware of it for many sessions. It had grown normal, and had not consciously broken through for some time.

A few ticks later he realized she wasn't going to ask. It so obviously required an explanation that she was simply waiting for him to provide it.

"A few months ago . . . ," he began. Then he paused. It was a place he did not enjoy going. So he stopped. Took a breath. Then he went there anyway. "Magic died."

"Oh, that's right. You said that in your first session. And I said we'd come back to it. And we haven't yet. I'm sorry. Go on."

"Well. He died. Natural causes and all. He was almost thirty-three. That's old for a horse. I was lucky he lived as long as he did. He had a good life."

"You sound like you think that should help you through the grief of it, though," she said. "I'm afraid it doesn't work that way."

"So I found out. After the vet came out and . . . humanely . . . put him down, I went into the house. I poured myself a shot and I slugged it down, just like always. And then I slugged down another. And that should have been it. Just enough to tip me over into not being able to feel much. But then something happened that'd never happened before."

"You couldn't stop," Hannah said. It wasn't a question.

He didn't ask how she knew. He had long outgrown that. Hannah knew all sorts of things Aiden didn't think she should be able to know. Asking about every one of them would only waste precious session time.

"I went on like that for a couple or three weeks. I mean, I was just drowning in the stuff. I couldn't work. I wasn't getting dressed in the morning. I was a hazard on the road when I drove out to get more. I'm lucky I didn't die. I was putting the stuff down so fast. Alcohol poisoning wasn't out of the question. But I guess I have a pretty strong constitution. I made it through. But then my girlfriend—my ex-girlfriend now—and my employees at the time, and my neighbors . . . well, they've known me a long time. They . . . intervened. I won't say it was anything like a formal intervention, because they didn't get together and hit me all at once. It was like this series of mini-interventions. Once I had three people come through my door in one day and tell me they weren't going to sit idly by and let me kill myself. So I just stopped. I don't know how exactly. I know I let Livie pour everything I had down the drain, and she sat with me until I cleared it out of my system. And then once I got my brain back a little, it was more my brain making decisions. You know. Rather than the booze deciding for me. And that was it. I haven't had a sip since. I haven't broken over even the tiniest bit, because I have this fear that once I start, it'll happen all over again and I won't be able to stop."

Aiden fell silent and watched her scribble notes on her pad.

It was probably close to a minute later—sixty ticks, give or take—when she looked up at him and spoke.

"And this was how long before you had that waking-up experience?"

"Couple weeks, I guess."

"Was that the first time you'd tried going hunting since . . . ?"

"Yeah. It was the first time I'd ever hunted stone-cold sober."

"That explains a lot. Doesn't it?"

They both sat on that moment, that turning point in their therapy, for an extended time. Aiden felt lost in his thoughts. And yet if someone had asked, he might have had trouble voicing what thoughts they were.

He glanced at the clock to see they only had six minutes left.

"I'm interested in your reaction to that," Hannah said.

"Right. I guess I'm wondering why in God's name I needed you to tell me that. I mean, I'm me. I'm the one having these experiences. And something as obvious as that . . . and you're the one who has to figure it out."

"I didn't figure anything out, Aiden. I just listened to you. You told me what happened. I just mirrored back to you what you were saying. We all need that sometimes. It's easier to see the big picture when you're standing a few steps outside it."

"I still have a question, though." Aiden crossed his legs. Uncrossed them again. He felt his breath go shallow, but he overrode it. Pulled in oxygen. "Let's say I'm one of these extremely sensitive people you talked about. Which seems really likely at this point."

"An empath," Hannah interjected.

"Right. An empath. That thing that happened with the deer. Feeling like I shot myself instead of him. I mean . . . is that normal? Is that within the range of what happens to these sensitive people? Seems to me it's a little above and beyond all that."

"It's . . ."—she paused, as if choosing her words carefully—"it's an unusually intense example."

"But not outside the range?"

"That's a hard question to answer, Aiden. You're right that it's an experience most people have never had. And never will."

"Even for an empath."

"I would guess, but it's hard to say. People have experiences that never go on the record. That they never tell anyone about."

"I feel like maybe it was still . . . kind of . . . bigger than anything in this world can explain. So I guess I just want to hear how you would explain it."

Hannah set down her pad. Set it on the end table beside her chair. She took off her reading glasses and connected her gaze directly with Aiden's eyes.

"Everybody explains things from their own experience," she said. "It just seems to be how we are. If you were talking to a psychic, they would probably explain it as a psychic experience. But you're not. You're talking to a psychiatrist. So you're going to get a psychiatric take on the thing. I think your subconscious played a trick on you to get you to see something you were trying not to see."

"Okay," Aiden said, and broke his gaze away. It still felt more comfortable to look at the patterned rug. "I can live with that."

"Then again," she added, just when he was ready to put the whole thing away, "to paraphrase what Shakespeare wrote, 'More things in heaven and earth than are dreamt of in our philosophies.' If you know what I mean."

"Yeah," Aiden said. "I'm afraid I know what you mean."

———

He was four-fifths of the way home when his cell phone rang. He glanced down just long enough to see that it was Gwen calling. He didn't want to talk and drive at the same time because it was illegal in this state, and this stretch of rural route was particularly well patrolled.

He reached an intersection just in time and pulled into the parking lot of a locally owned home and garden store.

"Hello," he said quickly, after sliding his thumb to pick up the call. "Don't hang up, Gwen."

"Oh, good," she said. "You're there."

"Just let me pull into a parking place here."

Aiden nosed his truck into an open space at the side entrance of the store. In front of his bumper sat an outdoor shelf full of brightly colored porcelain planting pots, a rainbow that caught his eye and held it as he spoke to her.

"Okay, I'm here again," he said. "Sorry."

"You're not home."

"No. I was at Hannah's."

"Oh. That's right. I forgot."

"Is everything okay?"

The silence that followed brought a burst of panic to his poor tired gut. As though someone had hit him in the stomach with shock and fear, and his skin had been incapable of stopping it from coming right in. It was only a second or two of silence. But it spoke.

"I'm at work," she said, "but I just got a call from the babysitter . . ."

There was always a babysitter now. Every minute Gwen was at work. Ever since the Buddy incident. Which is why she hadn't bothered to memorize whether or not Aiden would be home.

"What did he do?" His voice trembled slightly on the asking.

"Well . . . you know that really nice table in the cabin?"

"Table?"

"Yeah. Not the kitchen table. That nice wood coffee table. The one that looks sort of antique."

"He hurt a *table*?"

Aiden could hear himself nearly laughing, a breath of air coming out with the words that sounded almost like lightness. Like mirth. In truth, it was only a world of fear breathing out of his gut. Meanwhile his eyes remained fixed on those bright red and green and orange and blue and yellow pots.

"Yes, I'm sorry."

"Gwen. It's a *table*. I don't care about a table. Tables don't feel pain. We'll buy a new damn table."

"It was so nice, though. It was a nice thing."

"Yes," Aiden said. "Emphasis on the word *thing*. I think I got it at a swap meet. Or a garage sale. I didn't pay an arm and a leg for it."

"Well, I'll be watching those yard sales from now on. Maybe I can find a nice one to replace it."

"What did he do to it, anyway? It's a pretty sturdy table. I can't imagine he'd even be strong enough to break it."

"She . . . Etta, she accidentally fell asleep. Just for a minute or two. But don't worry that he could be out roaming the place if that happens, because she always has the dead bolt on when she's in the cabin with him, and the key is in her pocket. Anyway, I guess he got a paring knife out of the knife block in the kitchen and just scratched the hell out of the wood tabletop."

"Scratches could maybe even be sanded out," Aiden said, his eyes still on the riot of porcelain colors. "I could refinish the table."

"Scratches are the wrong word, I guess. I think it's more like gouges. But I'm still at work. I haven't seen it with my own eyes. She said it's really bad, though."

"It's only a table."

"Yeah, that's true," she said, something tight draining out of her voice, leaving it smooth and calm, as if all this trouble had never happened. As if they could just be two people, exploring being together. Without this constant fear of disaster. "It's only a table. But it's *your* table. So thank you for looking at it that way. For being so nice about it. Someday soon I'll tell you . . . you know."

He waited, but she didn't go on.

"No, I don't know. What?"

"What he went through. With his dad. And then you'll understand him a little better. You'll feel for him. I swear you will."

"When you're ready," he said with a satisfied sigh. Or it sounded satisfied, anyway. It was probably the last of the fear leaving him.

"I love you," Gwen said.

It was the first she had ever said it.

He said nothing for a moment. Just felt it. Just let it ricochet around in his gut, blessing every part of him it touched. It was a strange moment to have elicited such a declaration. But life was a tricky place, and he would gratefully accept her love without questioning its timing.

"I love you, too," he said.

They both listened to silence on the line for several seconds.

"Well," she said after a time. "I'll be home in less than an hour. And Elizabeth wants to cook dinner for all of us. That is, if you don't mind spaghetti. It's the only thing she knows how to cook."

"I love spaghetti," Aiden said.

"Okay. Good. See you soon."

And she clicked off the call.

Aiden sat a minute, feeling drained from everything he had just been through. The good and bad of it felt equally exhausting. He stared at the porcelain planters as he sat, and thought about what Hannah had said about Milo—and Milo's father—outer-directing their rage. Even though she'd said it many weeks earlier.

The sign over the planters read "Special Blow-Out Sale—Three for $1!"

Aiden bought five dollars' worth of them, loaded them into an open cardboard carton, set the carton in the bed of his pickup truck, and drove home.

—

"I actually brought these for Milo," Aiden said to Gwen, indicating the box of pottery with his chin.

They were sitting on the couch together in the cabin. Elizabeth was in the kitchen area, banging pots and pans around. Milo was staring at TV news with rapt attention, seeming not to know that anyone else existed.

Gwen craned her neck and peered into the carton. While she did, Aiden glanced again at the gouged and ravaged wood top of the coffee table. It made him wince, every time. The violence in the heart of the person who had attacked it seemed baked in, visible to anyone who viewed the damage. It made his stomach tip slightly.

"Oh, honey," Gwen said. Quietly, to keep her words private. "I wouldn't give anything like that to Milo. He'll probably just break them."

"Right," Aiden said. "That's what I figured he would do with them. That was the idea."

—

"I was thinking . . . ," Aiden said, and trailed off. "Maybe after dinner we could try something."

He was speaking to Milo, and trying to make that clear by looking at Milo, but Milo had his eyes trained down to his own plate of spaghetti, and so likely didn't know.

Aiden watched the boy take one tentative bite and chew the food as though it might be dangerous. Still, it was the first time Aiden had ever seen Milo eat. Even one bite.

"When I was a kid, Milo," Aiden said, a bit too loudly, dropping the boy's name awkwardly to get his attention, "I used to like to smash breakable things against a tree. My stepfather used to give me things it was okay to break. It felt great. And I think it really helped me when I was angry."

It was a lie. A total fabrication. Aiden had never broken anything on purpose. The truth—that he had no way of knowing where the pottery idea came from, and that it might be a silly and ineffective plan—was not something he cared to share. He thought if he made it more personal, it might take on greater meaning. It seemed to need meaning.

Aiden could tell Milo was listening, but he would have been hard pressed to explain how he knew. Milo did not look up.

A long silence fell, during which the four of them ate spaghetti without speaking. Milo even took a second bite.

"This is very good," Aiden said to Elizabeth, feeling that he was trying too hard but not knowing how to stop. He had complimented her on the meal twice already. "You're a good cook."

"I was thinking I could help you do chores around here," Elizabeth said.

In the brief moment before Aiden responded, it came into his head that maybe she was twice as good as any child he had ever met as a way of making up for her brother.

"Now why would you want to go and do a thing like that?"

"It's summer. And it might be fun."

"Chores are not fun," Aiden said. "That's why they call them chores. If they were fun, they'd be called happy extravaganzas."

Elizabeth laughed. Maybe a little more than the situation called for.

"I could go with you in the morning and help you feed all the animals."

"Right now the only ones I'm feeding are the rabbits and the horses in the barn. Other than the dog, that is." Aiden glanced quickly at Milo as he mentioned the dog. But if the boy had a reaction, Aiden was unable to see it. "The pasture is good now because it's early summer. Later in the year I'll probably have to supplement with hay, unless we get some early rains."

"So what do you do in the morning? Anything?"

Aiden glanced at Gwen, but her eyes and her attention seemed a million miles away from their dinner table.

"I go around and check all the water troughs. They have these automatic fill valves. But they can get stuck, or the line can rupture. Especially when it's hot, you have to check the water sources every day."

"Do you go in your truck or do you just walk around?"

"I take the truck or I go on horseback. Lately most often the truck. It's a little hard to walk. Pretty far. Well. Maybe not for you. But if you wanted to take on a chore, you could saddle Penny in the morning and ride around and check all the troughs. If your mom thinks it's okay for you to ride alone."

"Mom?" Elizabeth asked.

Gwen jumped, as if she'd been alone in a room when that voice startled her.

"What?"

"Am I allowed to ride alone every morning? Just around the property."

"Well, I don't know," she said. "Does Aiden think it's okay?"

"I think on Penny she'll be just fine."

"Okay, honey. If Aiden thinks it's okay, I trust his judgment."

"What do I get to break?" Milo asked suddenly.

All three of their heads came up and turned to the boy, and a moment of silence reflected their surprise. It was as though a person who had been mute his entire life had spoken. None of them could have expected it less.

"I brought home some porcelain pots," Aiden said.

"Why pots?"

"I don't know. Why not? They were on sale cheap."

"Okay," Milo said. "I'm done eating. Let's go."

206    *Catherine Ryan Hyde*

"Aiden's not done eating, honey," Gwen said.

"No, it's okay," Aiden said. "I'm done enough." He wound half the spaghetti on his plate around his fork and shoved it into his mouth. "I'll have a second helping later," he said, his mouth still full.

———

Milo stood in the late afternoon slant of sun with a bright-red pot in one hand. The first pot. His left hand, because his right arm was still in a cast. Aiden wondered about Milo's immediate choice of the color red. Did the boy respond to it the way an angry bull might? Or had Aiden read that bulls were color blind and that old theory wasn't true?

The boy stood facing a sturdy scrub oak tree, maybe four feet away, and wound up for a pitch. Then he froze and looked at Aiden over his shoulder.

"Really? This's not a trick?"

"I don't understand the question."

"I won't get in trouble when I break it?"

"No. I bought them for you to break."

"That seems weird."

"Why does it seem weird?"

"Why would you buy me stuff to break?"

"I thought it might help you."

"Why would you want to help me?"

"I'm not sure I understand that question, either," Aiden said.

In many ways, he did. He understood that Milo considered them enemies. And maybe he was struggling to reframe Aiden as someone who wanted to help him. Or maybe he was simply unwilling to try.

Mostly Aiden did not understand how a question like that one should be answered.

"Well," Milo said. "You asked for it."

He hurled the red pot with all his might. It missed the trunk of the tree and fell to the dirt a yard or two beyond it, where it rolled and did not break.

"Damn," Milo said.

Aiden could see the boy's face redden. At least, for a couple of seconds. Then Milo purposely turned his face down toward the dirt and away from Aiden. He stomped off to retrieve the pot.

Milo picked it up out of the dirt, and, as he came back by the scrub oak tree, simply smashed it against the solid trunk. No throwing involved. It shattered into dozens of pieces and fell to the ground.

Aiden and the boy just stood and stared for a moment, the sound of the crash still ringing in Aiden's ears.

Milo ran to the carton of pots, grabbed a green one, and ran back to a spot only two feet from the tree. He threw hard, and the pot hit its target and shattered into green shards.

Aiden dragged the carton through the dirt and set it under Milo's left hand.

For a minute or more, Milo bent, grabbed, threw. Bent, grabbed, threw.

*I should have bought more pots,* Aiden thought. *I should have dropped a twenty and bought them all.* Because Milo was already close to the bottom of the carton. He was just beginning to tap into some deep well of anger, and he was almost out of pots.

Aiden watched him smash the last one against the tree, then drop his hand into the box and find nothing. Milo fell to his knees and ran his hands around the bottom of the empty carton. Desperately. As though there could be more. As though there had to be more. Maybe they were invisible, or too small to be seen by the naked eye, in which case Milo was still determined to find them.

Aiden felt a twist in his full belly as he waited to see what the boy would do.

Milo froze for a long moment there on his knees in the dirt.

Then he jumped up, grabbed a baseball-size rock, and ran to the base of the tree, where he fell to his knees again and began smashing the shards into smaller shards with the rock.

Aiden heard a slight noise and looked over to see Gwen standing outside with him, watching.

"How's it going?" she asked. A bit warily, he thought.

"Not sure yet."

And he wasn't. Because he didn't know yet how the experiment was going to end. Then, just in that moment, it ended. It ended with a yelp of pain from Milo. He had brought the rock down at a bad angle and cut the heel of his hand on one of the pottery shards.

"Oh, honey," Gwen said. "Here. Let me put something on that for you."

He ran to her, and she used her own hands to try to stanch the bleeding as she ushered him into the cabin.

That left Aiden alone in the slanted sunlight, staring at a rainbow pile of broken porcelain and wondering if that exercise had accomplished anything, been worth anyone's time and effort.

"How did that go?" he heard a voice say.

He turned, startled, and saw Elizabeth standing in the open cabin doorway.

"I'm not sure," Aiden said. "I was just trying to figure that out."

She wandered over and stood at his side, and they stared at the bright litter together. The suddenly created garbage.

"It's kind of a shame," she said. "I mean . . . I know it was cheap and all. But it was worth something because you could do something with it. It could hold a plant. But now it's just all ruined and it seems kind of a shame."

Then she sighed, and left him alone.

—

Aiden spent the next fifteen minutes or so picking up every last shard with a rake and dropping it all back into the cardboard carton. He was being compulsive about catching every bit, and he knew it. Because Milo had already cut his hand on Aiden's idea. The last thing anyone needed was to step on a piece, in bare feet or insufficient shoes, and incur another preventable injury.

As he raked, he felt his mind go over and over the point Elizabeth had made. He felt as though he needed to find a use, a purpose, for the worthless rubble he had encouraged Milo to create. Except he couldn't imagine what use that might be.

It was pretty, though. In its own way. It was colorful and abstract, so it was appealing.

Maybe it could line the bottom of a fish tank. Or sit on the dirt in potted plants, to keep the moisture from evaporating.

Or maybe even an art project, he thought. He remembered suddenly that his sister, Bally, had brought home a cigar box from kindergarten that she had decorated with dry macaroni. Surely these colorful shards were more beautiful than plain, bland macaroni.

When he was satisfied he'd gotten it all, he carried the carton back to his house. He set it on the back porch and rooted around in the shed, even though he was quickly losing his daylight. He found a wood-framed window screen just where he expected to find it, carried it to the porch, and spread the dirty shards on the screen.

He was washing them off with the hose when he heard Gwen's voice.

"What're you doing, hon?"

"Oh," he said, looking at the scene in front of him as if for the first time. "I'm not sure yet. I'm kind of figuring it out as I go along. How's Milo?"

"He's fine. I just put a gauze patch on it."

"Doesn't need stitches?"

"No. It's not that deep."

"Good. Because it's awfully soon for another hospital visit. I can just hear what the deputy sheriff would say about that." Aiden turned off the hose and looked up into Gwen's face. "Let's go away," he said. "Just the two of us."

He watched her face change. Unbend and soften.

"What brought that on?"

"I just feel like we have so much on our plate here. Wouldn't it be nice if it was just us for a couple days? We could go to the coast. Morro Bay or Pismo Beach. Maybe Etta could take the kids to her house."

"It *would* be nice," Gwen said, bumping up against his shoulder with her own. "But I'm not sure if I could get time off work."

"But you could ask, though."

"Yeah. I could ask."

She moved close to Aiden and kissed him on the ear. His ear grew hot where her lips touched it.

"Goodnight," she said, and moved away.

"Tell Elizabeth dinner was good."

"Oh, she knows," Gwen said. "You made that plenty clear. Which is one of the many things I love about you."

———

A few minutes later Aiden sat on his back porch in the growing twilight, reading a web page on his phone. The page was a series of steps for do-it-yourself mosaics.

"Grout," he said. More than once.

The website listed the materials necessary for a mosaic project. Aiden was making a list in his head of anything he did not currently own. There did not seem to be a second item to add to the list.

He already had varnish for finishing it off. And his life was chock-full of what the website called "tesserae," the small items used to create the mosaic design. Examples mentioned were colored marbles, glass pieces, pottery fragments, or small tiles.

"I think we're pretty well fixed for pottery fragments," he said out loud.

Most of the other supplies listed—hammer, tile cutter, glass cutter, safety glasses—all seemed to assume that the tesserae would need breaking up.

"I think we have the breaking part covered," Aiden said.

He glanced at his watch. It was 7:40. The hardware store was open until eight. If he hurried, he could get there in time to buy grout.

———

Aiden was just stepping back out into the parking lot when he heard her voice.

He shouldn't have been surprised. The hardware store shared a parking lot with the salon where Livie worked. And the salon closed at eight, too.

"I loved you, you stupid bastard," the familiar voice said.

Aiden turned to see Livie staring at him in the last scrap of the day's light. The streetlamps had not yet come on. They would in a minute or two, most likely. So it was the darkest time of day during which he could have seen her, which spared him the details of whatever emotion he might have seen in her eyes. Aiden wondered if that was a blessing of some sort. A kindness from some unknown source.

Oddly, her voice had not sounded angry. Mostly hurt.

He turned and walked closer to her, his paper bag of grout tucked under his arm. When he was only a couple of steps from her, just as he stopped, she jabbed out with one fist and punched him in the shoulder. Fairly hard.

"I'm glad I ran into you," Aiden said, ignoring the blow. "I've been feeling like I owe you an apology."

"Oh my God, oh my God," Livie said, stumbling back two steps. "You were seeing her before we broke up. I knew it. I absolutely knew it." Her voice was breathy. Quiet. As if speaking only to herself. Not to Aiden at all.

"No. I wasn't. It's not that at all."

"Well, what is it, then?"

And on that line, she snapped more fully back into being Livie. As though she had seen him crossing the parking lot and reached for her shield, but had only just that moment snugged it into place. It felt familiar in a way that made him ache. That defensive posture and tone of hers. Not good, just familiar.

"I only wanted to say that I know now I was a terrible, terrible boyfriend. I have no idea how you put up with me. I mean, I was so shut down. I couldn't feel anything. And I can see now, looking back, how you tried everything to get some kind of reaction out of me. Some kind of caring. And there was just no getting through. No wonder you were always so frustrated with me. Anyway. That's all, I guess. Just . . . sorry. I was doing my best, I swear I was. It wasn't very good, though."

A long silence fell. Aiden tried to watch her face to see how his confessions were being received. But it was too dark. Whatever Livie was feeling was free to remain her secret. If she didn't tell him, he would never know.

"I have to go," she said, and peeled away in the direction of her car.

There seemed to be a light quaver in her voice. As though she was crying, or something close to it. But in the dark, Aiden would never know for sure.

# Chapter Eighteen

## *Boo*

Aiden began the morning by doing something he never did. He drove straight to the cabin. On the passenger seat of the truck beside him sat the carton full of clean pottery shards with cans of adhesive, grout, and varnish perched on top.

He carried the box to the door and knocked, and Gwen answered in her robe, a mug of coffee in one hand.

"I'm really sorry," Aiden said. "I think this is exactly what I swore I would never do. But I'm just kind of excited about this. I hope that's allowed. And that maybe you'll forgive me for it just this one time."

"Tell you what," she said. "This will cancel out the time I called you in the middle of the night. Now we're even."

But Aiden saw a definite shiny, light quality in her eyes, and could tell by her voice that she was not the least bit sorry to see him. It made his chest feel warm and buoyant.

"Now what have you got there?" she asked.

"It's a project I thought I could do with Milo."

"*With* Milo? Oh, I'm not so sure about that, hon. Milo's not a *with* kind of guy. But anyway, come on in and let's take a look."

Aiden stepped into the living room of the little cabin and set the carton down on the ravaged coffee table, covering as much of the damage as he could before settling on the couch.

"Coffee?" Gwen asked.

"I'd love some. Where are the kids?"

"Milo's getting dressed in the bedroom and Elizabeth is in the shower. Or maybe at this point it's the other way around. Jeez, honey, I just realized I don't even know if you take anything in your coffee. That's weird."

"Nothing," he said. "Just black."

She brought him a steaming mug and set it on the coffee table near the carton of potential art project. Then she leaned back and took a sip of her own coffee.

"Now let's see what we've got here," she said.

Aiden stole a glance at her face. She wasn't wearing makeup, and he had never seen her without it before. But she must not have worn a lot, ever, because she didn't look all that different. She looked nice, in fact. Natural and fresh. Someone with whom Aiden would enjoy waking up in the morning.

She caught him looking and he smiled shyly, and she smiled in return.

"These are all the pieces of those pots he broke up yesterday. I thought we could use them to do a mosaic project."

She leaned forward and stared into the box, as if needing to see everything with her own eyes.

"Aiden Delacorte, I swear," she said, her voice hushed with wonder. "If this was something you planned all along, you are a parenting genius. I can't believe how cool that is. It's like . . . it's like showing him that something can be broken all to pieces, but you can still turn it into something beautiful. Which for Milo is the perfect message. Did you figure all that out in advance?"

"Yes," Aiden said brightly. "Only . . . no."

He had phrased it that way on purpose to make a joke of it. And it worked. She laughed.

"Well, you figured it out in the long run, and that's pretty darn good. Milo can be really artistic. But I do have to warn you about one thing, though. He probably won't let you do it with him. He either won't get anywhere near a thing like this, or he'll get real compulsive about it and work on it for hours on end and not eat or sleep and not let anyone else get close to it."

"I don't care about that. If he wants to do it himself, he can. If he doesn't want any part of it, I'll do it. And then he'll still see that broken things can be beautiful."

Gwen surprised him by sliding her hand across the couch and under his hand, and he closed his fingers around hers and held them. It was warm, her hand, and it settled something that had been lurching around in his stomach.

"I don't know what I did to deserve you," she said, her voice dense with affection, "but if I ever figure it out, I'm going to do it again." Then, as if the emotion of the moment had grown too heavy, she said, "Now show me how you do one of these mosaic things. Don't you have to do it on some kind of surface? You can't just mosaic the air, right? Don't you have to have something to attach it to?"

"I thought I'd take him out to the shed where I keep scrap wood. Let him take his pick."

"And I hope you have a drop cloth. I bet it's messy."

"It might be messy. But you could do it on this coffee table. Nothing that happens to this coffee table could be worse than what happened to it already." He pulled the box down and set it on the rug, and stared at the marred surface. And there it was in his head, the whole plan. The correct course of action. Just like that. "We can do it *on* the coffee table," he said. "We can make a new mosaic top for the coffee table."

"Whoa," Gwen said. "Now *that* is a plan. I suppose you had that all figured out in advance, too."

Of course, it had been obvious that he had just thought of it. It had apparently been a gentle tease.

"Yes," Aiden said. "Except no."

They smiled at each other for an embarrassingly long moment.

"Let's go away *today*," Aiden said. Suddenly. He hadn't even known it was in there waiting to come out. Or maybe it hadn't been. Maybe it was an idea he'd had just as the words flowed out of him. "Today and tomorrow. These are your days off, right?"

"Well, yeah, but . . . that's a pretty short trip."

"It's only three hours to the coast."

"And short notice for Etta. But let me call her and ask her right now. It sure would be nice."

She rose and hurried out of the room.

Aiden sipped his coffee for a moment. Then he looked up to see Milo standing in front of him, dull reddish hair freshly slicked back with wet comb marks, wearing a clean white shirt and khaki shorts. In his hopelessly vulnerable-looking bare feet.

"What *is* all that?" Milo asked, pointing down into the box.

"It's a mosaic project."

"I don't know what mosaic is."

"I'll show you some pictures of finished ones. We're going to make a new mosaic top for the coffee table."

Milo narrowed his eyes and stared into Aiden's face for a brief moment. Aiden thought the defensiveness in the boy's gaze was due to the mention of the coffee table he had so badly damaged.

But Milo cleared up that misunderstanding with his next terse sentence.

"Who's *we*?"

"Could be you and me. Could be you. Could just be me."

"She can do it!" Gwen fairly shrieked, running back into the room. "She can take them!"

"Take us where?" Milo asked in that same defensive tone.

Gwen crossed the room to him, leaned over to his level, and draped an arm over his shoulder. "You and Lizzie are going to go to Etta's today and tomorrow. So Aiden and I can go on a little vacation."

"I don't *want* to go to Etta's," Milo whined. "Why do you need a *vacation?*"

"I need a vacation," Gwen said, her voice firm, "from exactly the kind of stuff you're doing to me right now. This is not negotiable. You're going to Etta's."

Elizabeth's voice came out of nowhere. Or seemingly so. "We're going to Etta's?" A moment later Aiden saw her, standing in the bedroom doorway in a thick robe more her mother's size, a towel wrapped around her wet hair. "Why? For how long? Oh! Aiden's here! Good morning, Aiden!"

She ran the three steps to him and sat beside him on the couch, staring down into the box.

"What's all this?"

"Milo and I are going to do a mosaic project to rescue this coffee table."

For a moment the girl said nothing. Just stared at the pieces of art project, as though building them into an imaginary mosaic in her own head.

Then words burst out of her with surprising enthusiasm. "Oh my gosh, that's brilliant! You're brilliant! So it does still have a use!"

"I think it's about to."

"And you planned that all along?"

"No. Actually." He glanced up at Gwen, then at Milo, who had given up on them and flopped in the chair in front of the TV. Which was not turned on. But the boy had a remote in his hand, so Aiden figured it would be. "Yeah, that would make me really smart. If I had. But you were the one who put that idea in my head."

The sound of cartoons drowned out nearly everything in Aiden's world.

"Still brilliant," Elizabeth said, raising her voice to be heard over the din. "Why are we going to Etta's?"

"So your mom and I can get away for a couple of days."

He tried to glance at Gwen again, but she was across the room talking to Milo. Fighting with him over the remote. Probably trying to turn down the volume, or get him to.

"Well, that's good," Elizabeth said. "You and my mom *should* get away."

"You think so?"

"Yeah. You've been really, really patient. You know. With Milo and me."

"No patience required for *you*," he said, fairly quietly.

Unfortunately, just as he said it, the TV volume came down ten notches or so. And everybody heard Aiden's private words.

"Teach me to check the water troughs," Elizabeth said. Brightly and suddenly. As if adult enough to know that the conversation needed a decisive turn.

"I need to take a shower first," Gwen said. "If both of you are going someplace, you need to wait while I take a shower. Please. Because I need somebody to be with Milo while I'm in the bathroom."

"He can come with us," Elizabeth said.

"Can he?" Gwen caught Aiden's eye as she asked it.

"Yeah. Fine. If he'll go," Aiden said.

"He doesn't get a choice," Elizabeth said. "Let me just get dressed, and then I'll put him in the truck, and then we're going."

———

They stood on the crest of a hill, in the dry tan rattlesnake grass, several yards from the parked truck. Staring into a watering trough in the corner of the farthest pasture. All three of them.

"I like the sound this grass makes," Elizabeth said. "The way these little . . . what are they? These droopy tops. Seed pods? They look a little like wheat. Not exactly, but a little. I like the sound they make in the wind."

"Something like seed pods," Aiden said. "They call this rattlesnake grass." Out of the corner of his eye Aiden saw Milo jump at the word. "Because of that sound," he added quickly. "It makes a rattling sound when the wind blows it. Or when you walk through it."

Milo extended both hands away from his sides, about waist high, and began to walk around in the grass, brushing against its tops to create more of the rattling sound. He stopped short when he saw cattle.

The cattle were drawing in closer, because Aiden was here. About forty head of them. The presence of people often meant the presence of hay. Aiden watched to be sure they stopped well short of the boy.

They did.

They stood about twenty paces away, staring with fixed gazes and lazily moving jaws. Big, dark, liquid eyes.

Aiden turned his attention back to Elizabeth and the trough.

"So, you see, it has this valve. Right here." Aiden wrapped his hand around the valve, which involved plunging it into the cold water. His hands had finally stopped shaking, he noted. "The valve has a float. When the water level goes down, the float goes down." Aiden yanked down on the float, pressing it below the surface. Water flowed into the tank with an audible hiss. "So then the water comes on. Fills it back up. And when the float goes up to the right level, the water turns off." He let go of the float and it popped back up to the surface. The hiss of flowing water fell silent. "So you look at the level of the water to be sure it's full, but it never hurts to work the valve by hand like I just did. Make sure it's not sticking. And that sound you just heard? The sound of water flowing? If you hear that when you come up to the tank, there's a leak somewhere. In this drought, we can't afford leaks."

"Got it," she said. "That's easy."

Aiden straightened up and turned to check on the boy. To his alarm, Milo had walked closer to the cattle. Much too close. He stood at nearly arm's length from a black-and-white cow and her calf. And the calf was looking inclined to take a step closer.

Aiden opened his mouth to yell the word "no." To tell Milo to slowly, calmly back up.

He never got that far.

Before he could even push out a word, Milo threw both hands in the air and rushed at the baby calf.

"Boo!" he shouted.

The calf spun on its haunches and skittered away.

Milo turned to Aiden, a small, twisted smile on his face. He cupped his hands around his mouth and shouted, "I didn't hurt him. I just scared him."

But while his back was turned to the cattle, the mother of the calf burst into defensive action. Which Aiden had known, for a split second, to expect. Because Aiden felt her rage.

"Milo!" Aiden yelled, and sprinted for the boy. "Milo, look out!"

Milo spun around to see what the danger might be. And saw it. Immediately. The cow was bearing down on Milo fast, seeming prepared to both stomp him into the ground and ram him with her head at the same time.

Before Aiden could take three sprinting strides she was on the boy, stamping hard at his sandaled feet. Aiden heard Milo let out a bellow of pain. Then she hit him hard in the chest with her forehead, and Milo went down.

The cow spun in her rage and came around full circle. And moved in fast to finish off the dangerous boy.

Aiden reached them. But he was still not sure if he had reached them in time. Aiden was leaning down, trying to grab a piece of Milo's white shirt, and the cow was moving in for the kill.

It was a toss-up. No one could have known at that moment. It was impossible to guess which would happen first.

Aiden grabbed a handful of shirt in his fist. He pulled hard. The cow's cloven hooves came down and landed in bare dirt. The shirt ripped, and the boy fell free again. But Aiden had moved Milo just far enough to make the cow miss.

He stood tall between the downed boy and the cow, raised his hands high—making himself threatening and big—and shouted at the animal.

"Git! Go on!"

The cow froze for a moment. Aiden looked into her eyes. She was furious. Rabid with anger. Aiden could feel it. She might be about to go after him, too. There was nothing he could do but hang in that moment and see.

What felt like minutes later, but might have been a second or two, she turned her head away. Broke off that deadly gaze. That's when Aiden knew it was over.

He scooped up the injured boy and slung Milo over his shoulder in a fireman's carry.

Then he looked back at the cattle.

The aggrieved cow had retreated now. Settled. She had gone back to her calf and was offering solace.

Aiden jogged all the way back to the fence and scrambled over, boy and all. He paid no attention to the fact that the barbed wire tore at his palms and made him bleed.

———

"Well," Gwen said. With a long, deep sigh. "There goes our vacation."

She sat on a hard plastic bench beside Aiden in the waiting area of the emergency room at the county hospital. That same familiar waiting room.

He looked over at her face and watched it twist with revulsion and shame.

"Oh my God," she said. "Oh, Aiden, please don't ever tell anybody I said that. I can't believe I even said that. I must be the worst mother in the history of the world. I am a terrible, terrible person."

"You're not," he said. "Not at all. You're a great mother. You're just upset and tired."

He looked up to see Elizabeth walk back into the room carrying a can of soda and a packet of peanuts from the vending machine. Beside him, he heard Gwen begin to cry. Quiet but audible.

"He'll be okay, Mom. It's just his foot. It's not anything he could . . . you know. He won't die from it or anything. It could've been bad. But Aiden didn't let it be. He was like a superhero."

And on that final, lovely word, two uniformed sheriff's deputies appeared in the doorway behind her. One was Jed Donovan, the other his sometimes-partner, Walter Mann. Walter was a tall, thin man with dark hair and a nervous tic under one eye. Quiet compared to Jed. Then again, just about everybody was.

"Well, well," Jed said, locking eyes with Aiden. "Anybody else got a spooky sense of déjà vu?"

Jed waited, as if expecting Aiden to say something in his own defense. But Aiden had been silenced by his own luck. His own life. The way his circumstances seemed to spiral downward, then break through the floor of what Aiden had assumed was the absolute lowest he could go. And spiral down further.

When he grew tired of waiting, Jed said, "Walt, you question the girl. And then the boy, when the doctors're done with him. But not in the same room. Separately. I'm gonna take our suspect here downtown."

He moved toward Aiden, and Aiden stood and prepared for the inevitability of this next undignified moment. For a flash of a second, he swore he saw Jed place one palm on the handcuffs hanging from his uniform belt. But the hand moved away again. Aiden had been wrong.

Or Jed had thought better of the idea. Jed took him by one elbow and led him to the open waiting room doorway. Aiden heard Gwen and Elizabeth arguing with the deputies. Pleading his case, most likely. But the words only sounded jumbled and far away.

"Downtown?" Aiden asked on the walk. "What the hell is downtown? This place doesn't have a downtown."

"Don't be a smart-ass, Aiden. You knew what I meant and you know it. Now cut the crap and come with me."

———

Aiden waited for what felt like hours in a drab, tiny room. Just a worn and scratched table with an uncomfortable chair on either side. There was no clock to help him judge the passing of time. Aiden wondered if that was purposefully done—a way to make the subject of their questioning feel his life ticking away without ever being able to gauge how much of it was sliding through his fingers.

Aiden's stomach jittered as he waited. His hands were shaking again, but he was so used to that by now that he was only just barely aware of it. More obvious to him was the fact that they were bandaged—that he had several stitches in two places on each palm, where the barbed wire had torn deeply into his skin. And that they hurt. He had said no to painkillers, and his palms stung and throbbed.

He fully expected to be handcuffed and taken to jail when Jed returned. On the one hand, it was all circumstantial. Just a bunch of coincidences. On the other hand, Aiden figured people went to jail over coincidences all the time. He just never guessed he would be one of them. *I suppose nobody ever does,* he thought, at the same moment Jed burst back through the door.

"Okay," Jed said.

He sat down on the chair across from Aiden. Then he leaned back, causing the chair to creak ominously, and propped his feet up on the table. It struck Aiden as overplaying his hand in the body language department. Jed had a cigar in his mouth, but it was unlit. In fact, it had clearly never been lit. Jed chewed at the base of it. Aiden assumed there was no smoking in the sheriff's office. If it had been allowed, he figured he'd be breathing noxious fumes right now.

Aiden didn't respond. What do you say to answer the word "okay"?

"Well now," the deputy said. "If that story you told me in the car is the truth, the whole truth, and nothing but the truth . . ." He paused. Chewed. "Then your new girlfriend's son is one stupid-ass little boy."

Aiden felt his jaw drop. Literally. "Hey," he said.

"What?"

"Don't be talking about Milo that way."

Jed pulled the cigar free from his teeth. It was grotesquely chewed at the base, and slick with saliva. It made Aiden a little queasy to look at it.

"Surprised to hear you say that," Jed said.

"Why would you be? It was a pretty rotten thing to say."

It struck Aiden that he had never much liked Jed Donovan. Seemed like something he would have known, and a thing that would not strike suddenly. Aiden had known the man for years, but only at the periphery of his life. He had never had any call to form much of an opinion. Jed was simply there. And Jed was what Jed had always been. But as the grind of Jed's tactlessness and overall unlikability settled in on Aiden, it came as no real surprise.

"I guess I more or less thought we were on the same page about the kid. So you don't think he's stupid? You have a right to your opinion. Just curious, I guess."

"I think . . . I think he was naïve. About cattle. He's never lived on a ranch before. I guess he thought they were spooky. Didn't realize they stand up for their young. But no. I don't think he's stupid. I think he's a smart boy. He just has problems."

"You can say that twice," Jed said, and then stuck the cigar back between his molars again.

"If you knew everything he's been through, you might see him with different eyes," Aiden said.

Then he hoped it was true, what he had just said. He was guessing. Taking Gwen's word for things. He hoped when he learned the truth about Milo's past he wouldn't be sorry he'd stuck his neck out.

"Be that as it may," Jed said, and then creaked his chair dangerously again. He was a lot of man on not much chair. But it was holding his weight for now. Aiden noted that the phrase "be that as it may" was usually only the first half of a thought. But not for Jed Donovan. The deputy struck off in a completely different direction. "While we're on the subject of why people do the things they do . . ." Jed paused for an awkward length of time. As though he'd given Aiden enough of a hint, and Aiden could now take over the conversation. But Aiden had no idea what he was driving at. "You take my advice about that . . . mental health professional?"

"As a matter of fact, yes. I did."

"Good to hear, Aiden. Good to hear. You want to tell me the person's name?"

"My psychiatrist?"

"Yes, that."

"Do you have a right to ask me that?"

"Yes and no. I can ask anything I damn please. You're under no legal obligation to answer. But let's just say if you cough up a name I'll be inclined to believe it's the truth that you're seeing somebody. If you won't answer the question, I'm left to wonder. If you know what I mean."

*A child would know what you mean,* Aiden thought. Jed was anything but subtle.

"Dr. Hannah Rutledge," Aiden said. "She has an office in Bakersfield."

"I'm sure she does," Jed replied. "I'll look her up in the white pages, of course, but I'm sure she does. So what did you find out?"

"Excuse me?"

"This big change you went through recently. What does this Dr. Hannah Rutledge think about it?"

Aiden just sat a moment, noticing that his mouth was open. He pressed his hands more deeply between his thighs to hide the shaking. Of course it was a mistake. It hurt terribly. It was all he could do to stifle a cry of pain.

"Isn't that between me and my psychiatrist?"

To Aiden's surprise, Jed broke into a wide good-old-boy grin. "Can't blame a guy for asking."

"I think maybe you can," Aiden said. "If a person couldn't do it, then I wouldn't be doing it right now."

Then he kicked himself for saying it. Because he was more or less at the mercy of Jed Donovan. But with guys like Jed, it didn't pay to be meek. They seemed to smell the weakness and move in for the kill.

Before Aiden had time to learn Jed's reaction to his words, the door opened from the outside. Aiden swung his head around and saw Walter Mann stick his head into the room.

"Jed, can I talk to you?"

Jed creaked his chair forward into a normal position and hauled his considerable bulk upright. He leaned over toward Aiden as he walked by, which made Aiden wince.

"Don't go 'way," he said.

Jed laughed, as though that had been a merry little joke they could all enjoy. Then he locked Aiden into the room alone.

———

"Seems you're free to go," Jed said, bursting back in. Startling Aiden. He sounded almost . . . disappointed.

Aiden stood and flexed his hands gently, feeling as he did that they were still shaking. He wondered how many days or weeks they would shake this time. Before he could shrug all this off and settle again.

He did not say anything in reply.

"You don't even want to know why I sprung you?" Jed asked as Aiden headed for the door.

Aiden stopped. Turned. Scratched his head.

"Yeah. I guess I do. Just seems like, when a guy like you says I'm free to go . . . I don't know. I figured that's not a moment to hang around and ask too many questions. But, yeah. Fine. I'll bite. Why am I suddenly being believed?"

"Well, all three of you had the same story. First off. Not proof positive, because you could've told them what to say on the way to the hospital. But Walt didn't think so. He didn't think the boy sounded rehearsed. Said he was pretty anxious to get the story out. Talked Walt's ear off, in fact."

"Milo? Talked somebody's ear off?"

"Yeah, I was surprised, too. Seems the kid was pretty impressed with you because you saved him."

"He couldn't have thought I would just leave him to get killed."

"You'd have to talk to Walt about that. Or Milo." As he spoke, Jed looked down at a folder he'd set on the table in front of him. Not up at Aiden at any point. Aiden wondered if Jed would have looked him dead in the face if he'd gotten to make an arrest. If he didn't have to let Aiden go. "Thing is, kid kept saying he saw you out of the corner of his eye, and he never saw anybody move that fast in his life. Girl said the same thing. Said you were like a superhero, moving at superspeed. Of course, she already thinks the sun rises and sets on you. Milo, now, he seems less inclined to be your fan. But today . . . I think the feeling Walt got is that the kid thought . . . the boy, I mean . . . you know . . . it being Milo and all, and all the trouble he's prone to causing . . . that he sort of expected you might have slowed your step just the tiniest bit.

Anyway, that wasn't the corker. The doctor sealed it for us. Said the kid has a bruise on the top of his foot that's a perfect outline of a cloven hoof. So there's no doubt that the damage was done by . . . well, I want to be perfectly politically correct like you're supposed to be these days, so let's just say a Bovine American."

He paused, half glanced up at Aiden, and seemed to leave space for Aiden to laugh. Aiden didn't laugh. Somehow hearing a good old boy make fun of political correctness did not strike Aiden as funny.

He realized Jed was looking more or less at his shaking hands, so Aiden slid them into his jeans pockets as gently as possible.

"Anyway," Jed continued, "the damage was consistent with said hoof being jammed down on the kid's foot at the same time as he got knocked over. Bunch of muscles and tendons torn right at the edge of that bruise. So there's just not a lot of leeway on what happened."

"Okay," Aiden said. "Good." He turned to leave. But then he stopped in the open doorway. Leaned on the doorjamb, one hand still in his pocket, the fingertips of the other pressed firmly to the wood to quiet the shaking. "Just one question, though, Jed. If all you had to do was talk to the doctor to find out what kind of injury it was, couldn't you have done that first?"

"First?"

"Before you dragged me in here like a common criminal. Yeah. How did you even get called in on this? If the doctor could tell what the injury was by looking?"

He was pushing his luck now, and he knew it. He should just go. But somehow a line had to be drawn in the sand. Because Aiden sensed they could walk through the steps of this troubling dance again if he wasn't careful. And if his life wouldn't give him a break.

"Actually, we . . . didn't exactly get called. We were at the hospital for a different reason and we saw you carry the boy in. Look. Aiden. It's like this, my friend." They were not friends, but Aiden let it go by. "A few minutes ago you were talking like you wanted to stick up for that kid. So if we have a choice of going too hard on a person who might be abusing him, or not going hard enough, which do you prefer we do?"

"I guess that's a valid point," Aiden said. "I just wish you'd been around when his father was abusing him."

"You and me both, Aiden. You and me both. I would've given that son of a bitch a taste of his own medicine."

An image flooded into Aiden's head. Milo, standing in his front yard with a lasso around his neck. Aiden's knuckles white on the knot.

"That never works," Aiden said.

Jed's eyes came up. Questioning. But Aiden knew he would never make Jed see the point, and he didn't intend to try. So he just walked out.

———

Walter Mann drove him back to the hospital.

"So what did Milo say to you, exactly?" Aiden asked in the first block or two of the drive.

Walter sighed. Aiden watched Walt's hands flex and release on the steering wheel. Flex and release. Another nervous tic?

"He described what happened," Walt said. "Same as you and his sister described it. He was feeling kind of embarrassed about it. He kept saying, 'I thought I could scare the cow. But it turned out the cow scared me.' He was almost laughing about it, but you could tell he felt the fool. Why?"

"It's just kind of odd. Usually he never says much of anything to anybody. Not if he can help it."

"Yeah, that's what Jed said. But he was talking a blue streak today. He knows he almost died. He gets that. You can tell. I think that's why he was so talky. Still all full of that adrenaline from looking death in the eye. It's not lost on him that you saved him. But it's more than that. More than just your saving him. Seems like you did the impossible to save him. Or the near impossible, anyway. I don't think he knew you held him in high enough regard to work so hard for him. I don't think he thought anybody did. I'm sorry we had you under suspicion. But you know how it is. At least I hope you do. What'd the boy want to go and scare a cow for, anyway?"

Aiden stared out the window, watching the town flash by. His town. The place he'd lived almost all his life. The place where he'd thought people knew him. Trusted him. But maybe even Aiden hadn't known Aiden until recently.

"Hard to say, Walt. He's different. I'll give you that. He didn't exactly scare a cow. He scared a calf. Little baby calf. And the mother went after him for it."

"He didn't tell me *that*. He made it sound like he scared a big, fat, dangerous cow."

"No, he was picking on someone more his own size. But I can see how he'd be embarrassed to say."

"I suppose." Walt pulled up in front of the hospital emergency room and shifted his squad car into "Park." "I'm sorry for your trouble with us today, Aiden. We try to get it right, but it doesn't work every trip out of the gate."

Aiden sat silent for a moment, feeling his palms throb with pain.

"Now would it have killed Jed to say that to me?"

"You know how he is, Aiden."

"I suppose."

Aiden climbed out of the car and shut the door carefully. Put the whole ugly incident behind him. At least, as best he could.

———

"You just missed the doctor," Gwen said when he sat down at her side again. "Is everything okay with the sheriff?"

"Yeah. Fine."

He leaned over to give her a kiss on the cheek but she turned her head toward him and offered her lips instead.

"Good," she said when their lips parted. "I don't even see why they hauled you in. It was perfectly clear what happened. You saved his life."

"They're looking out for the boy. They do that with kids. Give them the benefit of any doubt. Anyway, I got a decent apology. So what did the doctor say?"

He watched her face fall. *Collapse* would be a better word.

"Oh, it's bad, Aiden. It's a mess. He has a bunch of bones in his foot that are not so much broken as . . . well, crushed. And a very complicated fracture in his ankle from being knocked down while his foot was pinned. And a bunch of torn ligaments. They're going to have to do surgery."

"Oh," Aiden said. He wanted to say more, but he couldn't imagine what. He wanted to say, "Sounds expensive," but it seemed unforgivable to prioritize money that way. He wanted to ask if she was coming apart, but he couldn't think how to approach it. "When?" was all he could manage.

"Maybe this afternoon. We're waiting to find out. And look. Aiden. You had nothing to do with this. You don't need to bail us out this time."

"Not true," Aiden said, and shook his head too vigorously, and too many times. "I had everything to do with it. I was the one in charge of watching him."

"You were just a handful of steps away from him. It was all him. It was not you at all. Who runs at a cow and yells 'Boo'?"

And, at that strange juncture of events, Gwen began to cry openly.

"I hate to even ask, but how much longer do you have to work at the market before health insurance kicks in?"

"Almost another month. But it'll be okay. At least, I think it will. I've been thinking we'll apply for some kind of government assistance. But just . . . keep your fingers crossed I don't make too much to qualify."

"No," Aiden said. "No. It's not going to be like that."

"You can't cover this, Aiden. It's going to be huge."

"I'll sell the rest of my cattle. That's all. It's silly not to."

He looked up to see Elizabeth standing over their bench.

"I'm hungry again," she said. "Can I go to the cafeteria?"

"Sure, honey," Gwen said, still crying.

"Can you come with me? I hate to eat in a place like that all by myself."

"I have to stay here in case the doctor comes back," Gwen said. "But Aiden is the same way. So he knows just how you feel. Why, we maybe wouldn't even be together right now if he could walk into a restaurant by himself. So he'll go with you. Won't you, Aiden?"

"I would love to," Aiden said. "It's almost three in the afternoon and I haven't even had breakfast yet."

"Wait for him in the hall a minute," Gwen said. "Okay, honey?"

Elizabeth backed up a few steps, then turned and walked out of the room. Aiden waited, feeling a bit frozen, to hear what Gwen didn't want to say in front of the girl.

"I'm not sure I can ask you to do that with the cattle, Aiden. I know everything that's involved with it. You know. For you. On the . . . emotional side."

"It's as good as done, Gwen. We'll go away when all this dies down, and I'll have somebody come get them while we're gone. They're not a bunch of giant pets. I don't know what I think I'm doing with them. When fall comes I'd have to get a job just to feed them. No. I'm not a cattle rancher anymore. The cattle need to go."

# Chapter Nineteen

## Hope Wildly

Hannah was wearing a green jacket at their next session. A tailored blazer in a deep, rich shade that made something buzz in Aiden's chest. It was a strangely comforting sensation.

He had been here for almost fifteen minutes, telling her about the week's developments, but had just realized that the deep jewel tone reminded him of the green shards of pot that Milo was using in his art project at home. But there was more involved in his reaction to the color than that. He just couldn't get a bead on what it meant to him.

He didn't realize he'd been staring. He hadn't meant to stare.

"I give up," Hannah said. "Do I have a stain? Missing button?"

"Oh. No. Sorry. It's just that color. Partly it's the color of some of the pots in Milo's mosaic. Well. Former pots. But it's more than that. But I can't say what exactly. I just have a reaction to the color."

"That's not unusual," Hannah said.

"It's not?"

"No, not at all. Colors evoke feelings in people. Even if they're not consciously aware of it. Why do you think people have a favorite color? So, just clarify one thing for me. Milo is at home working on a mosaic tabletop *right now*? Didn't he have a very complicated surgery on his foot just a few days ago?"

"Yes. And yes. And I was surprised too."

"And his arm is still in a cast?"

"No, that's off now."

"Oh. Still. You'd think he'd have his foot up on a pillow and be resting."

"Well . . . ," Aiden began.

He stared out the window, breaking off his relationship with deep green. A woman in an office building across the street was standing with her hands on the glass, staring out onto the street. She was too far away for Aiden to see much more than that, but her body language made him feel lonely. He pulled his attention back into Hannah's office.

"He *is* resting *the foot*. He sits on the Persian carpet in the living room with his foot up on a pillow. But his legs are under the coffee table. And then when he moves from one area of the mosaic to another, somebody has to help him move. His mother or Elizabeth or the baby-sitter. I haven't seen him doing this with my own eyes. I've just been told about it. He seems to want to work on the mosaic in private as much as possible. He's very . . . *determined* about the project."

"How does it look?"

"I have no idea. He won't let me see it. I went over there to see how he was doing, and he wouldn't let his mom answer the door until they'd covered up the project with a drop cloth. So I guess she's seen however much of it he's done. And maybe Elizabeth has seen it. He doesn't have much choice about that. It's a small cabin. But he told me very firmly that *I* can't see it."

"Did you ask him why not?"

"I did. He said, 'It's not good enough yet.'"

"Ah," Hannah said, and scribbled a few brief notes. "A perfectionist. Poor kid. Have you thought more about whether to bring him in here?"

"Yes. We're going to. But Gwen wants to wait until she's been working long enough at the market for their insurance to kick in. I've covered them for the two hospital visits, because I really felt like the accidents were at least partly my fault. But she won't let me cover this. Believe me, I've tried."

"Did you ask if she's ever gotten him any kind of counseling?"

"Yes. She has. Or she tried to, anyway. It was when they were living with her husband. He was dead set against it. Vehemently against it. She had to take Milo in secret. She had to save the money from her household budget and sneak him into the appointments while her husband was at work. It was hard, but she did it for months. And then the therapist told her that Milo wasn't saying a word and he didn't think the sessions were accomplishing anything. And then a week or two later she took the kids and left."

He waited in silence while she scribbled. The conversation had turned away from something that felt important to Aiden. He wanted a chance to turn it back.

"That thing Milo told me," Aiden said. "About how I couldn't see his project until it's good enough. I've been thinking about that a lot. I feel like . . . like maybe he's saying . . . maybe he doesn't even mean to let on, but . . ." *Sooner or later you have to spit this out,* he told himself. "It seems like he wants to impress me now. Since I hauled him out of that bind with the cow. It seems like he's saying he wants to put his best foot forward for me on this art project, and do something I'll think is great. Which seems like kind of a breakthrough in our relationship. But then I think, well, maybe I shouldn't get too wrapped up in that idea. Because if I'm wrong . . ."

Aiden couldn't manage to finish the thought.

"It'll break your heart," Hannah said, sounding surprisingly matter-of-fact for such a weighty pronouncement of gloom.

"So that's why I think I shouldn't get too wrapped up in believing it."

Hannah set down her notepad. Leaned back in her chair. She had a cup of tea on a side table next to her elbow, and she picked it up and sipped at it. Aiden figured the tea must be cold by now. He stared at her jacket once more, and the deep green made his chest buzz. Again. It helped just a little.

"I know you don't have a lot of parenting experience," Hannah said. "So let me lay my thoughts out for you like this. You hope for the best for your kids. You want them to be happy, and you want to feel close to them and help them. So when you see them moving in what you think is a good direction, or think you see it, you hope. You hope wildly. And, as a result, having a child tends to mean getting your heart broken on a regular basis. It takes courage to hope for something you know you might not get. But the alternative is not to believe in your child or hope for great things for him. So I'm a big fan of the heartbreak method myself."

—

Aiden stood in the dirt, in the early morning light, not far outside the cabin door. Waiting. His pickup truck idled nearby, its driver's-side door wide open.

It was a little early to be making good on that trip he and Gwen had planned. Maybe. Then again, it felt as though they had been needing it for a long time. In fact, it felt as though they'd been needing it for years, which was impossible since they had only known each other for months. But still that strong feeling hovered.

After a minute or so of waiting, the door creaked open and Elizabeth stuck her head out.

"We have a slight . . . ," she began, ". . . well, what my mom called a complication."

"Okay. What sort of complication have we got?"

"He won't go to Etta's without his mosaic project."

Aiden felt his eyebrows inch up. "The whole coffee table?"

"Right."

"We could put it in the bed of the truck."

"Right. That's what we were hoping you'd say. But he won't do that until we get it all covered up. And I mean covered up so the wind can't blow the cover off it when we drive. Because then you would see it."

"And it's not good enough yet."

"Right."

"Okay. I'll stand here. You guys do the covering part. I can get it on the truck when the time is right."

"Thanks."

Her head disappeared and the door slammed shut.

Aiden stretched his neck and back while he waited. He looked down at the palms of his hands. The stitches had come out just the day before.

He glanced at his watch. They would be half an hour late getting out of town. He felt himself ruffle over that. Then he silently let it go. They would get to the coast when they got there, and being tense about it was exactly the opposite of everything the trip represented.

The door opened again, startling him slightly. He had been lost in thought.

Gwen slid out and pulled the door closed behind her. She threw her arms around his neck and kissed him on the cheek. Then she pulled back, dropped her arms, and looked into his face.

"It's too soon," she said. "Isn't it?" Her face twisted into something like a self-deprecating smile. "Or am I just being a mother?"

"Not sure," Aiden said. He cupped his hand around his mouth and shouted, "Elizabeth! Milo! Come out here a minute, please."

For a surprising length of time nothing happened. Even knowing there were crutches involved, it still seemed like too much delay.

Then the door swung wide. Milo stood braced on his crutches in the doorway, Elizabeth at his side. Milo had come out of the surgery with external metal rods holding the bones in place, with pins that went right through the skin. But the whole contraption was wrapped in something like a loose elastic bandage. Partly to keep it clean. Partly so no one had to freak themselves out by looking at it.

Aiden looked beyond them to see the coffee table covered in an old sheet and many wraps of duct tape.

"What?" Milo asked.

"Is it too soon?"

"Is what too soon?" Elizabeth asked.

"For us to go away. It hasn't even been quite two weeks since Milo's surgery. So I think your mom needs you to tell her it's okay." Then he took a deep breath, let go of his expectations and his anticipation of the trip, and added, "But only if it's the truth."

"It's not too early for me," Elizabeth said.

All eyes turned to Milo.

"I don't *care*," he said, as though all of this was simply too irritating and too slow. "Here or Etta's. It doesn't matter. I just want to work on my *mosaic*."

———

The hardest part of the trip to Etta's was getting Milo's foot in a position that he could sustain. Hanging off over the edge of the truck seat did not work out. It made the boy yelp with pain—just the weight of his foot, and the metal structure that supported it, pulling down on that broken ankle.

After experimenting with positioning Milo's rump off the front of the seat, feet resting on the mats, Aiden ended up seating Elizabeth in the middle and Milo on the outside with his back against the door, his feet propped up on his sister's lap.

"Is it back there?" Milo asked as Aiden pulled away. The boy craned his neck to try to see into the bed of the truck.

"Milo," Aiden said. "You watched me put it back there with your own eyes."

"I just *asked*," Milo said, a bit whiny.

Aiden mostly watched the road as he drove to the gate. But one time he glanced over at the boy, who was staring at the side of Aiden's face. Milo quickly cut his eyes away.

As he stepped out to open the gate, Aiden looked up to see a couple dozen head of his cattle grazing in the distance. At the top of a hill, under a stand of scrub oaks.

"I'm sorry," he said, barely above a whisper.

He might have been talking to the cattle, or he might have been talking to the late Harris Delacorte. It was hard to tell.

Then he turned his attention back to the task at hand.

Five times on the drive over to Etta's Aiden glanced over to see if Milo was staring at him. Five times Milo was, but quickly looked away.

———

Aiden and Gwen were driving down the 101 freeway over the Cuesta Grade—south before turning west again to the ocean—when he decided it might be better to question her silence. He had been going back and forth about it for dozens of miles. The discomfort growing in his gut finally overpowered him. He had to speak.

"You seem far away," he said.

She was staring out the passenger window, her head turned mostly away from him. Aiden could see wisps of her dark hair and the set of her jaw, but not much more. If he took his eyes off the road for a moment, he could see muscles working in that jaw. As though she were grinding her molars together.

For a strange and upsetting length of time she didn't respond.

Then, quite suddenly, as if sputtering up to the surface from a deep sleep, she turned her face to him.

"Wait. What?"

"Where were you?"

"Sorry. Did you just say something?"

"I said you seem far away."

"Oh. Right. I'm sorry, Aiden."

She reached across the seat and offered her hand for Aiden to hold. He took it. The roiling turmoil in his midsection drained away, just like that. Like water out of a tub when the plug is pulled. It swirled down the drain and it was gone.

"I've never left the kids," she said. "Thirteen years."

"I figured that was it."

"Oh, I mean I've *left* them. Obviously. To work. Only recently, though. Before I left home, I never had a babysitter. I was the babysitter. Always. My husband worked and I didn't. I stayed home with the kids. And he wasn't big on going out, either, my husband. So it would be the three of us during the day and all four of us at night."

A silence fell. Aiden felt compelled to fill it.

"What was his name?"

"My husband?"

"Yeah."

"Milo. The Milo you know is actually Milo Junior. But we dropped the Junior when we left home. Because there's no chance of confusion anymore. Why?"

"No reason," he said as they passed the sign that stated they were entering San Luis Obispo. "Just making conversation."

It wasn't entirely true. He wanted to get the measure of the man somehow, the way he might if presented with a photograph. He wasn't sure how the name helped, but it seemed the only available measurement.

Another long silence. From the north end of the college town to its southern border.

Then Gwen said, "I know I'm supposed to put all this aside. That's the point of the trip. That I'm so worn down from the kids . . . well, the kid . . . and I need a break from that. But I just keep feeling like something terrible could be happening."

"Why?"

"Because it's *Milo*."

"Oh," Aiden said. "Yeah. But you have your cell phone right where you could hear it, don't you?"

"Oh. Right. Yeah."

"So if Etta's not calling, then nothing terrible is happening. Right?"

Aiden heard nothing for a second or two, then a long, deep sigh.

"I'll settle down and enjoy this trip, Aiden. I will. I swear I will. Just . . . please, can you be patient with me if it takes me a silly length of time?"

"I'll be patient with you no matter what it takes," he said.

———

They lay together in a hotel bed in Avila Beach, on impossibly clean and crisp sheets. Aiden had one arm thrown over her, his chest pressed up against her back. He could feel her breathing through the soft motion of her shoulder blades.

In that moment every cell in Aiden's body, every inch of his internal landscape, felt clear and smooth. If he had been asked, he would have been unable to remember anything like a care or worry. If asked what troubled him, he might have puzzled over the word, no longer able to recall its definition.

He wasn't sure if Gwen was asleep. So it surprised him a little when she spoke.

"I'm going to tell you this now," she said, "because you're not looking at me. And I can only tell you this when you're not looking at me."

Aiden felt the muscles all through his abdomen tighten. He wondered if Gwen felt it, too. *Maybe that was my vacation,* he thought. *Maybe that's all the happiness I get.*

"Milo's dad . . . ," she began. Then she stalled for a time. But at least Aiden knew where she was headed. "He was hard on Milo, at least as he got bigger. Not so much on anybody else. He really singled Milo out. Elizabeth he loved. I think he loved Milo, too, but in this . . . *fierce* way. In this way that made the poor kid a lightning rod for everything he—my husband—didn't like about himself. He was hard on me, but verbally and emotionally. He never raised a hand to me. But he screamed at Milo and hit him. And in really unpredictable ways. Like Milo would do some little nothing thing . . . say something that was never meant to offend his dad, and my husband would stew over it for hours and then haul Milo out of bed in the middle of the night and smack him around. I know I should have done something. I knew it. But they loved each other. I swear they did. In both directions. It was just . . . in such a toxic way."

A pause. Aiden thought maybe he was supposed to fill it, so he did.

"That's why you don't want me looking at you. Because you're worried I'm thinking it's your fault for not leaving sooner."

"Well . . . yeah. *I* think that. So why wouldn't you?"

"I don't think it was your fault. I think it was his fault."

"I think it's both."

"What tipped the scales? Why did you finally leave?"

Aiden could feel her back change. The muscles tightened. Her breath froze into something that barely moved. The way Aiden's used to do. "I was seeing a counselor. Like I told you when I first met you. And she helped me with knowing I needed to leave. But I didn't leave right away. I . . . kind of . . . stuck for a time. And then Elizabeth told me something. Something I didn't know. But I should have known it. It was my job to know. It was my job to protect him. So much would be different if I had known. I should have known."

In the silence that followed, Aiden tried to hold her closer, more lovingly, to see if he could soften any part of her. But now she was made of gemstones and concrete. He didn't know when she would finally tell him what it was, but he knew she would—that she would not have started this if she didn't plan to go there. So he just waited, though the time seemed to stretch out forever. He felt as though someone had left him to hold something heavy, an anvil or a safe, until they came back to relieve him of it. He could feel himself growing shaky with the strain.

"Elizabeth told me he was going into Milo's room at night. And staying maybe twenty minutes. But a quiet thing. Not like hauling him out of bed to slap him around and yell at him. And then after he left she could hear Milo sobbing for the rest of the night. I guess she had insomnia by then, which was not too surprising."

Aiden could hear that she was crying. He wanted to do something to help. Anything. Wipe her tears away, at least. But nothing moved. And there was nothing he could do to help with this. It had happened. And now Gwen had to live with it. And Milo had to live with it. And nothing Aiden said or did would lift it away.

"I didn't want to believe it," she said. "But I took him to a doctor. And he examined him. You know. For signs. Of . . . And it was true. There was physical evidence . . ."

She never finished the sentence. Then again, she didn't need to.

As her words and their meaning sank in, something strange began to happen in Aiden's head and chest and gut. They filled with guilt. Guilt over not having protected Milo. Not being his champion and setting his life on a better course. But he hadn't been there. He hadn't even known Milo. But the feeling was so complete and so real. The grief was so utterly overwhelming. Debilitating.

It took a good minute or two before Aiden could understand that it was Gwen's guilt and grief. But Aiden was experiencing it. That had never happened with another person before. And Aiden hadn't thought it ever would. He had not seen this development coming.

He instinctively pulled his arm back from around her and rolled away.

He heard her sobs grow louder and more pronounced.

"You *do* blame me," she said.

"I don't. I absolutely don't. I blame him. You left as soon as you found out. I mean . . . didn't you?"

"Oh, God yes. That same day."

"I don't blame you."

*But* you *blame you,* he thought. He didn't say it.

"Then why did you pull away?"

"I just felt so bad for Milo I couldn't stand it," he said.

———

They sat outdoors on an upstairs patio of their hotel, drinking coffee and preparing to order breakfast. A surprisingly cold wind blew off the water, and Aiden stared transfixed at the view of the harbor at Port San Luis, with its long wooden pier and its breakwater jetty, dozens of dots of sailboats moored in between.

He knew he should feel light and happy. Free of the pressures of his life back home. He felt nothing of the sort. Instead, the image of Milo trapped in his room in the dark, helpless, played in and out of his head. And he could feel it. He could feel the sickening fear, the pain of betrayal, the degradation.

"You okay, hon?" Gwen asked, lightly setting her hand on his. "You look a little green."

"The cattle are leaving today," he said. Which was true, even if it wasn't the primary topic on his mind. "They're probably being rounded up right now. They must be scared."

She was looking into his face. He could see that. But he did not look back.

"Can you feel that? Or are you just imagining it?"

"It's a little hard to sort out the difference," Aiden said.

———

At dusk that night they pulled up to the curb in front of Etta's home, an ancient little farmhouse with peeling sky-blue paint, shutters askew where their hinges had rusted away.

"You'd better let me go in first," Gwen said. "See where we stand with the project."

"I'll walk with you to the door anyway," Aiden said.

They stepped out of the truck into the shocking heat.

"Damn," Gwen said. "I got used to being cool and I almost forgot."

They walked down a cobblestone path together toward the door. With every step Aiden took, a pressure in his gut grew heavier. But it was more than just heavy. It was sickening. His abdomen felt clammy—a glass of ice sweating on a hot day—and unwell, as though he were incubating something like a stomach flu.

But Aiden knew he wasn't getting sick. He recognized the feeling. It had been with him all day. It accompanied any thought of poor Milo in his bed in the dark, being forced to endure pain and fear and humiliation that nobody deserved. It was the same feeling, but it was getting stronger as Aiden moved closer to the boy.

Aiden veered off the path and bent over himself for a moment, resting his scarred palms on the knees of his jeans. He breathed deeply to try to pull himself together. Gwen's hand settled on his back, warm and steady through his thin shirt.

"You okay?"

"I will be, yeah. Just felt weird for a minute there."

"You getting sick?"

"I don't think so. I hope not, anyway."

A brief silence. Then he forced himself to straighten.

"I think I know what's going on with you," she said, and he avoided her eyes in case it was true. "I think ever since I told you about Milo's abuse, you're feeling for him like you do for the animals."

He allowed his gaze to flicker up to meet hers. Then he looked down at the cobblestones again.

"Guilty as charged, I suppose. That won't make life any easier."

"Might make it better, though. In the long run, anyway. I'm sorry if it's hard for you, but it gives me hope for you two. You wait here. I'll see what's what."

She stepped away, and Aiden stood. And breathed. And watched the setting sun at the horizon, obscured on and off by the blowing leaves of Etta's trees.

"Hey," Aiden heard a small voice say. Elizabeth. "You guys have a good trip?"

"Pretty good," he said, moving closer to the girl, who stood just outside Etta's closed front door. "It was hard. Leaving all this home stuff at home. But we did our best, and I think we managed. What's going on with Milo?"

But he knew. He could feel it. Milo was in a full-on panic. Aiden just didn't know why yet.

"He's kind of melting down. The table is done. He even put the varnish on it. So now he needs to show it to us. But he's scared it's not good enough, so he's just falling apart at his seams instead."

"Do *you* think it's good?"

"I haven't seen it lately. Etta has a den and he's been able to hide it in there. You can come in. It's in the den with the door closed."

Aiden stepped up onto Etta's front stoop and followed Elizabeth into the house. Gwen was standing in the living room talking to Milo, who was on his feet. Well, foot. Leaning his armpits onto his crutches, back hunched, face red with emotion.

"Honey," Gwen said, "we either have to leave it here or take it home. Those are the only two choices."

"I want to take it *home*," Milo whined, desperate and almost nasal, "but I don't want you guys to *see* it."

"Is it as good as you can make it?" Aiden asked.

Milo looked up and saw Aiden standing there. The weight of the boy's emotion hit Aiden's belly like a hard-swung baseball bat. For a moment they just stared at each other and nothing was said.

Milo was scared, but also sad and self-loathing and disgusted with everything he did. And sure that others would share that disgust if they ever got a good look at anything that meant something to him.

Aiden wished he didn't know all that. But wishing wouldn't change much.

For several seconds they just stood in that swirl of negative emotions, the ones only Aiden knew they were sharing. The boy's face turned sunburn-red. Then Milo nodded almost imperceptibly.

"Then that's all you can do," Aiden said. "I heard you put the varnish on it and everything. So it's done. So sooner or later you have to let us see it. You just kind of have to let the chips fall where they may. Know what I mean?"

For a moment, no one moved. Or even seemed to breathe. Aiden glanced up to see Etta move into the room from the kitchen.

"If you can get him to do that," she said, "you're a better man than all of us."

"I can't watch this," Milo said.

He moved for the kitchen with surprising swiftness. He had gotten quite proficient on the crutches, swinging his bad leg above the ground as he loped along.

"But I have your permission to open the den door?"

Nothing. Silence. Milo had reached the refuge of the kitchen. And he was not talking.

"Milo?" Aiden asked again. "Permission, please?"

"*Yes,*" Milo whined, sounding angry and terrified at the same time. Aiden opened the door.

In the middle of the den sat the coffee table. Its top had become a colorful sky full of suns. Milo had created a sort of sky background out of green and blue, like the surface of a sea shifting in tone and picking up highlights. Against this backdrop half a dozen suns shone, bright red at their cores, then going to orange and then yellow at the tips of their wavy, stylized rays. If Aiden had seen it in a store or a craft shop, he never would have questioned that an adult craftsperson had done the work. And the pattern itself was deep and compelling, like a fictional world. Like a fantasy that draws you in and changes the way you see reality just in that moment while you're staring at it.

He felt a presence behind him and turned to see Gwen, Etta, and Elizabeth crowded close to his back, staring with him. And a flash of Milo. At the open kitchen doorway, Aiden saw the boy poke just enough of his head out to look with one eye.

"Milo, it's amazing," Aiden called out.

A silent moment, followed by more of Milo emerging. A crutch, and half a body. Then the boy's whole head. Aiden could feel part of the weight, the cramp of emotion, lift from his own gut.

"You think it's good?"

"I think it's great."

"You did a beautiful job, Milo," Gwen said.

"But I want to know what Aiden thinks," Milo said.

"I think I couldn't have done nearly this good a job myself. How did you get everything so even? And get the grout in there without getting any on the porcelain?"

"It's called *tesserae*," Milo said, swinging closer on his crutches. His sister and the women stepped out of his way, and Milo moved over to Aiden and stood at his side, and they stared at the table together. "And the grout does get on it. You can't help that. You just have to wipe it off real good after."

"I still don't know how you did such a perfect job."

"It's perfect?"

The boy was looking up at him. He could see it in his peripheral vision. But Aiden couldn't take his eyes off the mythical suns.

"As far as I can see."

"Well, what you do," Milo said, suddenly the expert, the artist explaining his process, "is you just keep ripping it apart again if it isn't perfect. And you just do it again and again. And you don't leave it alone and put the varnish on until it is."

For the first time since Aiden had tapped into the energy of Milo's internal crisis, the landscape of that pain held still for one brief, grateful moment.

———

"So I think I had something like another wake up," Aiden told Hannah the following day, in a session he'd called her and asked her to fit in—as an extra—if she possibly could.

He sat on her couch, perched too close to the edge. Too tentative, and a little jumpy. A sudden move could have landed him on his butt on the rug.

"I didn't realize any part of you was still asleep," she said, nibbling on the end of her pen.

"Me neither, I guess. But did you ever stop to think about the fact that I feel with animals but not with people?"

"I have. Yes."

"And what did you make of that?"

"Hard to say at this point. I guess I see it as more of a situation where we take a couple of years or more and make something of it together."

"How can you not be curious, though? Take this, for example. Think about this. Ever since I had that experience at the roundup, I haven't eaten beef. I guess I've been feeling like some kind of vibration of what the animal went through at slaughter will still be hanging around the meat. Even though I have no idea if it's true or not, because I never get very close to any. But I eat chicken and fish. Chickens and fish feel pain. They have lives. Why cut off at mammals?"

"Because you have to cut off somewhere," Hannah said.

"Why? Why have a cutoff place for empathy?"

"I would think you could answer that question better than anyone I know, Aiden. Because it consumes your whole life. It's exhausting to feel the emotions of everybody and everything around us. It's hard enough to sort out our own. But why am I speaking for you? You're going through it, so you know. Let's say, hypothetically, that you somehow manage to extend your empathy to all forms of life, including the ones that are less like us. It's always easier to feel for those who remind us of ourselves. But let's say you find yourself empathizing with birds and fish. Then you have to be a vegetarian. But why stop there? Plants have a rudimentary form of consciousness. If someone is going through a room full of plants hacking them to pieces, researchers can use instruments to record a type of alarm on the plants' part. So now you have to extend it to plants. Now you have nothing to eat. Your house will be overrun with insects and vermin, because you won't kill them. They'll infest and contaminate what food you're still able to stomach, and there won't be a thing you can do about it."

She glanced out the window as if wanting to see what Aiden found so fascinating. But he was only looking away from the truth of her words until he could digest and accept them.

Seeing nothing to hold her attention there, she continued.

"At some point you just have to start prioritizing yourself, Aiden. I think there's a tendency to take a word like *empathy*—a *concept* like it, I guess I should say—and make it black and white. Empathy equals good. Lack of empathy equals bad. Yes, it's bad to have too little. But you're walking proof that a person can also have too much. It's one of those areas where we try to strike a balance. I do have to say, though . . . I think it's a form of progress, if you're saying you're open to people instead of just animals. I think people who relate to animals only are closed off from the people around them. I don't say it to insult them. It's just a fact, and they have their reasons. But I think this new development is some clue that you're more open to human interaction. And I like that."

They sat quietly for a moment, just looking at each other. There was not one other person on the planet, Aiden realized, with whom he could sit in silence while meeting his or her eyes. But now there was Hannah.

"So what was the new experience?" she asked after a time.

"While I was out of town with Gwen, she told me about Milo's past. What his father put him through. It was kind of a shock to hear it spelled out like that. And it changed something in me when I heard it. It woke something up. And all of a sudden I knew what Gwen was feeling. I didn't tell her that, though. Because that's just too weird. Or it might seem too weird to her—to be with somebody who knows what she's feeling all the time. It might feel like not having any privacy at all. Sooner or later I have to tell her, I guess. But I don't really know when. Or how. And then whenever I thought about what Milo went through, I knew what he was feeling, too. When I got home, and got close to him, I was carrying all his stuff on top of everything else. And that's a big one to have riding around on my back, believe me."

"I can imagine it is. What about other people? Elizabeth, say?"

"Not as I know of. Not that I can tell. Seems like it's Gwen and Milo. Maybe because they both have so much to feel."

She didn't answer. Didn't confirm or deny his theory. So he opened his mouth again and more words came out in a rush.

"At first I was just so angry. I wanted to go find the guy and pound him into the ground. But then I remembered what you said. About how the guy was probably twisted into that shape by some kind of abuse when he was growing up. And then it felt the same as it would feel to think about pounding Milo into the ground. I thought about the moment when I almost tightened that rope around his neck, and I saw in his eyes how scared he was. And I know now that he was always scared, that he'd been scared all along, and scaring him and hurting him was how we'd gotten into this mess to begin with. It sure as hell wasn't going to get us out of it. And then I just got really tired and depressed. And now I don't know what the answer is."

A silence. Hannah still did not fill it.

"Maybe *you* do," he added.

"Have the answer to all the hurt and fear in the world? Know the solution for generational cycles of abuse? I'm afraid not. I'd be a very famous woman if I did."

"So there's no answer?"

"You break the cycle in the case you have in front of you," she said. "You help this one little guy heal as best he can. Enough that he doesn't take it out on his own kids when he has them. And that's enough of a contribution for one person. And in case you hadn't noticed, you're only one person."

Aiden waited a moment before answering. Feeling the weight of that assignment ricocheting around inside him.

"That's no small order," he said.

"I never claimed it was," she replied.

# *Chapter Twenty*

## *Trust*

"Elizabeth's birthday is this week," Gwen called in from the bathroom.

Aiden was still in bed. Propped up, hands laced behind his head. Savoring the fact that they woke up together now. That they were together in the most literal sense of the world. It was their third morning all living in the big house.

"What day?"

"Tuesday. And before you say anything, you're absolutely right. I should have told you sooner. I'm sorry, Aiden. With everything that's been going on with the move and Milo starting therapy and all, I let that slip by me. And I don't just mean telling you about it, either. I almost forgot her birthday. I can't believe that, but it's true. I know you probably wanted more notice to think of something to get her. But if it helps any to know, so did I."

Aiden waited a moment to see if she would emerge from the bathroom. Or if she had more to say. When nothing happened, he decided to move forward with his thoughts. He had been planning to run his idea by Gwen, but there had been no real time frame for doing so. Now, suddenly, there was.

"I actually had something in mind for a gift for her," he called in.

Gwen stuck her head out into the bedroom. She was holding a toothbrush in one hand.

"But you didn't know it was her birthday."

"Right. I didn't. But I had an idea of something I wanted to give her. But it would have been for no occasion in particular, and I was worried that it would have been mean to do that without giving Milo something. I actually have a thought on that, too. But it's a wild thought, and I'm not sure I'm ready to do it. Or even *willing* to do it. But if it's her birthday, then it's okay to give something just to her. And then I can think about the Milo thing a while longer. But you need to okay my Elizabeth idea. It's kind of big. You might not want me to do it."

He watched her eyebrows lift slightly. She was wearing just a wrapped towel, a huge bath sheet. Aiden could have gazed at her all day.

"Okay," she said. A little tentative. "What is it, hon?"

"I was thinking . . . Penny."

Silence. Then Gwen let out a sputtering laugh.

"Is that a joke? I know money's a little tight, but . . ."

"No. Not *a penny*. Penny. That little gray mare she loves so much."

"Oh," Gwen said. "Penny. Wow." She moved over and sat on the edge of the bed beside him. "That *is* big."

"I know what you're thinking. At least, I think I do."

"Do you? What am I thinking?"

"Well. It's a weird thing to have to talk about. But we know not every two people who've been together for a few months will be together for the rest of their lives. Even though I honestly think we have a shot. But . . . she could always keep the horse here. And come ride here. I'd like to think we'd all still be friends no matter what. Actually, I'd really like to think we'll all be living here always. I mean . . . except that the kids'll grow up and go off on their own."

They sat together in silence for a time in a slanted beam of light that shone through the bedroom window. A strong wind blew the leaves of the scrub oaks outside. Aiden could hear it, and see the leaves whirling in place. It would be both windy and hot that day.

He could feel the turmoil Gwen felt, but nothing clear emerged. Nothing that would help him judge what she would say next.

"She'd love it," Gwen said. "I know she would. Thirteen is young to own a horse, though."

"On her birthday she'll be fourteen."

"Oh. Right. Duh. Still young for a horse."

"Not in ranching years, it's not. I got my first horse when I was seven. I'll teach her everything she needs to know. Just like my stepfather did for me."

"I guess . . . okay. Yeah." He watched her face soften into something like a smile. Not really a relaxed smile. But then, relaxation wasn't something either one of them expected of their lives together. "That will be really nice. Thanks." She almost rose to go. But then she stopped herself. "If you don't mind my asking . . . what were you thinking about giving Milo?"

"Oh. That. You know what? Not ready to go there. Is that okay if I'm not ready to go there? I'm so confused about it, and I'm thinking it might be the worst idea I ever had. I promise if it gets any more firmed up, I'll tell you."

"Yeah," Gwen said. "That's fine."

But she was disappointed. Aiden wished he didn't know that. He missed the old days, when he wouldn't have known.

"How much of a hurry are you in to get to work?" he asked her.

"I got a few minutes. Why?"

"I want to tell you the story of the horse my stepdad gave me when I was seven."

—

Aiden waited until 7:00 a.m. on Elizabeth's birthday, but couldn't bring himself to wait longer. He rapped on her door with the backs of his fingers.

"Hey, sleeping beauty. If you're gonna sleep the day away, this is not the right day to do it."

He heard what sounded like a muffled groan from the other side of the door.

"I'm awake," she said. But she sounded asleep.

"You decent in there?"

"Yeah."

Aiden creaked the door open and peered in. She was still in bed, wincing into the light from her window, and the hall light.

"Okay, I get it," he said. "I woke you up. But only to wish you a happy birthday and give you your present. And when you see your present, I expect I'll be forgiven."

Aiden watched her face come alive. Sleep fell away from her eyes.

"What did you get me?"

"You think you'll be able to learn that information from the comfort of your own bed? I don't think so."

She swung the covers back. Reached for a robe draped over the end of the bed to cover her white-with-bright-red-hearts pajamas.

"My present from *both* you and my mom?"

"No. Just from me."

She came sailing across the hardwood in his direction, but he blocked the doorway and halted her with a hand like a stop sign.

"Shoes," he said.

"Why?"

"Because it's outside."

"Even so . . ."

"Trust me. No bare feet around . . . this present."

Elizabeth sighed and began to dig through her closet.

"I'll meet you out on the front porch," he said.

—

He joined Gwen outside. She had brought two mugs of coffee, and she handed him one. Then she smiled at him, and the smile made every part of him—from his neck down—burn up and melt away at the same time.

"You're about to make a young girl very happy," she said, and kissed him briefly on the lips.

Aiden turned his head to Penny, who stood with her reins looped around the porch rail but not really tied. She was clean for the first time Aiden could remember. He had stayed up late the night before giving her a bath. He had conditioned her mane and tail and braided them. Or at least braided the top hairs of her tail so the braid trailed down, centered over the bulk of the tail. He had even clipped away the long whiskers around her lips and chin and nostrils. Both her saddle and bridle were adorned with comically large gift bows.

"Hear that, Penny? We're about to make a young girl very happy. Though I expect you'll be the one in charge of that on the average day."

Aiden reached down and patted Buddy on the head. The dog had a haze of hair growing in everywhere now, and only the slightest dark scar to mark the spot where the rope had burned his neck. The dog leaned against Gwen's legs and wagged his whole body, squinting his eyes with joy.

Elizabeth came bursting out the front door and onto the porch. Then she froze, and just stared. She was looking right at the mare, but couldn't seem to process what she saw. Or did not dare say out loud what the situation seemed to be, in case she was wrong.

"Happy fourteen," Aiden said.

A strange pause.

Then Elizabeth said, "You're giving her to me?"

"I am."

"She's *mine*?"

"She's yours if you want her to be."

The girl broke her statue-like pose and moved across the porch boards toward the mare. Penny picked up her head and nickered a greeting in her throat. Elizabeth burst into tears. She ran down the three porch stairs and threw her arms around Penny's neck.

"Is that *good* crying?" Aiden asked, leaning over to speak into Gwen's ear.

"I expect so." Then she projected her voice down the stairs. "Honey? You okay?"

"Okay? *Okay?* This is the happiest I've ever been in my *life*!"

"Yup," Gwen whispered back to Aiden. "Good tears."

Meanwhile Elizabeth had her helmet on—it had been hung on the saddle horn—the reins in her hand and her foot in the stirrup. She swung onto her new horse's back.

"Whoa, honey," Gwen called. "Seriously? In your pajamas and robe?"

But it was too late. Girl and horse were too far away to hear, loping off over the hills. Bows and all.

Just then Buddy whipped his head around and looked back at the house in alarm. His normally erect ears drooped and then pinned themselves back against his neck, and he bolted off the porch and slithered under Aiden's front steps.

Aiden looked around to see what had startled Buddy.

In the doorway of the house stood Milo, leaning on his crutches. The look on the boy's face stopped Aiden in his tracks. As Milo took stock of what was happening, his reaction—his emotions regarding the scene—built up like a gale storm, and Aiden felt it, too.

Milo was furious, but also deeply wounded.

Aiden tried to cross the porch to the boy, but he spun on his crutches and hurried back toward his room. Then he put on a burst of speed and tripped over his crutches—or his own feet—and fell sprawled on the Persian rug.

Aiden ran to him and tried to help him up, but the boy shook him off violently.

"Don't touch me!" Milo screamed.

He clambered to his feet, wedged his crutches under his armpits again, and headed for his room.

Aiden heard and felt Gwen move up behind him. They stood and watched together as Milo's bedroom door slammed. Then they heard two loud bangs that Aiden could only guess were crutches hitting the door, one after the other.

"I'll go talk to him," Gwen said.

At least the boy had an appointment to start seeing Hannah soon, Aiden thought. Maybe that would help. Then he reminded himself that the sort of help she could deliver might take years. If it came at all.

———

She emerged about twenty minutes later. Aiden was standing at the kitchen counter mixing up batter for the waffles they planned to have for Elizabeth's birthday breakfast. If she ever rode home and dismounted.

"How is he?" Aiden asked.

She sat at the breakfast table with a deep, deflating sigh. "Seems we have a whole different set of problems with him now. First he wouldn't accept you, and he wanted to act out against you. Now he wants your approval really bad. Like, more approval than it's reasonable to think he's going to get."

"He said that?"

"Not in so many words."

Aiden poured a fresh mug of coffee and set it on the table in front of her. Her old one was probably still on the front porch somewhere. Wherever it was, it was cold.

"Thanks," she said. "He just has to accept the fact that it's Elizabeth's birthday, not his. I think it was just hard for him because it was such a huge present. Really above and beyond what you would normally give somebody for their birthday. He knows Elizabeth is special to you, and that you two get along really well. And it hurts him."

"How much of that did he actually say?"

"Enough for me to get the idea. You have to give me credit for knowing him."

"I do. I think I should go in and talk to him."

"And say what?"

"Not sure," Aiden said. "But here I go. And we'll find out."

———

Milo was lying on his belly on the bed in his room—what had used to be the TV room—arms and legs thrown wildly out to the sides, his face pressed into the pillow. Aiden found it hard to understand how the boy could even breathe.

Aiden could feel that Milo's rage had drained away, leaving only the most heartbreaking loneliness and loss.

He knocked on the door a second time, even though he had already opened it. He knocked as an announcement that he was about to attempt to enter.

Milo turned his head to one side and peered at Aiden briefly through swollen red eyes. "What?" he asked, his voice artificially hard.

Aiden grabbed the back of the only chair in the room. Sitting on the bed with the boy would not do. It would have been a wrong move even to try. He pulled the chair close to Milo's bed, but not too close. He sat a respectful distance away. Not quite close enough to reach out and touch Milo's shoulder, had he wanted to. Touching was not on the menu when Milo was trying to be safe in his room.

"So when's *your* birthday?" Aiden asked.

"Not for *seven months*!"

"Oh. Well, that's too bad. But you know I'll do something really special and nice for your birthday, too. Don't you?"

"No you won't. You love *Elizabeth*."

He didn't go on to say, "And you don't love me." But it hung there in the air as if it had been said. And it was true. Ignoble but true. Aiden loved Elizabeth and did not love Milo. He was trying. And maybe he would get there someday. But so far Milo had just made it too hard.

"Tell you what," Aiden said. "We're still going to let Lizzie have her special day. Because it would be wrong not to. But first thing tomorrow you can get in the truck with me, and we'll go into town together. And we'll find some more of that . . . what do you call that stuff?"

"What stuff?" Milo asked. He had his head up off the pillow now, and was braced on his arms, half rolled over to face Aiden.

"The stuff you use to do mosaics. The pieces."

"Tesserae," Milo said.

"Right. We'll get you some really nice tesserae so you can start another project. And maybe we'll even go to a secondhand furniture store I know and get something you can work on."

Milo sat fully up on the bed, using both hands to swing his bad foot around. "What about *your* coffee table? Here in the big house? You don't want me to mosaic that one?"

"Well, it has that glass in the middle. Can you attach mosaic work to glass? If you can, I'd be happy to have an original Milo mosaic on my coffee table."

"I could look in that mosaic book you gave me. Maybe it says."

"Okay. We'll figure it out."

"What kind of tesserae can we get?"

It was clear that Aiden was ready to wrap up their conversation and move on to breakfast. And that Milo didn't want him to go.

"I have a friend—well, a guy I know, anyway—who sells tile. You know, like for counters and floors. All different patterns and colors and materials. I'm sure he has some broken ones. Or some scraps left over from cutting them to fit."

"Tiles would look nice," Milo said. The look in his eyes betrayed the fact that he had left the room in his head. Left the moment.

"There's one thing I'm going to ask you to do, though. I'm not going to say it's a condition. I'm not going to say you *have* to do it if you want us to go out and get all this stuff tomorrow. I'm just going to ask you nicely to do it."

"What?" Milo pulled himself back into the moment with clear difficulty.

"I want you to come to the table and eat something. You need to eat. Everybody needs to eat."

Milo shook his head. "I'm mad about Lizzie. It'd ruin her birthday."

"How about if I bring you in a waffle? Here in your room. Will you eat it?" Aiden paused, not sure if he was about to go a step too far. But the feeling, the truth he was about to identify, was there in the room. It was all around them. Gwen had even told him it was true, because Milo had more or less admitted it to her. He jumped in. "For *me?*"

A pause.

Then Milo nodded softly.

———

As they tucked into bed that night, Aiden could feel the weight of something Gwen wasn't saying. But he didn't know how to draw her out, and he didn't want to press any issues.

"You were amazing today," she said. "Great father stuff."

But that wasn't it.

"Thanks," he said.

Aiden turned off the light, and they lay in the dark for several minutes in silence.

"That story you told me before," Gwen said. This was it. He could tell. "About your first horse. Magic."

"Right. What about it?"

"You weren't . . ."

Then it seemed she would never continue.

"I wasn't what?"

"Thinking about that with Milo? About Misty's foal, when she foals?"

"I was thinking about it. Yeah. I was thinking it would be this huge statement of trust. And that maybe if I treat him like I think he's trustworthy, he might be able to find it in himself to step up to that."

She didn't answer for a time. Aiden felt he knew what she was thinking. Not because he was so deeply tuned in. Because it was what anybody would be thinking.

"But what if he . . ."

It was a sentence she left unfinished.

"That's why I'm not at all sure I'm willing to do it," Aiden said.

—

"Thank you for taking me," Milo said.

He was sitting on the passenger side of the bench seat of Aiden's truck, his bad foot propped at an angle on the seat, nearly touching Aiden's thigh. Aiden had placed the boy's crutches in the bed of the truck to get them out of the way.

"You're welcome. I think you did a great job on that first project."

"You do? Really? You're not just saying that?"

"If I didn't really think so, I wouldn't bring it up again if I didn't have to. I think you know it was good. And maybe it's time to believe what you know."

They drove along Aiden's country lane, board fences flashing by. The trees grew so tall and leaned so close together above the road that it felt like driving through a green tunnel.

"So what do you think of Hannah?" Aiden asked after a time.

"Who?"

"The psychiatrist."

"Oh. Doctor Rutler," Milo said, slaughtering her name. "She's okay, I guess. Why?"

"I just wondered. I like her. I was wondering if you liked her, too."

"You know Dr. Rutler?"

"Oh, yes. Very well. I see her, too. Didn't your mother tell you that?"

"I don't think so. I guess she told me you saw her, but I thought she meant just . . . you know. To talk to her about *me* seeing her."

"No, I see her on my own. For myself."

They drove in silence for a mile or so. Aiden glanced over at Milo. His hair was freshly combed, slicked back, and Aiden knew for a fact that Gwen had not been around to help the boy get ready that morning. And yet he was clean and groomed, in fresh clothing. As though the trip were something like a job interview.

"What do *you* have to see her about?" Milo asked after a time.

"Just . . . I have things I need to figure out in my life."

"Like what?"

"Like . . . feelings. Feelings are hard for me."

"You can't feel them?"

"I didn't used to be able to. Now I feel them too much."

Aiden glanced over to see Milo staring at him, eyes wide.

"Does it hurt?"

"Yeah. A lot of the time it does."

"Oh," Milo said.

Aiden thought the boy would say more. He never did.

———

Aiden wrapped one arm around the boy's shoulder as he guided him into the tile and linoleum shop. Carefully, so as not to knock him over. Then he pulled the arm back because he could tell Milo minded.

"Hey, Greg," Aiden said.

The older man looked up from some kind of catalogue. "Aiden. What brings you my way? And who's this young fella?"

"This is Gwen's son. Milo. Sort of my stepson, I guess you could say. Almost."

Greg walked out from behind the corner and offered Milo his hand to shake. It startled the boy. Aiden could see it and feel it, both. Milo backed up so fast on his crutches that he tipped himself over. Aiden had to catch him before he landed on the shop floor on his butt.

"Milo gets to know people in his own time," Aiden said, setting the boy back on his feet. Well, foot. And crutches.

"That's all right. What can I do for you two?"

"Milo is an artist," Aiden said. He felt the boy's swell of pride at the words. "He does really beautiful mosaic projects."

"Say no more. I've had the request before. Nothing quite as good as broken tiles for a mosaic project. Follow me out back. I'll get a couple empty cartons and you can go through my dumpster."

—

"Hmm," Aiden said. "Wish there was some way I could get you in here to see for yourself."

Aiden had climbed into the dumpster and was standing ankle-deep in broken tile and a few linoleum scraps. He moved the linoleum into one corner as best he could.

Milo strained to see over the edge of the dumpster, but he was just too small.

"Maybe you can lift me in."

"I don't know about that, Milo. It'd be kind of hard to keep your balance in here. Tell you what. I'll hold up some tile scraps. And you just say yes or no. Grab one of those cartons, and hold it close to the edge of the dumpster if you can. If you say yes, I'll drop them in."

It worked fine for about six double handfuls. Milo held the box with both hands, leaned it against the side of the dumpster, and leaned on the edge of the box. But it soon became clear that the word "no" was unlikely to come out of Milo's mouth anytime soon. He wanted it all. And the box quickly grew too heavy for the boy to hold, balanced on one leg as he was.

"Okay, new plan," Aiden said. "I just box up all the scrap tile he's got. And we put it in the back of the truck and take it home."

"Yes, please. But we need to stop at that furniture place like you said."

"Won't work on a glass coffee table?"

"I don't know yet. I can't figure that out. But I was thinking of . . . like . . . a really nice wood tray. Like the kind of tray people eat breakfast in bed on. My mom likes breakfast in bed. So I thought I could put a mosaic on that and give it to her as a present."

"We'll get one, then," Aiden said. "We'll get one if we have to go all over the damn county to find it."

———

Aiden sat in Hannah's office, listening to the clock tick. He wanted to say, "Tell me everything about Milo. Every word he's said to you. Every tic of his body language." But he knew he couldn't ask that. So he said nothing at all.

"How's it going with you two?" he asked, when staring out the window grew too heavy to sustain.

"Reasonably well, given that it's only been three sessions. But it takes time. I know I don't have to tell you that."

"I guess there's not much you can tell me about how it's going. What you're finding out. I know there's that confidentiality thing. I mean . . . is there? Or is it different with children?"

"That's a bit of a complex issue," she said.

She rose from her chair. For a strange moment, Aiden thought she was going to walk out of the room entirely. That he had offended her beyond repair. Instead she just poured more boiling water into her teacup from a hot pot on her desk in the corner of the room.

"It's most complex with adolescents," she said. "With a ten-year-old child like Milo it's a bit clearer, though not without its thorns." She stirred honey into her tea as she spoke. "Under the law, Milo is too young to consent to treatment. So it's actually his mother who entered into this verbal contract with me to treat him. And the law allows that she has a right to know something of the content of that treatment. But there's definitely a trust bond being formed between psychiatrist and child, and I burst that bubble at my own peril, as well as Milo's. And, just so you know, Gwen hasn't asked. She's letting it be between him and me."

She sat back down and stared openly into his face, and Aiden looked away, feeling as though he'd been caught doing something illegal. Or at the very least inadvisable.

"I'm sorry if I was wrong to ask," he said.

"You don't have to be. Just don't blame me for playing my cards close to the vest. I understand you have a huge investment in this, but you're not his parent in the eyes of the law. But I can and will tell you one thing, because it doesn't involve repeating anything he's said to me in the sessions. He needs your support. He needs you to believe in him."

"I know he does. I know."

Then they listened to the clock tick for half a minute or more.

"I just want to ask your opinion about something," Aiden said. "If it's something you're able to say. If Milo had . . . an . . . animal. And it was his. His very own. Do you think he'd take care of that animal? Or do you think he'd hurt it?"

He had hoped she would think about the question for a moment. Instead she immediately shook her head.

"I wouldn't even venture a guess, Aiden. I know you'd be a lot more comfortable with some kind of guarantee. But there are no guarantees to be had in this situation, and I think you know it. Why? Were you thinking of getting him a pet?"

Now it was Aiden's turn to shake his head without even thinking.

"Probably not. No. Forget I even mentioned it. It was just a stupid idea."

# Chapter Twenty-One

## Born

It was three days later when Aiden experienced the flip side of the pain of the wake up. It had never happened before, and he had not seen it coming. It had never occurred to him that he might be the recipient of an animal's joy.

He was mucking out stalls in the barn, starting with the brood mare, Misty, who was gigantic and ungainly with foal. He looked up from his shoveling to see Penny stick her head over the door of the stall across the aisle to look at him. Maybe even to tell him something.

She was happy. Not just not unhappy. Hugely, quantifiably happy.

He set down his pitchfork and shovel and crossed the barn aisle to her, and held out his palm, and she nuzzled it with her nose.

"You're welcome," he said. "Every good horse should have a little girl, don't you think?"

That was the moment when Aiden realized he had been guilty of an error in his thinking. He would have to be more aggressive about selling his horses. He saw that now. He had been holding back out of fear. Fear that the new owners would mistreat them. Or, even if it was the best new owner possible, fear of the terrifying unfamiliarity a horse has to weather after they've been sold.

But that wasn't fair to his horses, he now knew. He was protecting them from everything, including a successful bond like the one Penny had found. In trying to shield them from any pain, he was also shielding them from potential great happiness.

And he needed money, so it was a relief to make the decision. But the money was secondary, if a consideration at all.

Penny lifted her head and whinnied, and Aiden turned to see Elizabeth standing in the barn aisle behind him holding the mare's bridle.

"How long should I keep her in the barn?" the girl asked.

"How long? I'm not sure I understand the question. Leave her in here as long as you like."

"But you had her out in pasture. Is it better for her out in pasture?"

"There's really no better or worse about it. They're just different. In the pasture they have more room to move. They can run if they feel like running. In the barn they have more protection from the elements, and from each other. If you keep a horse in a stall, you have to take them out regularly and ride them. Or turn them out, or work them in some way, like when I turn Dusty out in the roping pen and let him run. Otherwise it's just cruel to pen them up so tightly. But you ride this mare every day. So the barn is fine for her."

"Oh. Okay. Good."

"I was just noticing how happy this little mare is, now that she has you."

Elizabeth stopped moving. She had been swinging the stall door wide, but she froze. She looked up into Aiden's face with wide, unguarded eyes.

"Really? You think so?"

"I know so."

"How do you know?"

Aiden ran the options through his mind quickly. Or maybe they ran through all on their own.

"Remember when I told you animals learn to read us when they have to live with us?"

"I remember."

"You asked why *we* don't learn to sense what *they're* feeling. I didn't tell you at the time, because I didn't know you as well as I know you now. But I'm one of some rare people who seem to have extra senses. Or just extrastrong senses. I can sometimes feel what the animals are feeling. Stronger they feel it, the more likely I am to feel it, too. Usually it's a curse. But this morning when I saw how happy Penny was . . . this was the first time I felt like it was a good thing to have."

Elizabeth was staring at him, and he was keeping his eyes slightly averted. She didn't seem to be judging him. Just leaning in to know more.

"What about people? Does it work with people?"

"Sometimes. Some people."

"Did you learn it from being around so many animals for so long?"

"No. I think I was born with it. Just more sensitivity than most people. Then I blocked it out for most of my life. And then I couldn't block it out anymore."

"Wow," she said, and her hands began to move again. Began to bridle her mare. "That helps a lot of stuff make sense when I think back on it. Like why you got so freaked out about the rabbits. And Buddy. You know. Getting hurt. Not that anybody wouldn't. But, you know. You were really freaked out."

"Yeah," Aiden said. "That's why."

"Can you tell when Misty's going to have her foal?"

"No. It's not like seeing into the future. I might know when *she* knows. If she goes into labor I might feel her pain from the house. I can tell you right now it's going to be soon, but not because of any special senses. I just know because I've watched a lot of mares go through the process."

Elizabeth led her horse out into the barn aisle. She stopped, looked at the enormous Misty, then back at Aiden. "Why is that a bad thing?"

"Why is what a bad thing?"

"Misty foaling."

"It's not."

"But your face got really dark when you talked about it."

"Oh," Aiden said. "Right. I just have a decision I have to make by the time she foals, and I'm having trouble with it. Maybe you can help."

"Me?"

"Yeah. You. You have good judgment. And you know your brother. If Milo had an animal and it was his very own . . . do you think he'd take care of it? Or do you think he'd hurt it?"

Elizabeth stood beside her horse for several long seconds, stroking the mare's face. Other than that one petting hand, no part of the girl moved.

"What kind of animal?"

"Horse."

"He'd be too afraid of a horse to get near enough to hurt it."

"Brand-new baby foal."

"Oh," Elizabeth said, drawing the word out, quiet and long, as the situation came clear to her. "I get it. Well, here's what I think. I think if he found a baby foal by the side of the road or something, well . . . I'm not sure. I think he'd be less likely to hurt it than he would have been back when he first met you. He was really scared of you then, and so he was acting out a lot. But I'm not positive enough. You know. If he just found it and it wasn't anybody's. But if you gave him a baby foal? I don't think he'd hurt it. I think he'd be all impressed because it was from you, and I think he wouldn't want to disappoint you. Thing is, I can't . . . you know . . . give you like an actual guarantee or anything."

"I know you can't. Nobody can. But thanks for your thoughts anyway. Oh. One more thing I wanted to ask you. When you guys came over that first night, I asked Milo if he liked horses, and he said no. Is that really true, do you think? I mean, he might not be interested at all."

Aiden tried not to sound hopeful. It probably didn't work.

"No. I don't think it's true. I think he's scared of them, and I think anything you said you liked he would have said he didn't like. But I think if he wasn't interested in having a horse at all, well . . . why would he have gotten so upset when you gave *me* one?"

"Right. Thanks."

Elizabeth nodded, and led her horse to the open barn doors. Out into the sun. Then she stopped and turned back to Aiden.

"Are you going to do it?"

"I don't think so," he said.

"Oh."

"I just keep thinking that when that new little life pops out into the world, it's my responsibility. I have a duty to make sure I don't put that foal in harm's way."

"I get it," she said.

But she sounded disappointed. Which was hard on Aiden, who never wanted to disappoint her.

———

When the sun went down that night, Aiden dug his camp cot out of the shed and set it up in Misty's stall.

Then he walked back into the house to find Gwen.

She was in the kitchen, doing up the last of the dinner dishes. He moved up behind her and swept her hair aside and kissed the nape of her neck.

"I might not be in tonight," he said.

"Really? Where will you be?"

"Out in the barn with Misty. I really think it's going to be tonight or tomorrow. Or maybe tomorrow night. I just want to be there in case anything goes wrong. Or in case she needs my help."

Gwen turned to face him. She almost put her arms around him. She started to. But her hands were wet and covered with suds. She looked at them for a moment, then smiled wryly and wiped them off on Aiden's shirt.

"Hey!" he said, jumping back.

But then they both laughed.

"Sorry. Couldn't resist. I think you're sweet to care so much about that mare. About all your horses."

"What would you think about . . ."

But then he trailed off and couldn't seem to finish.

"What? Go ahead."

"I was thinking maybe I'd take Milo out there with me. So he can see a foal being born. It's kind of an amazing thing to witness."

"Are you going to . . ." Then it was Gwen's turn to be unable to finish.

"Probably not. I don't know yet. I still can't decide. But I just thought it would be something he'd want to see."

"What about Elizabeth? She'd love to see it."

"Yeah," Aiden said. "She'd love it. But not this time. We have lots of births here, and we're about to have a lot more. And you're right, she should see this. But right now we have that 'Milo deficit' thing going on. He thinks Elizabeth gets much more of me. So this time I think it should be just me and Milo."

Gwen wiped her hands off on a dish towel, seemingly lost in thought. Then she nodded. "Okay. I'll explain to Elizabeth. I think she'll understand."

———

"Why do I have to do this?" Milo asked in his nasal whine. He had been moving over the rough ground between house and barn on his crutches, but he stopped and leaned. And complained. "I just want to go to bed."

Aiden raised his battery-powered lantern to better see the boy. "I have a cot set up in Misty's stall," he said. "If you get sleepy, you can fall asleep in there, and I'll wake you when the foal comes."

"I don't want to sleep in the *barn*. I want to sleep in my *room*."

"It's just this one night. Do this for me, Milo. It's an amazing experience to watch a new baby come into the world. It changed my life when I was a kid. Just try this with me, okay?"

Milo sighed, and slumped farther down over his crutches. "It's too hard for me to walk. The ground is all bumpy, and it's dark."

"Okay," Aiden said. He sank to one knee beside the boy. "Put one hand on my shoulder to steady yourself. And now I'm going to take your crutches." Aiden got both of them in his left hand, then turned so his back was facing Milo. "Okay. Hop on."

For a long moment, nothing. No movement. No words.

It was asking a lot of Milo, who did not care to be touched in any way. But if Aiden didn't push them into new territory, how were they ever going to get there?

A moment later Aiden felt Milo's spindly arms wrap around his neck. He stood, lifting the boy with him. Milo wrapped his good leg around Aiden's waist.

Together they moved to the barn for the night.

—

"What if we just sit here all night, and she never gets birthed to anything?" Milo asked.

He was lying on the cot in the corner of Misty's stall, too aware of the massive animal to relax much. Aiden was sitting with his back up against the stall partition, watching the mare and feeling whatever he could feel from her. He was sure she was close—that he could feel the pain of early labor.

"Then we just have to sit here with her tomorrow. And maybe again tomorrow night."

"But this is so *boring*," Milo whined.

But Aiden was pretty sure that "boring" was a euphemism for "scary."

"Why is it any more boring than going to bed in your room? Just go to sleep. I'll wake you if something happens."

A silence. Neither spoke nor moved. Then Milo put his head down on his arms and closed his eyes. A moment later the boy's eyes shot open.

"What if she steps on me in my sleep?"

"She can't step on you. You're not down on the ground."

"Oh. Right." He closed his eyes again. A moment later they shot open again. "Will you protect me if she tries to nibble on me or something?"

"She won't," Aiden said. "But yes. I'll protect you."

Milo closed his eyes and left them closed.

———

Sometime in the middle of the night, Aiden fell briefly asleep. But he didn't know he was asleep. Because in his sleep, in his half-dreaming state, he was sitting with his back up against the stall partition, watching Misty. It was exactly the same scene he would have been viewing if his eyes had been open.

With one dramatic addition.

Harris Delacorte sat with his back against the far wall, on the other side of the mare, staring into Aiden's eyes. Aiden felt his heart changing. Swelling. Growing bigger. It hurt, but not in a way he minded. He would not have squeezed it down to normal size again even if he thought he could.

"I think you need to do it," the dreamed Harris Delacorte said.

"I don't know if I can," Aiden replied.

"I think you have to."

"Why?" Aiden asked, thinking he sounded a little whiny. Like his younger self. Or even like Milo.

"Because of the worst that could happen either way. If you do it, you might be throwing away the life of a foal. If you don't, you might be throwing away the life of a boy. Pick the boy. Bet on the boy."

Aiden wanted to say more. He meant to say more. Ask more questions. But it was already too late. Harris Delacorte was gone.

"Dad?" Aiden called.

"Aiden?" The voice was sharp and high. It was not his father.

Aiden's eyes flew open. He looked over to see Milo half propped up on his cot, staring at him.

"Oh," Aiden said. "Milo."

"Are you okay? You sounded like you were talking to somebody."

"It's fine," Aiden said. "I just had a dream. Go back to sleep."

But before Milo could even put his head back down, Misty sank to her knees, groaned deeply, and dropped over onto her side. Aiden felt the sickening ache of a big contraction.

"I take it back," Aiden said. "Don't go back to sleep. It's starting. It's going to happen right now."

———

Aiden thought Milo was in the straw right behind him. But after many stressful—and painful—minutes watching Misty moan and heave, he turned to say something to the boy. Milo was not there.

Aiden raised the lantern and looked around.

Milo was on the cot, his back pressed into a corner of the stall, hugging his one good leg up to his chest.

"You don't want to see this?"

"I can see it from here," Milo said. But he didn't sound convincing.

Nothing more seemed to want to be said, so Aiden set the lantern down in the straw again and turned his attention back to Misty. He could see the front hooves of the foal emerge, covered in the loose white amniotic sac.

He was opening his mouth to tell Milo to come closer to see, when Milo surprised him with voluntary words.

"Does it hurt you, too?" the boy asked.

Aiden raised the lantern again to look at the boy's face. Milo squinted and turned away.

"Excuse me?"

"Does it hurt you, too?"

"Does what hurt me, too? I don't know what you mean."

He might have known what the boy meant. But he wasn't about to proceed without being sure.

"When she has a baby. It hurts her. I get that. But I'm looking at you. And it looks like it hurts you, too."

"Yeah," Aiden said. "It does."

"Why?"

"I don't know why. Just something I'm cursed with. Or blessed, on a few very rare occasions. More often it's a curse. Milo, you have to see this."

"What?" Milo asked, craning his neck.

"No, you can't see it from there. You have to come closer."

For a minute, nothing happened. Nothing was said. Then Aiden heard the light scrape of the boy's cutoff jeans moving across the taut canvas of the camping cot. Milo eased to his knees and crawled to where Aiden sat near the back of the prone mare. Milo leaned in close to look. Then he skittered backward until he could propel himself—with his one good leg—back onto the cot. He squeezed into the corner of the stall again.

"What *was* that?" Milo asked, his voice thick with dread.

"That was the two front hooves of the foal."

"Didn't look like hooves."

"It is, though."

"Looked like a bag. A white bag."

"That's the amniotic sac."

"I have no idea what that means," Milo said. "But okay."

"If you really come in close and let me shine the lantern on it for you, you can see the shape of the hooves right through the sac."

"No thanks. Thanks anyway. I can see from here."

Aiden knew he couldn't. But before he could say more, Misty gave a huge grunt. She pulled in air with a strange sound, then let it out in something like a loud, strained sigh. And with it came most of the foal. Aiden gently took hold of the front legs and guided it out. He didn't need to pull. He just made sure the foal was supported, and that it landed gently. Not that foals weren't dropping into the straw—or even the cold, hard ground—unsupported, all over the world. But at Aiden's ranch this little guy would get a gentle introduction to the world.

Aiden tore away the sac.

The foal underneath lay on the straw with its neck curved around in an arc, muzzle touching its own flank. *Like an oil painting of a newborn foal,* Aiden thought, but he wasn't sure where that idea came from.

It was a filly. Aiden could see that. She was coal black. On her forehead she bore a white marking that looked exactly like a crescent moon.

Aiden leaned back and smacked into Milo. The boy had been leaning over his shoulder, and Aiden hadn't realized. He had been too caught up in the birth.

"He's *born,*" Milo said. He leaned farther over Aiden's shoulder until his face was only a foot away from the baby's face. "You're *born,*" he said, directly to the foal.

"She's a she. It's a little filly."

"I don't know what a filly is."

"A colt is a boy, and a filly is a girl."

Milo leaned in again to address the foal directly. Aiden could feel the warmth of the boy's belly press against his shoulder.

"You're a girl," Milo said.

Then the boy backed up. As if realizing he had stepped into less familiar territory. His crutches had been left out in the barn aisle, and Milo struggled for balance, bracing himself by grabbing Aiden's shoulder. He hopped back to the cot and sat on the very edge of it, staring at the foal.

"What are you going to name your filly?" Aiden asked.

The words seemed to bang around inside Aiden, as if he were empty and hollow. They scraped and abraded everything they touched. Such dangerous words.

"What?"

"Your filly. Right here."

He indicated the newborn, who had her nose down in the straw, investigating its feel and smell.

"*My* filly?"

"Yes."

"How is she mine?"

"I'm giving her to you. So as of right now, she's yours."

No words, no movement. For several seconds. Then Milo pushed with his hands and his good leg and propelled himself back into the corner of the stall again.

"That doesn't make any sense," the boy said, his voice so small that it barely reached Aiden. "You think I hurt animals. Even though I haven't hurt one for a really long time."

"I think you can have this one without hurting her. I'm trusting you to take care of her."

"I don't know *how* to take care of her."

"I can teach you. I can show you everything you need to know. The only thing I can't help you with is . . . you have to have the right heart for it."

Milo had his head turned half away now, as if talking to the barn wall.

"What kind of heart is right?"

"Just . . . the kind that wants her to be okay. You just have to want to take good care of her."

Aiden waited for Milo to respond. While he waited, he searched for Milo's emotion. It dawned on him in that moment that the fear he had been feeling from Milo had morphed into . . . nothing. He could feel nothing.

In time Milo rose from the cot and moved closer to Aiden and the foal, dropping to his knees again for balance. He leaned in toward the new baby, and she stretched her neck out toward the boy, and they regarded each other close up for a second or two.

"I don't know what I want to name her," Milo said. "I can't think of a name."

"It doesn't matter. You can think about it for as long as you like."

"I want to go back to bed. Carry me into the house now, Aiden."

"You don't want to stay here with your new foal?"

"No. I'm tired. I want to go back to bed."

"Okay," Aiden said, tamping the disappointment down, keeping it from his voice as best he could. "Hop on, then, and we'll go back."

———

He was just coming out of Milo's room when he ran into Gwen. Quite literally.

"Oh, hey," he said, steadying her on her feet again. "Sorry."

"What happened? Did Misty have her foal?"

"She did. A beautiful black filly with a white marking like a crescent moon."

"Ooh," Gwen said. "I want to see! Let me run put my shoes on."

While he was waiting, Aiden mulled over the fact that she hadn't asked yet. Hadn't broached the obvious question.

———

They walked out to the barn together in the dark, and Aiden took her hand.

"Did Milo get to see it?"

"More or less. He was pretty much in the corner, as far away from the whole birthing thing as he could get. But he did see the foal when I first tore the sac away. And then he got a little closer and really looked at her. So I think he got the whole birth experience. At least, as much as he was willing to get it."

They stepped into the barn, where the battery-powered lantern still glowed in the new baby's stall. Misty was on her feet now, licking the filly all over.

They leaned on the stall door together, their shoulders tightly pressed to each other.

"She's *amazing*," Gwen said. "Oh my gosh, I've never seen anything that beautiful in all my life, Aiden. Look at those legs! She's all legs!"

Misty raised her head briefly and regarded the two humans. As if to say, "Yes. She *is* pretty amazing, isn't she?"

"Good job, girl," Aiden said to his mare.

Misty dropped her head and resumed licking.

"So . . . ," Gwen began, and Aiden thought he knew what she would be asking. But she surprised him. "I know you didn't give her to Milo, and that's okay. I get it. I really do. You're responsible for her. You need to keep her safe."

"I did do it," he said. "Actually."

"You gave her to Milo?"

"I did."

"Oh." A pause, during which Aiden could hear her breathing. As if every breath were a gasp or a sigh. "Am I the only one that finds that . . . terrifying?"

"You're not," he said.

"What was his reaction?"

"Not what I expected, I'll tell you that much. He looked at her really close up for a minute, and then he said he was tired and he wanted to go back to bed. And that was it."

"Hmm," Gwen said. "Maybe it's just a lot to process."

"Maybe."

"Or maybe he isn't going to take to having a horse, and you'll end up with her back again. And you can't tell me that wouldn't be a relief."

"I guess we'll see."

"But however it turns out, Aiden . . . whether he wants her or he doesn't, I really think it's going to be a great thing for him that you put this trust in him. I really have to thank you for that. It's stuff like this that makes me fall in love with you all over again, every day."

For a moment, Aiden thought they would be allowed to fall into that feeling of love. And just be together. But Gwen had one more thing to say.

"I just hope to God he lives up to your trust."

"Yeah," Aiden said, his eyes on the delicate, leggy new life. "You and me both."

———

In the morning, Aiden knocked on Milo's bedroom door.

"Don't come in, Mom!" the boy yelled out.

"It's not your mom. It's Aiden."

"Oh. Aiden. You can come in."

Aiden opened the door.

Milo was on the bedroom floor, sitting on the drop cloth left over from his coffee table project, arranging tile pieces on the wooden tray they had bought together at an antique store. Not adhering them down. Just arranging them into a design that could later be affixed. When it was good enough.

"What?" Milo asked.

"I thought you might want to come out and see your filly. She's standing up now."

"Can't. I have to work on my project."

"Oh. Well, when you can take a break, you should come see."

"Okay," Milo said. "When I can take a break."

But the morning disappeared, and Milo never stuck his head out of his room. Never indicated that he was able to take a break.

———

Aiden watched Hannah tap her pen for a moment before speaking. As if the rhythm of the sounds could help her put her thoughts into perfect order.

"I wouldn't make assumptions about his level of caring," she said. "I know he's showing it in a very different way than you did when you were seven. Bear in mind you were on the inside of that experience. So you felt your excitement, but it's hard to know how much someone on the outside of you would have seen."

"Except . . ."

But then Aiden didn't go on.

"Except what?"

"Except I've been feeling what's going on inside Milo for a while now. But all I'm getting these days is radio silence."

"He may very well be overwhelmed by the whole thing. And he might be responding to that overwhelm by shutting down."

"I thought of that. Yeah."

"I have no idea what he'll do in the long run, Aiden. But it was an amazing gesture. I'm sure, whether he wants the horse or not, it's going to make a huge difference that you put that kind of trust in him. It can't fail to impress him."

"That's what Gwen said. Then she let on that she was scared he might not live up to that trust."

"Even if he doesn't, I can't see how it could fail to help him, just knowing that you would make the gesture."

"With all due respect," Aiden said, feeling his stomach tip sickeningly, "please don't even say that. I don't even want to think what could happen if he doesn't live up to my trust."

# Chapter Twenty-Two

## Teeth

It was about three days later, possibly four, when Aiden walked into the barn and heard a gentle, breathy laugh coming from Misty's stall.

He walked over and leaned on the top of the stall door. Looked in on the scene. It wasn't Milo. Elizabeth had let herself in to see the filly. Aiden took a moment to nurse his disappointment before he spoke.

Meanwhile Elizabeth had not yet looked up and seen him there.

She was holding her fingers out to the filly, who was sucking on them as if she could nurse from them. Elizabeth giggled again.

"I know that seems fun," Aiden said.

The girl jumped. The foal spooked away and ran back to her mother. Elizabeth put one hand to her heart, then sighed out a breath of air.

"Oh. Aiden. You scared me."

"Sorry. I know that's kind of funny, how she'll suck on your fingers. But it's only fun now because she doesn't have her teeth in yet. They come in really fast. So be careful."

"Okay," she said, seeming a little embarrassed. "I'll watch out. She's just so adorable, though. I can't stay away from her. She's so *cute*!"

"Has Milo come down to see her yet?"

"Not that I know of."

"Right," Aiden said. "That's what I figured. I guess *Milo* can stay away from her. I'll go see what he's up to."

———

Aiden found Milo in his room, sitting on the floor next to—and staring at—what appeared to be a finished mosaic breakfast tray. When the boy looked up and saw Aiden standing over him, he made no effort to cover his work.

"Is it done?" Aiden asked.

"I think so."

"Aren't you the one who would know?"

"Well. Yeah. I put the varnish on it and all. But I'm just looking at it now and trying to think if it's good enough."

"Mind if I come take a look?"

"Yeah. Okay. But don't touch it. The varnish's still wet."

Aiden walked a few steps across Milo's bedroom and sat cross-legged on the floor next to the boy. He leaned over and looked closely at the mosaic tray. Milo had created an intricate tree, much like the trees that grew around and over Aiden's house and barn. The boy had had access to a number of shades of brown and green, and had varied the shades to create an effect of light hitting the leaves, and the bark on one side of the trunk. Aiden found it remarkable for a boy his age, assuming he had done it on purpose. The more Aiden stared, the less he could imagine how such an effect could have been created by accident.

"It's beautiful," he said.

"You're just saying that."

"Milo. Look at it. Can you really not see that it's good?"

"I think it's *good*," Milo said. "I just don't know if it's good *enough*."

"It's done. You have the varnish on it and everything."

"Yeah." Milo sighed deeply. Almost theatrically. "It's done, I guess."

"Then I think you need to come out and see your foal."

"You said she was a filly," Milo said, his eyes still glued to the mosaic tree.

"She's both. A foal is any baby horse, boy or girl. And then a colt is a boy and a filly is a girl."

"That's confusing."

They sat in silence for a moment, staring at the tree. Aiden wondered if he needed to haul the conversation back around to what he wanted Milo to do. But Milo got there on his own.

"What does she need me to do for her? Her mom feeds her with milk."

"She needs you to be her person."

"Why does she need that? Wild horses don't have a person."

"But she's not a wild horse. She's a domestic horse. And you have this amazing opportunity to bond with her now, so she's known you all her life. So you're the one person in the world she trusts more than anybody. When the time comes to ride her, it'll make such a difference. And school is going to start again soon, so this is when you really have the time to put into making her yours."

He watched the boy's eyes go wide at the mention of riding. Still, no matter how hard he tried to tune in to Milo, to leave himself open, Aiden could feel nothing. Either a window had closed on Aiden's sensitivity to people, or Milo felt no emotion at all.

"Don't you want that?" Aiden added.

"Yeah," Milo said. "I guess."

"Come on, then."

Aiden stood and waited. But Milo stayed down.

"Tomorrow morning," the boy said, "when the varnish is dry, will you help me make breakfast in bed for my mom? I want it to be a surprise for her like that. That's why I was working so hard on it. Because tomorrow is her day off. And I wanted it to be done by then. So we can bring it and say, 'Surprise!' And she'll think the surprise is just the breakfast in bed. And then she'll see the tray, and I'll tell her I made it as a present for her, and then she'll *really* be surprised."

Aiden smiled to himself, picturing the scene. "Sure. I'll help you."

"I was thinking scrambled eggs and toast. Because I *almost* know how to make those. I just need you there to be sure I don't make a mistake."

"You got it. But seriously, Milo. Let's go see that foal of yours."

Aiden helped Milo to his feet, and handed the boy his crutches. They walked together. Through the living room. Out of the house and toward the barn, Aiden slowing his steps unnaturally so as not to leave the boy behind.

They were halfway there when Elizabeth came trotting out of the barn on Penny, Buddy the dog tagging along behind. She waved as she urged her mare into a gallop, and the three headed up the hill.

"I still don't know what I'm supposed to do with her," Milo said as they stepped through the open barn doors. "How do I make her mine?"

"You can start by handling her. The more she gets handled while she's little the better."

"Like pet her, you mean?"

"Yeah. Like that. Get her used to having her head touched. And her ears. And you can run a hand under her belly and teach her to pick up her feet for you."

Aiden swung the stall door wide, and they stepped inside. Misty nickered to Aiden, a deep, satisfied rumble in her throat.

"She's standing up already," Milo said.

"She's been standing up since a couple of hours after she was born. I told you that. Don't you remember? You haven't come out to see her even once?"

"Not really," Milo said, his eyes fixed on the filly, who stood close to her mother's side, head high and nostrils flared, staring back. "I was in my room trying to think of a name for her."

"What did you come up with?"

"Nothing. I still don't know."

The foal stepped up to investigate Milo and his crutches. She reached out and pushed the middle of Milo's chest with her muzzle. Milo tumbled backward into the straw.

"Ow," he said.

Aiden reached down and helped him to his feet. Helped get his crutches under his armpits again.

"How 'bout if I get a soft brush, and you can see if she'll let you brush her?"

"I can't," Milo said. "I need both my hands for my crutches. I can't really do anything until I can stand up. You know. The normal way."

Aiden sighed.

It was a reasonable point. But at the same time, Aiden knew his young self would have been out brushing Magic on crutches if such a thing had been necessary. Nothing would have kept him away.

"Okay," Aiden said. "Let's turn them out, at least."

He took Misty's halter and lead rope down from its hook outside the stall door, and the mare politely presented her head for haltering.

"Where's the halter for the . . . I forget the word again. For a baby."

"Filly? Foal?"

"Right. That."

"She doesn't have one. She hasn't even been halterbroke yet."

"So how can you lead her outside?"

"You just lead the mother. The foal follows along."

Aiden stepped out into the barn aisle with Misty. The foal jumped straight up into the air in her excitement, then skittered to catch up. Aiden led them out into the sun. This would be the filly's first chance to look around in the sunlight. Feel it warm her skin through her coat.

He turned to see if Milo was following, and saw the boy leaning in the open barn doorway, dozens of steps behind.

Aiden opened the gate to the roping pen—the *former* roping pen—and led Misty and the foal inside. He unclipped Misty's lead rope, stepped out of the pen again, and closed the gate.

Misty ambled slowly from one end of the pen to the other. The foal followed sedately for about three steps. Then the wild enthusiasm of youth got the best of her, and she leapt straight into the air again. She bucked and danced on her comically long legs, and galloped in a big circle around her mother.

Aiden thought he heard Milo laugh.

He turned to see the boy making his way to the gate on his crutches. He stopped beside Aiden, leaned the crutches against the pipe fence, and steadied himself with his hands on the top rail.

"She's funny," Milo said as they watched her prance. "Only thing is . . ." Then the boy trailed off. For several seconds Milo did not seem inclined to say more. "She doesn't really seem . . . *mine*, though. It doesn't really feel like she's mine."

"I think that's normal. Especially since you haven't been down to see her since she was born. I don't think it's automatic. I think you have to *make* her your own. By putting in time with her."

"Oh," Milo said.

They watched in silence for a few moments. But the foal was settling now. Misty had her head through the pipe rails, grazing on some grass outside the pen. The foal had come back to her side and was bumping underneath the mare's belly with her nose, wanting to nurse.

"I'm going in now," Milo said. "She can be out here without me. It's not like she needs me to run around. Or have milk."

"You don't even want to stay with her for a few minutes?"

"I have to go in and see my mosaic again."

"But it's done."

"But I have to look at it again and see if it's good enough."

He picked up his crutches and set off for the house.

Aiden watched him go for several seconds. Then he looked up to see Elizabeth in the distance, watching from the back of her horse. She was up on a high ridge, under a stand of scrub oaks much like the one in Milo's mosaic. It was the place Aiden had last seen a few of his cattle. Back when he had cattle.

She reined her mare around and rode down the hill to him. She turned Penny toward the gate and sat there at Aiden's side, and they stared at the nursing foal together.

"I don't think this is going to work out," Aiden said.

"Maybe not," Elizabeth said, after a brief pause. As if needing to think carefully. "Only, don't give up on it just yet, okay? Sometimes things take Milo a long time. Like a really, really, abnormally long time."

———

They stood outside the bedroom door, Aiden and Milo. Milo fairly trembled with impatience and fear. The tray of scrambled eggs and toast shook with the boy's tension, and Aiden could hear the flatware rattle against the plate.

Aiden knocked gently.

"Aiden?" Gwen called through the door.

"Me and Milo. Yeah."

"Well, you don't have to knock. Why so formal? Just come in."

Aiden threw the door wide. In that moment he felt a blast of panic radiate from Milo like an electric shock. It almost knocked them both off their feet.

"Surprise!" Milo fairly screamed. His voice held a sharp edge of anxiety, mixed with the more pleasant emotions of the moment.

"Oh, my goodness," Gwen said. She sat up in bed in her nightgown and brushed her long, dark hair off her face with one hand. "What did I do to deserve breakfast in bed?"

"It was all Milo's idea," Aiden said. "And he did the cooking, too. I just supervised. Made sure nothing burned."

"You have to carry it," Milo said, not moving from the doorway.

It was an obvious oversight. Aiden had taken Milo's crutches and handed him the tray at the bedroom door, knowing he would want his mother to see him holding it. To know it was from him. But now, of course, the boy was stranded and couldn't move.

"Okay, I'm going to carry this over to you, Gwen. But we just need you to know none of this is from me. It was all Milo all the time."

Aiden carried the tray to their bed and set it on Gwen's lap. She stared at it in silence for several seconds. The smile fell from her face, and the mood in the room took on a serious tone.

"I've never seen this tray before," she said, lifting the plate of scrambled eggs and toast. "It's beautiful." She looked up and tried to meet Milo's eyes, but the boy looked away. "Milo, did you *make* this?"

Milo never answered. He seemed unwilling—or even unable—to speak.

"He did," Aiden said. "And he planned the whole thing by himself, too. He said he wanted to get you a tray like the kind people use for breakfast in bed, because he knows you like that. So we found one together, and then he made it into a mosaic for you."

Gwen looked down at the light-shaded mosaic tree again, then up at Milo. Still Milo leaned in the open doorway and would not look up.

Gwen began to cry.

"You don't like it?" Milo asked.

"I love it. It's the most wonderful present ever, Milo."

"Then why are you crying?"

"Because I love it so much."

"That doesn't make any sense," Milo said, screwing up his face.

"I know, honey. I'm sorry. Grown-ups are weird sometimes."

"It probably isn't good enough," Milo said.

Then he pushed away from the doorjamb, reached out for his crutches, and loped away.

Aiden looked at Gwen, and Gwen looked back.

"Should I go after him?" Aiden asked.

"I'm not sure. Let's give him a minute to burn off whatever he's feeling. Then you can see if he'll sit with me while I eat."

"Got it," Aiden said.

But he didn't wait long. Probably not nearly as long as Gwen had in mind.

He found Milo in his room a minute or two later and picked the boy up off his bed in one careful scoop, slinging him over his shoulder in a fireman's carry.

"What are you doing?" Milo shouted. "Put me down!"

"Nope. Sorry."

"Where are you taking me?"

"We're going to go keep your mom company while she has breakfast."

"I don't want to go in there!"

"Sorry," Aiden said. "But you're just going to have to deal with the fact that it's good enough, and she loves it."

———

"I honestly think the only reason I haven't given up yet is because of what Elizabeth said to me."

He watched Hannah's face for some reaction. But she was looking down at her notes. She didn't reply. Just waited for him to continue.

"I mean, it's been over a month."

"He never goes out to see the foal at all?"

"*See*, yes. I usually turn them out during the day, the mare and foal, and sometimes when he gets home from school he'll lean on the fence and just stare at her. They take the school bus, both kids, and sometimes if they don't come into the house right away, I won't know they're home. Elizabeth usually goes straight out to ride Penny. And then I'll start wondering where Milo is. If he got home from school okay. So I'll go out to look for him, and he'll be standing outside the pipe corral, leaning on the fence. Just watching her. It's happened four times. It scares me a little, because I don't know what he's thinking. The first two times I went out there and suggested I teach him to pick her hooves or get her used to the halter. But he always has something better to do. So now I don't even try. I mean, it's as close as he gets to her, so maybe I should just leave it alone. Maybe he's getting to know her in his own way. But he still hasn't thought of a name for her. Which is a safe enough thing to do. You know. It can be done at a distance. So I don't know what to make of that."

"What does Gwen think?"

"Gwen is so scared he's going to hurt the filly . . . I swear there's a big part of her that's hoping it won't work out. That he'll never go near her. She's ready to give up anytime. The sooner the better. I'm holding out because of what Elizabeth said."

"I'm going to give you another reason not to give up."

"Okay. I'm listening."

"At our last session, Milo specifically asked me to tell you something."

"Tell me something? Like a message?"

"Something like that, yes."

"He lives with me. Why didn't he just say it to me?"

"I have some theories, but it's not a question I'd want to answer off the top of my head. I'm noticing that the more emotional intensity there is behind a situation in his life, the more trouble he has communicating it. But he made me promise I would tell you this. And I wrote it down word for word, so I couldn't get it even the slightest bit wrong." She flipped back a couple of pages in her notes. "Ah. Here it is. In reference to the foal: 'Tell Aiden I said I'm not going to hurt her. I know he thinks I'm going to hurt her. But I'm not.'"

"Oh. Okay. Wow. Well, that takes a load off my mind."

A silence fell as he let the words settle more deeply. As he let them be heard and accepted not just by his ears, but by the places in his gut that had been afraid. They were only words. A promise. And promises could be broken. But it was a statement of intention, so it was a start.

"You know what I was thinking?" Aiden asked her. "What would you say to my bringing him in to one of my sessions? Or me coming to one of his? Maybe we could figure this thing out to the point where he could at least say a thing like that to me. Directly."

"I think it's an excellent idea."

"Okay. We'll have to figure out a way to schedule that."

She said something in return, but Aiden missed it. His attention had been drawn elsewhere. On her desk, something caught his eye. A four-sided pencil holder. Each side of it—or at least the sides Aiden could see—had been decorated in abstract mosaic work.

"I'm sorry," Aiden said. "I missed what you just said. I was looking at that pencil holder on your desk."

"I'm not surprised."

"It looks like the work Milo's been doing."

"It *is* the work Milo's been doing. Milo gave it to me."

"He made that for you?"

"He did."

"That makes me feel . . ."

But before he could finish the thought, Aiden had to stop and tune in to the feeling. It felt good—welcome—but he was having trouble identifying it more specifically than that.

Hannah waited.

An image filled Aiden's head. Not of Milo coming to this office and sulking in silence as he'd imagined, but of the boy coming here and opening himself and his life to Hannah. Learning to trust her. The way Aiden trusted her.

"It makes me feel hopeful," he said.

—

Aiden arrived home at about four in the afternoon and found Milo in the barn, leaning on his crutches, staring into the stall at Misty and the foal. For the first time since the foal was born, it didn't fill Aiden's gut with dread. Because Milo had promised. Because he had been so careful about sending Aiden that message through Hannah.

*Tell Aiden I said I'm not going to hurt her. I know he thinks I'm going to hurt her. But I'm not.*

Milo hadn't seen Aiden yet. The boy had not turned his head. He did not appear even to notice that Aiden was home.

Aiden stepped into the tack room and found a soft finishing brush, then walked up behind the boy.

"I think it's time to do more than just look," he said.

Milo jumped. Almost fell down, he was so startled.

"Aiden," Milo said, gasping for air. "I didn't know you were there."

"Come on. I know it's a little scary. But you need to get to know her."

He opened the stall door and stepped inside, then waited and held the door open for Milo. Milo just stood. Frozen. The boy's eyes went wide, like a deer staring into the headlights of Aiden's pickup along this lonely back road on a dark night.

"Seriously, Milo. It's like a wall, and you have to break through it. You just have to push a little harder."

Another frozen moment. Then Milo reached forward with his crutches and moved into the stall. Aiden closed the door behind them.

"Start on her withers," Aiden said. "Show her the brush first. Let her see what it is. Then go slow and give her time to get used to the feeling."

"What's withers?"

"At the top of her shoulders."

"Oh. Okay."

"Stick to her back or her sides until she gets used to it."

"Okay."

Milo balanced on his crutches, the toes of his bad foot barely touching the straw-covered dirt floor for balance. Aiden stood behind him to lessen the chance of his being knocked down.

Milo reached the brush out to the foal, and the foal reached her nose out to the brush. Then Milo set it gently on her withers and moved it, with the grain of the hair, down her side. The foal did not move or object. So Milo kept going.

"I think she likes it!" he said, his voice squeaky and high with excitement.

In that moment of distraction, Milo looked away. Craned his neck to look up into Aiden's face. Lightning-quick, the foal darted her muzzle in the direction of Milo's hand. Aiden saw it play out, but there was no time to stop it. It just happened so fast.

The boy shrieked in pain. His cry startled the foal, who spooked into the corner of the stall and then wedged in behind her mother to hide.

"She bit me!" Milo shouted.

Aiden tried to take the boy's hand, to look and see how bad a bite it had been. But it was too late. Milo had already turned and made his way to the stall door. He banged it hard with one hand. Aiden hadn't latched it, so it swung wide. Milo sailed along on his crutches toward the open barn doors, not bothering to close the stall door behind him.

"Milo, wait," Aiden called.

Milo did not wait.

———

Aiden found the boy in his room, crying bitterly. Looking absolutely desolate. Nearly destroyed.

"Can I see the hand?" Aiden asked.

Milo extended his left hand in Aiden's direction. The first knuckle of his index finger was turning purple and swelling fast.

"Well, now we know her teeth are coming in," Aiden said. "Sorry you had to find that out the hard way."

"Why did she bite me?" Milo howled through his sobs. "I never hurt her!"

"I know you didn't. I know. Look, Milo. I know it hurts. And I know it hurt your feelings. But you can't take it personally. She's just a baby. And she's not a person. She's a horse. She doesn't know any better. She's just figuring out the world the only way she knows how. She doesn't know what's food and what isn't. She doesn't know it hurts you when she does that. She just does what comes naturally for a foal. If you want her not to bite, you have to teach her not to bite. You have to teach her how you need her to act around you. She can do better if you give her time to learn."

To Aiden's surprise, Milo stopped crying. Or slowed to a stop, in any case. He looked into Aiden's face with a fierce curiosity.

"You're not mad at her?"

"I don't think it's right or fair to be mad at her. No. She doesn't know any better."

"So it's okay?"

"Not for you, it's not. It still hurts."

"But she's not a bad horse?"

"No. She's not a bad horse. She just needs to learn."

Milo struggled to slide off the bed. He grabbed his crutches from the floor, braced them under his armpits, and he was moving.

"Where're you going?" Aiden asked.

"I have to go tell her we're not mad," Milo said.

Aiden followed the boy out to the barn, and was surprised when Milo opened the stall door and moved right in, closing the door behind him. Aiden reached the stall door in time to hear the boy's words to his foal.

"You're not a bad horse," Milo said.

He reached a hand out to her, then jerked it back when her muzzle got too close. Then he reached it out again, cautiously. Aiden could feel the sharp pangs of the boy's fear. It was the first time he had felt anything from Milo in a long time—the first time the blank, silent wall of Milo had registered emotion in weeks, as far as Aiden could tell.

"And we're not mad at you," Milo added. "Are we, Aiden?"

"No," Aiden said. "We're not mad."

"Will you show me how to teach her not to bite?"

"Yeah. I will. But it'll take time. But if you stick with it, I know she'll learn it. I think you might want to come inside for right now, though, Milo. We should put some ice on that finger."

"Can't. I have to teach her how to get brushed."

"I really think the ice will help, though."

"Will you bring it out here?"

"Um. Yeah. Sure. Why not?"

Aiden turned toward the house.

He stepped out of the barn and into the afternoon sun. Elizabeth was riding up on her pony, Buddy wagging behind. She smiled at Aiden and he smiled in return.

"Where's Milo?" she asked.

"In the stall with his foal."

"Seriously?"

"Seriously."

"What changed?"

"You know . . . I was just trying to figure that out myself. At first it was because I insisted. And then she bit him. And now all of a sudden he can't get enough of her."

Elizabeth laughed one short bark. Then she scratched her head underneath the edge of her helmet. "That seems weird," she said.

"I know. I think so, too. But I'm not questioning it right now. I just have to go inside and get him some ice for his finger."

———

When Aiden arrived back at the barn with a bandana full of ice cubes, Elizabeth had put Penny away and was just walking out into the sunlight.

"You're right," she said. "All of a sudden he can't get enough of her. Did you know he gave her a name?"

"Just since she bit him?"

"No idea. I don't know when he thought of it. But he told me just now."

"What did he name her?"

"He wants to call her Tesserae, after the stuff you use to make mosaics. He said it always sounded like a girl's name to him. And he specially likes it because you can shorten it to Tess."

"Ooh," Aiden said. "That's good. I better go bring him this ice."

"Bet you ten bucks he'll just ignore it. He'll drop it on the stall floor and let it melt. He's really into brushing her, and it'll be like the way he gets when he does his mosaic projects. Nothing can tear him away."

She moved off in the direction of the house.

Aiden stepped into the barn and leaned on the stall door. Watched Milo gently brushing his foal.

"Ice for that finger?"

"No thanks," Milo said.

"I like the name you gave her."

Aiden saw the boy miss one brushstroke. Then Milo's hands picked up the motion again.

"How do you know what I named her?"

"Elizabeth told me."

"You really think it's good?"

"I think it's perfect. Did you think of it just now?"

"No. I've been thinking about it for a while now. But I didn't want to say it out loud unless I really thought she felt like mine. And also . . . I wasn't sure if it was good enough."

———

Aiden draped an arm loosely around Milo's shoulder as they walked into Hannah's office. He did it without thinking. The boy flinched and tightened, but did not explode. Aiden removed the offending arm.

They sat on the couch together, a respectful distance apart.

"So," Hannah said, "let's get some work done here today. Aiden, what do you most want to say to Milo?"

"Oh," Aiden said. "Give me just a minute to get my thoughts together."

It struck Aiden as strange that he hadn't anticipated the question and prepared for this session. It was almost as though he'd thought his words for Milo would take care of themselves when they sat down together with Hannah. And nothing could have been further from the truth.

"I guess I want to say . . . It's really nice watching him bond with Tess—"

Hannah interrupted. "To Milo," she said.

"Oh. Right. Sorry. To Milo." He turned his head in the boy's direction. "It's really nice watching you bond with Tess, Milo. It's . . . I don't know quite how to say it. It's so much like my own childhood. It's like coming around full circle on my life. And I appreciate the way you sent me that message through Dr. Rutledge so I would know you wouldn't hurt Tess. But I want to get to the point where we can say things like that to each other. Not need anybody else to help us communicate. If you know what I mean."

He waited. But Milo did not betray what he did or did not understand.

"But there's also something I want to ask you," Aiden continued. "Why did you like her better after she bit you? Usually you would expect a boy to like a foal less after she bit him. But that seemed to win you over, and I think we're all a little confused about that."

"Hmm," Milo said. "I sort of know why. But I'm not sure if I can say it right. But I guess I thought she was perfect. But she's not. She hurts people, but it's okay, because she just needs to learn to do better. I just have to teach her. That's what Aiden told me. And I liked that."

Aiden waited, hoping the boy would go on. But a silence fell, punctuated only by the ticking of the clock.

"I'm still not sure . . . ," Aiden began. But then he didn't finish.

He wanted to understand, because he wanted the communication between them to become clear. He wanted it to be something they could practice at home. Something they didn't need Hannah to intermediate, as if they spoke two languages and required an interpreter to translate. But Aiden didn't understand. Not yet.

"I think what Milo is saying," Hannah interjected, "is that it was a relief to know that someone else could do a hurtful thing and not be thrown away. I think when his foal hurt him and you felt like that was fairly normal, and to be expected, and you weren't mad at her . . . well, you tell me if I'm right, Milo, but I think it made Milo feel like there could be some forgiveness there for him, too. He's hurt living things. And maybe he liked the idea that he could learn to do better if someone would just take the time to teach him."

"Yeah," Milo said. "That."

Just in that moment, Aiden felt something from the boy that was not fear, or pain, or dread. It was not joy exactly, or even contentment. But it was another brief moment of respite from the negative feelings that dragged the boy down nearly every minute of every day. And if Milo could have a moment or two free from those things, maybe he could find a few more moments as time went on. It was a start.

"Milo," Hannah said. "What do you want to say to Aiden?"

"I don't know," Milo said.

Aiden could feel the boy shut down again.

"No," Hannah said. "Sorry, Milo, but that's the lazy way out. No more taking the lazy way. I understand if there's a lot you can't put into words right now. And I understand that you feel like you don't even want to try. But just say one thing. Big or small. Doesn't matter. Just pick one thing you could say to Aiden, and say it out loud in this session."

Milo sighed. He sat, rather darkly, Aiden thought, in a cloud of gloom and confusion that Aiden could not read.

The clock ticked while they waited. At least two full minutes.

Aiden almost stepped in to fill the void, but as he opened his mouth Hannah shook her head. So he closed it again, and weathered the silence.

It was awkward. Almost like eating at a restaurant all by himself.

"I guess . . . ," Milo said, startling Aiden, who had grown to accept the silence. "Just . . . thanks for getting me all the stuff for mosaics. And giving me Tess. I'm still scared of Tess. But not really in such a bad way. If that makes sense."

The boy fell silent again, and his face reddened. He stared down at his lap, then raised his eyes to Hannah without lifting his head. Strained to look up at her from under his eyebrows.

"Was that good enough, Dr. Rutler?"

"That was excellent, Milo," she said. "I think it's a very good first step."

It wasn't much. And yet it felt like a good first step to Aiden, too.

# PART SIX

AIDEN DELACORTE AT AGE FORTY-ONE

FIFTEEN MONTHS LATER

# *Chapter Twenty-Three*

## *Pride*

Aiden's uncle Edgar met them at the airport in Buffalo.

Aiden had skipped the previous Christmas going back to see his mom. There had been too much going on at home. Milo had been loath to leave his therapy and his filly. And, because Aiden's mother didn't tend to know who Aiden was when he visited anyway, they had let the traditional family Christmas visit slide. But only for the one year, because Aiden knew he did not have unlimited opportunities to see her.

Uncle Edgar waved to them as they stepped into the baggage claim area, and Aiden was struck by how much older he looked. As though he had become elderly in just two years. He wore a snow-white beard now. The skin on his face, and especially under his eyes, looked almost translucent in its thinness. He seemed a good two or three inches shorter than when Aiden had seen him last.

He grabbed Aiden in a bear hug, then turned his attention to Aiden's family.

"You must be the new wife, Gwen. So nice to meet you, darling."

He reached a hand out for her to shake, but Gwen moved in for a bear hug of her own instead.

"And these two lovely young people must be Elizabeth and Milo," Edgar said when she had let him go.

"I want a hug, too," Elizabeth said, and moved right in to take it.

Milo hid behind Aiden's back. Aiden could feel the strength of the boy's hand clutching at his coat, and the icy fear that crystallized around the boy's insides at the idea of interacting with a stranger.

Under his other arm, Milo clutched the two gift-wrapped breakfast-in-bed trays he had brought for Edgar and Aiden's mother. The trays themselves were exact duplicates of one another, so they nested together. But Milo had created a unique, original mosaic on the surface of each one, based on a thousand questions regarding what Edgar and May liked. And Milo had flatly refused to check them as baggage. He'd given up his carry-on bag to keep the gifts with him under the seat.

Aiden looked around and down to see Milo staring out the automatic sliding doors, which sprang open from time to time, blasting them with frigid air. There was snow falling outside.

"Aiden, look," Milo said, tugging at Aiden's coat.

"The snow, you mean?"

"Yeah. That."

"You knew there would be snow."

"Yeah. I know. But now . . . now there *is*."

They were interrupted by Edgar's booming voice. "And what happened to Milo? He was just here a minute ago."

"He's right behind me," Aiden said. "And I think I can safely speak for Milo and say he does not want a hug. Or even a handshake. Nothing personal, Uncle Edgar. He just needs time with new people."

"No problem," Edgar said. "No problem at all. You people don't look too warmly dressed. I think I should go get the car and bring it around. You can wait here for your bags to come down."

"We brought coats," Elizabeth said. "But we left them in our checked bags. Aiden was the only one who was smart enough to keep a coat with him."

"Aiden is the only one who's been to Buffalo before," Edgar said, and then hurried off to get the car.

—

Gwen had insisted that he sit in the front with Edgar. So they could "catch up." She had squeezed into the small back seat with both kids.

"How's Mom?" Aiden asked on the drive.

"Generally speaking, worse than when you saw her last. She does have her lucid moments. Sometimes seeing someone she hasn't seen in years will bring one on and other times not. But I'd say she's herself no more often than every week or two now, and the lucid moments are usually only a few minutes long. And, interestingly enough, if she does have a good moment, the memories she accesses are very old. She might say something about her first marriage, or our growing up together, but she won't remember what city we live in now. I would say don't get your hopes up too high. She might surprise you, but that way if she doesn't, you won't be too disappointed."

Gwen spoke up from the back seat.

"I think it's wonderful how you take care of her, Edgar. You don't see that in too many families."

"I've always adored May," Edgar said, his gray eyes misty and far away, ringed with dark circles.

"Totally foreign concept to me," Aiden said. "Nice, but foreign. A brother and sister who adore each other. Speaking of Valerie, she's not coming this year, is she?"

"No. She came last year, when she heard you weren't going to come. Terrible to have to say, but you know how she is."

"Yeah," Aiden said. "I know how she is."

"Did you and your sister have a fight?" Elizabeth asked.

"Not really. Not any one fight. We just never got along."

"Why not?"

"You know . . . ," Aiden said, and then faded. For a moment he searched around in the past, but he found nothing of use there. "I honestly don't remember."

———

"Look who's here, May," Edgar bellowed out, artificially cheerful, as if addressing a toddler. "It's company."

Uncle Edgar had told Aiden years before that he never identified visitors by name because it was just too embarrassing for May if she didn't remember them. It seemed better to let her treat company as new, unmet people if that was the best she could do.

Aiden watched her face light up. And, just for a moment, he thought she knew him.

"Why, it's just lovely to meet you," May said.

Aiden neatly folded up his expectations and tucked them away.

Milo stepped behind Aiden and clutched at his coat.

"Oh, my," May said. "The little boy is terribly shy."

"Milo takes new people at his own pace," Aiden said.

"Reminds me of my son when he was a boy," she said.

Aiden hoped she would go on. Maybe even go on to recognize the son in question. She never did.

———

Not an hour later both kids bundled up and ran out into the front yard to play in the snow. But the outing didn't last more than ten minutes.

"It's cold," Elizabeth said as they tumbled back through the door, a gust of cold wind and a puff of snow coming in with them.

"Yeah," Aiden said. "Snow is like that."

"It's all down in my *boots*," Milo whined, pulling them off and leaving them on the mat by the door.

"Come on, honey," Gwen said to him. "We'll go upstairs and change your socks."

"Not yet. I have to show them something."

Milo pulled his phone out of his coat pocket. Aiden winced, wondering if the snow had gone down into the boy's pockets as well. If they were about to have to buy him a new phone. But Milo tapped the screen on the device, and slid his fingers across it, and seemed to be finding what he needed.

He crossed the rug in his wet socks and held the phone out to Uncle Edgar. Way out. He stayed a good six feet away, leaning and reaching. When it was clear Uncle Edgar couldn't cover the distance from where he sat—especially considering that when Edgar leaned closer, Milo pulled farther away—Aiden took the phone and handed it over.

"Oh my," Edgar said in his booming voice, staring at what Aiden could just barely see was a photo of Tess. "What a lovely young horse. Is she yours?"

"She *is*," Milo said, his voice dripping with pride. "She's a *yearling*."

"She's quite a beauty," Edgar said, passing the phone to May. "Those long legs and that jet-black coat. And I love the marking on her forehead. It looks exactly like a crescent moon."

"That's what everybody says."

Gwen was at the boy's shoulder now, still hoping to steer him in the direction of dry socks. But Milo was off and running talking about his horse, in which case it was generally best to settle in for the long haul.

"Her name is Tess. Aiden gave me to her the night she was born. I was scared of her. But he taught me how to work with her and all. But . . . can I tell you a secret?"

"I think you should," May said. "I always like secrets."

"Don't tell anybody, though. Okay? Well, I guess you can't, because you live all the way out here in Buffalo, and you probably don't know one single person I know. So I'll go ahead and tell you. I'm *still* scared of her. But Aiden helps me. And I just sort of have her anyway."

———

It was only a few minutes later that Aiden found himself alone with his mother. Uncle Edgar had gone to the store to pick up a traditional Christmas Eve turkey dinner that he had chosen not to try to prepare on his own. Instead he had ordered it fully cooked from the supermarket, and was off to get it in the snowy darkness.

Gwen had taken the kids upstairs to get them unpacked so they could change into clean, dry clothes for dinner.

Aiden sat in silence with his mother for a time, nursing a feeling of shock over how much she had aged. She sat on the couch next to Aiden, still holding Milo's phone. Still staring at the photo of the yearling. Now and then she used her thumb to wake the display back up when the photo disappeared.

She was a handsome woman even now, and not terribly old. Seventy-four. Her hair was still a golden brown, but shot through with gray. She had age spots on her hands that Aiden could not remember having seen before. But all in all, she looked well for a woman her age, if not for her eyes. If her eyes had been clear and sharp, taking in the world around her, she would have looked essentially the way he remembered her. But every time he'd seen her in the past decade or so, her eyes seemed to have sailed further and further away.

"This reminds me of when we lived on the ranch with Harris," she said.

It startled Aiden. Partly because she had spoken at all. Partly because her words seemed full of facts. Memories of the world the way Aiden knew it.

Then he remembered what Uncle Edgar had said: that she would have access to very old memories if she snapped into any memories at all.

"I still live on that ranch," he said.

"That's lovely," she said, staring at Tess.

Aiden did not expect her to say more. For quite some time, maybe two or three minutes, she didn't. And then, out of nowhere, she did.

"The boy reminds me of you when you were little," she said.

"Milo?"

"Oh, is that his name? The boy who gave me this picture of the yearling. He's so proud of this foal, but he's afraid of her, too, just like you were when Harris gave you that colt."

Aiden sat a moment, feeling a tingling along his arms and legs. He couldn't decide if he should reply. He was sure his mother was remembering their past incorrectly. Maybe even sure that her window into lucidity had closed again. But he wasn't sure if he should correct her.

Still, the idea that he had been anything but successfully bonded with Magic was a statement he could not bring himself to let stand.

"I was never afraid of Magic."

"Oh, honey," May said, and looked up from the photo of Tess for the first time since taking hold of the phone. "You were terrified. Harris thought you might never get over it. He thought he might have made a mistake by giving him to you. That maybe he should have given you an older, well-broken horse. He said it all the time."

"I . . . I don't want to sound argumentative, Mom, but I took to that foal right away. I slept in the stall cuddled up with him that very first night."

May nodded with surprising vigor. "That you did," she said. "That you did. But then he got big and strong and frisky. He knocked you down, and he stepped on your foot, and he bit you. And then it was ages before you felt comfortable with him again."

"He bit me? Why don't I remember that?"

But his mother didn't answer. She seemed to be lost in the photo again.

"I want to ask you a question, Mom. While you're . . ." He wanted to say, "While you're here." He had almost said it. But it felt rude to point out how rare it was for her to be completely present, rather than physically with him but otherwise gone. So he took a different tack. "While we're together and talking like this. I wanted to ask you a question about my dad. Harris, not my birth dad. You know how he left me the ranch when he died. And the cattle, and his horses. But I sold off all the cattle last year. I don't run cattle on that ranch anymore. I just . . . I couldn't do it anymore. Emotionally. Sending them off to slaughter like that. And somebody I knew—somebody who knew my dad—said he'd be ashamed of me for that. And that's stayed with me this whole time. It's really bothered me. So I just wondered . . . do you think Harris would be ashamed of me?"

He waited. Watched his mother's cloudy eyes. They were still taking in the photo of the yearling, Tess.

He thought—or, perhaps more accurately, irrationally hoped—that she was putting together a thoughtful answer. But no answer ever came.

"Mom?" he asked after a time.

She did not look up.

"Mom?" he asked again. A bit more insistently this time.

Her eyes came up to his, just for a brief instant. And in them Aiden saw . . . nothing.

"I'm awfully sorry," she said. "Who did you say you were again?"

—

Uncle Edgar always smoked a pipe of cherry-scented tobacco after dinner, but never in the house. It didn't matter if it was dark and cold. It didn't matter if snow was swirling down, as it was that night after their Christmas Eve dinner.

May had insisted on doing the dishes, and Gwen had volunteered to stay and help her.

Aiden bundled up and sat out on the railing of the back deck with Edgar, a railing they had carefully cleared of snow with a whisk broom.

The only light on their scene was a soft glow from the kids' upstairs guest bedroom, and a soft beam from the streetlight on the corner.

"The boy seems troubled," Edgar said, blowing a blast of smoke out into the frigid air and accidentally into Aiden's face.

"He is," Aiden said. "I thought I'd shared that with you already."

"You said he was a handful. But that was a good year and a half ago. I was hoping things were better now."

"Oh, they are," Aiden said, his lips already surprisingly numb. "If you had known him back then . . . I mean, this is huge, where we are now. But he was seriously abused. He's not going to spring back from it overnight. In some ways he probably never will."

"He has a hole in his heart," Uncle Edgar said, and then puffed again. "So many of us do, but I expect his is bigger than most. We think we'll fill it up someday, somehow, but in most ways we never do. We just learn to live a good life with a hole in our heart. We make space for it. We work around it. You were a boy with a hole in your heart, and I'll bet anything it's still there."

"Not as big as Milo's."

"Big enough. It's really not so much a matter of degree."

"That's what my psychiatrist says, too. Anyway. It's definitely still a challenge with him. He's as much trouble as any three other boys put together. But we just keep putting one foot in front of the other, and we're still here. We survive each other. Against all odds, believe me. And every now and then there's some nice little moment that barely makes it all worthwhile."

The snow picked up, flurrying now, falling on Aiden's eyelashes and the little wisps of hair that extended beyond his warm knit hat. It threatened to dampen Uncle Edgar's pipe, but the older man just puffed more vehemently.

"She had a moment with me," Aiden said. "While you were at the store."

"Who? May?"

"Yeah. I think it was the combination of seeing me and then looking at a photo of a young horse. She started remembering when we lived at the ranch with Harris. But I think she got parts of it wrong. She told me I was afraid of Magic. That he got big and frisky, and he knocked me down and stepped on my foot and bit me, and I was afraid of him. But I would remember that if it had happened. I know I wasn't afraid of Magic."

Uncle Edgar laughed out a billowing cloud of smoke to be dampened down by the snow. "Oh, beg to differ, my boy. You were quite wary of going near that colt for almost a year. I don't know if it was fear. First of all, I wasn't there. I just heard about it over holiday dinners. And you were so shut down, I'm not sure any of us knew for a fact what you were feeling. I suppose May knew best. But that first year, Harris wasn't sure if it was a mistake to give you that horse. He didn't think it was going to work out at all. I don't know if the colt knocked you down and stepped on your foot, but he definitely bit you. When he was about six months old you came to Thanksgiving dinner with one thumb swollen up like a sausage."

"Huh," Aiden said. "Funny." The words sounded strange and dull to him, almost slurred by the numbness of his lips. "I don't remember that."

"Human nature. After something works out, we forget the frustration of the steps we took in getting there."

"Maybe," Aiden said. "I guess. Can I ask you a question? You knew Harris fairly well."

"Fairly well, yes, seeing as he was my brother-in-law for eight years. I didn't know him as well as you did, and of course May knew him better than anybody. But go ahead and ask your question, and I'll try."

"You know I don't run cattle on that ranch anymore."

"Don't you? I didn't know. How do you make your living?"

"Just breeding horses. It's tight, but I manage."

"Why did you stop running cattle?"

"I just couldn't do it anymore. Emotionally. The things you have to do to handle them. The tagging and roping and throwing them down and castrating them. And then knowing you're sending them off to be slaughtered. I just suddenly didn't have the heart for it anymore."

"Ah," Uncle Edgar said. He nodded to himself for a surprising length of time. As if shaking his thoughts into proper order. "I'm not surprised. All that sensitivity came back, didn't it? I always thought it would. I really didn't expect you could keep it shut down forever."

"Yeah," Aiden said. "It woke up. Anyway, I had a couple of employees. And of course they were disgusted with me. Didn't understand at all. One of them had known Harris. And he got right in my face and said if Harris could see what I was doing, he'd be ashamed. And, you know, it was more than a year and a half ago. Maybe closer to two years. And I never really shook that off. I still carry a little chunk of shame around in my stomach, wondering if maybe he was right. So I just wondered. I was just hoping there was somebody who remembered him well enough to tell me. Do you think he'd be ashamed of me if he knew?"

Edgar puffed on his pipe, then turned his face up into the falling snow. As if seeking to ask Harris directly. Aiden thought he saw something like a little smile at one corner of his uncle's mouth.

"I think you know the answer to that," Edgar said.

"I think I don't. Or I wouldn't be asking."

"Oh, come on, Aiden. As well as you knew Harris? What would he ask you if he were here right now?"

"I have no idea."

"He asked it all the time. He was practically known for it. When he started the sentence, people would roll their eyes because he asked it so much."

"I'm sorry," Aiden said, thinking he had reached the limits of his resistance to cold and would have to go in now. "I really don't remember."

"He would say, 'Are you doing what your heart says to do?'"

"Oh. Wow. That does sound familiar, now that you say it. Yeah, he did ask me that a lot."

"So . . . were you?"

Aiden looked up into the falling snow the way his uncle had done, and closed his eyes. He thought back to the awful time in his life when he had decided not to be a cattle rancher anymore. Then he stopped thinking about it and just felt it.

"Yeah. I was listening to my heart—as best I knew how, anyway."

"That's all any of us can do. And he would have been proud of you for it, and you damn well know that."

"Thanks, Uncle Edgar. I better go in now. I'm freezing my butt off out here. Besides, I have to tell Milo about how I was afraid of my foal. And how he bit me. He'll really get a kick out of that."

———

But the kids had gone to bed by the time he got back inside.

Aiden sat on the couch with Gwen for a few minutes, his arm around her shoulder. They watched through the window as snow piled up in the yard, illuminated by a soft glow from the streetlight.

"Our lives are so much better with you," she said.

Aiden wanted to say something in return. He meant to. But he was a little embarrassed by her words. More to the point, they created an emotional intensity so thick it was hard to push words through it.

"Especially Milo," she added. "The way you've stretched yourself for that boy. I'm not sure who else would have done all that for a guy like him. It's really above and beyond."

He still couldn't seem to manage words, so he gave her shoulders a squeeze.

Gwen might have been embarrassed herself. Because she kissed him quickly on the lips and jumped to her feet. "I'm going to go take a shower before bed."

"Okay, hon. See you in a few."

She trotted up the stairs, and Aiden sat by himself and watched the snow pile up. For about two minutes or so. Then he felt the bounce of somebody flopping on the couch beside him. He turned his head to see Milo settling in his pajamas.

"Aiden? You think they'll like their presents that I made?"

"I know they will. They'll love them. Those trays are absolutely one hundred percent good enough. What're you doing up?" But the question came out mellow and friendly. Not like the third degree at all.

"I couldn't sleep."

"Why is that, do you suppose?"

"I think maybe I'm excited that tomorrow is Christmas?"

It was a statement turned into a weak question, and delivered with almost no conviction. Plus it didn't match with anything Aiden knew about Milo.

"You weren't excited for Christmas last year."

"Okay." Deep sigh. "I lied. I get scared when I have to sleep in a new place."

"Ah. Got it. You want to sleep in the big guest room with your mom and me? I happen to know there's a cot. We could set it up at the end of the bed so you know we're close by."

"You would let me do that?"

"Sure. Why not? Come on."

But, oddly, no one moved. Only the falling snow outside the window.

"It's too bad about your mom," Milo said. "You know. How she doesn't remember people and stuff. She seems like a nice lady."

"She's . . . yeah. She's really quite lovely."

"Is she . . . ?"—it was a sentence that could have gone a hundred directions—"kind of like . . . my grandmother?"

"Yeah. I'd say so. She's your step-grandmother. I'm sorry you didn't get to meet her when she was more herself."

"I'm just glad I get to meet her."

"Come on," Aiden said, and pulled himself up off the couch. "We'll go get that cot for you." They walked toward the stairs together. "And while we're setting it up, I'll tell you a story."

Milo looked up at him, eyes full of skepticism. "What kind of story?"

"It's about a boy who gets knocked down and bitten by his own foal."

They climbed the stairs together.

Milo rolled his eyes. "I think I know that one."

"Oh no," Aiden said. "Not *this* one. You haven't heard *this* one. This is all new." He draped an arm around Milo's shoulders. The boy didn't yell out or flinch away. "And I just *know* you're going to enjoy it."

# *THE WAKE UP*
# BOOK CLUB QUESTIONS

1. Aiden has a deep level of empathy for both people and animals. Do you believe some people are more highly sensitive than others? Do you see this as an asset or a liability?

2. Early in the story, Aiden's life takes a drastic turn. What do you think was the final catalyst for Aiden's "wake up"? In the aftermath, Aiden begins to lose his friends, his girlfriend, and the life he's known. Do you think the benefits he derived from the wake up were worth the losses?

3. Aiden used alcohol as a means to numb his pain and memories for many years. Milo covers his pain through expressing outward anger or rage. In what ways do both coping mechanisms help them get through as a young child, but become a detriment later?

4. How do you think nature vs. nurture impacted Milo's acting out toward animals? Was Milo predisposed to violence and cruelty, or were those actions a result of his painful upbringing?

5.  Both Aiden and Milo come from a background of childhood abuse, and the story parallels their dual journeys. What things did they have in common that helped them to recover?

6.  In Gwen's marriage, she finally drew the line and left her husband after she learned he was sexually abusing Milo. Did she make the right decision at the right time, or should she have left sooner?

7.  Milo struggles with feeling that his work isn't good enough to share with others. Can you relate to his feelings of insecurity around being good enough? Ultimately, who needs to make that decision?

8.  Contrast the breaking of the pottery and putting the broken pieces back together with Milo's brokenness and how using his creativity assists him with coming back together.

9.  Running full circle from Aiden's childhood through Milo's is the bonding that occurs with the birthing of a baby foal. In what ways did this connection with animals reach deep within both of them and bring about a transformation that nothing else could?